*To, Debbie, Peter Rose & Joseph*

# The King of America

## By Rod Glenn

*To our good friends up in Sunny Scotland !*

*Rod Glenn.*

PublishAmerica
Baltimore

ISBN: 1-4241-3156-1
PUBLISHED BY PUBLISHAMERICA, LLLP
www.publishamerica.com
Baltimore

Printed in the United States of America

For Vanessa for her loving support and unwavering belief and for my family and friends for enriching my soul and fuelling my imagination.

*I would like to thank PublishAmerica for the faith they have shown in me. I will never forget. I would also like to thank my family and friends for being my harshest critics in the writing of this book. It is difficult for any author to be completely happy with a finished work, but as it is, with their help, I feel that it is a story to be proud of. Without their help, who knows how bad it would've turned out!*

# King of America

"Death comes as a heavy blow when,
known too well to others, you die unknown to yourself."

~ Francis Bacon 'Of Great Place'

# Chapter 1

## Fall of the Monarchy

Storming down the marble corridor like a whirlwind, a woman swept past, her ceremonial green Carama robe billowing up around her. The corridor within the White Palace was decorated with ornately carved oak panelling and adorned with countless finely painted portrait and landscape oil paintings.

Despite the gown, the woman moved with speed and lithe grace. In her early thirties, she was tall and in peak physical condition; a must being Commander of the Queen's Royal Bodyguard. Her red hair was functionally short, but still unmistakably feminine.

Reaching the end of the corridor, she swung the two heavy oak doors open with ease and strode into the Queen's chamber.

"Your Majesty, my apologies for the intrusion, but we must leave right away." Her voice was commanding but remained calm, despite the situation.

Queen Jennifer had been combing her long hazel hair at an imposing gilded dressing table set in a bay window over-looking the inner gardens. At forty, Jennifer was radiant with slender features and frame. Her usually warm, confident expression was startled by the sudden interruption. "Michelle, what's happening?"

Closing the door behind her, Michelle crossed the room quickly. "There's no time to explain. Please dress quickly."

Michelle assisted the Queen as she dressed in a simple day suit. As they finished, stomping footsteps could be heard approaching.

*Too late.*

Michelle swung to face the door and drew an automatic pistol from a concealed pocket within her robe as the doors burst open.

A startled cry caught on Jennifer's lips as six armoured clad Palace Guards marched into the room, assault rifles brought to bear. It took her a moment to recover as an officer followed the men in.

"What is the meaning of this, Captain?" Jennifer demanded as Michelle positioned herself in the way.

"You are under arrest," the Captain said coldly.

"Over my dead body," Michelle growled and aimed at his head.

"So be it," he replied side-stepping behind one of his men.

Michelle fired, putting a bullet into the forehead of the Captain's shield.

The remaining five soldiers opened fire, tearing open Michelle's green robes and dousing them with crimson. The gun dropped from her hand and she fell to the floor lifeless.

Queen Jennifer screamed.

The black surface skimmer limousine swung into the loading zone and came to a sudden halt with a whoosh of reverse thrusters. The rear of the monolithic Home Office building at 2201 C Street NW, Washington, DC was a hive of activity. With arms laden with boxes of files, dozens of suits and blue collar workers were dashing in and out of the service entrance over the watchful eyes of several security guards.

An elderly man with silver hair and a monocle stepped out of the building into the mid morning sunshine as the Limo arrived, flanked by two hefty bodyguards. Walking awkwardly with the aid of a plain silver topped cane, he made his way past a young office worker arguing with a delivery man over a collision that had scattered a box of papers across the pavement.

Carlton Brewster was a man who had spent most of his sixty-eight years of life perfecting the art of conflict resolution, but today he limped past without a glance. His skimmer had arrived in the nick of time with Republican soldiers already sweeping through the building.

As they reached the revving hover vehicle, the rear passenger door slid open to reveal a plush leather interior.

"Please hurry, Sir," one of his escorts said with one hand inside his suit jacket.

"Stop rushing me, David, I'm not as young as I used to be," the Home Office Minister replied, casting an irritated look at him.

Brewster eased himself onto the back seat as quickly as his old bones allowed him with his two bodyguards following. As soon as the door started to slide shut, the driver gunned the engine and headed back towards Virginia Avenue.

Relaxing slightly, David pressed the intercom button next to the partition to speak to the driver. "Take it slow, buddy. We don't want to attract any attention." Turning back to his charge, he said, "We've got a helicopter waiting in Georgetown to get you out of the city, Sir."

The limo pulled into heavy traffic onto Virginia with the Royal Plaza Hotel to their right.

Brewster allowed himself a sigh of relief and adjusted his black overcoat, settling back for the ride. As he made himself comfortable, he heard a distinctive metallic click. His eyes met those of David's and both men's expressions turned to horror.

The limo exploded in a dazzling fireball, casting burning debris across all six lanes of traffic.

*Fort Wayne (Consolidated Loyalist General Headquarters), Detroit, Michigan.*

The citadel of Fort Wayne rose like a great fist at the gateway to one of America's largest thriving metropolises. Built like an iceberg, its heart and strength lay deep underground, lending maximum protection against attack. The fortifications and the previously thriving community around it were scarred with the effects of a recent bloody urban battle. Smoke bellowed from unattended fires out of dozens of homes and businesses to the south of the fort.

It appeared at first glance that no living soul had survived the carnage, but here and there pockets of soldiers and armoured vehicles manned positions less than two kilometres from the fort's main gates and along the northern bank of the Detroit River. The wide murky swift moving river was lifeless save for two battered patrolling gunboats weaving carefully between the half sunken wrecks of dozens of vessels, military and civilian alike. Of its impressive 1,850 feet centre span, only around 100 feet of twisted metal and shattered concrete remained beyond the twin silicon steel towers of Ambassador Bridge. Amongst the rubble on both the Detroit and Windsor sides, dirt smeared civilians and soldiers alike were removing some of the less fortunate from the streets.

Deep within the bowels of the fort, General Bellamy Somms, Commander In Chief of American forces loyal to the King, stood over the strat-com map display and stared with fierce blue eyes at the nation. The broad circular chrome table displayed a real-time holographic image of installations and units throughout the American Province. Chips installed in vehicles and field radios uploaded position and status information via satellite into the headquarters mainframe to allow the senior command a bird's eye view of the entire nation. As his brain struggled to process the myriad of information, the normally subtle wrinkles in his ruddy face deepened into a perpetual frown. Anger grew within him like a cancer.

He shifted his heavy frame and rubbed his unshaven chin as the three officers standing near him waited with varying degrees of attempted patience. The Primary Command Centre was hot with apprehension and the only noise was the soft hum of machinery deep in the heart of the massive complex.

Somms finally looked up. "This is just the beginning." He withheld the fear and frustration from the words, but he did not conceal his anger or disgust.

The officers and the room's only other occupant—an armour clad soldier at the door—did not reply. The higher command shifted slightly, but the chiselled face of the guard did not twitch. A black visor masked the upper half of the soldier's face and a grey mane protruded from the top of his helmet. A huge, gleaming longsword was sheathed over his back and, to his chest, he held a squat, black assault rifle.

Somms broke the foreboding silence by stabbing the map with a powerful index finger. "Lexus forces have seized control of nearly all major cities and installations across the board. We have about twenty-four hours before they begin to assault our few remaining positions. We're outnumbered ten to one and our forces are scattered all over the northern continent, making it impossible to consolidate. And as for the south, we've lost all but two outposts." He paused for a moment to allow the statement time to sink in. The burden of his words was virtually unbearable. But it had to be said. He had to say it.

"Now," he continued, "Lexus has given the Brazilian Freedom Fighters his full support for their takeover of the South, effectively halving the Republic's problems."

He ran a hand through his balding blond hair and stared straight at each one of the officers in turn before saying, "This, gentlemen, is our situation. I'm not going to bullshit—it's a strategic nightmare and, after the events in Louisiana and Mississippi, the new Republic has an overwhelming public support." As an after thought, under his breath, he added, "Lexus timed it perfectly."

The Detroit garrison Commander, a tall Creole Lieutenant Colonel called Cussac, shook his head angrily at what he was hearing. "How the hell can the BFF even hope to take on the task of controlling and organising the South? The whole continent's in complete anarchy. They can't possibly be strong enough."

"Bob, I'm afraid IO totally underestimated, or more likely, fed us false information regarding the size and potential of the BFF." He looked hard at his friend. Lurking just beneath his angry exterior, Somms could sense the stress building up.

He made a mental note to talk to him later, then continued. "You know as well as I do, the reports that we received before the fall of Brasilia and Sao Paulo described thousands of well equipped and equally well organised troops storming them. We hold La Paz and Belem with not much more than a battalion in each. I don't believe we'll hold them for much longer."

Somms sighed deeply and leaned across the display. "Look, the Lexus Republic have us in a bad position; hell, very bad. But no matter how hopeless the situation looks you cannot lose hope. We've got a lot left to fight with yet."

The aging General had served with the officers that were gathered around him for up to a decade. Their eyes were filled with fear; but there was determination there too. *Damnit, they would fight to the death. They're good men, strong willed and loyal.* The Kingdom had been torn apart in front of their eyes, but they would not turn to the Republic like so many others had.

Grant Lexus...how he despised the man. He was a liar and a murderer, but most of all, a traitor. *He is the man responsible for all this. He will hang for it...somehow.*

But Bell Somms had lived a long life and now a small part of him wondered whether, even with his raw untamed stubbornness, he would live to see peace again like it had been; not so long ago. A peace that seemed a lifetime away now.

He excused himself from the meeting and examined the computer generated display. Using a laser pointer, he located Wyoming and enlarged the area. From Casper, his eyes turned north-east over the North Platte River until they fell upon the spot that concerned him. He watched, with grim, tired features, the innocent-looking place as the door opened with a whisper, admitting a slim officer.

The guard eyed the Major with caution, as he did everyone that entered, but otherwise did nothing.

In a tenth of a second, the Major whipped out a sleek, deadly machine-pistol from his jacket. The guard reacted a moment later. With the face of a man who was already dead, the assassin levelled the gun on the General. Somms gazed, almost dreamily, at the man that was about to kill him. He could not react, even if he had the time to. As the gun screamed, Cussac appeared in front of him and was instantly blown off his feet and catapulted into Somms. Both men collapsed as a single rifle shot rang out above the erupting chaos. The assassin dropped to the floor; dead, with a bullet through the temple.

Somms ignored the dead killer, as he did the soldier that appeared over him, half crouched. He held Cussac's limp, blood-drenched body to his breast, unaware that he was crying. The other officers were yelling, sidearms drawn. A siren wailed like a tormented banshee and running footsteps approached as the distinctive chatter of gunfire echoed throughout the base.

The General did not see or hear any of the mayhem around him. He wept. For Cussac. For the King. For America.

The darkened cell was lit only by a fist-sized window in the centre of the far wall. An acrid stench of urine clung to the air. The only occupant sat straight-backed on the only piece of furniture—a sagging bunk bed.

The man, in his late forties, wore clothes that had, only a few days ago, been all but priceless; jewel studded and gold embroidered. Now they hung to the broad-shouldered man torn and mud-splattered.

Duke Fredrick Frelon (less affectionately known as the Iron Duke) knew that he was to be executed; he had been politely informed of that fact. He had also been told that the same fate awaited his eldest son, Elias, a month after his twenty-fourth birthday.

A chill crept across his soul. Fredrick had always feared death, knowing that neither money nor power could prevent it. It was like an itch he could not scratch, coming and going seemingly with a will of its own, sulking in the dark recesses where you only visit in times of crisis. But, nevertheless, you know that it is always there, always within reach. And yet, now that death was indeed certain to him, he found himself strangely unconcerned with his own life. He had taken everything that he had in life for granted; wealth, power, family. He had lived only for himself. And now, of all times, his thoughts drifted towards his family.

Elias would die with him; that could not be altered. But his other two children—Bradley and Catherine—had some chance. They were survivors, just like he had been. Lexus would not get them.

As for his wife, Angelica…how he had despised her over the past few years. The constant bickering, the desertion, the affairs. What had she continually called him? Selfish, cold-blooded, heartless; the list was endless. And true. He had hated her; beaten her often for it.

This was the woman that he had loved…once. So long ago it had seemed so dream-like. Now, when he did not concentrate, that's all it ever appeared to be; a long forgotten hope without substance. This was the woman that he had risked the wrath of his father for by sneaking out one late night and stealing a horse to be with her. That night she had called him a fool; a wonderful fool. She had told him that she was falling in love with him. And the rose in his teeth! He had forgotten all about that. She had laughed at that; her soft all woman laugh that was beauty itself. How could he forget?

*What is this?* Now, on the very verge of death, long buried feelings—regret, sadness—the emotions mingled as they entwined his heart so that he could not begin to comprehend them. He had never regretted anything in his life, until now. He repeated that fearful question—How could he forget? And why does it all come flooding back now?

*I remember…like it was never gone. How did it get blown so much out of proportion? How could I have been so stupid? So damn pig-headed, to throw away what we had? How? Why? Maybe…*

His fist slammed down on the cold wooden surface of his bed. *God! Why is this happening to me? Why now? Is this my punishment for everything that I have done wrong? This is not fair! I do not deserve this.*

*Damn you, God. Damn everyone!*

He looked from the rags on his body to the tiny hole in the wall that gave him a pin-prick view of the outside world and concluded, *I am the one who is damned.*

His shoulders sagged with the weight of self pity, but it did not last long. Grinding his teeth, he forced it back down like foul medicine. They would not break him. If there was one thing that he was sure about, he would die with honour. And yet, even as he made the vow, he questioned it. What difference did it make? Did Lexus have honour?

He laughed aloud. It was a hollow, cynical sound that was instantly consumed by the very bricks and mortar that surrounded him.

His captors, guards that once would have died for him, would now see him die for them…or rather their ridiculous *Republic. Oh! Poetic irony.* They promised him that his brother, Paul—formerly the King of America—would be executed soon after him.

Paul, the stubborn old goat. He had known about the rising public resentment towards the Royal Family; the demonstrations turning to riots; the slumps in public living standards; the increased taxes; the crime surges; and the bloody environmental problems. He had also been warned about Lexus. He did not listen. Now there was a revolution.

He did not blame his brother for the people's anger; the damn peasant folk continually moaned about anything and everything. Some people could never be satisfied. But, as for trusting Lexus; that, he could never be forgiven for.

But what did it matter now? He would be dead soon, so would not get the chance to hold his grudge for very long.

Fredrick tried hard to smile. It was impossible. Then he felt an almost overwhelming urge to cry, something that he had not done for as long as he could remember. No, he did remember; after the battle of Atlanta. He had staggered, bleeding and exhausted, across the battlefield that was drenched in the blood of his men and the Kanaga and had wept the whole time. The single agonized cry that died before he managed to locate the source still, in his nightmares, echoed in his ears. That was twenty six years ago.

His entire emotion swelled up within him, threatening to drown him in self pity. Again he quelled it, though only just. He had to hold himself together. He repeated two words in his mind again and again— Dignity. Honour. *Dignity! Honour!* It was all he had.

The sounds of heavy footsteps approaching drew the Duke's eyes to the door. He stood and composed himself as, after a series of brief metallic clicks, the heavy barrier swung open. *It was time.*

Fredrick fought desperately to stem the flow of dread that seeped through every pore in his body. He was only steps away from his end, and he knew it. And it *was* his time. No miracle could save him now.

No Decker led Arion commando attack was going to appear at the last second.

He was led out into a huge parade ground that was packed with hundreds of civilians and soldiers alike. Everyone fell silent as he emerged into the cool bright daylight.

It was twenty six years ago that he had stood in the same parade ground in the Armed Forces Headquarters, only minutes from the White Palace in the Capital of America. But that had been for a very different reason. There had been other occasions since then, and others before, but that one time when CinC General Ira Bracken pinned the Lion Cross to his breast snapped straight into focus as he was marched towards the executioner's stand. He remembered the cheering crowds as if it were yesterday; for all the good it would do him it might as well have been.

The silence only held for a moment. A voice from the crowd screamed, "Hang the bastard!" It was hard to tell whether the voice was male or female. It was an animal cry. They wanted blood and that one voice was the catalyst for the rest. In seconds the crowds were surging forward, hurling abuse and whatever else was at hand. Snacks, bottles, stones; all became missiles.

In the middle of it all, at the centre of everyone's hate, Fredrick withdrew into himself. *Why so much hate? How can they despise me so much? What evil have I wrought upon these people to conjure up such hatred?* The questions were endless. The answers were beyond his comprehension. *I do not deserve this…*His thoughts were shattered as a small boy, of no more than eight, lashed out at him with a jagged sliver of glass. It tore a deep gash in the Duke's leg then he was swept away as quickly as he had appeared.

The escorts fought hard to keep the enraged congregation from the condemned man, but the occasional blow still struck home. A guard by Fredrick's side laughed as a small stone lanced the Duke's face. Seeing his face bloated with smug satisfaction caused something to snap within and Fredrick lunged for the nameless man who suddenly became the object of all his fury. The soldier's face changed to shock as the Duke laid two powerful punches into it. There was no chance to persist; he was clubbed to the ground with batons wielded by two of the other guards, then yanked back to his feet with a trickle of blood running down the centre of his forehead.

His head thumped like a Kanaga battle cry as, through his misted vision, he realised that he was finally being hauled onto the wooden platform. His eyes were drawn heavenward for a moment. The sky was a perfect powder blue without a cloud to blemish it. "Beautiful," he whispered to no one in particular.

There were two nooses suspended from sturdy beams; one was already occupied. The young man's eyes constantly flickered over the crowd. His face was stern and proud, but his eyes revealed much more. He waited until the Duke saw him, then said in the bravest voice he could muster, "Father." The single word was heavy with emotion, but remained steady. Fredrick was proud of him for that.

Their eyes met and thoughts of the hundreds of people crowded around them were dimmed. "Be strong, Boy," the Duke said, struggling to maintain an air of defiance.

"No talking," his escort snapped as he forced the second noose around Fredrick's neck.

"I-I'm trying, Sir," Elias answered, tears rolling down his pale cheeks. He attempted a smile but failed dismally. Father and son, standing side by side, waited to die. But death was not meant just yet.

A second procession pushed its way through the charged crowd. Surrounded by guards were two women, ashen faced and bedraggled. Duchess Angelica was crying, strands of her long raven hair were plastered to her wet cheeks. Still wearing the same suit as the day of her arrest and the murder of her bodyguard and friend, Michelle, Queen Jennifer held the Duchess's hand tight and kept her head held high. Once or twice she uttered soothing words to the agonized woman with her, but they were soundless in the roar of the crowds.

Angelica rushed forward as they drew close. Her heart made it further than her body. She only managed a couple of steps before her frail, screaming form was scooped up by two of her escorts.

"Angel," Fredrick cried out to her, "Don't give these bastards the satisfaction...*Please*." The last word was laced with emotion. She stopped struggling when that last word registered with her. It was not a word that her husband had ever used. Her eyes were big and pleading, staring up at her family.

Fredrick looked down at her as she cried, Jennifer's arm tight around her trembling shoulders. The barrier he had been desperately maintaining instantly dissolved and the tears finally broke through. "I am so sorry, Angel. Believe me." At that moment, he no longer cared about the throng of people that were gathered around him, wanting him to die. He did not care any more about his dignity. If that meant that they had finally broken him, so be it. The only things that mattered, that filled his heart, were Angelica and Elias.

A wiry officer strode forward. He was irritated and tired of listening to such emotional horseshit. It was all just a thinly veiled ploy to gain pity and forgiveness. Lieutenant Colonel Zedayal Corallis was not going to have any of it.

The Republican officer climbed onto the platform and cast his fox-like eyes over the people below him. *Beautiful.* Then he turned to the Frelons and revealed a glare of pure disgust. *Dictators…Greedy, Murderous, Dictators.* He strolled over to the trapdoor release lever then raised a hand.

The crowd fell silent. *Such power!* Using a loudhailer, in a thick Mexican accented voice, he said "The former Duke of Atlanta, Fredrick Thomas Frelon—brother of fugitive King Paul the Second—and his son, Captain Elias Paul Frelon, have been found guilty of treason by the new Republic of America. Their despicable crimes against the people have been fully documented in the new Republic Supreme Court and are far too numerous to list here, but let it be known that because of *these people* there are thousands of Americans living in squalor and starving to death. It is unsafe to walk the streets for fear of being murdered by someone desperate for enough money to buy bread. Because of their greed and arrogance we have had war after war with other nations of the world. *They* forced America to its knees."

He felt a familiar stirring in his loins in readiness for what would follow. Taking a deep breath, he bellowed, "The sentence is death!" The crowd roared their approval, obliterating Angelica's desperate pleas.

"Citizens of the Republic, you are free!" Long speeches were such a bore. His hand hovered over the lever for several unbearable seconds, teasing both crowd and victims alike. Then, at once, gripping it hard, he yanked downwards and could not suppress the smile that crept across his face upon hearing the simultaneous snaps of the two necks.

The crowd exploded with appreciation as the Duchess fell to her knees, sobbing. Jennifer stood anchored to the spot, the arm used to comfort Angelica, dropping limply to her side. Against her will she stared at the two limp bodies swaying gently in the breeze and could only imagine her own husband and son hanging there dead.

King Paul II sat staring at the bare, but clean, uninviting walls of his Wyoming hideaway. Dressed in a plain grey suit with an untied burgundy cravat draped around his neck, he looked more like the last guest at a wedding rather than the ruler of a nation. The only giveaway was the ruby inlayed gold signet ring, embossed with the royal crest on the little finger of his left hand, that signified his office.

The King was a broad-shouldered man, like his brother and his father before him, but they were turned in as he leant forward on the table and his face appeared gaunt. His hands were clasped tightly together in front of him on a basic oak dining table and a bowl of chicken soup lay cold and untouched to one side. Thinking about what was happening around him did not help at all in dampening the inferno of emotions that silently blazed within him. Rage pulsed through him as he considered the unfolding events.

He kept telling himself that it was just a nightmare; the nightmare that he thought would never, *never,* manifest into anything more. Yet, no matter how hard he tried, he could not awaken from it.

Simply put, he had been betrayed and now his country stood against him. The walls of Jericho that he had built up around him had finally come crashing down.

He would see to it personally that these rebels hang for their treachery. They would not get away with this. The insolence! And what of his wife? His son…his *family*? They could be dead. Slain by the hands of this rebel scum.

*No. They ARE safe. No harm will come to them while I live and breathe.*

Twenty-one years of ruling one of the five great provinces of Earth, and now a fugitive. A criminal. *In my own land. How dare they!*

*Damn it, they cannot do this. I am their King.*

He had been betrayed before, people in power always had enemies and sometimes they lurked in the most surprising places. But never by someone as trusted as Grant. They were friends. Grant Lexus had been his most trusted servant. His advice and support had been invaluable over the years, always a staunch ally of the Monarchy. And he had been rewarded handsomely for his service and loyalty. Why such betrayal? *Somms warned me, as did Fredrick and Brewster. They warned me about him. I ignored them in favour of friendship...of loyalty.*

Paul clenched his fists with the power of his anger and hate and only noticed the pain when a light tap on the door banished his tormented thoughts.

"Enter," the King muttered.

The door opened, admitting a uniformed officer of the Royal Guards. Major Reynolds slammed a fist to his chest in salute, then, in a rough, angry voice, said, "Sire, the scouts have spotted Republican forward recon units closing in from the east; less than a hundred clicks away. We must leave now. The men are ready to move on your command."

Paul remained silent for a moment and continued to stare at the wall. Then, without warning, he stood up and turned to the officer. "All right. We go now."

The single story stone lodge was of modest size with several plain brick utility buildings lining a dusty asphalt courtyard. Two surface skimmer APCs and three utility skimmers roared into life as their operators were given the go ahead. Engines revved impatiently as armoured soldiers hastily boarded.

Paul entered his designated utility skimmer in silence. Samantha Gordon, his personal assistant, followed. She paused in the doorway to glance towards the horizon. Beyond the grasslands and farmland rose the snow and pine-dusted peaks of the Bighorn Mountains. She turned away quickly and sat down beside Paul. Her hands were trembling ever so slightly as she buckled up her seat harness.

Reynolds came in behind them. He secured himself with practiced ease and adjusted his com-headset. Paul watched the younger man's face as he set about his job. Reynolds was in his late thirties with stern, solid features that never seemed to differ. He had been decorated for bravery five times, making him one of the most highly decorated soldiers in America. He was one of the best—that was why he had been one of a handful chosen from thousands to serve with the Royal Guards. To serve in the Guards had been the highest honour that could be bestowed upon an American soldier, much like the role of the Provincial Knights before they were disbanded so long ago. Now that honour had turned to disgrace in the minds of everyone except the men who served in the unit.

Paul ventured to touch the sidearm on his hip. He had been issued with it 'just in case'. Was there reassurance in such an implement? No. Some emotions were ignited by the weapon, but reassurance was not one of them. A sick aching crawled through him, dragging with it a deep underlying feeling of impending doom.

The King had refused to carry a gun for over ten years and had vowed never to use one ever again. It was a tool of destruction; something his subjects used for upholding Law and Order, not to be used by him personally. He had been given expert tuition in all forms of small arms and many forms of martial arts in his youth, but that was a long time ago. In training he had prayed that he would never have to use the skills he was gaining. His prayers were ignored (that may have been one of the many reasons for slowly eliminating the powers of the Church; a gradual erosion of faith). He had killed and despised himself for it. But such training was necessary—it was a part of human nature to prey upon the weak. The old saying '*The meek shall inherit the Earth*' never did come true. So his long gone father had forced the lethal teachings on him. But none of that mattered anymore. He was much older now and it was not just some lone assassin that was after him; it was an entire nation. His nation…

"Are you alright, Sire?" Reynolds asked, turning away from his command for a moment. The King looked up from his automatic pistol.

Somewhat irritated, he said, "Fine. Are we ready?"

"Almost," Reynolds replied. "We're just waiting for the scouts to get into position. The rendezvous point near Crystal City is still clear, so we're looking good, Sire."

Paul nodded. "With luck the passage to Europe should be open to us." After a moment's thought, offering justification to the plan, he added, "King Alexander has always been a strong ally to America. With his help we will stamp out this rebellion." He turned away to conceal his grim features and said, "You may give the order when ready."

"Yes, Sire." The Major listened to his headset for a moment, then said, "Affirmative. Speyer, move out."

Lieutenant Lucas Speyer, in the forward utility skimmer, acknowledged the order then took his team, an APC and his skimmer, out of the clearing. After two minutes the rest of the vehicles followed.

As the kilometres sped by, the only words that were spoken in the King's skimmer were orders and reports being constantly relayed between Reynolds and his men.

The tension was rising within Paul as he sat and watched the baron scrubland cruise by. Years ago, in terrain frighteningly similar to the rocky meadows that surrounded him now, he had visited such a place as a child. He had decided then and there that he loved the wilderness. The hardened land had struck him with an acute fascination and wonder; hardened by centuries of abuse from man and the elements.

As a boy, he had dreamed of escaping the mass of security that always surrounded him and running free like a wolf through the beautiful scenery. Sometimes in the dream he would be a peasant boy, hunting to fill his belly. Other times, and the ones he liked best, he was a deer, a wolf or a mountain lion. Each incarnation held a similar underlying feeling overflowing with joy and excitement. He always thought that the one place he could find peace was in countryside like that around him now.

He had not had that dream since the beginning of his manhood, until the night just past. He had been the white-tail deer, the animal he favoured the most, but he had not been running carefree under a clear moonlit sky. This time he had been fleeing for his life with hunters hungry for the taste of his blood on his heels. The sky had been filled with swollen black storm clouds, wind roared and fork-lightning lashed across the horizon. The chase seemed to carry on forever, and yet each time it seemed sure that they had him cornered, they allowed him to just slip through; mocking him, prolonging the hunt. When they finally had him trapped, cowering and exhausted, the sky turned blood-red. They converged on him like a sneering horde with every conceivable weapon thrust towards him—spears, guns, savage drooling dogs—and as they swamped him, he snapped awake with a startled cry caught on his dry lips.

It was no longer the sanctuary that he imagined it to be. It no longer held joy and wonderment. All that was out there were the hunters, closing in for the kill.

He had been cheated by his own people. *Damn it! They cannot do this to their leader. I am their King! Anointed by God. I control them.*

"Heads-up," the Major said calmly, cutting into Paul's thoughts. "Alpha scout under fire. Bravo and Delta pull 'round; flanking positions."

"What's happening?" Paul interrupted, grasping the Major's shoulder.

"Not now, Sire." Reynolds said and continued rattling off orders without missing a beat. "Alpha's down. Luke, pull your team forward and lay down suppressives. Watch for crossfire."

Paul stared fiercely at the Major as he calmly kept control of the situation. The officer's orders were flowing smoothly. One small interruption could cost lives. The King sat back, angry with Reynolds and himself.

"Second team, cut speed seventy-five percent," Reynolds said as more data appeared on the terminal mounted on a flip-down shelf in front of him. The skimmer immediately threw everyone hard into their safety harnesses as reverse thrusters ignited.

Samantha's hand gripped Paul's. He looked into her frightened eyes and gently squeezed it.

"Good work," Reynolds was saying, "keep them pinned and target mortars and turrets onto the area. Then move in and eliminate survivors." He sat back and allowed himself a few breaths.

Paul grabbed his chance. "Who are they?"

"Rogue infantry unit," the Major informed him. "They ambushed our forward scout and got more than they bargained for. There's no need to worry, Sire—just a minor interruption. No doubt the first of many."

The pristine street of modest detached brick houses in the exclusive Paramus district of suburban New Jersey was all but deserted as the first rays of bright autumn sunshine broke through the scattered cloud. The mature linden trees that lined the verges were thinning with the onset of autumn. Remnants of their lush summer coats were drifting lazily on the groomed lawns and sidewalks with the gentle cool morning breeze. The only sounds that threatened tranquillity originated from a dog several streets away, pining for attention, and the low hum of a light transport skimmer's engine ticking over on the driveway of one of the houses.

A face appeared at the open double-doors of the white unmarked skimmer. It was shadowed with concern. Duchess Madeline Frelon held her voice just above a whisper as she said, "Jason, hurry."

The young man who came out of the house at a jog was tall and solid with a distinct look of determination set into his boyish features. "Coming," he called to his aunt as he cleared the distance in a few strides and jumped in beside her. A young man sitting opposite handed him a pistol inside a holster. The Prince thanked him with a nod and slipped it around his waist, taking care to conceal it beneath his denim jacket.

The sliding doors shot into place as the skimmer pulled out of the drive and into the empty street.

There were four other occupants in the back of the skimmer, all dressed similarly to the Prince and Duchess, in casual nondescript clothes. They all held weapons ready and the air inside the confined space was tense and claustrophobic. A big man at the front of the compartment drew back the hatch to the drivers' cabin and said to the two men, "Keep to the back streets. There'll be patrols all over this place." The man riding shotgun had a calm, honest face, part of the reason why he was sitting where he was. He nodded without turning round.

After closing the hatch, the Sergeant turned back to the others. "We're doin' fine."

The plush streets of Paramus gave way to darker, huddled streets that were trash littered and less deserted. Here and there, hastily scrawled graffiti announced the *end of the monarchy* and *hail the new republic*. Grubby children played in the gutters with litter and debris they had picked up around them. A group of men and women of indeterminate age huddled around a burning trashcan. They glanced suspiciously at the transporter as it cruised by. Two children of about five rolled a trashcan under the clean, out-of-place transporter. It only just cleared the trims and was instantly flattened by the force of the anti-gravity field. They giggled uncontrollably as the skimmer passed by without noticing.

They drove for several minutes in silence until the man riding shotgun pulled back the hatch and, looking distinctly less calm, said, "Road block."

The Sergeant snarled. "Dammit, they'll search us for sure or cut us to ribbons if we try a u-turn. Side street?" The reply was an unsurprising negative. "Run it then."

There was a flurry of activity as everyone immediately secured their harnesses. As the Sergeant slammed the hatch, the driver muttered a curse.

The skimmer slowed as it approached. The Republican road block consisted of half a dozen men and a couple of vehicles. They were bored and taking little or no notice of the plain transporter approaching.

A corporal, acting post commander while the sergeant was away 'visiting' his 'sick mother', crushed his cigarette butt under foot and stepped out into the road. He loosely held his assault rifle in one hand as it hung from his shoulder and gestured 'halt' with his other.

The nonchalant look on his face turned first to a frown as the skimmer kept coming and then to one of horror as it started to speed up. The driver throttled full back on the thrusters and gritted his teeth as the transporter lurched forward and shot past the screaming corporal.

One sentry managed to fire a wild, short burst that prematurely opened a general store across the street, but the skimmer disappeared around a corner before any of the others could react.

Both men up front uttered sighs of relief as they left the road block behind them, but it was short lived. As they rounded a second corner they ran straight into a patrol. Three army utility skimmers were heading right for them. The driver managed "Oh shit" before the lead opened fire with a roof-mounted heavy machine gun and peppered the front of the transporter. The driver's head was blown apart with the first round. The man next to him joined him straight after, his chest ripped open by several more rounds.

In the back, the man sitting opposite the Sergeant took a hit in the neck, spraying blood across those by him. Panic swept over everyone as the skimmer swerved violently to one side and ripped straight into a closed Italian restaurant rather ironically called, Sempre Aprire…Always Open. The mangled transporter tore deep into the building, obliterating everything in its path, then it clipped a low wall and flipped on to one side. After demolishing tables, chairs and the bar, it eventually ground to a halt close to the far wall.

A couple of long minutes passed as the dust and debris settled in the darkness. It was a low groan that finally broke the silence, wavering over the smoky, fuel-drenched air. Movement followed.

"Out! Get out!" the enraged voice of the Sergeant barked.

Jason fell upon the door control and hammered it. As the doors strained back into the battered chassis, he fumbled in the blackness for Madeline's still form. His hand touched her forehead and he withdrew it instantly; it was sticky with blood. "No," he gasped aloud.

After a moment's frantic tugging at her harness, she fell into his arms. He quickly dragged her through the exit. The young man who was sitting opposite the Prince came after him, followed closely by the Sergeant, sporting a deep gash down his left cheek.

"You okay, Your Highness?" The young private asked.

"Yes, but Maddy—" he began. The Sergeant cut in before he could continue.

"Find us a way outta here, Davis," he ordered. The Private nodded to his NCO and headed for a pair of swing doors in the nearby back wall.

Absently wiping the oozing wound on his face with the back of his hand, Sergeant Travis eyed their surroundings with an annoyed frown and cocked his rifle. He was not having a good day and it did not look as though it would get much better. As a Royal Protection Officer (and Team Leader), his orders were simple. Protect the Prince at all costs and above all else; the lives of his men, his, and even the Duchess' were all insignificant in comparison to the Prince's.

Jason looked up from dabbing at the gash across Madeline's hairline. "They'll be all over us in a minute."

Travis responded with whispered agreement as he took up a defensive position behind what was left of the wrecked bar, his boots crunching over broken glasses and bottles. "Watch for a signal from Davis," he added then aimed at the huge ragged hole at the front of the restaurant where a wide window and a door had once been. Nothing remained above knee height between them and it.

The Prince frantically tried to revive his aunt as shouting and running footsteps approached. She coughed, then struggled; blind panic overwhelming her momentarily. He hugged her close and whispered, "It's all right, Maddy. It's me."

Madeline gasped out his name, filled with relief. She stopped struggling but maintained the embrace. After a moment he helped her to her feet and told her, "We've got to get out of here." She held the side of her throbbing head and gently nodded.

Davis re-appeared. "Kitchens. All clear, Sarge."

"Right." Without turning away from the entrance, Travis ordered,

"Davis, take point. I'll bring up the rear. Your Highness, follow Davis."

"Okay." He grabbed Madeline's hand and headed for the kitchens. The first Republican soldiers rushed through the opening before they were half way.

The Sergeant's rifle roared in the confined space. Four soldiers dropped instantly while several others scattered for cover. Jason ran to the door, half dragging the Duchess behind him. Then the Republicans returned fire.

The gloomy restaurant lit up like Hell as a dozen rifles wreaked a cyclone of destruction upon the entire room. Muzzle flashes licked the air like enraged cobras. Glasses and optics at the bar that had survived the crash shattered in the frenzy. Chunks were torn out of the section of the thick mahogany bar that Travis hid behind.

Jason threw himself through the door as a bullet sliced into his upper thigh. Another round nicked Madeline in the shoulder as she followed him through.

Glancing over his shoulder long enough to make sure that the others were clear, Travis cocked the rifle's under slung grenade launcher. He pumped three fragmentation grenades into the advancing Republicans, then with head tucked down, he sprinted for the door.

The Prince fell to his knees on the tiled floor, clutching at the fire in his wounded leg. The darkened room they found themselves in was a long galley-style kitchen, equipped with an array of chrome appliances and cupboards. Madeline, ignoring her own pain, grabbed him and hauled him to his feet. "Move!"

Davis came back through an exit at the other end of the kitchen and ran to Madeline's aid. A moment later the building shook and the Sergeant's bulk dove through the door and rolled across the floor. He jumped to his feet and yelled at the three struggling figures, "Still here? Let's go, they're right behind us!"

The loyalists piled through the next door and continued down a corridor with several doors leading off. Travis brought up the rear, continually urging them on. At the end of the passage they came to a heavy fire door. Davis shoved it aside and everyone, except Travis, fell out into a back alley.

An explosion followed by intense automatic fire signalled their pursuers' entrance into the kitchen. With lightning speed, Travis reloaded the grenade launcher from a belt around his waist. As the door to the kitchen was shredded by gunfire he unleashed the volley of deadly projectiles then hurled himself at the open exit.

Davis slammed the door shut behind the Sergeant as the grenades exploded. The fire door rattled in its frame.

# Chapter 2

## Hunt for Frelon

A man, black and sleek as a panther, sat cross-legged on the dirt floor beside a leafy fire, churning out a writhing mass of smoke into the dark, humid confines of his barren hut. The walls and roof were made of a hodge-botch array of ancient timbers and driftwood. A hessian sack had been nailed to the only window, allowing only a couple of isolated shards of light to gain purchase. The room quickly filled with smoke, distorting even that.

The man was naked and still. His auburn eyes burned through the gloom with an intensity that matched the embers at his feet. With each drawn breath his gnarled muscles tensed and relaxed. His entire body was crisscrossed with scars and marks, some intentional, others picked up along the way. In a tight fist, he held the skeletal remains of a chicken claw. It seemed mutated in its length and sharpness.

A low murmur rose above the soft crackle of the fire and grew in volume until it became a chant. Still the man did not move. His lips spoke words that only he could understand. As the chant grew still louder he brought the claw up to his chest.

He spat the final word through clenched teeth and at the same time yanked the claw across his chest. Blood gushed out of the deep slice and in seconds he was drenched.

The heavy breathing subsided and a sneer crept across his glistening face.

Paul watched, with hypnotic fascination, the sparse scrubland that surrounded them. The cracked and pitted asphalt road had seen better days; grass, weeds and the occasional wild flower were sprouting up from every rupture. Even though they were travelling at a steady 100km/h he could still pick out every detail around them. A twisted branch extended from a long dead pine, not unlike a serpent, pointing an accusing finger. A rock that bore an uncanny resemblance to a gravestone stood out hauntingly against a backdrop of twisted vines. Then his eyes met those of a half starved coyote standing bold on the crest of a rocky incline. He was positive that he saw sadness in those eyes before the animal disappeared from sight.

There was a war going on out there, just beyond view. He could scarcely believe it. This place seemed so quiet…untouched. And yet, not far away and all around him, people were dying. Americans…killing Americans. His people were killing each other and Lexus was to blame. There had never been such bloodshed at the hands of other Americans, not since the dark chaos years after the Great War. Anger once again began to boil inside, but before it could grasp hold it was abruptly cut off as the skimmer came to a sudden halt.

He turned to Reynolds, and in answer the Major said, "Forward scout has spotted an enemy camp ten clicks ahead, Sire. A Battalion Operations Base. Approximately 200 regulars; mainly on foot, except for a couple of transporters. They're co-ordinating patrols and outposts in the area. It'll be tough getting through."

"What do you have in mind?" The King already had a good idea.

"A minor disruption of their command and organisational capabilities."

Paul turned away. "Do what you feel necessary, Richard." He felt, for a moment, something surface. Guilt? For traitors? They deserved to die. He had sentenced people to death many times before the war started; it had been necessary. Capital punishment had always been at the heart of maintaining law and order. He found himself asking a disturbing question; are they to blame for this? Is it not just Lexus to blame? *No. They follow him. They hunt their own King. They are traitors.*

Reynolds watched his leader for a moment with what, on his unchanging features, could have been considered a frown. The man was in torment; that was obvious, and understandable. But there was something else, something different. The King had called him by his first name. That was something he had never done before, but that was not all.

He forced up a mental block against all the questions that were beginning to surface and turned away. He was about to contact Speyer when he noticed out of the corner of his eye that Samantha was watching him. His eyes were drawn to hers and some long dormant internal organ stirred. Looking back to his terminal, he forced business back into his mind. But even as he spoke into his headset, the thought lingered. "Speyer." The Lieutenant responded immediately. "We wait until twenty-one hundred. Prep the explosives tech and his team. They're to locate and eliminate officers' quarters and communications set-up. Kill as few grunts as possible. Got it?" He waited for Speyer to acknowledge before saying, "Alpha scout, find us a suitable spot to lay dog."

Samantha continued to watch him. Reynolds intrigued her. There was a cruelness in his eyes. He was ruthless and single-minded with no time for small talk or niceties. It had crossed her mind before that there must be more to this man, but in the brief moment that she looked into his eyes it made her positive. There was the merest flicker of a gentle, more caring side to the stone soldier. She had caught him with his guard down, an event most certainly less frequent than the coming of Haley's comet. A smile touched her lips for the first time in more than a week. He was human after all. She finally looked away when Reynolds turned and spoke to Paul once more.

The Republican Battalion Field Operations camp was quiet apart from a small group of soldiers standing around a cell-powered portable heater beside the main entrance. The road was blocked by a moveable section of steel fence with the word 'STOP' emblazoned on it. A further couple of sentries patrolled the perimeter, strolling casually, one occasionally stopping to draw on a cigarette.

The two patrolling sentries disappeared without notice. Shortly after, at nine thirty pm an explosion in the heart of the camp lit up the clear evening sky with devilish fury, signalling the end of most of the unit's officers and communications equipment.

The camp quickly fell into chaos despite the frantic attempts of NCOs and the last remaining officer to maintain control. Many of the less willing soldiers and conscripts took the opportunity to make a break for it. Half dressed troopers fled in all directions.

With the incursion accomplished, Reynolds ordered Speyer and the rest of his unit to continue. The passage ahead was open.

Grant Lexus was a small man. His straight, almost 'to attention' stance went some way to compensate for his lack of size. But what he lacked in stature, he more than made up for in the confidence that poured out of him through his stance and determined features. His tar-black hair was gelled back flat in a time efficient manner and his tailored suit clung tightly to his wiry frame.

The conference room with highly polished mahogany panelled walls and deep carpeted floor was empty apart from the small man who stood motionless at the window. Beyond the expanse of groomed lawns, landscaped gardens and perimeter fortifications, the calm, quiet streets of Washington DC surrounded him, basking in unseasonably warm sunshine. A flock of birds (they had feathers and wings, which was about all he knew about them) drifted lazily across the tops of the mature sycamore trees at the far end of the estate, silhouetted by the DC skyline. He saw a young attractive woman taking a leisurely stroll; probably one of the secretaries on a coffee break (obvious security reasons prohibited the use of the parkland surrounding the White Palace for anyone except staff from inside the fortifications).

For the first time in a while, his mind had wandered from the current events. It did not last long. A helicopter gunship swooped low over the Tidal Basin, then veered off over the Potomac heading towards Lady Bird Park. To Lexus, it felt more like stalking than patrolling; hunting out Loyalists where ever they hide. Glancing back to the secretary, he noticed that two soldiers had interrupted her walk. She was showing them her identification. One of the troopers shrugged moodily; 'Just doing my job, ma'am'. Yes, it all came flooding back.

He had taken Paul's Kingdom away from him. The American Province was under the control of the Republic now. After enduring hundreds of years of dictatorship, the people finally had a democratic government. Well, very nearly. He had managed to achieve what the Kanaga and the Khan in all their might could not...the fall of the Monarchy. The eyes of the country were upon him. The people, for the first time, looked to him. He had accomplished what, just a year ago, he could scarcely dream of.

And yet, with all his accomplishments, he was still uneasy. Fredrick was gone, as too was the worm-tongue Brewster; they had been two major hurdles to overcome. Capturing and then executing the arrogant Duke had been almost too easy. Somms wasn't going anywhere; Fort Wayne would become his tomb. It was only a matter of time for him. Decker was missing—the Arion Elite were still a problem, but one single unit, no matter how competent, were nothing to lose sleep over. That left Paul.

He still remembered the times that they had been friends. They would have been pleasant memories if they did not now make him feel sick. Friend? He could not stop himself from emitting a sharp, bitter laugh at the thought of Paul considering the two of them to be friends.

*Sure, he was the friend that used me to quell the Southern unrest; to unite the Province. I was the friend who averted the war with the Khan at a time when he could have crippled us. Then he was the friend who cast me aside for retirement; to be forgotten and worse, replaced by imbeciles such as Brewster who then poisoned the ear of the King against him. How fickle the King's favour was. I held the Province together while he did all he could to destroy it. I deserve this.*

So, after all that, lingering like a bad smell, why did he still feel some shred of guilt? *Once again, he succeeds in manipulating my emotions.* He always got what he wanted. There was only ever one way...his way.

Not this time.

Paul and the rest of the Frelons were finished.

A knock at the door drew the President out of his waking slumber. He continued to stare out of the blast-proof window as he said, "Enter."

Three men walked in, two in suits and the third in the army dress uniform of a five star general. The Defence Secretary, formerly the Defence Minister, Zain Namala, spoke first. "Grant, I have those reports that you requested."

Lexus turned away from the window and thanked him then greeted each man in turn—The State Secretary, formerly the Foreign Affairs Minister and Carlton Brewster's successor to the Home Office post, Kern Silus, and the Commander In Chief of Republican Armed Forces, newly promoted and boasting two extra stars on his shoulders, Orson Halburd. "Kern, Orson. Shall we begin?"

The four men looked dwarfed as they sat down, occupying one end of the room's centre piece, a huge mahogany conference table. Two serving maids, one middle-aged with a matronly look and the other barely out of her teens, entered the room with trays laden with a silver coffee service and china cups.

As they began serving the coffee, Namala retrieved a plastic folder from his briefcase marked FRELON, PAUL H. and below in large red letters TOP SECRET. He opened it and, after pausing to slip on his reading glasses, began to scan the contents. "Ah, here we are. On arrival at the Wyoming hideout, the 103rd Infantry Brigade, under the command of Colonel Chambers, found the area recently abandoned. They—"

Lexus interrupted, "What?" A flash of anger cut into his cool features for the briefest instant. The young girl, already nervous, clattered two china cups noisily onto the table, drawing a look of annoyance from her elder colleague.

"They proceeded to initiate an extensive search of the surrounding area," the Defence Secretary continued unperturbed, skim-reading the lengthy report. "It was while they were still carrying out this search that they received word of a fire fight that had flared up fifty two kilometres south-south-east of the hideout. A unit was immediately dispatched to the scene. On arrival, they discovered the remnants of the 62nd Infantry Battalion's Charlie Company, a unit with rogue status. Evidence pointed to the Royal Guards so they pursued this lead as well as several others." He skimmed through a page until he located more relevant information.

"There were no further updates until the 205th Infantry Battalion—assigned to law-enforcement duties in and around Amarillo, Texas—transmitted a priority call for 'immediate assistance' after being attacked by what was thought to be a Loyalist special forces unit. The hundred and eighty strong unit suffered sixty-five percent losses through death and desertion." Zain paused to glance over the top of his spectacles at his colleagues and friends, gauging their reactions. They were staring intently, waiting for him to finish. "Chambers personally headed direct to the location. He arrived there just over an hour ago and is in no doubt that the Royal Guards were responsible." He closed the folder and looked up. "That is all there is for the moment, Gentlemen."

Grant knew that it would not be easy to get his hands on Paul—his guards had been chosen out of the entire nation's armed forces—but nevertheless, it was still just a matter of time. There was only so much he could do to delay the inevitable. But still, he had hoped for it to be quick and decisive, for the nations, as well as his own, peace of mind.

He took a long deep breath and leaned back in his chair. "What reasons did Chambers give for drawing that last conclusion?"

Zain flicked open the report for a brief glance and nodded. "That whole county has been devoid of any significant effective rebel activity to date. Nothing like the calibre of those who struck the 205th (clearly a highly trained unit with experienced officers and a perfectly executed plan). There were also a few sightings of unmarked military vehicles in that area that fit the descriptions we have of the Royal Guards equipment signed out by Major Reynolds just prior to the King's escape."

The President gave a brief nod and considered his options. He would not be able to sleep until Paul was dead, that was nothing new, but the nation would not settle until he was brought to justice. "Yes, I believe he is right. That's fine, but unfortunately this is taking longer than I hoped." He stood up and walked around the table to Namala's side. "I want—the public want—this whole mess wrapped up. They want to rebuild and start afresh so that they can put this madness behind them. None of that can happen with Paul Frelon still running loose and stirring up trouble."

"With Frelon at large, the Loyalists have a channel through which they can still gain support. No matter what he and his kind have done to our country in the past, there are people out there who will still back him. But once he, as the figure head of the resistance, is gone we will have broken its back. They would no longer have a leader, and no longer have a hope. A leaderless resistance is no resistance at all." His breathing had grown harder and he stared at each of his advisors with sincerity and determination. *Did they understand the importance of this one man's life? No, not yet. But they will before the end.*

Sitting back down, Lexus made a decision that he had hoped would not have to be made. "If he is not dead or in captivity within forty-eight hours, announce his death to the world anyway."

"That would be dangerous, Grant," Namala warned.

"I understand the consequences of such a plan. But the pros, in this instance, heavily outweigh the cons. Paul Frelon is the symbol of their strength. The Republic has far greater military and public support, but they still fight on. Why?" He stared fiercely at the three men, needing them—willing them—to understand. "Because he is their *King*. They do not fight for honour or for the good of America, or even for love. They fight because they are brainwashed into believing that he is *the chosen one*. That he has been chosen by God to rule over the peasants. No matter what. Believing that means complete and total servitude. The term Loyalist was not given lightly—loyalty to their King above *all* else."

His friend was still not convinced so he smiled and added, "Zain, besides, if it did come to that and the public did find out that he was still alive; mistakes happen. Communication breakdowns…an officer after the glory of killing the former King; fakes his death to achieve fame and hero status. Something along those lines is perfectly understandable."

Namala nodded. It seemed like a big risk, but Lexus had obviously given it a great deal of thought and he was certainly no fool. They could use it to their advantage, if required.

Lexus noted the change in expression on the Defence Secretary's face and stood to pat him gently on the shoulder. They nodded to each other, then Lexus turned his attention to the General. "Can you spare another battalion, Orson?"

"I'm afraid not, Sir. At the moment the bulk of our forces are besieging Loyalist strongholds and maintaining law and order. Police and militia alone don't have a snowball's chance in Hell of keeping the peace in the present climate, even if they were at full strength, which of course they are not. They're experiencing high absenteeism through sickness and injury, desertion and military call ups." Halburd was apologetic in his words but as emotionless in expression as ever.

"That's right," Silus added, pushing his spectacles higher onto his nose. "And they're dealing with crime and public disorder levels that are through the roof, as well as subversive rebel activity. Many small towns have even resorted to hiring their own militia in the form of local thugs and mercenaries."

"Yes, I know that," Grant said evenly.

"However," the State Secretary continued unthwarted, "as each day goes by the crime figures decrease. The public are slowly settling down and adjusting to the new administration. I haven't been able to go through all of Brewster's old records yet, but I believe, judging by the current rate of decline, in the latter end of two months crime will, once again, be at a more realistic and manageable level, on a par with pre-Republic figures."

Lexus sighed and said, in a cold flat voice, "If Paul Frelon is eliminated."

The three men agreed verbally, whether silently they did or not.

"Well," Lexus concluded in a lighter tone, "thank you, my friends. We need to concentrate on getting this country back on its feet and back on a paying basis. The public need the security and confidence to return to their normal lives and work. Let's get Frelon out of the picture so this can be achieved all the quicker. I shall call another conference for an update on the situation in twelve hours time, unless of course, there are any major developments before then."

Since the brief interruption up in northern Texas, the King's party made it through Edwards Plateau without further incident. They had made swift progress, there having been less resistance than even Reynolds had thought. The Texan Gulf was only one step away and beyond that, the sanctuary of Europe.

The small group of unmarked vehicles lay silent in a depression in a dry riverbed thirty kilometres from the rendezvous point, each vehicle camouflaged with tank netting to further break up their profiles. It was late afternoon and a cool breeze was blowing in from the gulf. There was no civilization to be seen apart from an ancient rundown shack about two hundred metres further south on the steep bank of the desiccated river.

The scouts and several members of Speyer's team had been strategically positioned at a distance encircling the main group to give advanced warning of any dangers. None could be seen to the naked eye.

The King and his escorts waited in the confined skimmers for three hours, apprehensive and eager to move on. It was nightfall when the Major finally gave the order to move out.

They drifted through the night without lights and engines muffled; sticking to poorly maintained secondary roads. The illumination from the terminal gave Reynolds' face a blue tinge as he quietly relayed orders to the scouts and Speyer's team.

The lead scout spotted a patrol up front on an intersecting trunk road, but the heightened anxiety did not last long. The two army skimmers merely slowed down at the intersection before continuing across the horizon, without so much as a second glance in the direction of the darkened group of vehicles. They were only held up for a couple of minutes.

The telephone was ringing. Lexus snapped awake and fumbled in the darkness for the receiver. "What is it?" he asked as he sat up in bed. His wife, Fiona, stirred but did not wake.

It was Namala. "Sorry to disturb you, Grant."

"That's alright, Zain. Problem?"

"On the contrary. Orson has just received information that pinpoints where Paul Frelon will be in," he paused to check his watch. "One and a half hour's time."

Lexus blinked and any residual drowsiness instantly vanished. He flicked a brass light switch mounted on the wall beside the bed. Soft light from wall lamps illuminated the spacious regal bedroom. Next to him, Fiona moaned and pulled the covers over her eyes. "How?" he asked.

The Defence Secretary's smile broadened. Lexus could sense it. "The Commanding Officer of a small unit near Crystal City, Texas has informed us that his men are to rendezvous with the King and escort him to the coast. I've just received confirmation that his unit is an Agency Special Operations team with Loyalist status. They want to show their allegiance to the Republic by capturing Frelon."

"Has Chambers been informed?" Lexus asked evenly, concealing his excitement.

"His men are converging on the area now. They're going to keep at a distance until the SO team's got him, so they don't scare them off."

The President clenched his free fist and glanced down at his dozing wife. Her long red hair was splayed out across her pillow, the bed covers masking the rest of her face. "Good work, Zain. It looks like we may not need that contingency plan after all."

Inside the dark confines of a tent, a lone man sat at a foldaway table covered with crumpled hardcopy maps and reports, his face calm and emotionless. His powerful frame was dressed in desert fatigues, lacking both rank and insignia. After draining the contents of a plastic cup of coffee, he sat back in the light-weight camping chair.

His men were all behind him, as usual. This time he wasn't so sure about Connelly, but while disappointing, it was not a matter for concern. He was being watched anyway. The King was on his way with his platoon of the Guards. Now, granted, the Royal Guards were damn good; their skill bordered on insanity. But as long as they continued to take the bait, no level of skill could save them from the trap that he had set.

Chambers had put a company at his disposal (any more would have surely alerted the Guards) and the rest of his men at the ready to move in on the SO Commander's order. With his team co-ordinating the grunts they couldn't fail; even without Connelly's help.

The Captain had thought long and hard about the consequences of his actions. He was betraying his former leader; that was true. But the 'former' had to be emphasized. The King had had his chance and failed. It was time to give someone else a try. He told himself that it was not for purely selfish reasons that he was doing what he was doing; it was for the good of America as well. A new democratic Republic surely deserved its chance. That quashed his fickle conscience. And that was that.

His hand went instinctively to the field radio. He activated it and asked for all teams to call in and acknowledge that they were in position. They did and they were.

Lieutenant Connelly was starting to panic as he walked through the SO camp, comprising of eight scattered lightweight tents and three camouflaged utility skimmers. Dusk had quickly been replaced by night and cloud-cover obscured any moonlight. Apart from a couple of perimeter guards, the camp appeared to be lifeless.

But that wasn't quite true; Sinden had assigned someone to 'watch him'. He wasn't sure who as he had just had a brief glimpse of the person's silhouette in the trees, but he or she was out there. In the sanctuary of his own mind, he cursed his misfortune and stupidity at speaking out against Sinden's plan. He had mistakenly thought that he could persuade him out of it. How wrong he had been. Now he had made himself a target too and the King was virtually on top of them. Something had to be done. And it had to be now.

Unconsciously, his hand sought the butt of his pistol resting on his hip. It failed to improve his confidence, but did force his resolve. He took a deep breath and headed for Sinden's tent. The Watcher followed.

The last acknowledgement had just come through as Connelly entered the unlit CO's tent. Captain Sinden knew who it was before he was able to recognise the dark figure. His hand was already gripping the pistol that lay concealed under a map in front of him.

He threw the man, who stood half crouched just inside the doorway, a casual glance and said, "What can I do for you, Connelly?"

The Lieutenant had not had time to think through exactly what he was going to say or do. He took several deep breaths and gulped before he spoke. "I can't let you do it, Sir," were the first words that came pouring out. He had drawn his handgun as he entered and now he aimed it directly at his superior.

In the darkness, Sinden sighed. He had liked Connelly. Tightening his grip around the pistol, he said, "I didn't realise you felt so strongly, Andrew. But it's too late now anyway."

Connelly shook his head furiously, the pistol shaking slightly with it. "No. No it's not. You can warn them; there's still time."

Sinden smiled like a cat with a mouse caught firmly in its claws. It was impossible for the Lieutenant to make out his features. "Do you think so?"

"Yes! You can still do it." As a glimmer of hope rose up from the depths of Connelly's stomach, Sinden pulled up his pistol with lightning speed and fired.

Shock followed by an intense fire in his belly. Connelly fell to his knees with blood pumping out of his abdomen and gazed in disbelief as the Captain shook his head sadly.

"There's no going back," Sinden said matter-of-factly. He started to squeeze the trigger a second time but was interrupted as the entrance flap was yanked open. It was the Watcher with gun in hand. The Captain waved his gun casually at the man and said, "It's all right, Kane. Everything's under control." The man started to holster his pistol but did not finish. A hole appeared in Sinden's forehead.

With his strength ebbing away and his mind a whirlwind of pain and emotion, Connelly watched, as his CO fell forward off the chair and on to his face. The gun was like a ton weight in his trembling hand as he turned it on Kane. The Watcher managed to swing his pistol back to the prone Lieutenant but Connelly shot him twice in the chest before he could open fire. The force punched Kane back out of the tent and wrenched the gun out of Connelly's weakened grip. His former colleague emitted a low gurgling sound as he collapsed to the dirt.

The tent flap swung back into place, shielding the Lieutenant from the Watcher's final death rattle. Connelly had served with Kane for nearly three years. They had been friends. He had even met his wife at a charity event last year…

He heard shouting; the voices of his friends and colleagues would have been easily recognisable under different circumstances. A combination of pain and the chaos in the camp forced the thoughts of his dead friend out of his mind. He dragged himself over to the field radio.

It took several agonising seconds to reach the radio. Taking a moment to focus and hold together his floating senses, he groggily managed to change the frequency to the appropriate channel. A reply came through immediately.

Reynolds gawked at the terminal in front of him as he listened to the shaky voice over the radio. He was staring at the screen, but nothing it was showing was registering. For a moment he was stunned, unable to say or do anything. If Reynolds had been a man prone to nightmares, what he had just heard would have been the mother of them all. But this was no nightmare.

It took him a second to recover; that was nine-tenths too long for his liking. He rattled off a string of orders to Speyer and his men.

The two main teams hammered on reverse thrusters as the scouts were redeployed around them. Speyer's team performed a hasty u-turn in the narrow road. The utility had no problem, performing a sliding turn, but the APC slid precariously down the rocky slope towards the dry river bed below, almost tipping over. Near the bottom, the driver regained control and managed to complete the 180 degree turn. Opening up the thrusters, it roared back up to the road and passed the remaining vehicles. Once through, Reynolds ordered his vehicles to follow.

The man that had warned them of the impending trap came over the radio once more as they sped away from the rendezvous point. But this time he was not on the secure link; he was on open air. Reynolds' flicked a switch to put it on speaker.

His voice was weak and distant. "My name is Lieutenant Connelly...Andrew Connelly." He stopped as pain tightened its grip around his stomach, doubling him up in agony. He gritted his teeth and spat into the radio, "The King is the rightful ruler of America! My allegiance is to His Majesty. I will die for—" A burst of gunfire made the radio squeal with annoyance. Then it was silent.

Paul had been listening grimly, hands clenched in fists, but as he heard those last few words he held his head in his hands.

This man, Andrew, had sacrificed his life to save his King. It was the ultimate selfless act and yet, Paul had never known the man. He had always expected complete loyalty and through such loyalty, men had died for him before; thousands of them. But this time he had heard it first hand...felt his pain...listened to him die. And what had his King been doing? Running away.

He fought back the hot sting of tears before composing himself.

Reynolds looked at his leader. He was deathly silent, but his torment was impossible to mask with hands alone. His glance was then drawn to Samantha who was staring intently out the window. A tear slid down her already damp cheek. At that moment he was overcome with an overwhelming urge to take her in his arms.

Lexus had been sitting in the breakfast room, dressed in a robe and slippers and most of the way through his second cup of coffee when the telephone had rang again. He had picked it up halfway through the first ring with an excited "Yes?" The news that Namala gave him was not what he had wanted to hear; far from it. He had been apologetic— sickeningly so—but all Grant could do was listen and then hang up without another word.

Now, the President sat and stared at the telephone, his thoughts consumed by it. He willed it to ring again and for Zain to say that it had been a mistake; that they had caught him after all. But it didn't and Namala was not stupid enough to try to call again and explain in greater detail the reasons why Paul had escaped.

The elegant white porcelain device looked so innocent, squatting there on the clean marble worktop, unaware of the hideous tidings that it had been the harbinger of. It looked back at him, as if saying, *it's not my fault*.

He closed his eyes and told himself that it was just a minor setback. Nothing came easy in life and his was certainly no exception. He had fought his entire life to achieve his many accomplishments. So he could wait. He just had to push a bit harder for a little longer. That was all. Besides, he still had a few tricks up his sleeves.

The hunt for Frelon continues. He smiled and patted the telephone gently on the receiver.

# Chapter 3

## Samson

The cut across his chest still throbbed, but that was good; it allowed him to focus on the task ahead.

The small cabin swayed rhythmically with the beat of the ocean. It was a beautiful day outside—the sun was alone and strong in the sky and a gentle breeze stole away its harshness—but the blinds were pulled shut, shielding him from its glare. None of that interested him. He lay on his back on the hard bunk, his eyes searing through the gloom. In the writhing blackness of his mind, images began to form. There was a faint creak as the doors slid open a fraction. The man appeared not to notice.

The deck of the tired old trawler was grimy and stunk of fish, despite not having been a working fishing trawler for several years. What was left of the ancient coat of red paint that it had once known was either faded to a faint pastel pink or had flaked off a long time ago.

Its Captain, a broad weathered Hispanic with a broke nose and matching teeth, strolled across the deck and climbed the rusty ladder to the bridge. His step-brother was at the helm.

"How is our 'guest'?" The last word was loaded with sarcasm.

The Captain smiled, accentuating the busted set of far from pearly whites. "Sleeping like a bebé, Pico, mi amigo."

Pico, a younger man in his early twenties with olive skin, turned and stared at him with big almond eyes. "Are you sure you know what you're doing?"

"You saw how much money he had." He gripped Pico's arm in his powerful unyielding grasp. "Anyone with that kind of dinero who charters a battered old heap of mierda like this has got to be up to no good. And heading where he's heading is just asking for trouble." He relaxed his grip and smiled again. "Besides, you might be able to afford that Corsair you've always dreamed about."

Pico half-smiled at the thought of the Speedbike he had so long yearned for, but still felt sick deep down. Something was very strange about that hombre. The Captain's plan felt very wrong for all the wrong reasons.

The Captain slapped him on the back and turned to leave. "I'll get Marco and Jools. You slow her down to a crawl on the current heading and meet us below."

The other three were already gathered in the cramped confines of the corridor outside the spare cabin when Pico arrived. The Captain held his old revolver, Marco, a wiry man with an evil glint in his eye, had a machete and Jools, a towering Jamaican with a badly scarred face, a wrench. Pico held nothing but a cold sweat and was very conscious of it.

The Captain nodded to Jools who immediately shoved the door aside. Marco and the Captain rushed straight into the gloom with Jools right on their heels.

A mere couple of feet inside the room, there was a glimpse of steel as it flashed out of the darkness and sliced Marco's head clean off. Momentum carried his body several steps before collapsing on the bunk. As the severed head bumped against his boot, the Captain screamed and fired into the darkness. "Marco!" Seeing his friend's head bounce across the floor, the enraged Jools shoved past the Captain and stormed over to towards the bunk, swinging his wrench wildly.

A shadow appeared to the side of Jools. A whispered, "Jools." It was Marco's voice. He spun and gazed straight into auburn eyes; they appeared to be floating disembodied in the darkness. There was barely time for surprise as the dripping 14 inch dagger plunged into his stomach. His mouth opened to form a scream but the dagger ripped upwards through the centre of his chest, butchering him before a word could escape his lips.

There was an audible splatter as blood and entrails spilled onto the floor. The Captain saw Jools topple and fired in his direction. Pico stood frozen in the doorway. On the fourth shot the gun jammed. A wave of terror struck the Captain, anchoring him to the spot. The spell held for a few desperate seconds before he cast aside the revolver and dropped to his knees to pick up Marco's discarded machete.

A flicker of movement caused him to look up to see the black man looming over him. On reflex, he lashed out with the machete. The passenger caught the blade, seemingly effortlessly, with his spare hand and held it in an iron grip. With frenzied strength, the Captain ripped it free and observed, with pleasure, blood gush freely from the butcher's hand and spray across the timber floor. Glaring up into the passenger's face, he prepared to run him through. A contorted grin, all teeth and malice, gleamed back at him, causing an involuntary whimper to escape his dry lips. Staring into that predatory face banished all thoughts of the machete.

The man spoke for the first time since he had boarded the trawler. "My name is Carlos, Captain Sanchez. Meet the Soul Dagger."

From the doorway, Pico watched with hypnotic fascination as the blade exploded out the back of the Captain's head. It was all way too much. He collapsed to the floor, sobbing and begging for mercy.

Carlos gripped the Captain's greasy hair and drew the dagger back out of his face. He was still grinning as he walked with scarcely a whisper of movement over to the huddled snivelling form of Pico.

The chicken claw dangled from a cord around his neck. He casually pulled it over his head, saying, "Pico, mi amigo." The voice was strangely similar to the Captain's.

Shocked, Pico looked up in mid sob through tear-filled eyes. The dagger was no where to be seen. Instead, the passenger held out his hand. Pico took it and was helped to his feet.

When he was standing, Carlos thrust the claw into the young man's heart.

Pico gagged and his eyes rolled back into their sockets. As everything began to fade, he felt something move in his chest.

The corridor was plain with magnolia walls and lit only by a couple of naked bulbs with a staircase leading to the ground floor at the end and several doors leading off it. Jason, followed quickly by Davis, appeared at the top of the stairs and walked past two doors to the third at the end. The Private put a hand on the Jason's shoulder as they approached. "I'm telling you, man, it'll be for the best. You'll be at too much risk if you stay in New York."

The Prince shook his head. "Thanks for the concern, but I'm staying. There's so much to do and coordinate here. You'll need all he help you can get." He turned to the door. Davis stepped in the way.

"Jason, you're too important, dammit. You have to be protected."

Jason's face dropped and his shoulders sagged. When he looked up at his friend once more, he was filled with sadness. "Bobby, you must understand. I need to do *something*. My *father's* out there…"

"You have nothing to prove, Jason," Davis implored.

"He is my father and my King," Jason responded sternly.

Davis looked at him for a moment longer then sighed and stepped aside. The look of gratitude on the young Prince's face said it all. Jason patted his shoulder then walked into the room.

The only occupants, Madeline, Travis and the safehouse controller—a gaunt bearded man called Sykes—were seated around one of three plastic canteen tables. Boxes of supplies were neatly stacked against the far wall beside a compact kitchenette and ancient-looking vending machine. As Jason entered the two men stood, the latter pausing briefly to stub out a cigarette.

As he strode over to the table, the Prince wasted no time. "Maddy, before you start, I have decided to stay and help the resistance here."

Madeline crossed her arms and met his defiant stare. "I'm not going to argue about this, Jason. You cannot stay; it's far too dangerous.

We've already made the necessary arrangements to move you to the country."

"It's for the best, Jason," Travis added.

The young Prince stood resolute with his hands on his hips. "You can cancel them. I am not going anywhere. Everyone else is doing their bit for the cause, putting their lives in jeopardy. I am no different."

Madeline shook her head angrily. "That's precisely where you are wrong. You are different; you are the Heir to the Throne! We have to protect you at all costs and we are all charged with that one task, me included."

"That is horseshit!"

Madeline leapt out of her chair and slapped him across the face. "How dare you speak to me like that!" She immediately withdrew her hand to her mouth, visibly shaken. Travis and Sykes remained sullen. "I'm so sorry, Jason."

Jason took his hand from his reddening cheek and held Madeline's. His tone mournful, he said, "I'm sorry too, but you must understand. It is precisely *because* I am the Heir to the Throne that means I have a responsibility here. It's my duty as Heir to do whatever I can to help the Monarchy. I cannot hide from all this, even if I wanted to."

Madeline's eyes began to well up. "Jason, please…"

Jason gripped her hand tighter. "I need to do this for one other reason—the most important reason—I need to do this for my father. Maddy, he's alone out there…" His tone faltered for a moment. "They're hunting him down. I have got to help him."

Madeline pulled him into her arms and began to cry. Sykes lit another cigarette. Travis watched them and managed a tired smile.

The white-crested Sacramento Mountains thrust skyward, engulfing the horizon in front of the King's small group of vehicles, with lush oak and pine savannahs extending for miles from the slopes and the foothills. As they drew closer, cautiously negotiating their way along a little used secondary route, lined with mature pines, the 11,977 feet peak of Sierra Blanca poked through breaks in the cloud cover. The sight went some way to renew their weary spirits.

After the events in Texas, it had been decided that the West Coast would be far less risky than attempting anything from the Gulf. So now, they moved deeper into North Mexico State with those recent events far behind them, but still vivid in the forefront of their minds.

As they moved into the foothills, the forward scout relayed details of an approaching target to Speyer in the lead team. He instantly announced it to the Major.

"ID?" Reynolds asked.

The Lieutenant, often mistaken for a surfer when out of uniform, took a bite out of a snack bar, leaving it dangling in his mouth while he tapped instructions into his console. As information appeared, he discarded the snack before saying while swallowing, "Tracked cargo vehicle; armed and armoured. Forty-six metres long, twelve wide and nineteen high. A re-fitted old '20s Mammoth." He paused to lick chocolate from his lips and raised an eyebrow as armaments were listed. He shook his head and continued, "Front mounted 120mm quad cannon; front and back 20mm Machine guns and one roof mounted ground to orbit MED-6000 beam battery gun...thought they were all scrapped in the 50s."

"I'll be damned," Reynolds muttered, rubbing his coarse chin. "A Mammoth. Who?"

"No military markings; civilian, by the looks of it. Could've been recently commissioned though. No visible registration; just a name."

"What name?"

"Samson."

Reynolds considered his options. Such a vehicle could be handy. It had some heavy firepower, more than the bulk of military hardware around these days. They certainly did not build them like they used to. Even a hovernaught would think twice. "Right," he said finally, making his decision. "Move in; I want it. Alpha squad on foot—enter, capture crew and secure. Keep everyone else at a safe distance. Got it?"

Speyer smiled. "Yessir."

"Okay. Bravo and Charlie scouts take positions at the following grid reference and prepare to jam transmissions when the fun starts. Everybody else—"

"Wait, we got company." Speyer interrupted with the half-eaten snack hovering close to his mouth. "Four new targets approaching first. Civilian skimmers, lightly armed. Bandits."

"Scratch initial," Reynolds ordered instantly. "Observe and standby." He paused for confirmations, then turned to Paul and Samantha. "Sire, we've located a large cargo carrier which could be of some use to us. A small group of bandits are moving in on it. We'll wait and watch for now, just in case it's some kind of trap."

"I see," Paul replied. "You want to 'take' it?"

"The vehicles we have at the minute have become something of a hindrance, drawing a considerable amount of unwanted attention to us. We need a new look. This Samson could help us there." He smiled and added, "It's also carrying some powerful weaponry."

The Major concluded by saying, "As soon as we see what these bandits are up to we'll move in."

Paul nodded and, for reasons unknown to him, wondered how the crew would react to their vehicle being commandeered by force. But the vehicle was needed for the war effort and they should consider it an honour to have their vehicle commissioned by their King in person. He smiled cynically at that last thought and turned to look out of the window to conceal it from the others.

The first two dented skimmers shot into view as the wide dirt road snaked around a rocky outcrop. Sloping down and spreading out below on one side of the track was a wide expanse of sparse woodland. The oaks and pines, punctuated by the occasional fir, grew dense with the steep incline on the other side.

They appeared right in front of the old and rusted, motorized dinosaur known as the Samson. It had been trundling carefully as it squeezed its obese frame into the barely accommodating road, its tracks churning up great clods of earth. Roof-mounted machine guns flared and spat hot lead in waves at the lumbering transporter.

From inside the Samson's bridge, a somewhat shaggy trader in his mid thirties groaned inwardly. Casey Shacks rarely enjoyed the luxury of a good mood outside of a PASH high but, up until a moment ago, that was what he had been experiencing. "Shit," he muttered to himself with the resignation of someone who just knew the mood wouldn't last.

Several of the overheads had blown and never been replaced, lending gloom to the smoky atmosphere. The bridge was built to comfortably accommodate a crew of five for long journeys, however, Casey was sat alone at the controls, with his only company being a rusty disassembled maintenance droid dumped in the corner and...

"Four of'em, Jay," a metallic female voice with a distinct Texan accent yelled from a speaker on the console marked in faded lettering CHARLIE I. "Get'em!"

A second speaker, marked CHARLIE II, added in a soft male tone, "I reckon it ma'be wise if w'just sit tight. W'don't wan'any trouble."

"Shut it, th'pair o'ya," Casey spat. "One, gimme th'front '20. Two, keep it shut."

"Yeah!" One whooped.

"Huh," Two mumbled moodily.

A joystick popped up from the coffee-stained and trash-littered console. Casey grabbed for it instinctively, catapulting a half-filled coffee cup against the main screen. He lingered a moment, contemplating the dripping mass and then shook his head. "Okay, here'w'go." He hit a series of buttons in quick succession on the terminal in front of him. A front and back view from the Samson appeared on two monitors with a heads-up display on each.

He expertly manoeuvred the crosshairs on to one of the unsuspecting attackers who had now stopped firing and was approaching cautiously. As they centred on it he squeezed the trigger.

A shower of gunfire engulfed the first target, drilling a dot to dot pattern across the skimmer's left side. It spun off the road and down the rough decline, clipping a jagged rock in the process. A small explosion tore through the anti-gravity pack, throwing the doomed skimmer crashing into the ground. A fireball followed.

"Yarrr!" One roared triumphantly. Then quickly added, "Watch it!"

"W'gonna die!" Two whimpered.

"Miss'le lock!" Casey chorused. The huge transporter trembled as the screaming projectile struck its port side. "Sonuvabitch!" The culprit shot past, barely a foot from the Samson's side, and came into view on the rear camera. He snarled and ordered, "Switch t'rear gun."

Both monitors hissed static, throwing the trader back in his seat. He rolled his eyes heavenward. "Not now, baby, please." He thumped the console in front of the defective hardware. The screen crackled to life. "Thank you, Lord all mighty! Now you're hist'ry, bud."

He yanked back on the stick, drawing the attacker into the crosshairs. He fired instantly. The nimble little skimmer veered left, dancing aside the hail of bullets. Casey kept his finger tight on the trigger and angrily jerked it to one side.

Gunfire exploded all around the darting bandit for several long seconds before half a dozen rounds finally struck the windscreen. Blood and glass erupted from the destroyed driver's compartment. The out of control skimmer zigzagged wildly then swerved into a collision course with the Samson's rear.

"Aw shit," Casey uttered. "That ain't gonna do th'paint job no good."

The kamikaze bandit smashed into the rear access ramp with an earth shattering jolt. The trader recoiled from the blow as if he had been the one struck.

"Case!" CHARLIE I shouted, "'Nuther miss'le, babe."

He forced the thought of the damage to his precious Samson aside and tried to locate the two remaining bandits. "Screw th'damn miss'le! Gimme th'quad. I had enough o'these assholes."

"Right on!" One eagerly complied as the Samson shuddered with the impact of the second missile.

After a moment of deafening static, the front view appeared again. The trader poised his finger over the trigger and waited impatiently for both targets to show.

"Target One no longer returning fire," Speyer relayed to Reynolds as he observed the scene. He yawned, somewhat disinterested, before continuing. "Doesn't appear to have taken a hit to the weapons systems. Must be trying a new tactic."

"Continue observation, Luke," the Major replied as he checked his watch. They were wasting time.

"Target Two reloading the AT launcher. Target Four suppressive decoy action." Shaking his head, the Lieutenant added, "Rank amateurs, these guys."

"Blast th'bastards!" One yelled as the second skimmer shot into view.

"Bye-bye," Casey muttered and squeezed the trigger. Nothing happened. "What?!" he blurted with a mixture of shock, anger and desperation. Both bandits hung in view for one more teasing second, then disappeared.

"No," Casey said numbly.

"It ain't my fault!" One shouted despairingly.

"I tol'ya so," Two added just at the wrong time. His speaker was disconnected before he could say another word.

"Miss'le lock," One cautiously informed a still numbed Casey.

"Fuck off!" Casey spat at the electronic voice as the missile hit. The lights flickered for a moment, uncertain whether or not to kick the trader while he was down. For an instant Casey wilted and gave up, but then the power decided that it would be more fun to see what else could go wrong. It stayed on.

That was no consolation to Casey. "Jackass-heap'o'shit" he bellowed and gave the console an almighty thump. Both Casey and the Samson voiced their discomfort—more so from the former—as the two skimmers came back into sight.

The four 120mm cannons roared and recoiled back into the body. Everything forward of the devastating guns exploded in a mass of flames, dirt and debris. The two skimmers vanished in the destruction.

Reynolds watched, admiring the destructive capacity of the Samson's firepower. Paul and Samantha also observed the explosions from the Major's terminal. They were mutually stunned into silence. It was both awe inspiring and horrific at the same time.

Still rubbing his trembling bruised hand, Casey sat back in his chair, pale and sweating. Despite the onset of the shakes, with a satisfied smile, said, "Beautiful."

"Too fuckin' right!" One agreed.

His smile was quickly drowned by an angry glare. "Why the fuck don't anythin work' round' ere? W' nearly got diced, shit-fo-brains."

"It ain't my fault, Casey," One muttered sheepishly.

The trader uttered a few inaudible, non-complimentary words and reconnected CHARLIE II with a trembling hand.

"Waddidya do that for?" Two asked instantly, openly hurt.

"Cuz y' pissed me off. Just gimme a damage report."

If Two had breath, he would have muttered under it when he mumbled, "Y' never switch *One* off…"

Casey rolled his eyes. "Gimme a break here! Gimme the goddamn damage report."

The speaker emitted a click that could have been a tut and then Two grumpily said, "Hydraulics in th' rear are totalled; 'lecticals in th' garage' n' workshops are gone; Wheel Five is badly buckled; weapons systems are malfunctioning an' w' really need a new paint job."

Fumbling in his faded leather jacket that was draped over the chair next to him, Casey sighed and said, "Well, it was fun." His fingers wrapped around the cylindrical object in the pocket and the tremors seemed to ease just with the contact.

"It was?" If One could have cocked an eyebrow she would have.

"Yeah…it was. Right. No sweat."

Reynolds had waited long enough. Speaking into his mike, he said, "Move in."

"Right," Speyer replied eagerly with normal business being resumed. "Alpha squad; deploy and split in two. One on rear; two on side door. Scouts and turrets; cover and suppressives on my command. Blueprints transferred to wrist tac-coms. Be advised; subdue, do not eliminate. All units acknowledge." The Lieutenant listened intently to the confirmations, then replied, "All units go."

56

Alpha team's APC swung past Speyer's skimmer with a roar of thrusters, followed by one of the agile two-seater scouts.

After popping a pill, Casey chased it with an iced beer that he had retrieved from a well-stocked cooler and slumped back down in his chair. The leather was worn and split and it creaked under his weight, but it had been too many years in the training to ever consider replacing. He sighed with the comfort it afforded him and felt the ebbing of his adrenaline replaced with a rising spike from his stomach as the PASH started to take effect.

Smiling at the glorious tingling sensation, he dreamily told his two AI companions, "Repairs'll have t'wait. Let's git. I got'n'appointment t'keep and Dorian ain't the kinda guy to keep waitin."

Leaning forward with considerable effort, he stabbed several buttons and awaited a reaction. When the transporter continued to sit dumbly, ignoring the operators' instructions, Jay proceeded to hammer a separate button a number of times. When the only response was a dull whine from deep within the bowls of the Samson, he felt the rising high drop like a stone. He kicked the console in desperation and stabbed the button one more time.

With a grinding clamour, the Samson's engines turned over and the transporter slowly began to trundle backwards.

"Aw, fo'cryin'out loud!" The trader yanked at his haywire hair with blurry hands and thrust a lever to his left forward. After a brief clanking the tracks stopped then began to turn in a forward motion.

Casey shook his head in an attempt to clear his vision. "Nuthin'eva works right in this damn thing."

"That's cuz you always do th'repairs," Two pointed out.

Casey's eyes narrowed. "See! Now that's what I'm talkin 'bout! That kinda attitude's what gits you switched off, boy! You know, you'll talk real funny w'crossed wires."

"Yeah," One added smugly as a distant explosion rumbled through the Samson like an upset stomach.

"Now what?" Casey visibly sagged once more. "Carn'a guy git no peace no more? What's happ'nin?"

There was a noticeable pause as One mentally chewed her proverbial bottom lip. "Ermm, y'ain't gonna like this, but—"

"Jus'tell me, fo'Godssake."

"Okay. Unknown host'le forces enterin," One said quickly.

Casey sat bolt upright in his chair, casting the empty can of beer across the room. "What?! Shit! Where?" A feeling of nausea signalled the demise of the lingering effects of the PASH.

"How th'Hell'm I s'posed t'know?" One snapped back defensively. "Ya never fixed th'damn heat sensors."

"Shit!"

"Ya said that already," Two injected. His timing was perfect, as usual. He was disconnected before he was able to object.

One laughed. There was another explosion; much closer.

"Quit it," he snapped at One. "W'might have some real problems here." He drew his Harvey Wallbanger from his hip holster, checked the 8 round clip was full and flicked off the safety. After placing it within easy reach on the console, he considered his options. Nothing sprung to mind.

As he scratched his head, followed by the thick stubble on his chin, the thought of a second hit was both enticing and repulsing him. He glanced around the bridge looking for inspiration and to take his mind off a hit. After a second's thought, he asked, "What'bout th'sound sensors?"

"Nope," One answered, trying to be apologetic.

"Fo'—" He stopped himself, deciding that, for once, moaning would not help. "Bring th'elevator up'n'cut power to it. Screw th'cargo—Dorian can't kill me if I'm already dead—but they ain't gettin in'ere."

"Y'got it," One complied. The elevator slowly and painfully made its way to the top of the shaft. "Now what?"

"Access ladder; lock th'cover and th'doors to it."

"Right. What else?"

"Air ducts," Casey remembered.

"Oh yeah. I f'got'bout them."

Casey held his head in his hands and groaned. The headache was kicking in already. "I could git more help from a goddamn calculator. Seal'em."

"Right, d—" One was cut off in mid sentence as the two air duct grills blew off.

Casey went for his gun as two stun grenades hit the floor and exploded. Pain tore at all of the trader's senses at the same time and, with it, all thoughts of fighting were lost. Two armoured soldiers dove in straight after the grenades and two seconds later he was, gratefully, rendered unconscious.

# Chapter 4

## A Dead King?

*Fort Helina (West Coast Loyalist Command), San Diego, California.*

The sky was an angry grey over the Californian coastal city of San Diego. The clouds had yet to burst, so the atmosphere was humid with only a gentle breeze to stir the palm trees; or rather the few that remained.

More than half of the eastern side of the city and outer districts was shrouded in smoke and flames. Heavy artillery was currently bombarding the districts of Poway and Lemon Grove from emplacements stretching all along the edge of the greenbelt from the National Forest down almost as far as Boulder Oaks. Loyalist units were dug in along the western fringe of the two districts, but had taken heavy casualties. Not a single building had escaped the relentless battering.

Republican infantry and armour were slowly advancing their positions, aided by the artillery and air support from circling helicopter gunships. Sporadic exchanges flared up here and there across the stretch of no man's land between the two forces but fell short of escalating into a full scale battle…for now.

The Command Centre, in the belly of Fort Helina, was swollen with activity. Its open-plan design compensated for the cluttered appearance, but could not mask the overflowing waste bins, crammed work stations and unwashed bodies.

The San Diego garrison Commander, Major Daniel Yeoville, was only vaguely aware of the dozen or so other officers and staff rushing about around him, as he paced back and forth. They carried out their duties unceasingly, each one of them a picture of grim single-mindedness. The offices were a shambles, work surfaces covered with scattered reports, stats and empty coffee cups. The occupants were grimy, sweat-stained and dishevelled and there was no sign of polite protocol—they had no time for salutes or pleasantries—and yet despite everything the command centre purred like a well oiled machine.

The Major's shadowed face had given up trying to conceal his tormented thoughts. His situation was grave; Republican forces had him surrounded and heavily outnumbered. His supplies were running out and the few armoured vehicles that he had left were stretched hopelessly thin along his retreating lines. They were under constant bombardment from artillery and every other day the Republicans tried to punch yet another hole in his defences.

He was losing ground at a spiralling rate, and now, above all else, there was the latest intelligence report. It told him plain and cold that the one man they fought for was already dead.

The King was dead; that's what the latest news report from civilian media sources had announced. Yeoville did not believe it; it was just another Republican ploy to demoralize the opposition, but some of his men were starting to believe it and once that took hold it would spread like a cancer. Without their one shred of hope his garrison would fall apart.

They had already suffered crushing defeats and unprecedented hatred—it was enough to destroy the strongest soldier. They were cut off from re-supply or reinforcements from central command. And still it bore down on them like some indestructible beast; relentless and ravenous.

Somms had given him the simple yet horrifying command to just 'hold on as long as possible'. The General never did mince his words and for that Yeoville had the deepest respect for the man, even if it did terrify him at the same time.

His thoughts returned to his leader. On that front his emotions were in turmoil and for that he was awash with guilt. The events prior to the rebellion and the rebellion itself deeply disturbed him. Again he was doing the one thing he had been reprimanded for in the past—questioning. A soldier was supposed to obey, react and overcome. Questioning was not part of the process.

The last statement brought a half-smile to his recently depressed features. Throughout his entire career he had protested against such doctrine. He strongly believed that questioning and thinking for one's self would make a far more effective soldier in the long run. A soldier should not just obey but should also understand and (hopefully!) agree with the orders. It wasn't necessarily always a practical idea and it was rather a utopian outlook, but it was always something that he had believed in. Maybe he had been wrong.

This time he actually laughed.

One thing he was sure about was that if you swept away all the garbage—rumours, propaganda, prejudices—King Paul was a good man. He had his faults, that much was undeniable, but through it all he had remained honest.

His thoughts were doing him no favours. He needed to work; to keep his mind occupied otherwise the weight of it all would surely drag him down. He walked over to the tactical operations display of the city and surrounding area located in the centre of the room. Three officers—two men and a woman—stood by it, in deep discussion.

"OK, what have you come up with?"

It was the woman, Demoore, a tall olive-skinned Lieutenant who answered. "Out of the two possibilities—Poway and Lemon Grove—we believe their next push will be Poway." She tapped the north-eastern area of the map.

"Increased artillery fire in those areas rule out anywhere else," the older of the two men, Captain Palmer, injected. "Last time they tried a push without it their losses were way too heavy." He removed his glasses and rubbed his deep set eyes before continuing.

"Now, we know that Colonel Ryker is under a lot of pressure to take us without incurring heavy losses—his men are wanted down south. To facilitate this we know Washington have sacrificed some time to make sure that losses are minimal. They've never tried a push in Sector Five, but the last time they made a move on Sector Two they suffered substantially greater losses than other areas of advance due to our superior positions in the area. Given that, one would assume they wouldn't make the same mistake twice, instead they'd give the untried but relatively easier path through Poway a chance. Increasing the bombardment in Sector Two's got to be a ploy to dilute our forces."

The other man, a black captain called Jones, seemed unconvinced. "It still could be a double-bluff." He looked to his superior. Yeoville could see the young man's suppressed fear. "I mean," the Captain continued, "even with the defences in Sector Two it wouldn't take much to roll right on through if the bulk of our forces were in the north-east."

The Major considered his options, his tactical mind probing every possible approach to the dilemma. Ryker's plan was simple: choose the two areas furthest away from each other to maximize the time that it would take reinforcements to arrive from whichever target was the decoy. Two choices—hedge the bets and suffer badly either way or lump everything on to the favourite with the possibility of losing everything. Yeoville had never been a keen gambler, but sometimes life gave you no choice but to take a chance.

"Set up all units assigned to the counter-attack in Sector Five." Yeoville did not like half measures. "Position the gunships in Miramar; I want them refuelled and at the ready. Redirect all artillery and hold them until Ryker is fully committed, that way we'll maximize the effect."

"Right, Dan," Palmer replied, nodding approvingly.

As the three officers started distributing orders to the field, Yeoville excused himself and walked over to a computer terminal with a young woman sat at it, typing sporadically.

The Corporal turned to face him as he appeared by her side. "Sir?"

He smiled and asked, "Were you able to find out much on the Southern Continent guerrilla groups?"

"Yes, Sir. I managed to access a lot of data from the Intelligence Net plus a few civilian sources." She tapped several keys and paused a moment for the appropriate text to appear. "Here it is. The Brazilian Freedom Fighters came top of the list. They control the majority of the south now after getting the backing of the Republic. It's estimated at sixty-five percent control now. They're classified a military dictatorship and led by a General Ricardo Mendossa, a former lieutenant colonel in the Army—I haven't been able to access his personal files. They're steadily increasing in strength and support. Their strengths lie in their numbers, fanatical loyalties and organisation, but equipment is believed to be low-grade—stolen, decommissioned or civilian conversions.

"Next on the list is the Democratic Government of Ecuador; they have turned Ecuador state independent. The leader is President Fernando Maximillian, the former Guayaquil Mayor—I've managed to get elements of his personal files. Stable at the moment, but that will change when the BFF's borders reach them. Military stats are sketchy, but it's estimated that they hold a small number of regulars with high-grade equipment with strong militia and police support.

"Then there is the Argentinean Alliance; relatively strong in numbers, but disorganised. Another military dictatorship led by an ex-colonel called Juan Bequellez—again I have a small amount of information from his files. They currently have an unofficial non-aggression pact with the BFF but their relations are unpredictable at best.

"There is also an organisation known as the Aztecs, but there is very little information on them at the present apart from a possible name of the leader—Vasquez—and some kind of tribal structure. Their support seems to stem from villages and smaller towns all across the central states.

"Now, the smaller groups comprise of the following—the Guyanan Guerrillas; Paraguay Command; Montevideo Independence Group; Aires Breakaway group and the Recife Bandits. All have unknown loyalties; possibly none and have only localised influences. Mainly comprise of civilians backed up by small numbers of rogue military and militia units." The Corporal turned away from the screen and handed the Major a pile of documents. "This is everything I've compiled, including the extracts from personal files."

Yeoville stared at the screen for a moment, mulling over the information, then said, "Can you see if you can dig up anything else on Ecuador?" As an after thought, he added, "And try to find more on these Aztecs as well."

The young woman arched her stiff back. "Yes, Sir."

Pausing before leaving, he placed a hand on her shoulder and smiled reassuringly. "Thanks, Lyn." When he turned away, the smile was impossible to sustain.

He had almost reached the drinks dispenser when the lights dimmed and turned red. For an instant the room fell silent, then Jones shouted, "The assault's started!" and the siren began to wail.

A knot tightened in the Major's stomach and the thought of coffee was drowned into insignificance. He told himself to stay cool as he headed straight back to the tactical operations display. "Where?" he asked as he approached.

"Sector Five," Palmer replied.

"Units in position?"

"Just," Demoore added as the siren cut out, leaving human voices to fill the void.

Yeoville clenched a fist and allowed himself to breathe. Looking to the other captain who was listening intently to his headset, he said, "Talk to me, Dez."

Jones continued to listen for a couple of seconds, then said, "Approximately a battalion of infantry; backed up by an armoured company and three or four gunships. Into no mans land and engaging. Our 'ships already on intercept."

After sweeping between Woodson and Iron, the two dark forms halted above the Poway skyline. The heavy cloud cover lent the evening early purchase, allowing them a phantom-like appearance. It was only the whump-whump-whump of rotor blades that shattered the illusion. Below, Loyalists troops had taken up positions inside the battered buildings and behind sandbag and barbwire walls blocking the streets.

Without warning, rockets erupted from the armoured helicopter gunships and engulfed the battered suburbs and Loyalist frontline. In seconds the scene in front of them was awash with flames and destruction. Small arms fire scattered across the sky illuminating it in glowing tracer technicolor. A couple of rockets screamed heavenward.

The gunships did not linger; they broke, banking left and right. As the roar of their blades faded, the battle below took hold.

Yeoville stood tense, sweat standing out on his forehead as he endeavoured to think and issue orders at the same time. Just on their doorstep the battle raged, but, to the occupants of the Command Centre, the destruction was soundless apart from the soft, rhythmic thump of artillery shells falling above them.

Apartment blocks burst into flames, shops exploded, churches collapsed while all the time over head and all around helicopters buzzed the skies, locked in erratic dog fights. Tanks tore through everything in their paths, turrets blazing relentlessly while soldiers picked their way through cratered streets and crumbling buildings, their comrades and friends dropping around them with every heartbeat.

Outside, the battle continued, while Yeoville gave more and more orders. He knew what was happening out there; to the city, the people, his men. His chest heaved with it, but he had a job to do and he had to get on with it otherwise it would get worse; much worse.

The casualties mounted. Jones, just relaying the information and refusing to actually listen to it, said, "Lieutenant Bowan dead. Bravo Company; fifty percent losses. Second L. requests abort hold and regroup."

The Major's mind reeled. "Pull back to Sector Four. First and Second platoons from Charlie reinforce. Concentrate artillery to cover." Jones instantly relayed the orders. "Any more skimmers available from Recon?"

Palmer shook his head grimly. "Not a chance."

"Hovernaught status?"

The Captain contacted the hovernaught as Jones continued to relay reports and orders to and from the field. Palmer spoke briefly to the captain of the vessel and then turned to Yeoville. "Svenson reports they've taken several direct hits; continuing rear guard action to cover Bravo's withdrawal."

"They've taken enough of a pounding; pull it back to Miramar. Use their artillery and mortars to cover." The Major paused to down the coffee some kind soul had brought him earlier. It momentarily eased his coarse throat. "Skimmers report?"

Palmer raised the company commander as the base trembled with a direct hit. The lights flickered for a split second, but in that time Yeoville's heart stopped and leapt into his throat. He breathed a silent prayer and looked back to Palmer.

"Seven—no, six—remaining," the Captain informed him. "One damaged. O'Cleaf is dead. Platoon Sergeant Geron reports Republican forces still pushing forward with everything they've got. They're playing cat and mouse with their armour."

"Right, pull them back to their RV point; scatter mines behind them. Tell them to use everything; we'll have to worry about re-supplying later."

"Blue 4 down," Jones injected. "Hovernaught taken another direct hit from artillery—crippled and in flames."

"Get them out of there!" Yeoville shouted.

"Svenson refuses to abandon. He's continuing to cover retreat with remaining weaponry," Palmer said, rubbing his throbbing temple.

"Dammit, Beau!" Yeoville cast the empty coffee cup across the room. To Demoore, he said, "Do we have anything left in the field that we can use?" He already knew the answer. She shook her head; the gesture was complete and utter dejection.

"Please," the Major uttered scarcely about a whisper, "just a little longer. *Come on.*"

"Blue 7 badly damaged; returning to Miramar," Jones said bitterly.

"Bravo on Charlie's position; seventy-five percent losses. Taking hits from armour and one gunship."

"Hell," Palmer spat, "when the infantry reach them they'll be overrun in seconds." He paused to listen to his headset. "Four skimmers left. Mines proving effective; heavy losses reported from Republican units."

Jones interrupted. "Contact lost with 2nd Platoon."

"Their remaining 'ship's returning to base; probably to re-arm," Palmer said.

Jones held up his hand. "Wait! Svenson reports enemy infantry no longer advancing; they're consolidating their position. Armour disengaging and pulling back to reinforce them."

Yeoville stopped pacing and shouted, "Target everything onto them! Pound those positions into the ground." Jones and Palmer simultaneously rattled off orders to all relevant units.

As acknowledgements came in another explosion sent a shiver through the base. Demoore's headset captured her attention for a moment. She replied in short then told the Major, "A collapsed ceiling and electrical fire on A-Level. That last hit breached us. Reported to be three dead and several wounded. Fire Control on their way."

Yeoville ran a hand through his closely cropped hair and was about to curse when Jones interrupted him.

"Spotters report Republican forces withdrawing; all attempts at digging in abandoned."

"That's confirmed," Palmer added. Longing for a cigarette, he dropped into a chair and let out a long deep sigh. With trembling hands, Jones picked up his long forgotten cup of cold coffee and downed the lot.

Yeoville closed his eyes to utter a short prayer but the blackness filled him with dread. It was merely a temporary reprieve, not a pardon. Next time they could stroll up and knock. He did not hear anyone else cheering either.

The cell was small, but thankfully, clean and relatively bright. Queen Jennifer sat at a plain bare table and listened to the soft hum emitting from the light panels in the ceiling. She longed for a window to look out upon rolling plains like she used to do on quiet afternoons in Montana. That was a luxury long gone—the ranch had been burned to the ground and the staff incarcerated or executed. The only thing left to cling on to was the memory. Of her family, friends, life…Memories were all that remained.

The artificial light was beginning to aggravate her migraine problem; not that a migraine constituted any kind of real trauma given the current predicament.

In front of her, the afternoon meal she had been given lay cold and untouched. It had looked appetising enough and her body yearned for the food, but eating was the last thing on her mind. With the meal they had brought news of her husband's death.

He had supposedly been found dead when, shortly after refusing to surrender, government troops moved in to capture him only to find that he had already committed suicide. His last few guards had joined him. And that was the end of that.

When the officer first uttered the words, with just a hint of satisfaction, her mind instantly believed it. A lump formed in her throat and tears distorted her vision. She knew that Paul would rather take his own life than be captured. God knows, at the time she had contemplated the very same. Angelica had tried the day after her husband and son had been put to death. She did not succeed; they refused to let her die, to ease her suffering. Instead they forced her to live on in misery. They would have stopped her too, if she tried. But that was not the reason why she decided against it.

Ignoring her head, deep down her heart dared to whisper an alternative. He was alive. He had to be. With that, came the thought that one day he would come for her. There was not much she could do for him—that made her feel utterly useless—but there was one thing still within her power and that was to stay strong for him.

His position had, of course, over the years caused a strain on their relationship. The last two had been particularly bad, spending very little time together, usually only to make an effort for Jason or as part of an official engagement. A long string of events and problems had just gotten in the way, causing an ever widening gap between them. But that did not change the fact that he was still her husband and that they still loved one another.

Paul would always portray the characteristics of a rock—that was his nature, inherent from his father—but Jennifer had also seen a more frail side to his nature, one that she alone knew existed. There had been times after making difficult decisions (some that she had not agreed with) in the darkness of early morning that he had cried out in what she could only describe as misery. In those quiet moments she would hold him. They would never talk about it when they arose and, the one time she had mentioned anything, Paul had denied all knowledge.

What had the media and the new authorities described him as? 'A callous dictator.' One newspaper had even gone as far as 'Evil'. Paul? How could they say such things? They did not know him as she did.

Her hands trembled as she gently caressed her silk handkerchief. Tears trickled down her cheeks, but she made no attempt to dab them.

General Somms looked up from the field reports on his desk to acknowledge the Colonel that had just entered his cluttered office. "Well?"

Colonel Henderson's eyes were downcast. "Contact has just been lost with Portland and Belem. Presumed overrun." The man was in his late thirties, but the thick black beard, the stress lines and the bags under his eyes aged him a further ten years.

Somms remembered the tanned and clean-shaven Major striding into his office two years ago ready to take on the world. It could not be the same old man that sagged in front of him now.

Somms looked away from the haunted face; it was an all too familiar sight to him these days. His gaze settled upon the photograph of his wife, all rosy cheeks and smiles. Her face emanated a warmth that was unequalled. He turned back to Henderson a fraction too quickly and immediately offered the Colonel a seat. "What about Diego?"

Henderson took out a carton of cigarettes, offered one to Somms, who failed to refuse as quickly as he usually did, then clumsily lit one for himself. He savoured it for a moment before answering. "Their situation is rapidly deteriorating. They have approximately a battalion of regulars plus the same again in support staff, less than a company of assorted armour and a couple of gunships. They have the back-up of around a thousand poorly equipped civilians-cum-militia and the 103rd Attack Squadron has been permanently grounded—Miramar has lost ops, radar and all remaining launch sites. They pounded it into the dirt."

Somms remained expressionless as Henderson gave his report, silently regretting not accepting the cigarette. His doctor had all but put a gun to his head to force him to give them up four years ago; 'life or death,' he had said, 'it's your choice.' Dorothy had needed him then— the illness had sapped most of her strength. He had to be there for her, so he banished them from his life forever. Although now that she was gone, forever seemed pointless.

"A Republican garrison at Division strength with armour and air support are besieging them. There's also a sizeable element of the Pacific Fleet offshore." Henderson forced a smile. "On the plus side for them now that Miramar has been incapacitated, the elements of the 101st that were carrying out air raids across the city are being relocated."

"Which unfortunate sonuvabitch is going to have them knocking on his door?"

"Us."

Somms nodded. "Figures."

"Also," Henderson added, "Lieutenant Colonel Decker has been in contact again. No sign of the Falklands being compromised. He wishes to know, 'how long his men will have to sit on their butts?' His words, Sir."

The General sighed. "The Arion Elite are the only counter-attack force we've got left. They're going to be crucial in the coming weeks. Mike should exercise a bit more patience and a lot less bloodlust. Make note of my reply." Henderson pulled out a battered note pad. "Mike, you are to remain on standby, along with the naval contingent, until the King has been located and secured, as per previous communication. I will stress this point one last time—there will come a time in this conflict when your men will be the spearhead of the King's counter-attack. That time is not far away and you can rest assured that you will be the first to know. Until that time is upon us be patient." Somms drew in a deep breath, partially to inhale some of Henderson's passive smoke and massaged an irritating ache in the back of his neck. "Code and scramble it and send it immediately."

"Yessir." The Colonel stood to leave, tapping ash into the grubby ashtray on the edge of the desk.

"And Henderson." Their eyes met. "It doesn't look good at the moment but hang in there. We have a long fight in front of us, but at the end of it the King *will* be victorious." Somms' face was stone-serious, but when Henderson sighed and nodded, his features lightened into a fairly convincing smile.

The door clicked into place behind Henderson and Somms eased back in his chair. Thoughts of missiles and carnage filled his mind and pain, misery and death followed in its wake. Thousands were dying with every passing day for what they thought was right…or wrong. Nothing ever changes. This war was no different to countless wars before it—the African war or even the Great War; the war that ended the Old World and started the New. That was over five hundred years ago and still nothing had changed. Man builds from nothing, destroys it, then builds again. And so the cycle will continue till the end of time. If mankind was indeed the most intelligent life form on the planet, then our self destructive nature walked hand in hand with it.

He stared at the door for some time before his eyes strayed back to the photograph of Dorothy. He was almost glad that she was not alive to witness these turbulent times…almost.

The sadness was quickly replaced by anger. He stood up and slammed the chair against the back wall. *An entire life in the army! Four wars, not including this one. And for what? To end up fighting ourselves.* He leaned against his desk with more than just his own weight. *Haven't we been doing that all along?* He attempted a cynical smile but it turned out to be a grimace. Philosophy was not usually his forte.

Who was he trying to fool? Did they really have a hope in Hell? Was there anything this sad old excuse for a soldier could do? The answer to the latter questions was probably no. As for the first question, Dorothy was no longer with him and she was the one he used to fool. That only left himself.

He straightened up and slowly pulled out his sidearm—a sparkling clean nickel automatic. Along its side, in elaborate italics, it read 10mm ELITE MODEL 66. The weapon had been given a name, much the same as an owner gives his dog a name. Man's best friend.

Somms turned the gun over and over in his hands. It had been given to him thirty-two years ago along with the Lion Cross for Bravery by King Luther, Paul's father. It was one of his most treasured possessions; something he had always been proud of. That was far from the case now. In fact, his previous feelings towards it now felt ridiculous.

He pressed the magazine release and checked what he already knew. It held its full twenty rounds. After easing the clip back into position, he flicked off the safety catch. His hand trembled as he pulled back the well-oiled breech.

As he looked down at the pistol, his thoughts were drawn back to another day, almost three years ago. Dorothy's pale, pain-racked, beautiful face staring up at him from the hospital bed. *"I love you, Bellamy...Don't leave me."*

The gun went out of focus as tears blurred his vision. The same brief picture of the day his wife passed away had come to him many times in the past—on a dark windy night or a calm summer afternoon or when making a coffee late at night (*Bellamy, that'll keep you up all night, hun*)—but this time he actually heard the bleep of the heart monitor, he smelt the old disinfectant poorly covering the scent of illness and decay; he sensed the cold hand of death. He remembered turning round, searching desperately for someone to share his grief, but he had been alone with her. No children to embrace. For years she had prayed for a child, but biology had conspired against them. There was no shoulder to cry on. Then she had just drifted away, like the night slowly extinguishing the day.

As he raised the gun up to his chest another memory flashed before him. A few days earlier. Her smile, like it had been before the illness. *"Remember to look me up when the time comes. Mind you, that won't be for a time yet, Bellamy Albert Somms."* She had highlighted the Albert, as she used to in the early years. *"You still have so much to do. And don't you go fooling around with that racy secretary of yours."* A little wink. Arianne was sixty and loved only two things; poetry and her cats. *"I love you, Bellamy. I can wait."* He remembered kneeling by the bed, holding her warm hand, crying. It must have been so hard for her to say, but she said it anyway; that was her way.

He disarmed the pistol and placed it back in its holster.

Casey Shacks was slouched back in the co-operator's chair, holding a damp rag to his throbbing forehead. He thought the day had hit its lowest point with the bandits but now it was dropping like a stone, and it wasn't even midday yet. He was madder than Hell in a snowstorm and a PASH fix was all that he could concentrate on. And one of these bozos had nabbed his jacket.

There were three men and a woman standing around him. He had recognised one of the men instantly and just knew that things were going to get a whole lot worse. The woman was his secretary, but a real looker all the same. The other two were soldiers—one of which immediately struck Casey as not quite working on a full maintenance crew.

Reynolds folded his arms, quickly growing impatient. The clock was ticking while they were wasting time with this smuggler.

Shacks noted the officer's agitation and smiled inwardly. He wasn't the only one who was having a bad day; that made him feel just a little bit better. He cast the rag aside. "Look, Mister, I don't care who th'hell you are and I don't rightly know what any of this has to do with me— and I mean no disrespect—but I got a job t'do. I got a customer waiting for this cargo."

Reynolds could not believe what he had just heard. "We're at war here and you're worried about your job and your mob customers!"

"It ain't my war, General."

Reynolds stepped forward. "What the hell is your malfunction, boy?"

Paul interrupted, his low, even voice instantly cutting through the tension. "Richard, please."

The Major stopped and took a deep breath. "My apologies, Sire." He turned away from the defiant trader to find a seat on the edge of the grubby console.

The King had watched the brief exchange with sombre eyes. After initially feeling anger, he realised that this man was just trying to get on with his life, such as it was. The commissioning of his vehicle had seemed like a good idea until he had come face to face with its owner. His actions had a direct affect on others; it was a revelation that had not previously been considered. Had he ever considered it? "Mister Shacks, we will not order you to help us."

Shacks was about to shoot off another wise crack, but something in the King's tone and eyes stayed his tongue. After a pause, he muttered, "That's mighty decent of you, sir...your highness."

"All I ask is that you listen to what I have to say and then make your decision."

Casey plucked a half smoked cigarette from behind his ear. It was a quick movement to try to hide the tremors, but Mr Gung Ho saw for sure. "OK."

"Thank you. I am here to ask for your help and I know that the method we used was extreme, but believe me when I tell you that there was no other way, given the circumstances."

The trader shook his head and smiled grimly as he lit the cigarette with careful deliberation that seemed to banish the hand-demon temporarily. "Yep, wrong place at th'wrong time. Story o'my life. Like the time I was in Reno with these two hookers—" He stopped himself when he caught the expressions of his audience.

"Sorry, sir-sire, you w'sayin?"

Paul took a moment to gather his thoughts, before continuing. "I truly sympathise with you, Mister Shacks." The words were out of his mouth before he realised that he actually meant them. Suddenly he felt compelled to apologise. "I do not know whether you support the

Republic, but if you inform me that you do, then you have my word that we will leave you this minute with no further inconvenience to you. You are a civilian and entitled to your own opinions and beliefs, so do not feel in any way obliged to help us."

Casey studied the man. Man? This was the King he was talking to. He had always been portrayed as so powerful—no, mighty was the word. Years ago, in a dive bar in Kentucky, an old timer had likened the King to a mountain. Shacks had smiled then in a bourbon-fuelled haze, but afterwards the image had stuck with him. The man—he felt that he could call him that now—in front of him seemed to emanate that same authority, but he had the feeling that if he scratched the surface he would expose a deep layer of uncertainty.

This revelation seemed to be a lifetime removed from the Monarchy's iron fist rule that he had always know prior; that almighty mentality and the treatment of human beings as an exploitable resource (he had read it on a leaflet once). He had also caught the odd underground newspaper with stories of human rights atrocities and miscarriages of justice. Back then and right up to yesterday none of that had concerned Shacks—it had been none of his business. His business was trading (or smuggling as the authorities preferred to call it). Yet something deep inside persuaded him to listen. It was an instantaneous result that Casey did not feel a part of; it happened and that was that. "Go on," he heard himself say.

The King self-consciously rubbed his bristly chin and then focussed all of his attention on the trader. "This is very difficult for me to say…I have made a great many mistakes in my life—mistakes that weigh heavy on our nation and on my own heart. I want to rectify those errors and your vehicle and expertise would help us immensely." The words poured out like a speech one of his advisors might have written, but the most surprising thing was that he meant every word. He had so much to say—he needed to explain, to apologise even—but he did not have time for all that now. Instead, he knelt down in front of him and said, "I want you to know—damn it, I want everyone to know—I will put right my wrongs. I just need a second chance." His voice faltered on the last word and he realised that his heart was beating furiously in his chest.

It is strange how an awakening can happen; it either takes a lifetime or occasionally, like now, in a moment prostrated before a simple smuggler. Realisation washed over him. He had dragged the country down and held it there in his stubborn grip until it could take no more. This revolution was his fault and his alone, and it was up to him to make it right.

Until the King knelt down in front of him, Casey thought he had seen everything and that words were cheap. He was speechless long after the King had finished. Suddenly a new King knelt before him. But not many people were given a second chance. He did not know whether the King would get it, but he felt this man may actually deserve it.

"Let's just git one thing straight, Your Mightiness," Casey said as the King rose to his feet, looking somewhat embarrassed. "Samson's my vehicle and I got final say on what happens to her."

Paul wanted to hug him but instead he took his hand and squeezed tight. "Thank you, Mister Shacks."

"Nuther thing. M'name's Casey."

# Chapter 5
## Closing In

After acquiring his civilian skimmer in New Orleans, Carlos made his way north-west, sticking to main roads where he could maintain high speed. His auburn eyes focussed on the cracked asphalt that stretched to the horizon, but his mind was fixed to playback.

The Zombie-husk that had once been called Pico had served him well, getting him not only to New Orleans but also past the Inward-bound Inspectorate. It held no further use for him so, not wanting to prolong its torment, he smeared salt on its lips and released him permanently to the grave. It would be days before its carcass would be found.

All thoughts of past action were then discarded as his mind conjured up images of last night's vision; the same one he had experienced in his tonnelle the night before he left Haiti, except this time it had been the most vivid yet. He remembered it frame for frame as if he had a celluloid copy to be played at will. It showed him where to go and what to do.

Jason entered the Canteen/Briefing room without a word and gently closed the door behind him. This time Sykes sat alone at the table, halfway through his second packet of cigarettes and fifth coffee of the morning. He appeared pale and even thinner since their previous meeting. The room was hot and smoky.

"Take a seat, Your Highness." The Controller was in no mood for small talk, his bulging eyes piercing the Prince's. Jason was reaching for the back of a chair as Sykes got started. "Now, you'll be acting as observer and second (he chose the word carefully—this kid wasn't commanding anything yet) on a low risk op to take out a storage depot in the Queens district of the city—here's the address." He handed the Prince a scrap of paper. "Memorize it then destroy it. The team will comprise of yourself, an Explosives Tech—Jim Cowie, who will be commanding the mission—and three cover men. Cowie has his brief to rig the depot in two pre-determined positions on external walls."

After taking in the information on the paper, Jason tore it into small pieces and deposited it into the already bulging ashtray. Sykes eyed the rubbish in his ashtray with annoyance as he finished off another cigarette and jammed it amongst the pieces. He lit another as its predecessor still smouldered.

"You go at zero-hundred," he said between drags, "and after execution, hike it to the safehouse at Maddison Avenue. You'll lay up there for two to three days before returning here. Any questions? Good."

Getting up, Jason asked, "Is Sergeant Travis still on that reconnaissance?"

Sykes flicked ash and nodded. "Not back till tomorrow night."

In the corridor, Jason took a deep breath. This was what he had fought for. Now he had a job to do. His stomach was in knots and he felt clammy, but it was the best he had felt since the beginning of this horrible mess. He would make his father proud.

At the far end of the corridor, Madeline appeared at the top of the stairs. She called out to him.

He met her half way and hugged her.

Holding his hand, she asked him, "Are you sure you want to go through with this? Travis didn't get a chance to finish your refresher training. There'll be other operations, you know, and your leg isn't fully healed yet."

Jason shook his head and smiled. "I spent two years with the Marines remember and the leg's fine too, Maddy. The only reason I'm being allowed to go on this one is because it's low risk. I know that, but at least I am being allowed to do *something*."

"You always put on the brave face, but I know you better."

This time he laughed and hugged her again. "You think you're so clever!"

Reynolds and Shacks were the only two in the bridge of the Samson, the former speaking into his com-link and the latter at the controls. Reynolds no longer wore his insignia or red trims on his uniform and his helmet with its proud red mane had also been disposed of, leaving his uniform plain black.

"And serial numbers on the equipment?" Reynolds was saying.

"All erased. I'll send Cook up with your sidearm," Speyer replied.

"Good. Now, as soon as that portable power cell is connected allocate 50% of output to primary systems. We need more power to bring all the sensors on line." Reynolds paused to check the printouts splayed across the console in front of him. "Yes, we'll keep the remaining 50% in reserve just in case we need the heavy artillery—it's the only way we'll be able to power it up."

"Sounds good. Oh, Anderson's squad have just returned from dumping the APCs and Cobek's team have finished stripping the utilities. We'll be all set when the server reboots. We're ready when you are."

Reynolds thanked him and signed off. He smiled; everything was going like clockwork. Turning to Shacks, he said, "We can get moving again now."

"'Bout time."

Reynolds turned his attention back to his com-link. "Okay, Luke, the next thing is—"

Speyer interrupted. "We've got company."

Reynolds sighed; spoke too soon. "What is it?"

"Republican scout—it's spotted us but not the scouts. He'll have reported in for sure."

"I will want to know which scout was responsible once we've sorted out this situation," Reynolds muttered as he considered his options.

Casey was watching the Major carefully as CHARLIE I crackled into life. "Case—Militia Patrol wants a word wi-ya."

"We'd better surrender," Two was quick to add.

"Any ideas, Major?" Casey asked, considering a rummage in his jacket as his best option.

Reynolds scratched his prickly chin. "We need to avoid a confrontation, if possible. Talk to him—see what he wants. Speyer; stand by."

Casey shook his head and turned to the mike on his console. "Patch'im thru." Static squealed for one deafening moment then made way for a deep authoritive voice.

"This is Republican Militia Sector Guard one-nine-four. Identify."

The trader leaned into the mike. "Erm, yeah, this here's Casey Shacks—commercial shippin'licence Bravo-Lima-two-two-oh. Can ah help yall?"

"Prepare to be boarded."

Casey's mouth worked without forming words for a couple of seconds until his mind caught up with the situation. "C'mon, bud. I gotta deadline t'keep—I'm already runnin'late. Can't ya cut me sum slack here?" He looked to the Major's stone face as he felt beads of sweat starting to rise on his forehead. He felt the fluttering calling. The soldier did not blink—he listened and waited. *God, I need a fix.*

"That's a negative, Mister Shacks. I'm sorry, but we have orders to search every vehicle."

Casey switched off the mike before saying, "Whaddawe do?"

"Go along with it, but stall him," Reynolds said evenly.

"And what the hella you fellas gonna do?" Reynolds was already heading for the elevator.

"Disappear."

"Disappear? Just like that? The great frickin Boroldus! Great! Just fuckin'great!" The doors were already closing on the Major. He turned back to the mike and, after taking a moment to compose himself, switched it back on. "Look, Sector Guard whadever—"

"One-nine-Four," CHARLIE II muttered.

"This is one-nine-four. What's the problem?" The voice was even less patient this time.

"Well, I s'pose it's kinda funny, ya-see I—"

The Republican cut in. "If it's smuggling it's not a problem. We're after bigger fish."

Casey feigned a sigh of relief. "Thanks bud, I really'preciate that. Now, m'hydraulics are shot on th'rear access ramp. I ran into a bunch of bandits'bout thirty clicks back east."

"I didn't hear anything on the emergency channel."

"Yeah, I was in a hurry'n'wanted t'git some distance first." Casey shook his head. *Shit, that's lame.*

"The emergency channel is there for your benefit, Mister Shacks. You're required by law to inform the authorities immediately after the incident." The radio was silent for a moment while the Republican considered his options.

Casey continued to sweat. His mouth was dry and the tremors were returning with a vengeance.

"Report it as soon as we have finished. Lower the steps on your port side entrance."

"Y'got it." It was difficult to contain his relief.

"Good. You know, for a guy in a hurry you sure do dick around a lot," the Republican said matter-of-factly.

Casey smiled. "That's what m'wife used to say…and there was these two hookers in Reno…on second thoughts forget it. See ya in five."

Two troopers in grey uniforms with sidearms at their hips stepped out of the elevator and eyed their surroundings. The skinny, younger man looked openly bored. The older of the two, a robust, pot-bellied man holding sunglasses in one hand and resting his other on the butt of his pistol said, "Mister Shacks." It was not a question.

Casey swung around in his chair. "Yup." He checked the soldier's name tag. "Sergeant O'Malley."

The Sergeant switched his stare from the room to Shacks. "Now that formalities have been dispensed with, would you be so kind as to escort Private Dooley and myself around your vehicle. Then we can get this over with as quickly as possible."

O'Malley sympathetically patted Casey on the back. "I'm sorry for the delay, Case."

As the sergeant followed the lanky form of Private Dooley down the steps to his grumbling patrol unit, Shacks said, "Don't worry'bout it. You guys're only doin'ya job."

O'Malley looked to his skimmer—insectile against the Samson— and then back up to Shacks. "We'll be off then. Thanks for your time."

"Glad to oblige."

The Sergeant slipped his sunglasses back on despite the lack of sunshine. "And remember to report that incident. There could be a reward for those scum-bags. I'll put in a word for you—least I can do in return for that Eagles tip. I'll be putting a hundred on it."

"You bet." He waved to them as they returned to their skimmer then turned to go back inside, intending to get himself a well earned hit.

O'Malley exchanged a couple of words with one of the crew men inside the patrol unit and called after him, "Hold on, Casey."

The trader paused in mid step. *Uh-oh.* Something twisted in his stomach. He turned slowly to look questioningly at the sergeant.

O'Malley was mad—it was plain to see. He threw the radio hand piece back into the skimmer and stomped back over to the bottom of the steps. "The CP Commander wants me to requisition the Samson and draft you. I tried to overturn his decision but he wasn't having any. I'm sorry, Case. I've got no choice." There was genuine sorrow in his ruddy features.

Casey stared down at him, unable to reply, his mind a sudden tornado of panic. A voice to his side spoke before he was able to make any sense of his scrambled mind.

"Be angry, but go along with it," Reynolds whispered.

Casey blinked a couple of times to focus more than just his eyes. "I- I gotta contract t'keep. Whadda'bout my customer? I'll get cut up for fish bait, man. What about me, Russ?" His voice rose a few octaves towards the end of the sentence. There was no doubt what that psychotic Major had in mind. Full blown shakes politely took over from its lesser cousin.

O'Malley shook his head solemnly. "There's nothing I can do—it's martial law and the area commander has absolute authority. I can put an appeal in writing for you when we get back to the CP, but that's it I'm afraid."

Gritting his teeth to stop them chattering, Casey said, "This is great, bud—I'm ruined. My customer ain't the forgiving type. He has serious anger management issues, man; I weren't kiddin bout the fish bait scenario. You tell that boss o'yours that I'm comin'under extreme protest. I wanna speak t'him in person. He might git away w'this sort o'thing with other folk, but he sure-as-shit ain't gonna do it t'Casey Shacks."

O'Malley nodded and turned back to his patrol unit.

"...when he's acknowledged," Reynolds was whispering into his headset.

At the skimmer, O'Malley exchanged brief instructions with the radio operator then trudged back towards the Samson.

"Wait," Reynolds muttered.

The Republican reached the bottom of the steps. Pulling his sunglasses back off, he said, "I'm to ride with you."

As Casey opened his mouth with the express intention of being flippant, the Major's emotionless voice ordered, "Now."

In the blink of an eye the Republican patrol skimmer was a pile of smouldering metal and Sergeant Russell O'Malley was flat on his back with blood trickling out of a hole in his forehead.

Dumbstruck and pale, Casey turned, his ears ringing from the gunshot six inches from his head and looked at the Major's smoking pistol. Even as he watched, Reynolds simultaneously holstered the weapon and barked orders. As soldiers emerged out of foxholes and undergrowth, Casey switched his gaze to O'Malley. He had died instantly, so there was only a little blood.

He did not even have time to change his expression—no shock, no fear—just a hint of weariness.

"Shacks, let's move it," Reynolds' voice drilled into him.

As a light is switched on, so too was Casey's rage. The trader glared at him with hellfire in his eyes, noticeably shaking. "You bastard."

Reynolds had to check himself so as not to take a step back. "He was a Republican—a traitor. We had no choice," he said flatly. The words came out before he could stop them. He had neither the time nor a reason to explain his actions.

"Don't you get it? He was an American, dammit. Nuthin' more... nuthin' less." Casey returned the Major's glare for a moment longer before storming off to the bridge. He would need to make that stop at his cabin first for a double helping to alleviate the shakes.

Reynolds looked down at the life he had just taken. It was the first Republican he had killed and the first time he had been up close to one. It struck him for the first time that they were actually Americans too. He had hardly considered them as human until that moment.

The Samson's bridge was hot and stuffy, despite the attempts of the air conditioning. Casey was forcing the groaning giant up to its limit of 100km/h along a rough secondary road that had never heard of the term 'Road Maintenance'.

"Scouts Charlie and Delta pull back and draw fire," Reynolds ordered into his com-link. He then shot a quick glance at Shacks. "Can't this tub go any faster?"

"She ain't built fo' speed," Casey replied curtly and spat his half smoked cigarette across the room.

Reynolds shook his head in annoyance and turned back to his portable tac-com, showing on its illuminated display dozens of enemy units. "Speyer, there's a lot more than just local boys converging on us."

"You're not kidding," the Lieutenant answered. "Even if we were still in the skimmers there's no way we could lose them—not without a diversion or delay of some kind."

"Yeah, I'm working on it. Scatter the mines for now." Reynolds was interrupted by Charlie Scout.

"Delta's down—fast attack skimmers are all over us." The tense voice was barely audible over the racing engine and patter of gunfire.

Reynolds clenched his teeth and replied, "Use smoke and pull back on a north parallel two clicks wide." As the scout acknowledged, Reynolds stood up and arched his stiff back.

"Well, y'sure throw a helluva party," Casey muttered as the elevator doors opened. Paul and Samantha stepped out.

"How is everything going," the King asked as he crossed the room.

Reynolds looked at him and frowned. "It's much safer for you to stay in the garage for emergency evac, Sire—just in case."

Casey glanced at the Major. There was deep concern in his voice when he spoke to or about the King; it was hard not to notice how strongly he felt for his leader. The controls shuddered and Samson uttered a deep groan, drawing Casey's attention.

Paul smiled. "I know, but I could not sit around any longer. You did not answer my question, Richard."

Reynolds stared at him. The King had aged so much in the last couple of weeks. His features were greyed and his usually stocky build now seemed shrunken and frail. It was impossible to overlook the strain on Samantha's face too—she seemed almost in physical pain, though he knew that was not so. They both had too much time on their hands, giving the brain too much to think about.

He exhaled, then said, "We've taken a few casualties and Republican forces are closing in, but I'll be damned if they have us yet." He tried to shut out the present image of the King and remember him as he used to be only a short time ago.

"Now, Sire, please return to the garage."

"Thank you for your candour." Paul agreed and patted the Major's shoulder before leaving. Samantha smiled weakly at the Major, then followed silently. Reynolds watched until the elevator doors closed behind them then, reluctantly, returned to the terminal.

The Bronx back alley was shrouded in darkness and the funnelled wind whipped up trash and litter into an elaborate dance, as if performing a magical ballet. A clanking alarm echoed several blocks away and a cat yowled out of sight further down the alley. The streets had been a lot quieter than normal due to the curfew—no taxis, drunks or insomniacs—just the occasional patrol or transporter.

Bob Davis, on point, signalled the five man team to stop and take cover. At the street entrance, standing just out of sight on the sidewalk, he had heard two voices.

Jason Frelon and the tall red-headed explosives technician, Jim Cowie, edged closer. "What is it, Bob?" Jason asked.

"Couple of guys—probably a foot patrol."

One of the faceless voices, a young man probably still in his teens, said, "So, didya catch the Eagles/Wolverine game?"

"Nah, my mom was watching a goddamn re-run of 'Cindy' of all things—'How to get ahead in a man's world!'" The second voice was only slightly older. "I heard about Gillespie's shot though."

"Ya had to see it to believe it, man. Ya ain't seen nothing like it."

The second man paused to grind out a cigarette butt. In the relative quiet it sounded like scraping sandpaper. "Well, he's gotta be the highest paid Forward Blaster in the League."

The black clad group of Loyalists listened and waited in silence until Jason decided that they could not wait any longer. "We should retrace our steps and circle around."

"I agree," Cowie whispered and all three rejoined the rest of the team.

As they crept away, the first voice spoke again. "You know, after the game, they were talking about how the Council are considering putting pro sport matches on hold until all the trouble's over. Something about the heightened anxiety leading to more unrest."

"That's just nuts, man.," his colleague uttered with disgust. "They do something like that and I'll riot for sure!"

The conference room, somewhat stuffy after the recently adjourned meeting of the High Council, now harboured only Lexus, standing by the window reading the contents of a folder and Namala, Silus and Halburd sat at the closest end of the table. Empty tea and coffee cups littered the table punctuated by half eaten plates of biscuits. A slightly stale smell hung in the room caused by too many people sat in suits and uniforms for too long a period. There was a press conference full of reporters waiting for them but, "Let them wait," had been Grant's curt response.

The President, in a hushed tone, said, "It is him." He walked back to the table and handed the folder back to Namala.

"How can you be so sure?" Silus asked just a little too quickly for the President's liking.

Lexus eyed him with a flicker of distrust. "I know."

Cutting through the awkward silence, Halburd said, "OK, what do you want from me?"

"The Cheyenne and Lieutenant Colonel Corallis."

The General's eyes widened. "The 42nd are the toughest unit we've got—it took them just three days to take Las Vegas and Nellis. They're going to strengthen the Illinois garrison ready for the assault on Chicago. With their backing we'll have Chicago in less than a fortnight. It'll stretch Somms' hold to breaking point."

"The whole division?" Namala asked incredulously.

Lexus nodded. "He must not escape again." The concern on his colleagues' faces was unmistakably obvious. They still did not understand Paul Frelon's importance. They could not see past the politics of the situation. They did not realise that the Province would never be totally under the Republic's control without the King— Frelon's—death. Still he thought of Paul as King. *Damn him.*

"Why Corallis?" Halburd asked.

*Imbecile*, Lexus thought angrily. "His loyalty and determination is without question—he carried out the *Iron Duke's* execution impeccably. I want him to assume immediate command of the Cheyenne—their existing CO will have to answer to me if he has a problem with it. As soon as they link up with Chambers, send him up to Chicago. Hopefully he will prove more useful there."

With his voice laced with suppressed anger, Halburd said, "The 103rd aren't enough to guarantee victory in Illinois. This will put the whole campaign in jeopardy."

This time the President's annoyance was clearly visible. "You told me two days ago that they were pulling troops out of Chicago to fortify

Detroit and that the current contingent would be able to overrun it without too much difficulty. Another brigade should guarantee it."

Halburd silently cursed himself for being so optimistic in his previous appraisal. Swivelling his chair around, he struggled to maintain eye contact with Lexus as he strode round the table to hover over him. Looking up, he said, "With all due respect, Grant, the 42$^{nd}$ would significantly reduce our losses and allow victory in a shorter timescale."

Lexus slammed his palm onto the table beside the General, his face reddening. "Victory in Chicago means nothing!" He glared at the three men before fully digesting their stunned looks. Clutching his stinging hand, he closed his eyes and took a moment to regain his composure, before saying, "My friends—Orson—I apologise." He placed a hand gently on the General's shoulder. "We are all under a lot of pressure and I too feel what you are going through. I know you're all doing your very best for the Republic and that's all I can ask of you."

The three men watched him grimly. "You all must understand that the capture of Paul Frelon is of the utmost importance, rescinding all other priorities. As I have said before, we will never gain complete control until the leader of the resistance has been taken out of the picture completely. He is their only reason for fighting." He could make out a glimmer of understanding in Namala and Silus, but in Halburd there was no change.

Lexus looked directly at Halburd. "His being on the run was advantageous for a short time—now it only serves to fuel the resolve of the resistance. That is why we had to take a risk in announcing his death in the first place. We must act fast and make sure that he is eliminated before he is able to cause any more harm.

"So, we have some time, but not a lot. With every hour that passes the public will lose confidence in us, thereby weakening the Republic and by default strengthening the resistance. We must not let that happen."

With his piercing eyes, Lexus visually interrogated his companions. He could sense their probing questions with regards to his conduct, ability, even sanity. Were they really as loyal as he had first thought?

He had spent three years engaging their loyalty as he planned the revolt. They had been all too eager to back him at the start, but why now did he have visions of rats escaping a sinking ship? Maybe Halburd had military rule in mind. Maybe Zain was having second thoughts altogether.

Was he becoming paranoid? Mad, even? What was Paul doing to him? This was yet more of his mind games and manipulations. Twisted revenge for betrayal? *No!*

The President let out a long drawn breath and said with conviction, "Times are hard—the whole province is in uproar. You must understand that, at times, I will grow frustrated, as I'm sure you will, but we must stick together.

"All this will end soon, and as long as we hold firm and maintain our resolve, the Republic will be triumphant."

The three advisors rose from their seats in silence and, in turn, shook his hand.

Private Davis crouched at the entrance to a derelict scrap yard, looking through partially open rusted gates into the badly lit street beyond, waiting for Jason's signal. The other three team members crouched amongst the abandoned debris of rusted engines and machine parts, barrels and broken crates. The mission had gone as smooth as it could have. No confrontations. No difficulty in planting the charges. They were only a few blocks from the safehouse, so the team had relaxed a little. Cowie had even allowed Jason a short spell at point duty.

"C'mon, Jason." There was an edge to his voice. In contrast to the others, the closer they got to safety the more nervous Davis felt, especially when Cowie had agreed (under duress) to let the Prince take point.

Across the street, at the entrance to an alley, Jason finally appeared and gave the all clear. Davis signalled the man closest to him, a big bearded man with the SAW, who instantly moved in a hunched sprint and crossed the street swiftly, despite his size.

Cowie, then a short Mexican called Perez followed, with Davis bringing up the rear.

When they were all safely across, Cowie tapped the Prince's shoulder and said, "Good job, Jason. I'll take point rest of the way. Powers, you watch our backs." The man with the beard nodded, adjusting the weight of his machine gun on his shoulder.

As they picked their way through the deserted back streets, hugging the walls and staying in the shadows, the Loyalists remained silent.

One block away from the safehouse, snake-like lightning lashed out across the heavily laden sky. It was brief and it was not repeated, but to Davis it was an omen. As a thought like a bad smell persistently nagged at the back of his mind, the rain started. At first it was only a few bloated drops, but, like a rollercoaster, it quickly gained momentum.

In the downpour, visibility was reduced to mere feet. Almost immediately Jason lost sight of Cowie. He started to move faster, but something out of the corner of his eye ensnared his attention. A flash. Second floor window; no lights or blinds.

In a moment the team were prone. Davis approached him, wiping the free-flowing rain water from his eyes and plastering his fringe back onto his head. "What's wrong?" A feeling of dread crouched near by.

Jason pointed out the area that bothered him. "I've lost sight of Cowie. Something's not right. Thought I saw a flash from that window."

Davis squinted in the rain and the darkness, but could not see anything, but still the feeling persisted. "I'll move up to that next doorway and try to get a better look," Davis whispered just above the rain.

"I don't know, Bob. I don't like it. Where the hell is Cowie?"

"I'll check it out and if I can't see Cowie we can backtrack and come round from the east."

Jason chewed his bottom lip but reluctantly agreed.

As Davis moved cautiously forward it started. Machine gun fire poured down on them like the rain—tracers and muzzle flashes lit up the night like an electrical storm.

Perez screamed, "Ambush!" as Powers roared, "Rock'n'roll!" and let loose an arc of flaming gunfire into the heavens. They all broke into a sprint.

Davis, yelling, "Go-go-go!" sprayed wildly into the air as Perez was cut down with the descending curtain of bullets.

As the rain hammered and the guns blazed, the three remaining Loyalists ducked and dived and fired furiously up at the unseen enemy. Their return fire was feeble in comparison and a combination of the rain and the flashes disorientated and blinded them.

Powers slammed straight into a trash can, sending him sprawling to the ground, his SAW clattering across the puddled asphalt out of reach.

A ricocheting round caught Davis in the knee. An explosion of agony instantly took his legs out from under him. Panic swept over him and he screamed, "Jason!"

Barely able to heard him over the bedlam, Jason spun and ran without pausing to the dark prone shape. "Bobby, no!" He scrambled to his aid, his sub machine gun empty and cast aside.

Powers sprung to his feet and looked back to the others. "Frelon!" As he started to run, two bullets struck him in the chest and abdomen, punching him back onto the toppled trash can. Bent over it, his dying gurgles were lost in the midst of the gunfight.

The Prince did not see Powers go down, he saw only his friend in agony and the bullets clattering around him. A metre from him, a round caught Jason in the shoulder, causing him to spin and lose his footing. As he collapsed in front of Davis another bullet struck him in the lower back, thrusting him into Davis' arms. "Father—"

Davis caught him and they fell backwards as one, gunfire cutting up the ground all around them. The two friends embraced as death engulfed them.

The Briefing room walls were drawing in around Madeline and pulsating in time with her head. Her whole body shook uncontrollably and, despite having wept continuously since hearing the news, the tears kept coming.

She kept telling herself that it was a mistake, that it was not Jason. But it was no good—she knew that she was only trying to fool herself and no amount of denial would change it. Jason was dead, along with Davis, Perez and Powers. The only one unaccounted for was Cowie.

Did he betray them? Did he just run at the first sign of trouble? They were questions that she would never know the answers to.

She alone had been charged with his safe keeping. She had failed her brother, Jason and herself. But above all else, a kind, loving, innocent boy was gone. Savagely murdered.

She stood up and grabbed the chair that she had been sitting on. As it bounced off the wall, she kicked out at the table, sending it clattering across the floor. With her breathing short and rasped between dry sobs, she stood in the middle of the room. She held her head in her hands and screamed.

The door swung open. Sergeant Travis paused in the doorway only a moment before rushing over to the Duchess. His big arms enveloped her. "I'm so sorry."

Samson's garage was quiet, except for a group of guardsmen talking in low voices among themselves at a workbench by the elevator doors. It was lit only by a couple of low wattage overheads and the courtesy light in one of the dormant utility skimmers. Paul sat, alone with his thoughts, in one of the dimly lit skimmers.

He had just turned the radio off after hearing a news report. The bulletin had informed him about a number of developments. For one, King Alexander had declared a neutral stance towards the civil war, not wanting to get involved with what was ultimately an internal issue, but promising to reopen relations once the crisis was over. His involvement ended with a short message hoping for the situation to be resolved as quickly and as painlessly as possible with his thoughts and prayers going out to every American.

The second report had detailed poverty statistics over a ten year period up to the start of the civil war. They showed a steady increase in citizens living below the poverty threshold and a steady decrease in the size of the population who held the greater part of the province's wealth. At the time of the revolt less than one percent of the population possessed a staggering three quarters of the entire nation's wealth.

Such statistics had never concerned him before. After all, he had been at the pinnacle of the less than one percent, surrounded by servants and splendour. Until recently, he had never worn the same item of clothing twice, other than his ceremonial robes and crown. Until now he had lived a life not even dreamt of by the rest of the nation. And every day that he picked at a banquet, half of America was hardly able to eat at all.

He had taken it all for granted.

But even as the enormity of the statistics still buzzed in his mind, a third report interrupted the scheduled sporting fixtures; a news flash. It was brief and seemingly emotionless and it struck the King like a sledgehammer. Within the midst of an emotional hurricane inside his cracking sanity, he came to the most horrifying realisation of his mistake-ridden life—it was no lie.

His son was dead.

He hung his head and cried softly to himself. He had, in some way, prepared himself for losing his power and even his own life, but deep down, no matter how anxious he became, he had not considered for a moment that he would lose Jason. With thoughts like that, he would never have made it this far.

*My son has died for my sins. Where is the justice in that? When will this nightmare end?* As he wept, he asked himself one more question. Did he deserve a second chance? After all, the madness would end as soon as he was dead. Everything would go back to normal and the entire nation could go back to their lives.

*If* he gave up. But it was too late for that, giving up now would mean that Jason and all the others had died in vain and he would be betraying the friends and supporters he had left. And there was more than just his life and his friends' lives to consider. For now, he still held the title, King of America, and as such it was his duty to look after the interests of the nation as a whole, not just his supporters.

He tried to dismiss his next question as soon as it began to surface, but something inside him allowed it purchase. Could Lexus and the new Republic achieve more for the good of the people than the Monarchy could?

There was no way of knowing for sure. He had been weak and made many mistakes through greed and power, there was no denying it, but he did still truly believe that he could make a difference, right the wrongs and give the whole nation a new lease of life. It had been his duty all along. He had strayed from the path, but for no longer.

An image of Jason formed in his head and the only discernable feature was his eyes and the sadness thàt they shrouded. Then the image was gone and in its place was, at first anger, and then rage. *I will come for you, Grant. Mark my words.*

The elevator doors opened, admitting Paul and Samantha. Casey had his hands full at the controls, so did not acknowledge them. Reynolds stood and saluted.

He too had heard about the Prince's death in New York, but the situation did not allow them (probably a good thing) to dwell upon it. "Sire, we've received news that the 42nd Mech are moving in on us. They're a rapid response unit and as such wipe out any chance of escape without a major confrontation."

"What the Major's sayin'is," Casey added, "w'can't run, w'can't hide and there ain't no way w'can take on an entire division."

Reynolds glared at him as Paul said, "Thank you, for the overview, Casey." A quick succession of freeze-frame images of Jason laughing snapped into his mind's eye. Blinking in a desperate bid to quell them, he continued. "You served with the Cheyenne before joining the Guards, Richard?"

Reynolds nodded. "They're good."

Samantha had been chewing her lip, but now she asked, "What are you saying? That's it, we don't stand a chance?"

"No way." The words were thick with conviction and immediately stemmed her growing panic. "I'm saying that it is time for action."

"What do you suggest?" Paul asked.

Reynolds glanced briefly at Casey, before addressing the King's question. "With your permission, we will drop off Alpha squad to allow them to set up a defensive position and await the main brunt. An ambush should give us the time we need."

"Suicide fo'them though," Casey muttered without turning away from the controls.

The Major's face reddened. "The Guards—to a man—will lay down their lives for their King without hesitation."

"Yeah, real honour for'em."

Reynolds clenched his jaw and turned back to Paul. Whatever excuses he gave, the damn smuggler still struck a nerve. And that was getting to become a habit.

During the brief confrontation, Paul had been battling his own demons. He met the Major's eyes and said, "Is there no alternative?"

"I wish there were, Sire." They both saw reflections of their own torment in each others eyes.

With the images of Jason returning, the King nodded and excused himself without another word. Samantha caught a glance from Reynolds. It was brief, but she too sensed his torment. She felt that Shacks was being far too hard on him and decided to talk to the trader the next time she could catch him alone. Richard deserved much better.

As Samantha followed the King into the elevator, Reynolds' eyes lingered on her. His heart was beating faster than it had been a moment earlier. *She understands.*

As the elevator descended and Casey continued to wrestle with the controls, Reynolds addressed his com-link. "Anderson, kit up your squad and be ready to move in five."

Her combat boots felt like leaden weights as Madeline stomped up the concrete stairs. As she reached the top, the first thing she noticed was that one of the overheads was flashing, on the brink of extinction. Her gaze fixed on it for a moment before becoming aware of the young couple standing two doors down, holding hands and assault rifles. They were chatting with hushed voices, the girl pressed close against the young man. As she continued to observe, the girl broke out into fits of giggles and kissed him on the cheek.

Madeline stormed past them, causing a brief interruption to their intimacy. Her obvious hostility drained their harmony, for a moment. She went straight to her room, hoping to avoid Travis.

She slammed the door behind her and flung her kitbag and sub-machine-gun onto her bunk. The room was dim and sparsely furnished and Travis was sitting in the one faded armchair.

"What do you want?" Her words were razor sharp.

The Sergeant leaned forward and rested his chin on his clasped hands. "Madeline, you've got to ease off."

She bent her face down close to his. "I will die before I quit." The words were whispered, but filled with venom.

He met her glare with compassion and said, "No one's asking you to quit."

She turned away from him and caught her reflection in the mirror above the wash basin. She saw a haunted old woman staring back at her. Her eyes dropped to the floor. Perching on the edge of the bunk, she asked wearily, "Well, what are you saying?"

Travis leaned closer. "We're kicking them where it hurts, Madeline, make no mistake and you've done more than anyone. Hell, you're on patrols and ops nearly every night—you're physically and mentally exhausted." He moved off the edge of the chair and sat down beside the Duchess.

Taking hold of her small hand, he said, "All I'm asking is that you slow down a bit. You're taking on so much and—"

Madeline squeezed hard on his hand. "They killed Jason and you want me to slow down! I'm fine, thank you. I can take whatever they throw at me and send it right back to them."

"It's killing me seeing you like this. You did everything you could—it's not your fault." He gripped her shoulders and wanted to shake her until she snapped out of it, but instead he hugged her. "He's gone, Maddy."

As Travis whispered the last three words, Madeline sagged in his arms and cried, every last drop of aggression draining away.

After a couple of minutes, she sniffed and wiped her sodden face. "I'm sorry, Karl." A few more tears escaped out of the corners of her eyes.

Travis smiled. "Now what in the Hell have you got to be sorry about?"

"I'm coming apart. I'm turning into a liability—I could—"

"That's bullshit, and you know it. Without your leadership and commitment, this cell would collapse. You've been concentrating so much on keeping the rest of us together, you haven't left enough time for yourself. That's all."

She managed a weak smile. "You're not one to put up with self-pity, are you?"

This time Travis laughed. "God no. I'd lose my membership to the Hardass Society."

The sun-baked valley was barren and lifeless. A gentle breeze carried with it the beginning of another cold night. The sun, low on the horizon, cast long shadows from the twelve men that squatted amongst the scattered brittlebushes and boojum trees on the valley floor.

Royal Guard Sergeant Anderson yanked back on the cocking lever of his assault rifle and licked his dry lips. After surveying the valley for a second time, making note of defilade, fire and displacement positions he nodded. Yes, it would do.

The wiry black sergeant gathered his men around him and checked his watch. "Right, we'll have contact in eighteen minutes from the forward scouts. Kennedy, take your section up to that ridge over there; spread out and dig in. Two man teams."

The Corporal arched his freckled face and squinted, looking high up the north face to pick out the best positions in advance. After a moment, he said, "OK, let's go."

Anderson watched the six men move quickly away from them for a couple of seconds before turning to his section. "Let's double-time it. Rand, take point." A muscular lance corporal spat at the dirt and headed towards the south face without a word.

Corporal Kennedy scanned the far end of the valley with image-intensifying binoculars, the device managing to magnify what little light remained. He was heavily camouflaged with desert netting draped over him in a recess behind a jagged crag. After confirming that there was still no sign, he spoke into his headset, "Second, to First; we're in position."

Across the other side of the valley, crouching in a narrow crevice, Anderson replied, "Affirmative. Should have them on scope in three minutes." His eyes did not stray from his I-I binoculars for a second.

Another voice crackled in his earpiece—it was muttered, but purposely recognisable. "And Christmas comes early this year."

Anderson closed his eyes just for a moment; he had been expecting something. "Stow that shit, Roberts. Radio silence now till I give the order. All confirm."

As he listened to the confirmations, it started to sink in to him that he would not leave this valley alive. He would die along with all of his men and there was no way of avoiding it. Judging by Private Roberts's last comment, they were all arriving to the same conclusion.

He told himself that it was what they had all signed up for, that it was just the waiting that was hard. But there was always that annoying part that kept saying, *No, I can't do this. I don't want to die.* Why is it that sometimes the smallest voice grabs the most attention?

With the seed of doubt very much planted, he racked his brain for an alternative, some other option as yet unthought-of. But of course there were none. No ingenious plan or miracle would save them. But, perhaps they could save the King. He refused to die for nothing, for his life to have had no meaning. But to die to save His Majesty…well surely that was the ultimate sacrifice.

He had sworn allegiance to the Throne and in that had sworn to protect it with his life.

After a moment's contemplation, it all seemed to settle into focus. His mind was clear and his heart was true.

The two utility skimmers sped across the uneven wasteland, one in front of the other, sweeping up clouds of dust in their wake. The two forward scouts were dented and dirty; their occupants, tired and nervous.

Both skimmers—commissioned from civilian life to replace losses already incurred—had been hastily fitted with light armaments and armour. In the lead scout, Sergeant Bender was not as nervous as his two companions, but he was unhappy. He did not like being issued, at the last moment, with a dissected civvy vehicle with some guns welded to it.

He watched, incredulously, the roof mounted grenade launcher as it rattled in its bracket. He cursed, not for the first time, the motor pool acting jack for lumbering him with such a piece of shit. It must have been that last card game that did it. He would have to let him win a couple of hands next time.

Shaking his head, he turned to the speed gauge. He immediately slapped the buck private sitting in the driving seat next to him on the side of the helmet. "What damn speed I tell ya t'go, boy?"

The young man flinched and quickly decelerated. "Sorry, Sir- Sarge."

*Draftee asshole,* Bender thought. *A fucking replacement for some of the swinging dicks that bought it in Vegas...hardly a fair swap.* "Just keep'n'eye on this hunk o'junk, Private." As the draftee apologised again, the Sergeant looked over his shoulder to the third crewman, sitting amongst a web of entangled electrical wiring and panels.

"Hol, pick up anything on that sorry excuse fo'a scanner yet?"

The Com-Tech flicked an irritating wire out of his face and muttered, "Zip, Sarge. I ain't even sure if this garbage would pick anything up."

"Well what a fuckin surprise." He grabbed the radio hand piece from the dash board and pressed the transmit button. "Ranger Two, this is Ranger One; copy?"

"Roger, Sarge," a crackling voice answered. "Go ahead."

"Drop back'bout twenty metres and stay frosty. We gotta be almost on top o'them, so we might hit them before we reach our ceiling."

"Roger that, Sarge. Say, does your scanner keep blacking out every couple of minutes?"

"Tell me ya kiddin'?"

"No, Siree. Keeps goin fubar on us."

"I'm gonna kill that Jaunders," Bender muttered, again, thinking of the motor pool Sergeant. The Sergeant was a veteran of many scrapes in his time, the most recent of which was the assault on Nellis followed by some bloody street to street action in Las Vegas, so was not overtly scared of combat (everyone was a little scared; you'd have to be crazier than a loon otherwise, but you learned to control the fear, harness it), but this time he prayed that they would not come across the enemy; not tonight. "Do what ya can, Willie-P."

The wind was picking up in the valley. Anderson wiped away dust from his binocular lenses and adjusted the range-finder. The wind was emitting a low moan that seemed to drift up from the valley floor. As an after thought, he inched his headset mike closer to his still dry lips.

The Private next to him checked that his rifle was cocked and the safety was off. Satisfied, he looked to Anderson and said, "Sounds like the dead are already restless down there."

"You're a bundle of joy, Minetti." The Sergeant was still mulling over that last remark when the first Republican scout appeared on the scope. A second followed and they were coming in fast. "Wait for it," he muttered.

He wet his lips and then tensed as the targets entered the kill zone. "Now."

The first missile struck Ranger 2 and tore the lightly armoured vehicle to shreds with a dazzling fireball. They were gone before they could see it coming.

Bender saw the explosion through his wing mirror, and for a moment was stunned. It took him a second to recover. "Evasives!" It was all he managed. A second missile struck the skimmer in the rear, flipping it end over end like a giant Catherine Wheel.

It hit the ground on its roof at nearly 90 km/h. In the next moment, the flaming remains exploded and scattered across the valley floor, igniting several brittlebushes along the way.

Anderson watched the rapidly fading flames and muttered, "Two down. Reload and get ready, the rest of'em will come down on us like a ton of bricks. Expect skirmishers both sides of the valley at elevation."

He tucked the binoculars back into a pocket on his webbing and switched on the laser scope on his assault rifle.

Mortars hit them five minutes later, followed by skirmish teams, then a full assault shortly after.

The Samson's bridge was quiet; even Shacks and the two AI clowns had not said a word in quite some time. Maybe all three of them were contemplating the same things as Reynolds while he stared blankly at monitor in front of him. The changing information it displayed seemed to have lost all meaning and he made no attempt to digest it.

No matter how much justification he afforded himself, he could not get Anderson and the others out of his mind. He had left them behind. In his entire career, he had never left a single man behind; he had never been faced with the dilemma before.

His men, including himself, had been chosen for their unshakable loyalty, as well as skill. But to drop them into a situation with absolutely no way out, no hope…

He could still picture their faces as he briefed them prior to their drop. As he explained, not one of their faces betrayed any kind of fear or anger. They had taken it as part of the job—in their stride, at least on the face of it.

Reynolds then remembered how he had felt when he had been sent on a long range strike deep in the heart of the Amazon jungle as a young lieutenant. His unit were supposed to take out a group of guerrillas, torch their base of operations and then hike it to the extraction point. It had been a high risk operation, deep into hostile, lawless terrain, but it was by no means a suicide mission. And yet, he could not forget the sense of betrayal he had felt at being ordered on such a dangerous operation. As it transpired, he lost over half of his platoon on that operation, but they achieved their goal and managed 138 confirmed kills. And into the bargain he had been awarded his first medal. He was proud of some of his medals, but that first one was not one of them.

So how must Anderson, Kennedy and the rest of Alpha feel?

He wanted to tell them how sorry he was. Instead, he had told them how proud he felt. Proud! Would that really make them feel better for being sent to their deaths? He reminded himself that it had to be done. It was a sacrifice that had to be made.

The silent statements had as much substance as they had volume.

The evening sky was prematurely black with smoke and the entire valley was engulfed with it. Gunfire and sporadic explosions were clearly audible but only briefly illuminated, like ghosts, in the grey shroud.

Anderson smeared the mixture of ash and sweat from his forehead across the sleeve of his muddy jacket. The clatter of gunfire was constant, all but drowning out the shrill voices at the other end of his com-link. After the short pause, he aimed his rifle into the swirling blackness and picked out another target. He had plenty to choose from, figures, barely recognisable as human, picking their towards his position from all levels, moving then firing, moving then firing, keeping the pressure on.

As he fired, Roberts' voice came over the com-link, wavering just above the malevolent cry of the battle. "Kennedy's dead, Sarge!.Only me and Suwalla…"

Anderson ducked back behind the rock as several rounds ripped chunks out of it. "Continue holding."

Another voice, barely discernable, cried, "We're gonna die!"

Anderson scrambled to the other side of the boulder and aimed around it, emptying his sixth magazine with a short burst. As he reloaded, he shouted, "We'll die fighting, Rand!"

Minetti had been blown into two pieces earlier when their position had taken a direct hit from a rocket. Anderson had managed to dive out of the depression in the nick of time. The Sergeant knew that Dowell, too, was dead. Torq had not replied to his last call, so he was probably dead or dying also. That left Sheldon and Carlton out of his section left who were just in sight, reloading the AT launcher. The latter's face was just as black as his West Indian counterpart's.

After inserting a missile into the back of the tubular launcher, Sheldon slapped Carlton's shoulder and shouted, "Let'er rip!" The Private paused to aim at the shadowy form of a skimmer (it was impossible to discern the type) on the valley floor, then squeezed the trigger.

The armour-piercing missile punched a small hole into the side of the slow moving APC and an instant later exploded inside, splitting it open like a tin can. Flames and broken, charred bodies spilled out.

Bullets peppered their position, driving both men flat against the ground. With no more missiles, Carlton cast the useless weapon aside and scooped up a combat shotgun from the dirt beside him. Sheldon, thrusting the butt of his rifle hard against his shoulder, popped up with him to return fire on the advancing shapes.

Anderson finished off his last clip then, drawing his pistol, shouted, "Displace!" He rolled past the edge of the rock, and, half-crouched, disappeared in the darkness.

Sheldon grabbed his shotgun-wielding friend. "Let's go!"

Carlton stared back at him with wild eyes and cried, "Yeah!" Shoving him aside, he leapt over the ridge and charged blindly down the slope, emptying shells all the way.

"Carlton!" Sheldon yelled after him, but he had already been swallowed up by the smoke and darkness. Intending to follow, he began scrambling out of their shallow dug-out just as the whole world around him erupted in a ball of flames and shrapnel. The percussion blew him several feet away from the dug-out and left him in a twisted pile.

The Lance-Corporal lay there as the blood pooled around him, watching, with detached curiosity, as his guts spilled out of a huge gaping wound in his stomach. He died before realizing that both his arms were missing.

The sweat was streaming down his face as Anderson ran through the darkness. A soldier appeared right in front of him. The Republican's eyes were like a rabbit's caught in the headlights of an oncoming car. The Sergeant shot him twice in the head without pausing to think about it. It did not break his stride.

*Muzzle flashes licking the air, searching for blood to taste... writhing smoke, masking the enemy, searing the lungs...Broken, mutilated bodies...Enemy...Death...*

A voice, deep within the quiet confines of his head, screamed out, *You're losing it!*

He stopped, half crouched, with his chest heaving and his stinging eyes darting left and right, and attempted to regain his composure. As his heart slowly eased its pounding and his senses returned to him, a stray bullet struck him in the chest.

Anderson dropped to the ground, bleeding.

*Gun!*

While gritting his teeth to suppress a scream, his hands desperately fumbled in the darkness for his discarded pistol. Only slimy earth greeted his scrabbling fingers.

A Republican emerged from the smoke and stood over the wounded Loyalist. He levelled his rifle to Anderson's upturned face. The Sergeant closed his eyes as he heard the soldier mutter an inaudible word. Then he pulled the trigger.

# Chapter 6

## The Battle of San Diego

Major Yeoville's office was small and cluttered. Sitting at his disorganised desk, his chair was swivelled to face the San Diego city map that was pinned to the wall. He studied every block and street of the city that had been his home for half a decade. The map failed to show any of the destruction it had suffered from the Republican bombardments and assaults. He checked the date on it—less than a year old. It was a very different place out there now.

He checked his watch; Duke Fredrick's younger son and daughter would arrive shortly. What in the Hell had possessed them to come to a city on the verge of collapse, he could not possibly fathom. But he would certainly find out.

Catherine lingered in his mind. It had been six months since he had met Catherine at a formal dinner dance held at the recently levelled Miramar base. His date, whose name he could not remember, had stood him up and the Lieutenant Colonel from Washington who had been with Catherine had been too busy greasing his path ahead, to take any notice of how stunning she had looked.

He had watched her for a time, smiling politely, broken only by the occasional 'hello' or 'nice to see you again'. He remembered how she had gently circled the rim of her wineglass with her index finger. He remembered the wistful look on her porcelain features.

Then, after what seemed like an eternity, he had plucked up the courage to talk to her. They had ended up talking and laughing together undisturbed for the entire evening. It had been a magical evening.

Thankfully, his thoughts were cut short. The door shot aside to admit a young tall and tanned, self assured man in combat fatigues with a broad smile planted on his face. The slightly older woman who followed him had inherited the long raven hair of her mother, together with an unrivalled gentle smile.

As his sister closed the door behind them, Bradley Frelon spoke first. "Hi, Major. Small world." Without pausing for a reply, he dropped down into the seat in front of Yeoville's desk.

Yeoville hardly noticed the Captain's distinct lack of military protocol and basic manners. It was the same lack of respect that he had received when he had first met him at the same dinner dance, only he had been a lieutenant then. Instead, his eyes were set firmly upon Catherine. It felt like hours not months since they had last met. He stood up smiling and feeling suddenly very awkward.

"Hello, Daniel," she said and then cast her brother a stern look. Bradley rolled his eyes and stood up, taking an 'at ease' stance.

"Nice to see you again, Catherine," he replied, immediately disregarding 'Captain' Frelon's behaviour. Still, it was hard to ignore the fact that most commissioned officers of his age had just finished training. Yet, Bradley had already skimmed through the ranks of second lieutenant and lieutenant within three years of entering the service. Having a duke as a father must have come in pretty handy; although not any more. He almost cringed at that last thought and instantly felt a stab of guilt.

He sat back down and rubbed his freshly shaven chin. "I'm sorry about your father; he was a fine man. And your brother, Elias, too."

"That makes me feel much better, Sir." Bradley over-emphasized the 'sir' but lacked the conviction behind it. The first time he had heard it had been once too many, but he had been hearing it ever since.

"Thank you," Catherine answered sincerely, but not wanting to dwell on the painful memory, she asked quickly, "How bad is your situation?"

Yeoville motioned for them both to sit down. "Bad. Ryker is getting stronger while we get weaker, and there's no longer any way for Somms to get help to us." He smiled, then added, "You picked a great time to visit."

Catherine looked at the wall map, and after a moment's consideration, asked, "Do you think that you can hold for a couple more days?"

"If they don't try another big push in the mean time...yes." He started to pull himself back out of his chair, but the room suddenly dimmed and went out of focus. He sat down again in a hurry and rubbed his eyes.

Both Bradley and Catherine noticed. The former simply shook his head and folded his arms. The latter frowned, but refrained from commenting.

It took him a moment to compose himself before asking, "Any specific reason for holding a couple more days?"

"We have reason to believe that our uncle, the King, is on his way here."

"Why?" Yeoville said, openly shocked.

Catherine sighed and admitted, "I don't know."

More cautiously, the Major slowly stood up and said, "I don't know why coming to a besieged city on the brink of falling would be a good idea, but I am sure there is a damn good reason. We will hold; no matter what."

Catherine was touched by his unshaken loyalty; it was rapidly becoming something of a rarity these days. He seemed very different to the easygoing man that she had first met, yet that just seemed to fuel the emotions that she had kept bottled up over the months.

Yeoville's last remark seemed to instil new life into Bradley too. He jumped to his feet and in three strides had paced the room. As he fidgeted, he said, "I have a squad of damn good men that are ready to muck in. We got through without so much as a single shot being fired— the ceasefire saw to that—but they're tried and tested, every one of them."

"All the wounded should have been recovered by now, so it won't hold much longer."

Bradley stopped pacing. "We will be ready for them."

The statement was in earnest, so the Major let it pass without comment. *Let him enjoy his ignorance for a little while longer,* he thought cynically.

He looked back to Catherine; her eyes were already upon him. As their eyes met he felt her mind probing his. It was a strange feeling that was gone before it was recognised. He had to swallow.

Bradley clapped his hands together, banishing the moment to future dreams. Catherine's face had become hot with embarrassment and their awkwardness was clearer still. Definitely time to go. "Well, sis, hadn't we better get settled in?"

Catherine nodded without taking her eyes away from Yeoville. With a wave of his hand, Bradley left them alone. Catherine lingered for a moment, before saying a brief goodbye and following him.

Yeoville watched the door close behind her and then slumped back in his chair under the barrage of emotions that bore down on him. The last few minutes had confirmed everything to him, and it was all too much to take.

Feelings were surfacing that he had not felt in a long time; feelings that he thought he would never touch upon ever again. Right from when he first met her something struck him, and he had been unable to shake it since.

And yet he had promised that this would never happen; to himself and to Mary. *God, how would she feel?* Guilt began to eat into him. It was slow, but merciless.

To appease its appetite, he told himself that it would never work anyway. Apart from her being Royalty and fifteen years younger, they were in the middle of a revolution. And then Mary...

He squeezed his eyes tight shut and rubbed them hard, in a vain attempt to banish the memories that were starting to reappear after a long hibernation.

As his final defences crumbled, the alarm sounded. The tormenting memories instantly vanished and in seconds he was out the door and running towards the Command Centre.

He was sweating by the time he reached the Command Centre. It had been three minute since the alarm had sounded, but already the room was in uproar. Palmer instantly caught sight of him and waved frantically.

As Yeoville cleared the distance between them in a few strides, Palmer told him, "They're storming Sector Five again."

"I knew he wouldn't wait long after the ceasefire," he replied, wiping the beads of sweat from his face. "Reports?"

"That's not all, Sir," Demoore added, her voice laden with fear. "They're dropping paratroops right on top of us as we speak."

"Dammit, he got some help. Where's Jones?"

Palmer interrupted a sentence on his com-link to say, "Out in the field—acting CO of the Recon Company."

Yeoville checked the tac-com and saw that the unit marker for C Company, situated in the north-east sector, was red—engaging the enemy. "What's Charlie's status?"

Palmer relayed the order and listened to the short reply. He had to cover his other ear to make it out. "Heavy losses; up to thirty percent. Forward CP compromised, but holding."

"Phased rearguard action back to Four. Use artillery and mortars to cover." As the Captain relayed his orders, he asked Demoore, "What about the gunship and Bravo?"

She checked her watch. "The gunship will be up in five. Bravo has three full platoons operational—they've topped up from the civilian reserves."

"What have we got to fight with?"

"We have the two remaining platoons from Alpha, then the Battalion staff and MPs. That's it. They're dropping about a company on us.

"Can we take anything from Miramar or the border posts?"

Demoore shook her head instantly, expecting the question. "Miramar's down to a skeletal staff of ground crew and comms. And the remaining reserves and elements of Delta Company at the posts are stretched as thin as they possibly could be."

The situation was escalating out of control and Yeoville needed time to think; time that was not available to him. His mind screamed out. He had to make a decision. Hesitating would cost lives. "We'll have to hold with what we've got. Alert Captain's Frelon's men and tell them that we may need them sooner than we thought." As Demoore shouted to the operator nearest to them, Palmer also relayed more reports from the field.

"Use all three platoons of Bravo along with the remaining skimmers from Recon to fortify Sector Four. Once in place, Charlie to hold on their position." As Palmer passed on the orders, Yeoville consulted Demoore again; this time regarding the status of the Hovernaught.

"Most essential repairs completed but it really is just a temporary patch up. She's firing and moving around Sector Three providing artillery support. Being targeted by artillery and one gunship."

Palmer's eyes widened as another report came over his headset. "The outer perimeter's breached—storming A level. The remains of 2nd Platoon are scattered around the perimeter. 1st Platoon engaging and holding."

Yeoville wiped his forehead and said, "2nd Platoon regroup and hit them from behind. Use the MPs and anyone else we have spare with a gun to set up a secondary line of defence on B level."

As the Major finished his sentence, an explosion shook the base, dislodging chunks of plaster from the ceiling. Dust and debris rained down on them and the room plunged into darkness. Smoke and screams filled the air.

A man, unrecognisable through the smoke and darkness, staggered into Yeoville, coughing, "Help me." The Major eased the bleeding man into a seat, then squinted to see his colleagues.

"Wes?"

"Over here," Palmer shouted from only a few feet away. Yeoville moved carefully towards him.

From the other side of the room, a woman was crying and a man repeatedly shouted, "What the fuck happened?" Then a female sergeant yelled, "Everyone calm down! Get some flashlights operational ASAP."

As he reached Palmer, a couple of flashlights swept across the murky carnage. Yeoville could just make out several figures moving around, inspecting damage and casualties. There were moans and cries from several people scattered around the room. Forcing himself to focus on the critical situation in the city above him, he asked, "Have we still got comms?"

"Yes. Charlie have linked up with Bravo and both are now under fire; holding well, for—" He paused to listen to a new report, and then said, "1st and 2nd Balboa Artillery Batteries under fire from section to platoon strength paras. Also, the Naval Hospital wing has taken a hit."

"Dammit, the gun emplacements are virtually defenceless. Redirect 2nd Platoon onto them. We'll have to hold without them. The Hospital will also have to cope on their own." Yeoville started to pace as he wiped sweat and dust from his face. Ryker was successfully diluting his defences with the newly acquired paras and there was nothing he could do about it.

As Palmer continually spoke over the com-link, Yeoville suddenly remembered about Demoore. He began scrutinizing the murkiness around him as the dull red of the emergency lighting finally kicked in, bathing the wreckage in a blood-red glow.

There were three partially bandaged operators, the Sergeant helping one with a badly gashed head, and two others unscathed who were working there way through the room. Strip lights, wiring and chunks of plaster lay strewn and dangling everywhere, but the main ceiling supports had held. They had been very lucky. Lyn was bent over a motionless figure who was, at first, unrecognisable beneath the chunks of debris and dust.

Realisation struck him and he ran to the Corporal's aid. "Liz," he muttered as he swept the fragments from her unconscious form.

As Yeoville took out his personal med-kit, Palmer said, "1st Platoon have lost their hold on A level; pulling back to B. Secondary defences in position. 2nd Platoon engaging one platoon of paras. 2nd Artillery batt destroyed."

Looking up from the wound on the back of Demoore's head, Yeoville asked, "What about Charlie and Bravo?"

"Under heavy fire, but holding. Blue 7 and Hovernaught still supporting."

The Major left Lyn to finish tending to Demoore's injuries and rejoined Palmer beside the littered map display. Before turning his attention back to the city, he shouted to the sergeant, "Tully, you got everything under control here?"

She glanced over to him, her face smeared with muck and blood from a graze above her eye. "Yessir."

"Okay." Turning back to Palmer, he said, "So what we up against?"

"Their main push comprised of around a brigade of infantry backed up by armour (unsure of numbers) and two gunships. They've also got a couple of ground support planes—T60's, we think—that came in with the dropships, but they can't stick around for long."

"How much damage have they taken?"

"We haven't hit them half as hard as last time. Their point infantry battalion has heavy losses and their armour isn't coping well street to street—as before, but there's no sign of them letting up this time." He stopped to listen to another report and after a brief reply, said, "That was Jones. His skimmers are playing the usual cat and mouse tactics with their tanks, baiting them for the AT units. He has three remaining and can't keep them at bay much longer."

Behind them, the Sergeant flung down her headset and shouted to them, "Major, they've broken through to C level. Remaining defences are trying to intercept but are scattered. They don't hold much hope of stopping them before they get to us."

Yeoville cursed and instinctively drew his sidearm. Palmer and several others followed suit. "Barricade the door and get everyone organised."

"Yessir." She drew her pistol and began yelling orders to everyone able to hold a gun. Casualties were moved unceremoniously to the other side of the room as Tully, with the help of a young man, began barricading the door.

Yeoville felt a new level of panic settle over the room. To Palmer, he said, "Tell Svenson and Jones they'll have to co-ordinate the battle from now on as we may not be on the air much longer." After a moment's thought, he added sternly, "Tell them to fight on at *all* costs."

Palmer had spoken to Svenson and was just raising Jones when the emergency lighting and the remaining electronics went dead. With the room once again in darkness, the tension lifted a notch closer to hysteria.

The Sergeant was quick to switch her flashlight back on and order everyone to remain calm. In moments, two more beams swept over the room and the preparations continued.

Palmer resumed communication with what was left of the Recon Company, but not before muttering, "Bloody lucky the radios have their own back-up cells."

As Palmer spoke to Jones, Yeoville turned to the Sergeant and said, "Good job, Tully. Any luck above us?"

Pausing between orders, she shook her head grimly. "Sorry, Sir. It's chaos up there."

The Major snatched a second's thought and then flipped over a desk, smashing the computer terminal and scattering papers across the already littered floor. Crouching down behind it, he shouted, "Everyone take cover." Then to Palmer, "Wes, get down here."

Palmer glanced around him and realised his own mortality. He quickly ducked down beside his CO. Tully was still snapping orders at a couple of dawdling subordinates when the main doors were blown out of their frame, dislodging the desk and cabinet that had been hastily shoved in front of it.

Several handguns boomed in the confined space before three intruders flew through the shattered door-frame; SMGs chattering a reply. The paratroopers were laden with weapons, ammunition and webbing, but they moved with feline speed.

Yeoville and Palmer popped up in unison. They both fired a three round volley, then ducked back down as the return came. The desk was shoved into them with the force of the multiple hits.

The Major glanced to his side and saw Lyn and a young male private both take hits. It was too dark to see if they were fatal, but neither got up again. He gritted his teeth, then rolled away from the desk, firing as he moved.

Palmer dove in the opposite direction and disappeared out of sight.

After another hail of machine gun fire, Yeoville heard the distinctive sound of a grenade clattering across the floor towards the far side of the room. As he thrust his head in his hands, the blast seemed to wrench the building from its foundations. The fragmentation grenade spat out thousands of tiny metal shards, shredding everything in a three metre radius. Palmer and Demoore were over there somewhere.

He came up screaming and firing at the same time until the pistol clicked empty. A couple of small fires had ignited where papers had piled up and, coupled with the smoke from the blast and the darkness, reduced visibility to less than a metre. It was impossible to tell if he had hit one of them.

Another volley of automatic fire confirmed that at least one was still alive. Then a couple of pistol shots to his right. With his dulled hearing, still ringing from the grenade, he could not be sure if he had heard a cry after the last shot. He could hope.

As he fumbled in the darkness reloading, while trying to muffle his coughing from the thickening smoke, he saw a figure emerge in front of him.

The Republican Paratrooper was crouched and held his sub-machine gun to his hip. It was aimed right at him. He hesitated with the magazine half inserted into his pistol. The para had him dead to rights.

A gun discharged, but it was not the Republican's, for he dropped to the floor. Yeoville turned to see Palmer crawling towards him. He had suffered a shrapnel wound to the leg and had a number of cuts and abrasions, but he was smiling all the same.

His initial relief was replaced by horror as he noticed the faint outline of a hunched figure behind the Captain. He started to shout a warning, but the Paratrooper's SMG spoke first, pounding several rounds into Palmer's back. He was dead before he hit the floor.

"Wes!" The magazine clicked into place and the weapon was cocked and firing an instant later. He fired repeatedly into the

Republican's chest, abdomen and face until the dead body toppled out of sight.

Sensing movement to his side, he spun and aimed at the head of Sergeant Tully. She instantly recoiled and raised her hands.

"Sir, you ok?"

He looked back at his fallen friend and only then did he begin to feel a deepening pain in his shoulder. Glancing down at it, he realised that it was soaked in blood and his vision began to blur.

Tully gently held his uninjured shoulder as he sagged against a waist-high partition wall. With his head swimming, the Sergeant quickly told him, "The base has been re-secured—these were the last of them…" Then her words appeared to grow farther and farther away until blackness engulfed him.

Major Yeoville gingerly opened his eyes to a smudged and distorted world. There were two people sat at his bedside in the small private room, but he could barely recognise them. It was not until the closer of the two leaned forward and spoke that his senses were given a jump start.

"Daniel, Daniel; please speak to me." It was Mary, and she was delicately holding his hand like she used to. His heart sounded like it was beating right in his ears. How could this be? Was he dead?

Desperately, he tried to tighten his grip on his wife's small hand and with it, his grip on this hazy reality. But, try as he might, his useless limbs refused to cooperate. "Don't leave me," he rasped.

As his eyes slowly began to focus on the face that had uttered the soothing words, he realised that he was not dead. The sorrow did not last more than a moment, for Catherine's eyes lit up at the sight of Yeoville's focussing upon hers. Elizabeth Demoore was sat in the chair beside her, fresh dressings on the back of her head and above her left eye.

"Thank God you're back in the land of the living again, Sir." the Lieutenant said, barely above a whisper.

He forced a weak smile as he glanced around the room. Recognising the base infirmary, his attention strayed back to Catherine; she had sounded—and felt—so like Mary. It had unsettled him.

San Diego was on the verge of collapse. Forcing his thoughts back to their immediate problems was a welcome respite from the turmoil of emotions swelling inside him. "How we doing?"

Catherine shook her head, but the concerned smile remained. As usual, he was straight back to business. But for a moment there…his pleading words had hung in the air for what had seemed like an eternity. At the onset of the revolution, she had realised that it was unlikely that she would ever see Daniel again. She had always been very practical. So she had raised a barrier, for her own good. She could not bare any more hurt; her father and brother were gone and her mother imprisoned. The thought of losing Daniel too was just too much to even comprehend. So the barriers had come up. Yet looking at him and listening to his words, cracks were instantly revealing themselves in her defences. In that moment, she had a glimpse of how the rest of her life could be with this man and what she saw she had been delighted at. It was like a near death experience, instant, but all revealing.

The vision disappeared with his semi-consciousness, but its memory would never be forgotten. She mentally shook herself and said, "I've been liaising with Captain Jones and Captain Svenson while Elizabeth has been receiving some medical attention here." Before explaining their situation, she felt that she had to add, "I'm sorry about Captain Palmer. I know he was a good friend."

Yeoville thanked her, but could not prevent the image resurfacing of Wes dropping lifeless to the floor. It was only a mere snapshot of the fatal moment, but it was startlingly vivid, down to the droplets of blood splattering the floor next to the Major's feet.

"The Republicans have advanced another two kilometres on the main front, taking the fighting to the outer perimeter of Miramar," Catherine told him before he had a chance to dwell further on Palmer's death. "And, on average, we've also dropped back about a kilometre along the rest of the boundaries."

While attempting to haul himself into a sitting position, he asked, "What time is it?"

Catherine gently restrained him and eased him back down. "No, Daniel, you have to rest. Elizabeth and the others have everything under control. You've prepared them all well."

He only resisted for a moment. With a sigh, he repeated his question.

Demoore checked her watch and said with some trepidation, "One twenty AM."

Yeoville choked and rasped, "I've been out for four hours!" His coughing lent renewed potency to the pain in his shoulder, causing him to grit his teeth.

Catherine winced at the hurt in Daniel's face, but managed to say, reassuringly, "Yes, but don't worry." After a moment, she reiterated, less convincingly this time, "Everything is under control."

Without taking his eyes from Catherine, Yeoville relaxed back in his bed. The curtains had been raised on a deeper concern that Catherine had previously been concealing. Instinctively, he squeezed her hand. "Where's Bradley?" He felt a tremble briefly disturb her seemingly tranquil surface.

"He, erm…" She had to swallow before continuing. "He took his men and…left."

The Major's first conclusion was of cowardice, but that was immediately discarded as she explained.

"He had some foolish counterattack in mind. He was just leaving when I found out…I tried to stop him." She bowed her head while fighting back tears.

Demoore rested a hand on her shoulder and said, "He'll be alright, Catherine."

Yeoville closed his eyes and mustered all the conviction he could. Gently raising her head to look her in the eyes once more, he said, "Liz is right. Bradley's a good soldier and he knows what he's doing." His words sounded genuine enough, he only wished that he could believe it himself.

The streets of southern Poway were in ruins. Artillery and street fighting had laid waste to the once affluent area. Stucco coated single and two story detached homes were now just burnt out shells, their ample lawns now cratered and scorched. Sycamores that had lined the street were now either scorched bare or splintered and felled. Small fires still burned in the carcasses of a few homes and, here and there, bodies lay in and amongst the debris. The killing had been seemingly indiscriminate, snaring man, women and child. Amongst the death, also lay animals; both domestic and wild. Killed either in flight or shelter, the sheer terror would have been universal.

The mass devastation was against a backdrop of sporadic gunfire and explosions just out of sight, but by no means out of mind. The Poway summit was more a gravestone than a landmark.

Bradley's team were the loyal remnants of the Company that had been under his command when the revolution struck. One platoon had remained loyal to the young royal officer, but escape and evasion had cost them dearly. Only ten men remained from the thirty three strong platoon.

Dressed in overalls and work clothes, they drifted silently through the wreckage, their faces sombre but alert. They had slipped through the Republican lines amongst the hundreds of fleeing refugees struggling along the Pomerado Road and were now approaching the rear echelon units of the main attacking force. At this higher elevation, they could just make out the nucleus of the battle around the foot of Fortuna Mountain.

The ranking NCO, Platoon Sergeant Lee Farber, signalled the squad to halt. As they complied, he moved close to Bradley and asked, "What do you think, Sir?"

Bradley nodded as he surveyed the area. "Looks perfect."

Farber pulled off his black woolly hat, revealing shaggy ginger hair and wiped it across his sweaty forehead before replacing it. "Okay."

After setting trigger-mines and explosive charges along the route, they quickly took up positions in the shells of the houses and behind partially demolished walls. They made the most of elevation and defilade to maximize their impact. Once in position and displacement sites were set, they lay in wait.

The Loyalists had been waiting for fifteen tense minutes when the first elements of the convoy reached them. Like sailing ships caught on a breeze, supply and logistics vehicles drifted unhurriedly by punctuated by the occasional utility skimmer. Foot soldiers skirted the edges of the wreckage as they traipsed along side them. Bradley and his men let them pass without incident. The heart of the advancing Republican force, and their target, had yet to arrive.

Following the forward supply and logistics would be the Command and Control column, and behind them, reserves and medical units. Scouts and troops would interlock the chain in between and along its edges.

As the C&C units reached them, they counted a utility skimmer, scout and APC at the front of the procession, followed by three Command and Control vehicles—essentially extended APCs with tracking, comms and the tac-com network server—separated by utilities, then a scout and two more utilities to the rear. In range, there were approximately two platoons of foot soldiers, looking a little weary and bored, but still alert.

As the centre of the convoy entered the kill zone, Bradley gave the order.

The mines and explosives erupted in three waves, the first obliterating two of the C&C vehicles, the next took out the third and also the APC. A scout and two utility skimmers disappeared in the final volley. In the carnage, the triple blast also killed or maimed half of the foot soldiers.

Amidst the smoke, flames and screams, order swiftly gave way to chaos. As the routing survivors scattered, the Loyalists caught them in a web of crossfires. The remaining vehicles and soldiers were overwhelmed in minutes.

Bradley surveyed the destruction without comment. The battle had been short but fierce and his adrenalin was swift to ebb away with it. After a moment, he counted that six of his men remained plus one who was too badly wounded to move. They bid him good luck then left him with a morphine injection along with the dozen disarmed wounded Republicans.

The seven men double-timed it back to the Pomerado Road and found it far less crowded than it had been only an hour and a half ago. The fighting around Fortuna had died down to that of a camp fire in the early hours of the morning. Sporadic flashes, out of sync with their voices, were all that was evident.

Two kilometres down the road, they had only seen two small groups of people taking advantage of the welcomed respite. They hurried past with meagre possessions, dark clothes and down-cast faces. Civilization had abandoned them, leaving a transparent shell consisting of fear and instinct alone.

The sun was planning its impending ascent when a private, just ahead of Bradley, glanced over his shoulder and spotted the hawk-like T60 bearing down on them. As they scattered, its twin rotary cannons ripped up the asphalt all around them.

Scrambling away from the road, Bradley saw one of his men hammered to the ground in a shower of blood. The plane was over the interstate by the time a couple of the Loyalists half-heartedly returned fire.

"Don't waste your ammo," Farber snapped at them as he dusted himself off, his hat lost in the scramble. "You alright, Sir?"

Bradley found his feet and nodded. "I'm fine."

Lance Corporal Terrino stood over the dead private and muttered, "Louie weren't so lucky."

"C'mon, let's move," the Sergeant said, slapping him on the shoulder.

Bradley paused to look at the dead private before following.

Bradley and his five remaining men had skirted around the easterly side of Fortuna and were nearing the San Diego River. The homes and businesses on this side seemed to have escaped most of the devastation, but were abandoned nonetheless. The only sign of life they had seen since the Pomerado Road was a single stray cow strolling down the middle of the road. Looting and one or two stray shells accounted for the majority of the damage.

"After crossing the River," Bradley said as they paused to catch their breath, "we should be out of the danger zone."

"Then about two hours to get back to base," Farber added.

Terrino, a couple of metres in front, turned and asked, "Whose round is it?"

"Well, we know whose round it won't be," said the private in front of Terrino. "Yours. It's never your round."

A hushed laugh rippled through the line, briefly lifting their spirits and temporarily concealing their fears. Bradley laughed with them and suddenly realised that the men were finally starting to accept him; well, the few that were left. It had been an arduous task, as had the rest of his short but colourful army career, fighting prejudices from the likes of Yeoville. For a time, he had been the youngest in his company, a fact in its self hard to overcome, but coupled with being the Iron Duke's son, made it virtually unbearable.

Their current predicament snapped back into focus as machinegun fire cut down the point man. Everyone dove for cover as the private in front of Terrino was struck twice in the chest and shoulder.

"Ben!" Terrino yelled as he hit the floor behind the burned out shell of a recreational skimmer. He returned fire, his curses lost below the din.

Bradley and the remaining private dove behind a decorative stone garden wall and popped back up in unison to reply. Farber, finding limited sanctuary behind a sycamore to Terrino's left, yelled, "I saw two muzzle flashes. Trees in the park eleven o'clock. Anyone confirm?"

Terrino ducked back down as gunfire drilled holes along the wrecked vehicle's flank. With a clenched jaw, he said, "Three SAWs in dug-outs just inside the tree line. Sitting just fuckin' waiting for us!"

The parkland, once offering fun for children and sanctuary for lovers and friends, now harboured death from the three machine gun crews. It had looked at first almost tranquil; bordered lawns with interlocking pathways, a separate enclosed play area with swings, climbing frames and roundabouts and in the centre a small wooded area. A peaceful place for Sunday picnics in the sunshine watching the kids at play…

"Stay cool." Farber squinted to see the three positions. "I see them. Cap, you see'em?"

"Got them," Bradley replied whilst pointing out the third fox hole to the private. Several rounds tore chunks out of the low wall in front of him. Between bursts, he said, "Concentrate fire on the central position. Anyone got any smoke left?"

Not waiting for a confirmation, he crawled further along the wall then popped back up to empty the remains of the clip at the central position. The others, except for Farber, followed suit, firing then changing positions.

The Sergeant had one smoke grenade left. Unclipping it from his webbing, he squeezed the arming lever and threw it up the street. As it bounced and clattered, releasing thick smoke along the way, a plume of crimson marked the central gunner's death.

Aided by the partial smokescreen, Farber grabbed his rifle and sprinted across the grass verge towards a side gate between two homes. One of the gunners zeroed in on him and at once the grass and dirt tore up around him. One bullet struck his shoulder as he crashed through the wooden gate.

Ducking back down after finishing his last rifle clip, Terrino glanced over briefly to see Farber clutching his shoulder now out of range of the remaining gunners. Ben's body and rifle were two metres away. "Cover me!" he yelled. Before the smoke dispersed, he scrambled towards the discarded weapon. In seconds, he grasped the rifle by the muzzle and turned to head back. A ricochet sliced a gash in his forehead causing him to stumble and drop the rifle. He landed heavily on his hands and knees as a second bullet blew the heel off his boot. Screaming, he collapsed onto his side, clutching his leg.

"Terrino!" Bradley howled. He made an attempt to dive back over the wall to help the stricken man, but a shower of bullets forced him back down.

In the next moment two more rounds struck the squirming Loyalist and he moved no more.

The exchange continued for another two desperate minutes.

Bradley's assault rifle clicked empty with the demise of the second machine gunner. "Dammit, I'm out." He turned to the Private. "Scott?"

"About half a mag, Sir." His face was dirt smeared and his eyes were wide-eyed with suppressed panic.

Using the wall and gate for cover, Farber fired one more time, then clumsily ejected the spent clip. He retrieved a fresh one from his webbing and mouthed, 'last one' to the Captain.

Bradley took a deep breath, drew his sabre from its sheath strapped across his back, and said, "Covering fire."

Farber started to protest, but it was too late. The young Captain came up from behind the wall in a low sprint. With his head down, he ran zigzagging towards the final machinegun. Farber and Scott opened fire simultaneously.

Bradley had reached the low iron railing that marked the boundary of the park when Scott's rifle fired its last shot. That gave the Republican his chance. It took a fraction of a second to get the Loyalist in his sights and squeeze the trigger.

There was a distinctive twang as the machinegun jammed. Panic overwhelmed him as his target loomed closer and his shaking hands tried to snap open the top of the gun.

He had cleared the breach and snapped it shut as Bradley reached within a couple of metres of him. A cry escaped his lips as he cocked it then squeezed the trigger. A three round burst zipped past Bradley's head as he dove onto the Republican, slamming him against the crudely dug back wall of the fox hole.

"Move!" Farber yelled at the Private as he staggered to his feet.

Scott reached the dug-out ahead of the Sergeant and found Bradley lying on top of the Republican with his blade buried into the man's chest almost to the hilt. Neither man was moving.

Lieutenant Demoore was running down the dim battleship grey hospital corridor. Her peak fitness days were over, but the news she carried drove her on past her usual physical barriers.

As she rounded the final bend, her boots squealing like an over protective sow, she slammed headlong into an orderly with his hands full of clean bed linen. Being the larger of the two, Demoore went through him as if he was only there in spirit rather than body, knocking him to the floor and scattering the linen.

Yelling an apology over her shoulder, she skidded to a halt outside Major Yeoville's room. She paused only to take in a few deep breaths and to push strands of damp brown hair back under her cap.

Inside, the Major was sat up looking through some reports with Catherine perched on the bed beside him.

"Liz," Yeoville said, shaking his head, "you're going to do yourself an injury."

She smiled at him, taking the opportunity to take in a couple more breaths. Conscious of her burning cheeks, she got straight to the point. "They've halted the advance, Sir."

Yeoville sat bolt upright, ignoring the discomfort it brought. "How? Why?" he asked with a cocktail of excitement and suspicion.

"Captain Frelon." Her own astonishment was as clear as the Major's.

In an instant, Catherine was on her feet and clasping the Lieutenant's hands in hers. "Is he alright?"

Demoore squeezed her hands and said, "He's alive, but he's wounded." With a thousand questions about to erupt from Catherine, Demoore continued without giving her a chance. "They've reached one of our border lookouts, so they'll get here within the hour. Until he arrives, we really don't know anything else."

The Lieutenant did not know Catherine very well, but as tears emerged from the corners of her eyes, she immediately threw her arms around her.

Yeoville watched them from his bed, as guilt gave him another wake up call. Mixed with the delight at hearing the news, for an instant he had also thought how much more unbearable this would make the young Frelon. It was inexcusable.

He wanted desperately to hold her; to tell her everything was going to be alright. Instead, he just watched, feeling awkward and stupid.

Only when Catherine left them to go and wait for Bradley's arrival did Yeoville get the full story of how Bradley and his men had struck a decisive blow against the Republic's forward Command and Control. A large multi unit force with badly disrupted C & C would be just as likely to damage itself as to inflict damage on to the Loyalists. Ryker would have no choice but to cease the advance until sufficient replacements and restructuring could be managed.

Guilt again surfaced. Bradley and just a handful of men had managed to stop what his whole garrison could not and all he could think of was how cocky it would make him. The kid deserved a medal.

Yeoville swung both his legs off the side of the bed.

Demoore moved to stop him. "What are you doing?"

The Major stared at her. "I want to be there when they bring him in." She started to protest, but, seeing the determination in his eyes, instead just nodded and walked to the closet.

It was early afternoon before Catherine was allowed in to see her brother. No one had been permitted to accompany her, so the ten minutes that had gone by since she went to him were beginning to feel more painful than his bullet wound.

Daniel Yeoville had seen a great deal of pain and anguish, but nothing had struck him quite so powerfully as the haunted expression on Catherine's face as she followed the doctor out of the waiting room.

He had sent Demoore back to Operations, so his only company was the sporadic passing of the occasional nurse or orderly. Whether he liked it or not, it gave him time to think.

Even in frailty Catherine bore an enormous strength. It was not apparent to the casual observer, not that he could imagine any man just glancing at her. He remembered how, at the Ball, men would catch sight of her, become transfixed and then quickly look away. Later, he would catch sight of them sneaking another glimpse. At that point he had not even met her, yet even then he had felt a twinge of jealousy, although he did not recognise it for what it was until the following day.

Yes, she had strength, but it was equalled in weakness. With most of her family either dead or imprisoned, it was only natural to feel not just love for Bradley, but a responsibility and possibly even dependence.

Bradley's current condition must have been torture for her. Again, his heart went out to her and again he racked his brain of some way to ease her pain. Again, no miracle answer surfaced.

The faces of Wes and Lyn flashed in front of his eyes, they were followed by others; soldiers, friends, family. Mary appeared to him last. They were all gone…dozens of people that he had shared his life with…including his best friend and his wife.

# Chapter 7

## Sacrifice

The ground was muddy from recent rainfall and barren save for a few vicious rock formations and the occasional cottonwood or juniper, sagebrush or grass. The roar of the Samson preceded its physical form by several minutes. When it did appear, the transporter was coated in thick muck and was dripping wet from its ascent through the forested eastern face of Donohue Mountain deep in the San Ysidro Mountain range.

At the two thousand feet elevation, they could see past the Jamal Mountains to the outskirts of San Diego. Most of their view was obscured by the greater peaks of Otay and San Miguel, but parts of El Cajon and Lemon Grove were still visible between them. Even from nearly thirty kilometres out, they could see the smoke. It hung like a veil over most of the city, attempting to conceal the devastation.

From inside the bridge, Reynolds leaned closer to the monitor and said, "San Diego." It was laced with relief, but there was an edge lurking under its surface that was difficult to hide.

Casey glanced from Reynolds to the King and asked, "So what now?"

The Major looked for confirmation from Paul.

In reply, Paul said, "Well, we have come this far. The situation is as we expected, so the plan still stands." He did not take his eyes away from the monitor. Its image was by no means a new one—with familiarity, war and destruction, like anything have the tendency to appear all too ordinary—but of late it had become impossible to ignore, never mind quell, the voice inside his head that repeated, *This is your fault.*

Reynolds noticed, all too clearly, the distant look in the King's eyes. Again, he sensed his leader's pain. "I'll make a move then," he said, as if only to himself.

"S'what 'bout me? Waddaya need from the Case-man?"

Paul looked at him with a hint of surprise escaping his grim features and then managed a sincere smile. "You have helped us more than enough already, Casey. I could not possibly—"

"Wo-ah. Y'ain't dumpin'me now—ah said ah'd help yall and ah don'do nuthin in half measures." The trader's rubber-like face shifted to defiance. His eyes were wide, but not due to a PASH hit, but with genuine conviction. It had erupted out of his mouth without actually thinking about it, but now that it was said, he did actually mean it. No one was more shocked than Casey Shacks.

Two things struck Reynolds. Interrupting the King was normally unspeakable, but he could see that Paul did not mind, and he too did not take offence. In addition, he had shown in just a few words the true strength of his loyalty—equal, at least, to his own. What surprised Reynolds more was that this new revelation did not surprise him at all.

"Damn right!" Both CHARLIEs were saying in unison, Two albeit a little more tentatively.

Paul had to catch his breath before saying, "You are a true and loyal friend Casey Shacks. Thank you, thank you all."

An uncharacteristic seriousness settled over Casey's face. "I...thanks, Sire."

The Samson's mess room was more like a mess cupboard, but it served its purpose for the three men that currently occupied it. Reynolds and Speyer were both seated at the table, examining the portable tac-com. Shacks was too wired to sit, so instead he was prowling, taking time out only to stub out a cigarette and light up a fresh one. The air purifiers had packed in, so a blue haze hung in the air.

"Yes, that has to be the best route," Reynolds said. "We're only going to make it so far in the vehicles, so we'll have a bit of a hike the rest of the way."

Speyer nodded and said, "So if we set off the diversion at El Cajon, we should distract the brigade there and also draw a sizeable amount of their forces from Lemon Grove." He took a sip of coffee before adding, "The risks for the incursion should be reduced significantly."

Reynolds had known Speyer a long time and had never known him to reveal any sign of fear, but he saw it in him now. He had not seen it in his eyes or his mannerisms, but instead, in the way he had picked up his cup. It was like someone turning on the light to his darkened mind.

"Yeah, don't ya worry, Reynolds," Casey said, sensing the change in mood. "We'll keep 'em busy fo'ya."

Reynolds looked up at Shacks. The smuggler was a lot worse at hiding his fear. His bravado was totally transparent. "Look, once we get into position, we will need thirty minutes to get clear. The second that time is up I want you to either escape or surrender, which ever you can."

The Lieutenant locked eyes with his commander. "You know we can't do that."

Shacks started to object, but Reynolds beat him to it. "I don't give a damn about the regs, Luke. There is no need for you to 'evade capture at all costs.' If you can't escape, I am ordering you to surrender."

"But personal feelings—"

"Bullshit, personal feelings. There's nothing of importance that you can tell them, if they could make you talk, so I'll be damned if you're to lose your life over a Royal Guard Directive." He shot a sideways glance at Shacks. "That goes for you too, Hero."

"That's the nicest damn thang anyone's ever said to me," Shacks cooed whilst clutching his heart.

Reynolds smiled, despite himself. Speyer took another sip of coffee.

Reynolds and Shacks walked in silence to the elevator. Speyer had left them earlier to brief his team. It was not until they entered and the doors closed behind them that one of them spoke.

Shacks muttered simply, "Guess I was wrong 'bout you."

"Ditto."

Once the preparations were complete, Reynolds caught up with Speyer in the garage. The two officers stood aside from the group of soldiers milling around a hastily scrounged light transport skimmer parked in front of the main exit, packs and weapons strewn around them.

"All set?" Speyer asked him.

The Major nodded and grasped his friend's shoulder. "Look after yourself, Luke."

"Hey, if you think you can get rid of me this easily, you've got another thing coming." His tone was jovial, but Reynolds knew him well. "Just take care of the King for me."

Reynolds cast a glance over his dim surroundings. Several of the soldiers near the door broke out in laughter at the conclusion of a murmured joke from one of the privates. The Major's keen senses identified the culprit as being Private Cook. The scrawny-looking Private, whom Reynolds knew to be an expert at both marksmanship and close-quarters combat, glanced their way.

Reynolds turned back to Speyer and said, "Listen, I know Shacks and I haven't seen eye to eye much, but watch out for him; he's a good man."

Speyer smiled at that. "I knew you'd come round. You can count on it."

The elevator doors to their left parted to admit the formidable form of Staff Sergeant Cobek. "Ready, Sir," Cobek said. Paul and Samantha, dressed in grey jumpsuits, and a rather sheepish looking Shacks followed.

Reynolds turned to acknowledge Cobek, but Paul intervened. "There is one duty I would like to perform before we leave, Richard. That is why I have also brought Mister Shacks down here."

Reynolds and Shacks exchanged confused expressions. "Sir?"

Paul smiled and said, "Bear with me, Richard. This sort of thing would normally take hours with all the pomp and circumstance, but I will condense it given our situation and time constraints. I have decided to reinstate the Order of the Provincial Knights, an order that was disbanded by my Great Grandfather, King Thomas."

Samantha appeared as surprised as everyone else, but the surprise was quickly replaced by a proud smile as she guessed what was coming. Reynolds was totally confused.

"Richard, Lucas and Casey, please kneel before me."

The three men were open-mouthed as they duly complied. Paul unsheathed a gleaming longsword, its hilt a carved ivory wolf's head, the symbol of the House of Frelon. He gently dubbed each shoulder of each man and uttered the words, "Advance, Knight, in the name of God." Having dubbed each man, he then stepped back and said, "Arise, Sir Richard. Arise, Sir Lucas. Arise, Sir Casey." The three men rose in unison, looking first to one another then back to their King.

"There would normally be a medal," Paul added with a smile. "But we will have to sort that out another time." A murmur of laughter broke the serious mood.

"I-I don't know what to say, Sire," Reynolds uttered.

Paul placed a hand on his shoulder. "There is nothing to say. I believe it is time to go."

"Yes, Sire." To the congregated men, he then said, "Let's move people."

"See you later," Speyer managed, rather dumbstruck, whilst backing away.

Paul took hold of the Lieutenant's hand before he moved out of range and shook it firmly. The look that passed between them said more than any words could. "Good luck, Sir Lucas." As Reynolds beckoned, Paul turned one last time to Shacks. "You have been an inspiration, Sir Casey. Good luck."

Shacks headed back to the bridge, still somewhat embarrassed, leaving Speyer to watch in silence as the King and his escorts boarded the transport skimmer. Even as Reynolds paused in the doorway, the garage door began its weary descent to form a ramp for the skimmer's escape. The Major lingered for a moment, their eyes meeting, and then was gone.

The battered skimmer lurched down the ramp and out of sight.

Speyer was alone apart from one Private standing near the now ascending ramp. He knew from assignments, without recognising the man's features, that it was Meek. The soldier, whose name was somewhat ironic given his stature, nipped the end off his half-smoked cigarette and stuck it behind his ear for later use. Glancing one last time towards the exit, he trudged off in the direction of the workshop.

The Lieutenant drew in a deep breath then headed for the elevator.

The Samson's dishevelled Bridge was hot and tense. As Casey wiped sweat from his brow, another missile rocked the straining giant. "Hell'n'damnation, they're all over us. The ol'girl is 'bout ready to bust right open."

Speyer was concentrating on the crackling rear camera view. The four lane street was strewn with rubble and debris, as well as more than a few bodies. Shops and offices on both sides were bullet ridden, some with walls and doors blasted in. A utility skimmer had careered into a convenience store, leaving only its smoking rear sticking out onto the sidewalk. A couple of flattened vehicles also lay in the mammoth's wake, unable to avoid its path.

The image of devastation failed to register, only targets mattered, and they included two recon skimmers, one utility skimmer and at least a dozen clusters of frantic infantrymen. His finger would have been firmly glued to the trigger, had it not been for the jamming warnings irritatingly flashing every few seconds on the console.

The street was a snug fit for the Samson, tearing down street lighting and traffic lights, flattening bus stops and litter bins. Had it not been getting shot at from every angle by small arms fire, rockets and grenades, the scene may have been vaguely amusing.

The transporter, with flames and smoke enveloping it, spun on its axis and ploughed through a fenced outdoor rest area, churning up the groomed lawn and obliterating the wooden tables and benches. Several Republicans were caught off guard and routed in different directions.

Continuing its path of destruction, the Samson crashed through the frontage of a café, taking roof and walls with it and carried on through the adjoining office before finding another four lane street.

"Keep us moving," Speyer muttered absent-mindedly as he launched several grenades at the gaping hole where the offices and café used to be. The camera view spun to reveal the street and more Republican soldiers. Speaking into his headset, he said, "McGuire, report."

The Corporal's voice was barely audible as two more blasts, one after the other, shook the whole transporter. "We've got fires breaking out everywhere and hull breaches in at least two—" The radio emitted an ear-splitting squeal at the same time as Casey let out a string of curses.

"W'lost all power 'cept 'mergency backup." On cue, the lights and consoles flickered and the deep growl of the engine died.

Casey and Speyer's eyes locked, but before either one of them could speak, the radio found life. "...ded, LT. Do you read?"

Speyer turned back to his station, and in doing so, had a brief glimpse of dozens of soldiers swarming all over the Samson's rear. Then the monitor died. The beast was down—they were coming in for the kill. "McGuire, say again."

The Corporal opened the channel again, but over the gunfire, he directed his attention to someone else. "Fall back...t...vator! No, Chris' dead!" The radio went silent for only a few seconds, but it seemed like minutes. "LT, we're being boarded. Meek and Jefferson...dead. Me an...ler are pulling back to the elevator."

Speyer noticed that Casey was watching him; grim and silent. He shook his head before saying, "Our mission's accomplished, Corporal. Surrender immediately."

Casey noticeably slumped in his chair. "Damn."

After staying uncharacteristically quiet for some time, CHARLIE I announced matter-of-factly, "W'screwed." The lights dimmed for a second time then blacked out to be replaced after a moment by the red emergency lighting.

"I'm scared, JAa…" The voice of CHARLIE II went baritone then faded out. Casey simply stared at the dead speakers. Lights blinked out all over the console.

Once McGuire had acknowledged, Speyer, too, eased back in his chair. Without turning, he said, "We put up a helluva fight."

Casey plucked the last cigarette out of a crumpled pack from the breast pocket of his leather jacket and, with it dangling from the corner of his mouth, said, "Yer damn right, Soldier." With a smile, he added, "Or should I say, Sir Luke?"

Speyer's smile vanished as a new voice, with panic stretching it to breaking point, erupted over the air waves. "Sir…Guire's dead!…Not letting us surrender!"

In tandem, the two men sprung to their feet. This was an outcome they had not considered.

Speyer frantically tried to think as Casey grabbed his holster and cap. As he slipped them on, the Lieutenant replied, "Fowler, get to the stores. Use whatever you've got to slow them down. We'll meet you there." He took a moment to check that his own pistol was holstered and loaded.

Shacks had drawn the same conclusion; he already had the grill cover off the air vent as Speyer joined him. Without a word, he drew his Harvey and scrambled in the grimy shaft.

Speyer rushed after him. "Hang on; I'm supposed to be watching out for you!"

"Y'can worry'bout savin' me later," was the tinny response.

The duct was one shade off pitch black, but judging by its slimy feel, the impairment was a blessing. The smell was an almost physical cocktail of mould and oil.

Five metres in, Speyer stopped. In the darkness, his slippery hands groped about his webbing, seeking a smooth cylinder.

"Speyer?" The trader's muffled voice seemed to drift back from a great distance, but it was scarcely a few feet.

As his fingers grasped the object, he replied, "I've got an idea. Just keep going." He heard a faint grunt, then Shacks resumed his journey. With that, Speyer yanked the grenade off its hook and threw it back the way they came.

It clattered back towards the hole, as the distinctive groan of the elevator sounded, growing louder and louder. The grenade disappeared through the tiny opening and skittered across the floor of the abandoned bridge.

Speyer was already scurrying after Shacks when the explosion jerked the Samson like a final dying rasp. He caught up with him squatting beside a vertical shaft.

"Damn good idea. They won'look fo'what they think's already dead."

Speyer bent over the hole and scrutinised it. "Is it this one or the next that leads to the stores?"

"This's it, s'gonna be real slippy-like, so be careful. You go first, that way if I slip, yall break my fall." The darkness could not disguise his grin.

"Funny guy." It was said with sarcasm, but he smiled too.

Half way down the shaft, Speyer came across the grill for the mess room. Judging by the charred and smashed remains, a grenade had been tossed into it. The destruction was partially illuminated by the red neon of the emergency lighting and smoky shards of light squeezing through the shattered porthole.

The image of Reynolds' stern features, demanding their surrender, snapped into focus; he submerged it just as quick and carried on without comment.

Shacks also paused at the grill. Before he could move on, a weary sadness settled over him. His eyes moved from one of the mangled chairs, to a corner piece and leg from the table and finally to the vending machine—still smoking—with its innards hanging out. Suddenly he felt very tired.

It was Speyer who broke the spell. "Come on, Sir Casey." he whispered harshly.

Before they reached the stationary fan at the bottom of the shaft, they found the grill, behind which lay the store room. The room had been similarly redecorated to the one above, but had no emergency lighting or window to illuminate it; the only murky light spilled in from the partially open doorway.

Speyer, only now, realised how quiet it had become. Immediately after this revelation, he saw the crumpled corpse of Private Fowler in the doorway. He refrained from cursing, instead listening for the slightest noise—a scrape, a muffled exhale, an itchy trigger-finger. Silence.

He could sense Casey's growing impatience, when he finally moved. Without a sound, he eased the grill cover off its bracket and lowered it down to the bottom of the shaft. With his pistol leading the way, he slithered out of the hole and down the wall, quickly righting himself the second his palm touched the floor.

As the Lieutenant inspected the battered boxes and crates, Shacks followed him out, landing in a far less graceful heap on the floor. Whilst rubbing his shin, through gritted teeth, he uttered, "Sonuvabitch." On seeing the disapproving glare from Speyer, he continued the rest of his cursing in silence.

After checking that the hallway was clear, Speyer bent down and closed the dead private's eyes before stripping him of his rifle and one spare clip. "Anything we can use in here?"

"Ah could use a damn stretcher," Casey said, now gingerly testing the weight on his injured leg.

"Get serious."

"No, nuthin'."

"Right, let's go then." He cautiously stepped into the hallway and, keeping to one side, made his way towards the blown side entrance. Several dead Republicans paved the way. They paused only to retrieve more ammunition and a rifle for Shacks from the dead.

They were half way to the exit when a Republican appeared crouched in the doorway and fired instantly. Speyer threw himself to the floor as he returned fire.

The Republican slumped forward, leaving Speyer clutching a glancing bullet wound to the top of his shoulder.

Shacks rushed to his aid. "How bad's it?"

"I'll live," Speyer said, suppressing the pain as Shacks helped him to his feet. He glanced at his rifle, then unceremoniously cast it aside and drew his pistol instead.

"We gotta go, bud. They're gonna be all over us."

Speyer nodded and they both moved on with Shacks giving as much support as the Lieutenant would let him. Less than a metre from the door, they both stopped and listened.

"Waddaya think?" Shacks whispered.

"That one," Speyer nodded to the young man slumped in the doorway, "was a private. There must be at least another plus an NCO. If one of them is seasoned, he'll be at a distance ready to pick us off."

"Well that's just dandy."

"On the plus side they're infantry, so he won't have a scope." After a moment of thought, he said, "Get Fowler."

Casey considered querying the order, but thought better of it and ran back to the stores. He returned, struggling with the body over his shoulder, his grimy face glistening with sweat. Breathlessly, he said, "Now what?"

Staring down the barrel of his assault rifle through the smashed lounge room window, Corporal Slovak willed the Loyalist bastard to show himself. He hadn't known the cherry long, just having been transferred in, but he had seemed like a good kid. Only eighteen and full of fake bravado. A walking clusterfuck if there ever was one, but he had been brought up not a million miles away from Slovak's old home town of Boulder. The other guys in the platoon had never heard of Canfield, Colorado, a small mining town north east of Boulder. But Slovak knew it well and they had both attended the University of Colorado in Boulder, albeit five years apart.

He asked the black private squatting next to him leaning against a floral sofa sprinkled with shards of glass, "That numb-nut CO of ours replied yet?" His eyes never left the lifeless smoking transporter.

"No, man." He pushed the headset mike away from his mouth in disgust.

"Jesus, we got us a situation here and the rest of the company's decided to take some R&R. Why does this shit always happen to me? Those dipshits in First Platoon said it was clear. Assholes!"

A sigh was caught on his lips as a face slowly emerged from behind the doorframe.

Holding his breath, the Republican waited.

After a moment, the torso began to follow. Half way out of the door he jerked and started to withdraw.

Instinctively, Slovak realised that the Loyalist must have seen him, so on reflex, fired. He was rewarded by a crimson plume erupting from the head as it disappeared from view.

He turned to the private, grinning from ear to ear. "Y'see that, Dave! That's what I'm talkin' about!" He had only turned away for a couple of seconds, but the pistol was already aiming right at him. He saw it as it fired.

The bullet burst open his nose. As he fell backwards onto the beige carpet, he started to choke on his own blood. Before his gloved hand had settled on his chest he was already dead, crimson discolouring the carpet in an expanding circle around his head.

As two figures jumped clear of the transporter, Private Dave Little panicked and started running before he had properly found his feet. His toe clipped his own boot heel causing him to stumble and crack his head off the corner of a heavy pine coffee table.

Speyer did not allow him the luxury of dwelling on his fatal error, rapidly clearing the distance to the house front despite his injury. The drop from the Samson had jarred his shoulder still further, but did not stop him from popping up at the window and emptying several rounds into the groaning dazed soldier. The Republican was instantly silenced.

Wincing at the renewed pain, he shouted to Shacks who was hot on his heels, "Keep going. Got to get to cover."

Casey's body reacted, but not before catching a glimpse of the two dead Americans in the remains of some poor bastard's lounge. *Kill or be killed*, he told himself. It did not help. Despite their situation, PASH whispered for attention.

They quickly followed the wall till they reached the side alley of the once sizeable detached house. Before going through to the back garden, Casey glanced back one last time to the blackened—still smoking—wreck that had been known as the Samson. The shell that remained was hardly the sanctuary and home that he had previously known, the scene of countless adventure and drama, enacted with the help of CHARLIE I and CHARLIE II. He felt naked without her and lonely without them. Over the last few days, the PASH had increasingly lost its allure, but he felt the aching returning with renewed lustre.

"So long," he uttered before turning to follow Speyer.

The El Cajon district, over the past month, had seen fierce fighting, so was mainly deserted. As the two recently appointed Knights picked there way through litter and rubble strewn gardens and back streets, Speyer's thoughts, more than once, turned to the people caught in the middle of this conflict. Men, women and children who were just trying to quietly live their lives were lost amongst the destruction. Jobs, schools, hospitals…homes…all were being damaged or destroyed in the crossfire.

He recognised, not for the first time, the stark contrasts that war could reveal. On his journey with the King, he had witnessed whole towns that had been literally obliterated and also, merely a couple of kilometres down the road from one such flattened town, he had seen a town completely untouched but similarly bereft of life. And yet, in some towns, even in the thick of battle, he had also witnessed life continuing in a semi-normal fashion. Papers being delivered, hair being cut…life being lived.

In the end it came down to one thing; human resolve, or the lack of it. When you tried to analyse it, it made no sense at all, but if you just accepted the reality, it seemed to be completely reasonable.

He wondered what Richard would make of his thoughts and smiled, picturing the look on his face. He also considered how they would be doing; it would be no parade, that much was certain. Yet the King was in his charge, so failure was out of the question. Deep concern surfaced regardless.

The night was cold, but by no means quiet. On reaching the outskirts of La Mesa, they discovered far more Republican activity and found that a company CP had been set up in the local medical clinic. They were on high alert and very jumpy.

Resting in an empty garage, in the darkness, Speyer took a moment to pull back the Velcro from his wristband. It revealed the illuminated dial of his wristwatch, the digital display reading 2:12AM. After replacing the cover, he said, "We'll take five, then get going. We need to be over the line before sun-up, so it doesn't give us much time."

Shacks insisted on changing Speyer's field-dressing, then after a brief rest, they left the garage and continued towards Loyalist territory. They had only been travelling for ten minutes when the relative peace was shattered.

They had been making their way along a cluttered back alley, over-shadowed on one side by a three-storey office block and a domestic skimmer dealership on the other when several gunshots, in rapid succession, rang out. Speyer collapsed with them.

Shacks dropped on one knee and opened fire at a second floor window in the office block where the flashes had come from. The Harvey Wallbanger boomed like a cannon, two shots going through the window and the other two blowing chunks out of the sill. Whether permanent or not, the Republican did not return fire.

He scrambled over to his prone companion. "Luke?" he whispered as he reached him. The Lieutenant was on his side, with his face obscured, so he eased him on to his back and repeated his name before seeing the damage. The high calibre sniper round had struck him in the centre of the chest, killing him instantly.

Shacks cradled his head, staring in disbelief at his pale, slack features with blood smeared on his lips and one cheek. He wept in silence for some time, oblivious and uncaring of his own vulnerability. Speyer had been leading, not Shacks, so he had been killed and Shacks had been spared. They had survived so much together only for it to end so abruptly. There was no logic or pattern to it…it was random and final.

A few hours prior to Lieutenant Speyer's death, monitoring the radio in the partially re-constructed Command Centre, Captain Jones heard something that immediately struck a chord. He turned to Yeoville, who was pacing around the recently repaired tac-com, openly agitated.

"I think the King is trying to break through."

As he digested the information, the Major took a moment to glance at his surroundings. The doorway was just a jagged hole in the wall, only two terminals were operational—the others had been gathered together and placed on two tables at the far end of the room with their insides on show and cables splayed amongst them. Still more cables dangled from the ceiling and rubble and debris had been piled up in two corners of the room. Two maintenance staff were still engrossed with repairs while two operators manned the terminals, leaving Yeoville and Jones as the only others present.

Other than those few minor blemishes, the room and its grubby occupants were in fine shape. "What makes you think that?" The question was asked more out of habit, than necessity. He had a feeling and, judging by the sudden stillness and expressions on the operators and engineers, he was not alone.

"All Hell's broken loose behind Republican lines around El Cajon."

Yeoville glanced at the tac-com. The screen showed Republican forces to be estimated at a brigade in that sector. "Diversion?"

Jones merely nodded, but Yeoville could see a gleam in his eyes that revealed a whole lot more. "What can we throw into the mixing pot?"

"Svenson was just saying how bored he was," Jones said, a smile creeping across his lips.

Yeoville scanned the map once more, before saying, "Get the hovernaught and Bravo to mount strikes all along the front. We'll have to be careful though, we only know the location of their diversion, not the King's party. Stress vigilance against friendly fire, but no specifics."

"Yessir."

"It's about time we gave Ryker something to worry about."

Paul and his remaining companions had been on foot for some time with only one incident behind them, leaving two Republicans dead and Private Hamilton with an arm wound. They had managed to avoid several larger patrols, so although Reynolds was by no means complacent, he was acutely aware that they were doing far better than he could have hoped for.

The district that they had been moving through for the past half an hour was in total darkness; no street lights, neon signs or residential lighting. If there were inhabitants with private generators, they were, understandably, keeping any signs of them well hidden. It left the group feeling cold and isolated.

The sky was mainly clear, lending some illumination from a crescent of moonlight. Distant sporadic gunfire, accompanied by the occasional explosion replaced the normal sounds of territorial cats, lonely dogs and late night revellers.

On point, leading the group, was a young black soldier with a stance that bore the weight of the world on his shoulders. Lance Corporal John Alistair Joseph, better known as AJ, paused by a wrecked shop front. The door was lying on the floor, amongst a bed of broken glass, from both the door and the huge window. Only a few discarded packages remained—a squashed loaf of bread and a ripped bag of flour being the ones by the door he could recognise—to reveal the shop's former identity.

Looters had been responsible for the sight in front of him; the effects of war appeared in many guises.

He had only paused briefly, but Cobek, maintaining radio silence, motioned for Cook to approach him before allowing the rest of the team to continue. "What's up, m'man?" Cook asked in a hushed voice.

"It's cool," AJ replied without turning to him. He lingered for only a moment longer before moving on.

AJ continued to lead the group through the dead streets. Despite stopping every block or so from a noise here or a shadow there, they made good progress. With the passing of each new block, the not-so-distant fighting grew in intensity. The guttural rhythmic thump of a gunship sounded in the black sky and diminished before it could be spotted.

In the time that they had been walking, for the majority of it in silence, Paul had been given ample chance to see, first hand, the extent of the devastation. He felt a bitter concoction of anger, disgust and shame, which was washed down with an underlying feeling of deep sadness. Past decisions that he had been all too eager to make, resurfaced now to haunt him. Quick to instigate, but they would take more than his lifetime to rectify. It was all too clear. But was it all too late?

He tugged at his shirt collar to stem the advancing cold, but it was more an inner chill than a physical one. Picking up the pace, he forced himself to catch Samantha's attention. He smiled at her, well aware of her need for reassurance and desperate for some of his own. The circles around her eyes had grown steadily darker, lending a haunted sheen to her former bright features.

He looked at the road ahead and his thoughts drifted once again to his wife, and then his son...

AJ caught sight of the concealed gun positions a moment before they opened fire. He had time only to signal an ambush before he was cut down across the thighs. Still he managed to let off a single shot before the agony overwhelmed him, leaving his rifle forgotten.

"AJ!" Cook cried, already on the ground.

"Cover fire!" Cobek barked. The soldiers opened fire simultaneously while Reynolds and the Sergeant positioned themselves in the line of fire of Paul and Samantha, both of whom were stunned into rigid silence.

"Ten o'clock; rooftop," Private Swede shouted over the clamour from a crouching stance against the wall.

Cook cocked the under slung grenade launcher on his rifle and fired. The grenade arched through the air and landed out of sight on the rooftop position. The subsequent explosion blew one of the Republicans clean off the roof, hitting the ground headfirst with a gut-wrenching crack.

Crouching in front of the King, with his rifle ready, Cobek said, "First team, suppressives. Second team advance ten. Move!"

Cook, Swede and Hamilton began firing single shots in rapid succession at any possible hiding place. At the same time, a Puerto Rican PFC and a Native American Corporal rushed forward.

They reached the moaning form of AJ when another Republican opened fire, popping round the street corner fifty metres ahead of them. He only managed to get off one wide shot before the largest of Cobek's team hit him in the head.

"Nice shot, Swede," Cobek said. "Chey, get AJ into cover. First team, continue suppressives."

The two soldiers swept up the injured Guardsman with ease and dashed into an open doorway. As Chey gently laid AJ to the grimy tiled floor, the PFC—Rodriquez—quickly made a sweep of the darkened lobby and short hallway. Two elevators—disabled—and one door, which led to the wrecked Super's office.

The Puerto Rican emerged from the apartment building and motioned for the others to advance as he took up a covering position.

Once inside the relative safety of the lobby, Samantha began trembling uncontrollably. Hugging herself and biting hard on her lower lip proved futile in keeping the tears at bay. Without warning, Reynolds abandoned his command and wrapped his arms around her. She instantly sagged and, with her face buried in his shoulder, sobbed for some time.

The show of unprecedented affection only stunned Cobek for a moment. He recovered by barking a string of orders at his remaining troops. On turning to Chey, he noticed Paul on one knee beside AJ. His hand was resting on the LC's forehead.

"You're going to be alright, Son," Paul said to him. In response, AJ's eyes focussed on him and his trembling eased.

Once he had finished the field dressings on both of AJ's legs, Chey said to both Cobek and Paul, "He lost a lot of blood and he's in deep shock."

The Sergeant nodded. "You've done all you can for him. We'll have to continue without him."

The King jumped to his feet with uncharacteristic agility. "No!" The force with which he spat that one word caused everyone to stop and look. Reynolds, and a more composed Samantha, moved towards them.

Concealing his own shock, Cobek said, "But Sire—"

"We are not leaving this man or any other man behind." Glaring, he added, "Not any more."

In a low voice, Reynolds asked, "May I speak with you, Sire?" Paul angrily agreed and was led into the Super's office.

"Sire, nobody wants to leave Lance Corporal Joseph, but he is too badly injured to continue with us."

"I don't care, Richard. I'm sick of this, damn it. Sergeant Anderson, Lucas, Casey. Where will it end? I cannot bear the burden of all these lives any more." The last sentence seemed to draw away the last of the King's anger. He slumped down on the edge of the dusty metal desk, eyes downcast.

The Major glimpsed a chair on its side in the corner of the room. He grabbed it and sat down beside his King. "I never thought I'd tell you this, Sire, but there were times in the past when I did not agree with certain decisions you made as our King." Their eyes met and for one moment Reynolds thought that he had made a fatal mistake, but Paul's response was that of silent agreement.

"But now, seeing you like this; you're different. The change is almost physical; it started back in Wyoming. I believe, given the chance, you would be a far better King now than you ever were. Don't get me wrong, I would have died for you then as I would do now, but before it would have been out of duty alone."

Ignoring the obvious emotion welling up inside both of them, Reynolds leaned closer. "I need to make sure that you get your second chance, my lord. Not for the Monarchy or because of Lexus, but for the good of the people. You are the best man for the job."

The CO of the Republican garrison besieging San Diego, a portly man in his mid forties, took a moment, while yawning, to look around the splendour of the oriental dinning room that surrounded him. Soon after the rise of the Republic, the Torrey Pines Palace had been liberated from the hands of the Royal Family. Being one of the four Royal Palaces, and the Duke of Atlanta's formal seat, it had grandeur to spare and fortifications that matched. If the company commander in charge of its security had not been a Republican, it would have been extremely difficult to take, even from just one company.

He turned back to the portable tac-com, set on the low standing table and scratched his belly under the wrinkled t-shirt he had hastily donned. "What the hell is Yeoville playing at?"

His tactical adviser, Major Wilson, looking as pristine as ever, had, up to now, remained silent. The wiry officer shifted his 'at ease' stance and said, "He's showing his desperation. He has finally realised that his situation is now unsalvageable, so he is testing our lines for weak spots for a possible route of escape." He smoothed a hand over his greying goatee beard as he awaited a response.

Colonel Ryker glanced up at him. "That would be a possibility if we were dealing with someone rash, but sadly Yeoville is not. He knows his forces don't have the mobility—they'd be cut to pieces. And he's not the type of man just to cut and run and leave his men behind."

"But he also knows that we are suffering the temporary inconvenience of a lack of forward C & C."

"Inconvenience? That's hardly the way I would describe it. It's thrown the schedule all to Hell and I'll have General Halburd asking some very serious questions in a day or two." He quelled the urge to stress the point further, stemming his irritation. "No, they must be diversions linked to the rogue Loyalist attack in El Cajon. Maybe Somms managed to send some reinforcements after all. There'll be Hell to pay with IO if a Loyalist force has managed to get all the way here undetected."

A knock at the door interrupted the brief silence that followed. A young second lieutenant entered, followed closely by Lieutenant Colonel Corallis.

"Sorry Sir, but Lieutenant Colonel Corallis demanded to see you immediately," the staff officer said with genuine trepidation.

Without taking his eyes off Corallis, Ryker said, "Fine. Leave us."

Corallis grinned like a child with candy as the young officer left them.

"This should be interesting," Wilson murmured under his breath.

Ryker ignored the comment and said, "What can I do for you, Corallis?"

Still smiling, Corallis walked towards them slowly. "Funny you should say that, Ryker, but it's more what I can do for you."

He did not like the way that sounded or the manner in which it was spoken, but he graciously asked, "How so?"

"Well it would seem that the fugitive, Paul Frelon, has decided to use San Diego as the place to flee America from."

Ryker kept his tone even, but his expression grew harsher. "Do not play games with me." Corallis smiled again and Ryker wanted to punch him for it, but he controlled himself, as he knew that the scheming wretch was in favour with the President...for the time being.

"I'm flattered that you credit me with such a playful nature, but alas I kid you not. The King is breaking into San Diego and I am here to catch him or kill him." He moved still closer to Ryker, silently daring him to question him further.

Ryker knew he was serious, so did not push it further. Leaning forward against the table, he asked, "So what did you have in mind?"

Corallis relaxed his posture and took a moment to offer cigarettes to the other two men. Neither accepted even though both smoked, but if it annoyed him he did not show it. Instead, he lit one for himself and drew on it before continuing. "I have the Cheyenne with me, but it's hardly worth wasting their energy on a crumbling Loyalist outpost such as this, so I want your men to punch a hole through and make their way straight towards their HQ. That should sufficiently occupy the majority of their defences while I lead the Cheyenne in from a different sector to hit his escape routes—Miramar, the civilian airport and the harbour."

Ryker shook his head and feigned surprise. "Well, I've got to hand it to you, Corallis, you've got it worked out beautifully. My men do all the work and you steal the glory."

Corallis drew on his cigarette once more before dropping the ample remains onto the immaculate sandalwood flooring. After crushing it underfoot, he pulled out a letter sealed with the Presidential Seal. "I assumed that you would feel this way, so I took the liberty of asking our esteemed leader to draw up this document, authorising me to take complete control of the San Diego contingent." He paused, more for effect than for necessity.

Ryker pondered on this latest development. His initial reaction was going to be that of outrage, but that would have been futile and further gratifying to Corallis. Instead, he actually felt somewhat relieved. He glanced towards Wilson, who in keeping with his post, had strategically withdrawn to the room's fringe. As usual though, he remained expressionless.

Turning back to Corallis, he said, "It's all yours." His flippancy was rewarded by the briefest flicker of anger.

AJ was a good hour behind them, but he was still at the forefront of Reynolds' mind. The King had struck a nerve in their brief confrontation, dredging up painful memories. They were events that had scarcely had time to settle, but already they seemed a lifetime ago. Snapshots of Anderson and Kennedy, Lucas and Shacks and now AJ all paraded by.

*So much sacrifice.* His thoughts were shelved as soldiers around him dropped to the floor. He went down with them, shielding Paul and Samantha as best as he could.

Rodriquez, on point, had signalled everyone prone. Now, from his crouched position against the crumbling wall of a gutted post office, he trained his rifle on the row of battered condos over the road from the t-junction they were approaching. He had seen, or maybe even just sensed, some movement in the doorway of the central building. He aimed, unblinking, for one very long minute, before carefully making his way back to Swede.

He exchanged brief whispered words with the big man, before returning to his position.

Swede approached the main group. Still speaking in a hushed voice, he said to Cobek and Reynolds, "'Riquez has spotted a possible target up at the junction and thinks this route is compromised."

Reynolds nodded and said, "He's right, we can't risk another exchange. It'll delay us, but we'll double-time it back to that last right and pick it from there."

"We only have a couple more hours till dawn," Cobek warned.

As the group re-organised, a dozen or so foot soldiers came into view from the direction they were about to head in. They were nervous and trigger-happy, so they opened fire immediately, even before they had confirmed that they were not friendly.

Everyone, except Hamilton, was quick to take cover. Hamilton, with his previous injury, reacted a moment later and paid the ultimate price. A bullet tore into his stomach and he dropped to the ground, writhing in agony.

The remaining Loyalists gave him cover fire, as best they could, killing or seriously wounded at least half of the group, but the Private was in the open. A second round struck him in the side and drove his screams up another octave, and then another caught him under the chin, blowing his helmet clean off and silencing him for good.

Drowned by the roar of gunfire, Cook could be seen, red-faced, mouthing a string of obscenities whilst firing non-stop.

They had the last three Republicans pinned when Rodriquez, covering their rear, yelled, "Incoming on our Six!"

Everyone momentarily glanced over their shoulders to see at least another two squads advancing two by two. Rodriquez had already cut down the first two, but cover fire pounded the lamp post he was crouched behind, interrupting his defence. One round, glancing off the post, clipped his upper arm. He gritted his teeth and spat in their direction before returning fire.

Without needing to be ordered, Swede switched his field of fire to their rear, backing up Rodriquez.

Cobek, his voice raised but still even, said, "Once that second team get into position, they'll cut us to pieces."

"I know!" Reynolds snapped in between two round bursts from his pistol. "We can't go through the buildings—they'll surround us in no time—so our best chance is to hit them head on." He stole a moment to check Paul and Samantha. They were holding on to each other, frightened but alert. It was going to be damn risky, but as if to counter his doubts, Paul chose that moment to mouth the word 'Yes' to him.

He turned back to Cobek. "Right, we go the original way and use three grenades to cover our back."

Cobek actually smiled at him. "Sounds good to me, Sir."

The plan was set into motion immediately with Cook, Chey and Cobek all throwing grenades in unison at the three remaining Republicans to their east. At the same time, Rodriquez launched a smoke grenade to their west.

In the next moment, everyone was on their feet and running. As they ran, Paul and Samantha were the only ones who were not firing. The triple explosions behind them produced a deafening roar that sent a tremor along the road.

The smoke did well to obscure them for the first few metres of their advance, showing muzzle flashes as orange smears, but the breeze took hold of it, luring it away and thinning it out. Amongst the gunfire, strangely distant voices and echoing footsteps filled the darkness.

Then the Republicans decided to give them a piece of their own medicine. Even amidst the din, Reynolds still heard the distinctive clatter of the grenade just a couple of metres in front of him. He dropped to the ground as it exploded.

The blast threw someone back at him. The body landed in a twisted heap beside him. On his knees, he bent over and pulled the body towards him, revealing the bloody face of Corporal Chey. "No," he muttered feebly.

"Major!" Cobek's voice briefly raised above the mayhem. He sounded further away than he actually was. Through the quickly dissipating smoke, he could make out several figures up front. Then the white hot pain in his leg registered.

While gripping it with his free hand, he choked back a cry. Then suddenly Samantha was beside him. Crouching down, she tugged at his combat jacket. "Come on," she implored. "You can make it."

There was no time for hugs, but he was going to make damn sure that they made up for it later. Instead, with her help he struggled to his feet and they were soon moving again.

They had reached the point where the grenade had exploded when Samantha stumbled forward, taking Reynolds with her. He pivoted and, half crouched, caught her before she hit the ground.

Her face was only a nose width away as she uttered one word. "Richard…" There was no pain or anger in the word, just sadness and longing. A trickle of blood oozed from the side of her mouth.

Reynolds held her, his head shaking furiously. "Samantha, no. Please…" The bullet had struck her square in the back, she was dead as her final word left her lips.

He pulled her limp body to his chest and sobbed.

Cobek and Swede got to him a moment later. With Swede covering, the Sergeant grabbed his CO. "She's gone, Sir!" The officer ignored him, desperately holding on to the dead woman. It took all of the sergeant's ample strength to wrench him up.

As he was dragged to his feet, resigned, he laid her body against the ground. He was still holding her slender hand as Cobek started to pull him away. He managed to hold on a moment longer before she was gone.

As his shaky legs began working again, he swallowed hard on his anguish and forcibly replaced it with rage. They ran that night through the darkness and bullets, and with every step Reynolds' hatred grew stronger, the pain in his leg only serving to fuel it.

Having managed to survive and evade the remaining Republicans who were responsible for the deaths of Samantha, Chey and Hamilton, the Loyalists did not encounter any further resistance for another kilometre. After listening to a few garbled messages over the radio, they determined that they had finally reached the belt of no-man's land.

It was only one kilometre more or less that separated them from Loyalist forces. It seemed bereft of life, but they knew that both Republican and Loyalist snipers and gun positions would be scattered along it. Their nerves would already be stretched, and possibly their judgement as well. No-man's land may well have been this particular mission's last hurdle, but it would surely prove to be the most difficult yet.

Reynolds ordered a five minute rest, driving exclamations into the end of each word like a stake. None of the soldiers had ever seen him like this. Cook and Swede glanced at each other with mixed expressions of embarrassment and concern.

A soldier did not have too many definable fears, as a rule. One, certainly for some, was death, another, more often greater than death, was the fear of the unseen enemy. Torture and capture were other tangible fears, but the one least spoken of was that of a Commanding Officer teetering on the edge. For all soldiers joked about them, questioned their competence (behind closed doors) or plain hated them, the officer, whether directly or not, held their lives in his or her hands. So, personalities aside, when it came down to it, they had to trust their officer. For that trust to be put into question, was concerning to say the least.

Cobek knew what the other three must have been thinking, Hell, it had crossed his mind too. But Cobek had fought alongside Reynolds a lot longer than anyone else and he knew deep down that nothing could affect the man's judgement. His command and his men meant everything to him and nothing could change that.

He thought then of Ms Gordon and then of his ex-wife, Jackie. He found no comparisons, due mainly to the fact that he hated Jackie for growing sick of his army career. She had left him several years ago and taken their son with her. Living in Boston, she was remarried now to some Sales Executive.

He wondered, absently, how bad the fighting had been there. He had heard that most of the east coast had fallen under Republican rule quite bloodlessly, but hoped that a stray bullet might have…He canned that train of thought, angry at himself. With it, he laid to rest the appraisal of his CO.

Paul had not been blind to the obvious affections Samantha and Richard had begun to feel towards each other, so he temporarily stored his own grief to go and offer whatever comfort he could muster to the tortured Major. Reynolds, however, just politely thanked him for his concern and insisted that he was fine. Before he could stress the point any further, Reynolds stood up and announced that it was time to move.

The area of no-man's land that they were heading through comprised of blocks of demolished undistinguishable buildings. There was nothing left standing above waist height and the small parts of road that were still visible bore the deep scars of artillery bombardment. The small group of Loyalists seemed to be the only living creatures around.

As they picked their way through the devastation, they came across the occasional half buried body or vehicle. Paul stumbled and fell to his knees in front of a battered and blood-encrusted helmet. As he hauled himself back to his feet, he could not help but notice the big jagged hole in its side.

The fact that most of the bodies had been collected in the ceasefires did not dampen the images that his mind conjured up. Death surrounded them, engulfed them…beckoned them.

Rapid fire jolted him back to the situation in hand. "Cover!" Cobek was yelling as he dove on top of Paul. They landed heavily, knocking the wind out of Paul, but Cobek made no attempt to apologise. The Sergeant was already returning fire before the King realised that he was on the ground.

Reynolds and the others were also firing in short controlled bursts; luckily the gunner's initial volley had gone wide, tearing up the ground just ahead of Rodriquez.

The machinegun was positioned around two hundred metres at four o'clock and was well dug in. Even the muzzle flashes were hidden, only smoke and trajectory giving him away.

"Can anyone take him?" Cobek asked, ceasing his futile attempt. He received negatives from everyone.

He was about to rattle off a string of orders when Rodriquez injected, "I'll double back and take him from behind."

Cobek looked at him for a moment. The Private grinned back at him, his brilliant white teeth a sharp contrast to his boot-polished face. Still staring at him, Cobek said to the others, "Cover him."

Even before the M had trailed off, the Private was up and moving with Swede and Cook laying down suppressive fire.

Several drawn out minutes passed with the machinegun firing every few seconds at the huddled Loyalists. On occasion, born more from anger than reason, either Cook or Swede would briefly return fire, each time attracting a scowl from Cobek.

It happened to be Cook's turn. "Cook, hold your fire, goddammit!" Cobek growled, regulating his tone as best he could, given the circumstances.

The Staff Sergeant could not fool Reynolds. That shadowed look had become all too familiar to him over the years, more so now than ever. He glanced over at the King, expecting a similar expression.

"Get your fucking head down!" he snapped.

Paul stared at him for a moment, shocked and lacking comprehension. But the fury laced with fear engraved on the Major's face drove it home. He immediately flattened himself back down against the rubble. In the next moment, a fresh volley of gunfire tore into the battered low concrete wall above him.

A sprinkling of dust and fragments covered his chest and hair. He looked from them to Reynolds. The Major's face was shameful.

"I apologise for my outburst, Sire," he said with deep conviction.

Paul was aghast. The man had just saved his life, for the umpteenth time, and here he was mortified at the way he had done it. He never ceased to amaze him. "There is most definitely no need to apologise." The needless apology had lent the King a few precious seconds to allow him to stabilize his breathing, so he spoke in an almost convincingly calm voice. "You were just doing your job."

"Not very well, given recent events."

It was Paul's turn to preach, giving him renewed vigour. "Nonsense! There is not a living soul on the face of the Earth who could have achieved more than you, *Sir* Richard. You are doing a fine job." He emphasised the 'sir' as a reminder and, as an after thought, added, "And for once, will you kindly call me Paul. You are a Provincial Knight after all."

Reynolds stared at him for a moment, his first intention to strongly object. But instead concluded that it was in fact ok, and not just because the King had said so, but it also felt right. Under certain circumstances, power and station found themselves to be secondary. Mutual respect had the habit of overshadowing them every time.

Inactivity, even in the most dangerous situations, had the tendency to breed complacency. Cobek noticed a rather sheepish-looking Swede groping around his webbing and to his amazement, the private pulled out a pack of class one ration biscuits. He then amazed himself by accepting the one that was offered to him. Only Reynolds refused.

"How much longer do you think we should give Rodriquez?" Swede asked as he finished off the oatmeal biscuit.

"Dumb Spick's probably dead," Cook muttered. "Any more them cookies, Swede-o?"

"Nope."

Cobek shifted his weight on to his right buttock, as the left had gone numb. "He ain't dead, he's got the Devil himself watching his six. He'll just be helping himself to their rat-packs and ammo before coming back."

"We sure could use some extra ammo right now," Swede said and patted his rifle. "Down to thirty-eight rounds."

Without checking, Cook said, "Last mag, but it's full."

Cobek checked his supply and found that he had about a clip and a half—75 rounds. He emptied the half-filled magazine and split them evenly so that both privates had equal. "How about you, Sir?"

Reynolds glanced at the counter on the pistol's handgrip by his thumb. "Ten rounds; enough."

"I'll say, Sir." The words were a whisper on the breeze, but instantly recognisable.

"Riquez!" Swede exclaimed, unable to contain his relief.

The private's dark form slithered among them. "You miss me, big boy?"

Swede slapped him on the shoulder. "Yo mama."

Grinning, Cook said, "Can we please get the Hell outta here now?"

The door silently eased open, casting a soft beam of light into the darkened room from the hallway. Grant Lexus crept into the bedroom and hovered over the bed of his sleeping child; eight year old Adam.

The young boy slept soundly with the tip of his duvet touching his small nose in the way that always comforted him. His breathing was soft and regular.

Grant smiled, drawing comfort from his contented son. Brushing a few strands of sandy hair from the boys face, he whispered, "Sleep tight, son." He turned to leave, but then looking back, added, "This is for your good, my son, and for the good of America. I only ever wanted to do what's best..." his voice trailed off. He didn't know what he wanted to say or why he suddenly felt an overwhelming urge to say it.

After an uncertain moment of hovering in the doorway, he let out a deep tired sigh, then left the room as silently as he had entered.

# Chapter 8

## Spurious Sanctuary

As Major Yeoville eagerly awaited the arrival of the King, he made a futile attempt at straightening his grubby appearance. After running his fingers through his hair and struggling to tuck in the only clean shirt he could find (that happened to have two buttons missing), his wound making one arm less than useless, he found himself fidgeting. For a little while he actually felt like a kid again.

He noticed that, without being told, the rest of the command centre staff, and various other base personnel who had appeared to fill the room to virtual breaking point, had also made similar attempts at improving their appearances and for that he was proud of them. There might be a war on, but you still had to make an effort.

It was as that thought still lingered that King Paul II entered the room. His grimy features and muddy and torn jumpsuit hardly detracted from the man's presence. Apart from a scrape on the left cheek and the loss of a little weight, his features were fundamentally unchanged from the dozens of public and television appearances Yeoville had seen him on. But, whether it was meeting the man face to face or something else, there was a subtle change. Something that made him more real…more defined.

On a physical level, the weight loss suited him; his jowly chin was gone and his waist had shrunk a couple of sizes. The lines had deepened somewhat around his eyes and on his forehead, but overall, he looked younger and fitter than he had done in maybe ten years...Except for his eyes. The deep hollows told a completely different story.

"Your Majesty," Yeoville said whilst stiffly managing a bow.

The King had never been cursed with the verbal ramblings that most politicians were infected with. His words had always been straight to the point, cold and detached. What he said that day, however, in the cold early hours in that battered command centre in what remained of San Diego remained direct, but of an entirely different manufacture. They projected warmth that Yeoville swore on later he could almost feel. They were spoken with both the humility of a shepherd and the wisdom of a sage.

The King started by strongly shaking the Major's fully functional hand whilst asking, "Major Yeoville; Daniel, if I may?"

"Of course," Yeoville agreed, more for the fact that it was asked in earnest, than because of who asked it.

As he thanked him, Paul glanced around the dishevelled room and its equally bedraggled occupants. By their expressions alone, he could begin to see the ordeal that they had endured. And that, coupled with their obvious delight at his arrival, touched him deeply.

"Daniel, I am indebted to you and every member of your command for your unwavering courage. Thanks to you and others like you, you are fighting to give the Monarchy a second chance; more specifically *me* a second chance. We have all lost people very dear to us..." He faltered and again stole a glance at the attentive faces. Reynolds had silently entered after him, and he too was staring intently. As their eyes met, he offered the King an encouraging smile that was doused with sadness.

What he knew he had to say was going to be far from easy. A time when he had to inform Jennifer that her mother had died without warning of heart failure immediately sprung to mind. Jennifer had nurtured a close relationship with Constance since she had been a baby, not once having crossed words. The news that Constance had died had hit him like a sledgehammer, for he had known that absolutely nothing he would be able to say or do would possibly console her. He had known that it would be agony for her and he would feel utterly helpless.

For that, suddenly for the first time, he felt a pang of guilt. It occurred to him now that, five years later, his motives at the time had been purely selfish. He had not wanted to be put in such an awkward situation and had certainly not been happy about feeling helpless...In the moment that it took the thoughts to pass he made a mental note to somehow, sometime apologise to Jennifer.

Drawing courage from his previous failure, he continued, addressing the whole room. "It is hard for me to admit this, and you are only the second group of people that I have told this to, but I have made a great many mistakes in the time that I have been your King." He fought hard to overcome the urge to cast his eyes down with the shame that rose up like some great titan awaking from an ancient slumber. "This revolution is my fault."

Yeoville was stunned and his face made no attempt to conceal it.

"You have all stayed loyal to me despite my shortcomings; my arrogance, my greed and worst of all—my indifference. It was loyalty that I have come to realise I did not deserve. And yet, thanks to it—to you—you have given me the chance to right those wrongs." He clenched a fist and his eyes now focussed purely on Yeoville's.

"This has been a painful voyage, both mentally and physically, and I have discovered a great many things about myself, some of which I will be eternally ashamed of. It has been a bitter pill to swallow, and I'm sure that it is far from over. But I need to tell you all here and now that I have learnt from my mistakes—and I'm still learning—and feel that finally I can hope to be a leader worthy of your loyalty. I know now that as King I should be honoured to serve America, not the other way around. America's strength is in its people, not in its leader—I am just the figurehead." His voice was straining and his body trembled by the time he finished.

It was by no means a spectacular speech, neither eloquently spoken nor portrayed, but it was spoken from the heart and every person in the command centre knew it to be true.

Yeoville could not contain himself; he embraced the King, ignoring the protests from his shoulder. As he did a cheer arose from the congregation—including Reynolds—a cheer that sounded like hope.

Paul walked briskly through the corridors of the last functioning wing in the Naval Hospital. He felt a renewed strength coursing through his once tired limbs. The junior doctor leading him had a beam on his face that seemed to light their way along the gloomy halls. And for a time, the King even mused that Rodriquez might be finding it hard to keep up.

Once inside Bradley's private room, his smile matched that of the doctor's. The young Captain was sitting up in his bed, his bandaged chest the only clue to his recent misfortune. He was laughing with his sister as he entered and they both turned to him with faces mixed with shock and relief. Rodriquez and the doctor remained respectfully outside.

"Uncle Paul!" Catherine exclaimed, jumping up to embrace him. He held her for some time, before reluctantly letting go.

As she stepped back from him, she wiped a tear from her eye. "We've missed you." She said 'we' because Bradley would never admit it.

He smiled at them both, tears welling up in his own eyes too. "I have missed you too." There would be a time later for sadness, apologies and consoling, but for now they could just be glad to be together.

Bradley, on the other hand, could not help but consider the fact that half of the Royal family were now stuck in one city on the verge of collapse. He was annoyed at himself for thinking that way; it was not like him. But the observation remained all the same.

The whole of Fort Wayne appeared to breathe a sigh of relief at the news of the King's well-being. It was tainted only by the frailty of his location, but thankfully only Somms and his immediate aids knew of the King's exact situation.

Sitting behind his desk, the said General grinned despite the flipside. He could sense the impending struggle, but for now he took solace that, at least for the time-being, he knew how things were. The worst torture of all was always not knowing. After the Lexus propaganda machine got moving, he found that even he had started to doubt whether the King had still been alive, so God alone knew how the men had felt.

The boost had arrived in the nick of time, for defeat had been gouged into the faces of everyone around him, and if the truth be known, in him also. Men had been deserting and some had even turned to suicide, Henderson just two days ago, among the latter. Defeat had seemed inevitable. The news had most certainly yanked them back from the edge of the abyss.

Over night, the morale had shot up; they had even gained a few men from the other side (nobody cared about their previous misguided loyalties, least of all Somms).

As he pushed back his chair and stood, he thought of all the men that had died not knowing whether their King was alive or dead; those that had died without hope. He remembered Henderson's weary face, saying he was going to try to get some sleep, and some hours later being discovered with both lower arms sliced all the way to the bicep. He had left the Command Centre that evening with one thing on his mind—death. Henderson, and all the others, had died believing all to be lost.

Somms shoved the chair back into its niche and headed for the Primary Command Centre.

Three words cried out in his head. Time to act.

The Command Centre was pulsing with renewed activity. Despair had been replaced by resolve and they were not about to relinquish it. The change hit Somms like a heatwave as he stepped into the room. A residue of hope was left on his lips.

"Drake," Somms called to a brawny colonel.

The officer turned to reveal a latticework of deep old scars across his face and neck. His left eye was half closed in a permanent frown. "Aye, General?"

Somms did not break his stride until he was standing beside him. "Get Decker on the horn."

Drake grinned at him, exposing a gap where two incisors should have been. "Yessir." He excused the senior communications officer and hailed the Arion Elite Commander personally. Decker was on the other end of the line in a matter of moments. "Mike, it's Drake, I'm handing you over to the General."

Somms took the headset from him and said, "You've heard the news?"

Decker half laughed. "You bet your ass, Sir."

"Well you'll have to celebrate another time."

"I figured. But, as it happens, my men party in different ways anyway, Sir."

Somms shook his head, but smiled all the same. "Now's their chance. You move now—your orders will follow."

After a brief pause, Decker replied with open gratitude, "Thank you, Sir."

"That is all, Colonel. Good luck. Out." Somms dropped the headset back onto the console, then asked, "Panama Commander?"

"I've already informed Major Richly," Drake said as he motioned for the communications officer to return to his post.

Somms rubbed his chin. "Good. The Elite will have no problem getting there, but the King's party are going to need to utilize every bit of their meagre resources to break out of San Diego. Still, once they link up, the main bridge has already been crossed." His stony features concealed the true extent of his concerns well. "We can put the destroyer and two frigates that we've been hiding in the Hawaiian Islands to good use finally."

"What's the latest on our borderline outposts?" he continued before Drake could sense his ill-ease.

"Jacksonville, Montreal, Merida and La Paz garrisons have been upgraded to critical. The Merida commander, Captain Shaeffer, has reported brigade strength forces engaging his perimeter defences. He has two companies and a small amount of militia remaining. He expects to hold for another three to five days max."

He paused to grab the attention of a passing technician. "Can we get a couple of black coffees over here?" As the young technician headed for the vending machine, the Colonel continued. "Major Topus in

Montreal is down to battalion strength, holding out against a brigade, but they're also contending with a flight of T60s. Since losing Toronto they've been completely cut off, so their supplies are also down to a minimum.

"Major Copalar, in La Paz—"

"Copalas," Somms corrected. "Juan Copalas."

"Right," Drake agreed, unperturbed. He noticed the technician returning with their drinks, so paused to thank him and take both plastic cups. He handed one to Somms and after taking a sip, said, "La Paz is under heavy assault from BFF forces estimated at up to two brigades. His garrison, including militia and re-enforcements, is at around two battalions. He said he's held out so far mainly because of the poor tactics and training deployed by the BFF.

"Benwell, at Jacksonville, is well fortified with two full battalions, but his supplies are severely depleted. He's up against a brigade plus an armoured battalion, but as yet they've only been probing his lines." He gulped some more coffee, but did not take his eyes off Somms.

Somms risked a taste of his coffee, hated it—as he knew he would—but drank more anyway to dull the taste buds. After a further moment of contemplation, he finished off the coffee and cast the cup into a nearby receptacle.

"We can do nothing about La Paz and Merida and we can't do much about Montreal, however hitting that column of Turtles leaving Buffalo tomorrow should help. We can do something for Jacksonville, though." He paced as he spoke, the caffeine seeming to take an immediate effect. "Contact Captain Hernandez in Nassau."

The idea now clicked with Drake. "Of course, he's got all those trawlers and leisure boats at his disposal."

"And he is well supplied and under no threat, at present."

"Orders: I want him to start shipping supplies into Jacksonville one boat at a time under the cover of darkness. As much supplies as they can spare, but no men. There's no reason to further reduce Nassau's contingent yet. Is it a company he has there?"

"Yes, but as well as fortifying the island, he's been training up locals to aid in defence. The islands are all heavily pro royal. He's expecting to have a second operational company within the next week or two."

"So be it. Make sure he's aware of that flotilla from the Atlantic fleet patrolling the eastern Florida coast. Liaise with Benwell so he can have men ready."

"Yes, Sir." Drake began to turn away, but changed his mind. He looked back at Somms and smiled again. "Things are looking up, eh?"

The General returned his smile and thought better of lecturing him about not speaking too soon and that Drake was smarter than that. They both knew that crap all too well, but that little thing called hope kept popping up to say 'maybe things ain't all that bad'. So instead, he said, "Yes, they are."

The convoy of Republican Turtle Troop Transporters had passed through Hamilton without slowing and were now heading towards Mississauga. The wide grey expanse of Lake Ontario was to their right and the charred and muddy remains of Bronte Creek Forest to their left.

A battle between Loyalists out of Toronto and Republicans from Buffalo had left the majority of the woodland and the surrounding towns of Burlington and Oakville ruined. The fierce week long battle had claimed the lives of some three thousand soldiers, along with several hundred unlucky civilians.

From a distance, the low olive drab transporters with curved armoured hulls appeared deceptively small, despite the fact that each one of the twenty vehicles was capable of a carrying a full combat ready platoon. It was only at the sight of the intermingled utility skimmers and scouts that betrayed their true size.

In the cab of the turtle second from the front, one career soldier and a draftee were arguing about the extremely serious subject of speedbikes. The driver, Corporal Mitchell, could not believe the bullshit that the young private, Martuk, was trying to make him swallow.

"I'm tellin'ya, man," Martuk was saying, "I've driven my brother's Corsair thousands of times and I've beat his pal, Felix—the one with the Supa Nova I was tellin'ya about—hundreds of times."

Mitchell did not take his eyes off the road for fear of not being able to resist the urge to wedge his fist into the Kansas City asshole's face. What the Hell had he done to deserve being saddled with a bullshitting jerkoff like this? "You can say what you like, numb-nuts. Trials and competition have proved that the Nova can beat the Corsair every time. The Corsair's top speed alone is 458 and the Nova's 475, for Christsake." He felt his face reddening. The last time his face went red he had ended up winning himself an all expenses paid trip to the stockade. So he quickly added, "End of discussion."

Martuk shook his head, but was smart enough to keep his mouth closed.

From inside his heavily camouflaged utility skimmer, deep in the Bronte Creek Forest, the commander of the Loyalists' last remaining intact armoured battalion (109th 'Marauders'), Major Griffin Pike, stared intently through the range-finder at the passing turtles.

His Rhino MBTs were staggered all along the kill zone in 'V' formations, poised and ready to strike. It took a further few agonising seconds before the lead utility hit the marker.

Through clenched teeth, he uttered, "Hit the ordinance and fire all sections."

Neither Mitchell nor Martuk registered the impact on the side of the lead turtle. The armour-piercing shell punched a hole into the main compartment and exploded a fraction of a second later inside the packed cargo area. The hatches, side doors and rear ramp all blew open, releasing a torrent of flames from all orifices.

As human fireballs fell out in all directions, Mitchell wrestled with the controls to stop his transporter from slamming into the back of the burning wreck. It was beginning to comply when he felt the impact. The intolerable roar, together with Martuk's single cry, reverberated around his mind even after he lost consciousness.

The first volley obliterated all but one of the scouts and utilities and a third of the turtles. The second and third volleys took care of the rest, leaving only the scattered survivors fortunate enough to vacate the transporters in time.

One final turtle, its rear a mass of smoke and flames, made a run for the lakeside, more symbolic than realistic. It hit the waters edge as two more rounds struck it, the second punching straight through to the cabin and ripping it apart. With all power lost, it dropped to the water, the heat momentarily boiling it on contact, whipping up great gusts of steam. Then it slid deeper into the lake and the flames and bubbling abated, leaving just the blackened roof on show.

Pike continued to observe the blazing wrecks, his face solemn and absorbed. Then, without warning, he ordered, "Let's haul ass to the RV. Bravo, take the lead."

Madeline sat back in her faded easy chair. Gazing around the room, it appeared that the once poky and gloomy room of hers had taken on a slightly more agreeable disposition.

Since Jason's death, despite Karl's increasingly frequent chats, she had begun to believe that all was indeed lost. She had found herself not wondering whether Paul might be dead, but whether Paul might be alive. The faith that she had so desperately tried to cling on to had slowly slipped through her fingers, leaving her empty and spent.

But now, as fast as her decline had started, she now suddenly felt the desperation going into recession. Paul was alive. Her only lingering regret, and a regret that she would keep with her till the day she died, was that Jason was not with her to share in her new found hope. On reflection though, Jason had always been filled with enough hope for everyone. The thought probably never crossed his mind that his father might die or be already dead. His hope and optimism had been infectious.

The innocence of youth or the power of love? Or just bad song lyrics? She laughed, but it was not cynical, not this time. For once it was light-hearted, easy…She had forgotten how much she had loved to laugh. Like so many things, it was quick to lose, but very slow to recoup.

Now that it was back, she vowed never to let go again. And she was talking about a great deal more that her sense of humour. "Take care, Paul," she muttered to her own four walls.

She spent the next hour contemplating the future, something she had not been able to face in such a long time. She also lingered over fond memories of both Jason and Paul; the three of them together. Smiling, she recalled how, along with Jennifer, they had spent a month long holiday at the family island in the Bahamas three years ago. It had been a magical month and their last holiday together. It was scarcely twelve months later that the rioting began in earnest.

Her thoughts were interrupted by Travis bursting through the door.

"Karl?" she exclaimed, startled and concerned.

"We've got to go," he said. The assault rifle in his hands and the expression on his face revealed the true extent of the urgency.

Without needing to be told twice, she jumped up and grabbed her boots. As she endeavoured to tug one on, she asked, "What's happening?"

"One of Sykes' men is missing and they've seen suspicious activity out back. Sykes thinks we've been compromised—possibly by the missing guy, Lieber—and I'm inclined to agree with him."

Madeline looked up from lacing up the second boot. "Lieber? You sure?"

"Nothing's for sure, but something sure doesn't smell right."

She finished and sprung to her feet, grabbing her submachine gun off the dressing table-cum-desk at the same time. "What's the plan?"

They left the room with Travis in the lead. "Sykes' sent a scout down into the escape tunnel to check that it's clear, but he's already given the order to evacuate, so we're going one way or another."

They reached the bottom of the stairs, which led onto the first floor and saw seven people grouped together outside the briefing room. Sykes and the young lovers, Todd and Carla, were among them.

As they drew near, Sykes handed manila envelopes to four of the group and said, "You know the drill. Check your destinations then thoroughly dispose of the brief. Do not discuss your destination with anyone, not even your partner. And watch your partner's back. Now get down to the tunnel." The three men and one woman all nodded solemnly and then headed for the stairs to the ground and basement levels.

Todd and Carla stayed with Sykes. "Here's yours," he said to the newcomers, handing them identical envelopes. "And yours." Carla and Todd received theirs, leaving one left for himself.

"I don't need to repeat myself, so let's move it."

As they hurried towards the stairs, Travis asked, "What if the tunnel's out of action?"

"Then things are going to get ugly," Sykes replied without looking around.

He considered stressing the point further, but there was no point. If the tunnel was out, the only thing they could do would be to fight their way out. The idea of that contingency becoming a reality left him cold, so he chose not to dwell on it.

As sometimes happens, decisions were made for him. As Todd reached the bottom of the stairs, ahead of the others, the strengthened front door disintegrated in a deafening roar. The flimsy glass inner door imploded right along with it, blasting hundreds of deadly shards across the hallway to the dumb-struck Todd.

He dropped to the floor, screaming and holding his hands to his face. Carla, oblivious that her own beige trousers were rapidly darkening from several shards in her thighs, rushed to his aid. "Todd!"

Sykes, his pistol now drawn, also dashed forward. Without turning, he yelled, "Get her out of here, Travis!"

The Sergeant spun and in one fluid motion, hoisted Madeline over the hand-rail and onto the floor, facing the rear of the house. "MOVE!" he snapped and leapt over after her.

Shoving the Duchess forward, he paused to catch a glimpse of the scene behind them. What he saw caused his heart to skip a beat. Dark figures were surging through the smoke-filled ragged opening. Sykes started firing. Todd's cries were quickly turning to pathetic gargles. Carla was wailing, not in pain, but in despair. Two of the Republicans dropped with Sykes' first volley, but then the others behind them returned fire.

The Sergeant swung his rifle off his shoulder and into his sweaty palms as gunfire boomed in the confined space. Todd was not fortunate enough to be hit straight off, but Carla took two shots in the chest at close range. Blood erupted out of her back, drenching Sykes.

Madeline and Travis crashed through into the spacious kitchen and breakfast room, partitioned by a breakfast bar with several stools scattered around it. Glancing over his shoulder one more time, Travis saw Sykes still firing with an enraged scream caught on his lips. The gun smoke was thickening fast, but not fast enough to obscure the safehouse controller being catapulted back against stairs by several shots to the chest. He slid down the remaining few steps to finish up in an undignified squatting position.

Travis pumped the under slung grenade launcher and fired back the way they had come. Bullets tore into the door and wall around him as he slammed the door an instant before the blast struck it.

Madeline was already halfway across the room and right outside the pantry door which led in turn to the escape tunnel. Travis ran after her, instinctively glancing towards the shuttered kitchen window. As he did, the pantry door flew open, catching Madeline full force on the shoulder.

The heavy door cast her aside like a rag doll, jarring her to stunned silence. Travis saw the two Republican soldiers with their rifles at hip level as the back door began to rattle in its hinges.

Two words struck his mind like lightning. *Game Over*. His rifle clattered onto the tiled floor at the same time as mentally deciding to order his hands to do it.

The younger of the two Republicans fired on instinct. To Travis, the three round burst felt like a bag of hammers being thrown at his chest. For some reason, his mind refused to linger on that thought. Instead, as his vision blurred and the terracotta floor grew close, he took once last glimpse at Madeline. She was dazed and staggering backwards from the pantry door, her SMG dangling loosely by her side. As his head smacked off the tiles and the lights went out, his mind or his lips or both whispered, *Don't fight...*

The gunshots seemed to register after the wet thwack of head hitting tiles. A wave of horror swept over Madeline before even turning to see what had happened. Travis was face down on the floor with a pool of blood rapidly spreading out from his torso across the floor. She could see one of his eyes staring up at her and a word seemed to be caught on his dead lips.

Just before she screamed, she dimly heard one of the killers shout, "What are you, a fuckin'moron? We're s'posed to at least try and take some goddamn prisoners."

Then another voice; shaky, "I'm sorry, Tony...I lost it." Then the screaming alerted them to her presence behind the door.

Her anguish turned to fury in mid-scream and both hands clenched her SMG. The soldier known as Tony dove out into the room as she opened fire into the door. In seconds she had emptied the thirty-round clip, disintegrating the centre panels and beyond it, most of the chest and abdomen of the second soldier.

As his comrade dropped, wide-eyed and dead, Tony, sprawled across the floor, cried out, "Johnny!" Before he had finished the second syllable he was opening fire.

*Grant was smiling as he bowed then sat down in front of King Paul II; it had been two months since the two friends had last met. Paul was dressed in his official crested red and blue embroidered robe, obscuring the rather plain (but extremely expensive) suit underneath. His friend appeared shrunken and a little uneasy as he shifted position in the finely crafted oak throne.*

*"It is good to see you, old friend," Paul said.*

*"And you, My Lord."*

*"You have served me well, Grant. And this occasion has been no exception; the new trade agreement that you have managed to negotiate gives us a superb foothold into the Oceanic market."*

*"As always, it is my pleasure, Sire." As he uttered the words, he thought of how hurt he had felt at being sent away yet again on some minor errand that one of the junior ministers could have easily handled. He had been back in DC less than two weeks after returning from Delhi and then had been packed off to Queensland. His patience was wearing thin. Why was Paul doing this to him?*

*"That is why I have chosen you to chair the conference in Bogotá next week to ensure that the Crown's interests are thoroughly protected."*

*Lexus could not believe what he was hearing. Surely this had to be a joke.*

*The King continued, unaware of his aid's dismay. "The unrest and resentment of the Monarchy in the South has become a serious concern. We have traitors and terrorists running rampant. Groups calling themselves the Brazilian Freedom Fighters, Aztecs and Recife Bandits seem to be gaining popularity with each passing day. That is why it is imperative that you take charge down there for me."*

*Choosing his words carefully, Grant said, "Sire, I am honoured, but I feel exhausted from my trips to Australia and India." Attempting to make light, he added, "Fiona and Adam scarcely remember what I look like."*

*"Grant, my friend, you are the only one I trust for such an important mission."*

*Lexus desperately sought the words to object, but of course found none. Instead, he agreed and even thanked him for the honour...*

The conference room seemed to shrink with the passing of every unspoken and lingering moment. The term 'caged tiger' crossed the agitated mind of Kern Silus and not for the first time. Grant Lexus was pacing with a glare that was only broken by the occasional look of disgust, aimed more and more frequently at his three advisors.

General Halburd had started the meeting by explaining the current situation. The discussion had quickly turned heated and had ended with Halburd making the holy unwise observation that the President had perhaps been too hasty in informing the public that the King had been killed. Now the room was silent, holding its collective breath.

Zain Namala had remained quiet thus far but, feeling the rising grumble akin to an awakening volcano, was enough to snap him into action. He had to diffuse the situation before things got really ugly. He cleared his throat and said, "I feel that we're all guilty of underestimating Frelon and his followers." Grant was not looking at him, like the other two were, but he felt he commanded more of his attention than the other two combined. "Grant, you warned us and, at the time, none of us truly understood. I too thought that all this would be behind us by now and that we would have been starting to re-build now, not continuing to destroy." He was rewarded with a brief glance from Lexus as he tore his attention away from the window for a moment.

"I think we're all a little tired and frustrated," Namala concluded with a sigh.

"I'll agree with that," Silus added, just a little too quickly, as he was prone to.

Namala waited for a response from Halburd and was surprised when one was not forthcoming. He was about to continue when Lexus abruptly swung around to faced them.

"You're absolutely right, my friend. I have been foolish and naive to think that Paul could be stopped so easily."

"Well, it's surely just a matter of time now," Silus said.

"And what makes you say that?" Lexus asked him, some of his former glare resurfacing fleetingly.

Seeing the renewed confrontation in his eyes, Namala quickly injected, "What Kern is trying to say is that Frelon has nowhere to run this time. He is trapped in San Diego and its collapse is assured." If he was grateful for his colleague's injection, Silus did not show it.

Lexus shook his head, discarding the glare. "Sadly, given recent events, I do not share your optimism, Zain." His shoulders seemed to sag and he slowly sat down, suddenly seeming weary. Rubbing the bridge of his nose, he addressed all three, but stared at Namala. "No, for victory to be assured we have to be totally committed."

"What the Hell's that supposed to mean?" Halburd snarled, his patience teetering on a knife edge.

Lexus shifted his gaze to the General. It was even and yet somewhat provocative. "You tell me, Orson. You seem to know more about it than I."

Halburd, refusing to back down, leant closer. "My men are doing everything in their power to kill that bastard."

Namala, now tiring of his peacekeeper role, said, "Orson, I think you misunderstood Grant's meaning."

"Did I?" He did not take his eyes off his superior.

Lexus turned away from him, muttering, "I'm sure you did." He took a moment to compose himself, before saying, "I have taken the liberty of drawing up plans to reduce garrisons in Arizona, Nevada, Oregon and North Mexico to flood California with enough troops to ensure that even the rats cannot escape."

"Do you realise what you're saying?" Halburd asked, his tone still aggressive.

Speaking with a new level of conviction, Lexus said, "Be very careful, General Halburd." As he turned back to Namala, he continued in a lighter tone, but the threat still hung like a Sword of Damocles.

Halburd sat back, a sudden sweat on his brow. He told himself that it was all anger, but that was only partially true.

Lexus jabbed a finger at the plastic folder on the desk in front of him. "The exact numbers are in there, along with a list of further installations and garrisons throughout the Province who can spare further men and equipment to be flown in to California as soon as possible."

"Isn't that risky?" Namala asked carefully.

"Yes. However, the fall of a few demoralised outposts can wait, whereas the demise of Paul Frelon cannot." He stood up, the weariness shaken off, and, for a moment, Namala feared a renewed confrontation (aimed at him, this time), but instead his tone was more relaxed than it had been for some time.

"Kern, hold a press conference to inform the public that we did believe him to be dead and use something along the lines of him having one of his personal guards made up to look like him to discredit the Republic. Add that now we know the truth we will bring the fugitive to justice as quickly as we possible, bringing all our resources to bear."

"I thought you would want to deliver the statement," Silus said, eyeing Lexus with marked trepidation.

"You thought wrong," he replied evenly.

The red touring recreational skimmer that Carlos had acquired just west of Tucson, Arizona was caked in desert grime and had taken a couple of minor knocks, but was otherwise in peak condition. The engine's low hum relaxed to idle as he brought it to a halt in the centre of the deserted freeway.

The early evening sky over San Diego was an unnatural dark grey, despite making allowances for the time of year. Even from his position, looking over the smoking vestiges of El Cajon, he could see (*feel*) the death and destruction that clung to the city like a shroud.

As he waited (he *was* waiting for something, not merely admiring the view), two gunships skirted low above the suburbs of Poway, heading south towards him. It crossed his mind that these petty people may have finally detected his presence and figured out his agenda and that now they would try to stop him, instead of unknowingly aiding him. Of course that was ridiculous, and he laughed out loud to stress the point. The guttural snort warped his slender face, allowing it, for a moment, to discard its usual features and hint at the beast inside. It was not quite a physical change, but more like a desperate wish yet to be granted.

If anyone had been observing they would have had to look away then look back again to ensure that their eyes were not deceiving them. On nervously glancing back, they would have seen nothing more than a calm, maybe even wistful, slim black man dressed in a black silk shirt with what could be a chunky pendant around his neck.

Then the waiting was over. He was not going in to San Diego after all. Instead, he performed a U-turn and headed back to the last exit several kilometres east. There was a secondary road that led south.

He made swift progress along the largely deserted route and it was not until he was nearing Hermosillo when three fools made the mistake of delaying him.

The two men and one woman turned out to be Army deserters. Right from the start of the revolution, under the expert guidance of Private Tom Ruddle's 'Number One' motto, he, his girlfriend, Private Loretta Clancy and friend from junior high, Private Lenny Lubowitz, had decided that the Army had turned out to be not quite the meal ticket it had been in 'peace' time. So, with stuffed kitbags and a stolen army utility skimmer, they had checked out of Villa De Boot Camp and headed for the happy memories of 22hour parties back to back with two hour drug runs for Gonzuala, the local Police Chief.

As with most things in life, on arrival they had found that a great deal had changed in the two years they had been away. For one, Gonzuala had been gunned down by one of his deputies who had then promptly attempted to take over his business interests. Three days was not all that bad for a rookie crime boss. He had been hung and left to rot in the town square as a warning to others who might upset the natural order. Since then some gang violence and then a government crackdown had left the party town a shrivelled shell of its former glory.

So it was time for Ruddle Master Plan B—rob the city jerkoffs passing through doing their wandering salesman bit. The bandit-business had turned out to be a lucrative one right up to the moment that Tom Ruddle spotted the dirty red rec-skimmer.

From the cab of the battered utility skimmer, Ruddle smiled and lowered the binoculars. "That sap looks like he's been on the road non-stop since the start of this shit."

His gangly friend chuckled. "Ya think we should make him see the error of his ways, eh Tom?"

Lying on her belly across the back seats, kicking her legs in the air, Clancy muttered, "I'm tired, Tommy. C'mon back here and fly with some PASH."

Ruddle spun and snapped a powerful hand around a slender dangling ankle. "We're on the job, Lore. How many fucking times do I have to tell you not to pop on the job?"

The slackness in Clancy's face dissipated as his grip tightened. "Tommy, you're hurtin!"

He thrust her leg away in one angry jerk and turned back to the rec-skimmer that had now passed their elevated position. "Just get your shit together, Bitch." Without another word, he gunned the engine and shot them over the ridge and down to the dusty potholed road.

Carlos was aware of their approach before seeing the dust trail racing up from the rear. Their intentions were clear. Not prepared to risk damaging his transport, he pulled over and stopped. The utility skimmer performed a far less graceful manoeuvre, its reverse thrusters screaming and billowing up clouds of dust as it jerked to a halt right behind the rec-skimmer.

Carlos smiled as two men jumped out, the driver sporting a stumpy combat shotgun and the other wielding an assault rifle. The third occupant—a woman—scrambled into the driver's seat to keep the spluttering engine running. Her eyes were wide, a sight he was quite used to.

As they bore down on him, his lips began to move, soundlessly formulating ancient words. Everything around him blurred and the two men suddenly seemed to be running through treacle. Neither shock nor fear marked their faces however, for to them, nothing had changed.

It was not until the black stranger unexpectedly appeared outside the skimmer, with the movement of the door only the possibility of a blur, that the two men realised the enormity of their situation. Ruddle had less time to worry, for the stranger was upon him in the blink of an eye.

Lubowitz fired from the hip, but the stranger had already grabbed Ruddle and swung him into the line of fire with time to spare. Three rounds punched into his friend's abdomen. Lenny had time only to gape as the 'city sap' swept over the roof of the skimmer like a breeze on the wind and appeared right in front of him. He held a huge gruesome dagger to his parched throat.

"Sir, I…"

"Lenny," the man said like a whisper in a library, "I would like you to meet the Soul Dagger." With that he thrust it up through his chin until he felt it impact off the inside of the top of his skull. There he allowed his hand to twist it almost full circle whilst staring calmly into the dead man's eyes.

Loretta Clancy only began to register the last few seconds of events as the stranger dropped Lenny's body to the asphalt and headed towards her at an oddly leisurely pace. That was her queue to take the skimmer out of neutral and apply the thrust. Unfortunately for her, in her panic, she tried to do both at the same time, causing the struggling engine to stall.

She started screaming as he arrived at the driver's door and, as his arm reached in to drag her free, she passed out. She would never know how lucky she was for that.

# Chapter 9
## Explorer

Major Yeoville entered the Command Centre with an unmistakable grin firmly planted across his face. His arm was still in a sling, but he had hardly given it a second thought since the arrival of the King. And after the latest event it could not be further from his mind.

The four people hovering around the tac-com—Sir Richard, Paul, Jones and Demoore—all turned, seemingly aware of the newcomer's identity before seeing him. They all held similar expectant expressions.

As he approached with an almost comical spring in his step, he could contain himself no longer. "It's confirmed. The meeting with Major Sleeper was just a formality; he had already held a meeting with his officers and NCOs and he has their full backing. The 402nd Infantry Battalion has now joined the garrison."

After the hugging, shaking hands and whooping from the whole room had subsided, a stillness gently draped itself over the room once more. The silent thoughts were almost audible like the hum of the distant generators.

A moment passed before Jones uttered, "It's a damn miracle."

Paul turned to him and in a low tone said, "No, it's just exactly what we needed."

The Captain knew what he was implying, as did the others, but it was too soon for such leaps of faith.

"Yes, Sire," Reynolds said in a tone that was neither committal nor mocking.

"Along with the hundred odd men and twelve assorted skimmers that have joined us from other Republican units, this has strengthened the garrison three-fold," Yeoville added. "Ryker will have to wait for re-enforcements before he'll be able to launch another assault."

Not wanting to spoil the mood, but being unable to stop himself, Reynolds said, "Yes, but I'm sure once Lexus knows he will send every spare unit he has straight over here. He'll not be happy until this entire city has been erased from existence."

"Thanks for sharing that," Yeoville muttered sarcastically, but he knew that he was right. It was his timing that was way off.

"Richard is right," Paul said, placing a hand on Yeoville's good shoulder. "We must always be aware of the bigger picture, even in times of celebration, but it should not deny us a small moment of joy. We have our work cut out, but our situation has certainly improved." He caught the corners of a few mouths rising at that last remark; even Reynolds'. He patted Yeoville's shoulder a couple of times and then turned back to the Tac-com.

"Well said, Paul." Yeoville marvelled not only at the way he spoke, but also in the effortless way he first assumed and then relinquished control of the discussion. "Jones, liaise with Svenson and Sleeper to fortify both inner and outer defences to the limit of possibility; I want everyone on it round the clock. Ryker could have units in from Frisco, Angeles, Vegas and Tucson within forty-eight hours, and units from further a field within a week."

"We'll be ready for them," Jones said, his smile undeterred.

Over the next hour, activity in the Loyalist Command Centre hovered around fever-pitch. As well as managing the strengthening of the garrison's defences, Yeoville and Reynolds mulled over contingency plans, as ultimately they would be needed. It was as several ideas were circulating that Demoore interrupted. "Detroit is intercepting dozens of communications from DC to Republican units across the entire Province." She faltered with a growing look of anxiety spreading across her face. "Orders for units between company and brigade size to head directly for us via air, land and sea using, military and civilian transport alike."

"What?" Reynolds uttered, his tone incredulous.

Resisting the urge to echo the sentiment, Yeoville asked, "Estimated numbers and arrival times?"

"Mainly infantry—in the region of three thousand—but also additional units of light and heavy armour, at least three more gunships, two T60s and another flotilla of combatants from the Pacific Fleet."

A young male operator, eves-dropping the hushed conversation, on registering the sheer size of numbers involved, could not help himself shouting out, "Holy shit!"

Reynolds swung around at him a moment sooner than Yeoville, growling, "Get a grip, Private!"

The private's face was pale and awash with fear, but the Major's tone cut straight through to his training. Still acutely aware of the gravity of the situation, the young soldier quickly understood the need to avoid panic. "I-I'm sorry, Sir."

Yeoville spoke less harshly. "We'll talk about this later, Barrett. There are no surprises in any of this, so go about your business."

"Yessir," the private responded, his pitch slightly more stable. They had attracted a few more sideways glances, but nobody appeared to have understood the reason for the brief confrontation.

Yeoville led Reynolds further out of earshot from the other occupants of the room. Demoore followed.

"Well, we knew they'd throw a lot at us," Yeoville said, "I just didn't think it would be quite so much."

"It doesn't really change anything," Reynolds said evenly, once again completely composed.

"How so?"

"The assumption was that San Diego would fall."

Yeoville shook his head, despite himself. "No, I knew that the King could not stay here regardless, but with the extra units, I hoped that we could hold out until..." His voice trailed off. In fact he had no idea how to end the sentence.

"Exactly, until what?" Reynolds asked, his tone hushed but no less harsh. "There's no way we could get this war turned round in time for General Somms to punch through with reinforcements. And there's no way Lexus would let this city stand after the humiliation he's suffered. He's got an example to make and San Diego just drew the short straw. All that matters now is timing."

Anger flared in Demoore as well as Yeoville, but it was the Major who spoke. "These are my men for christsake! Only timing matters? Bastard!" He jabbed an accusing finger into Reynolds' chest. "They're human-beings that have gone to Hell and back only to find out now that they've only been delaying the inevitable all along." He had managed to keep his tone low but his jaw was clenched and he had stepped right up close to the larger man. Reynolds, as was his nature, stood his ground.

"Dan," Demoore injected, "we're attracting attention again." More than half of the room were now openly watching them with varying degrees of concern.

"You know better than that, Yeoville," Reynolds replied, ignoring the Lieutenant. "What your men have done and will do is vital to the entire war, but you have to face facts. San Diego will fall."

Partly because of their audience and mainly because of an intolerable itching feeling that Reynolds was right, despite his tornado-tact, Yeoville turned away. "We'd better get to work on plan B then."

Acceptance had replaced his initial anger, but bitterness remained. Yeoville sat back in his chair and drained the tepid remains of his coffee. "Major Sleeper has no problem with Svenson being left in command. He said given the length of time he'd been on our side he didn't expect anything else.'"

"Good," Reynolds said, acutely aware of their uneasy truce. "It would hardly be appropriate for a chain of command row to flare up."

Yeoville nodded but his features were still deeply frowned. Leaning forward on his elbows, he said, "You know, I'm grateful for the King's intentions, but what he concocted about it being too much of a risk to allow me to stay because of the information they could wean out of me is bull. There's nothing I could tell them that they wouldn't already know anyway."

Reynolds shook his head in earnest. "I don't think you're giving him enough credit. The fact that he likes you has little or nothing to do with it. He knows damn fine that you're a bloody good officer, so he doesn't want to lose you and there *is* a great deal of sensitive information you and your advisors are privy to." As an after thought, he added, "And before you get on your high horse about your men, he knows damn fine the sacrifices they are making and the courage they are showing, but you will serve America better elsewhere, another time."

Yeoville considered arguing further, but to be honest, he did not have the energy. He felt old and drained and guilt was just another emotion stacking up with the others. It would just have to take a number and get in line. "I'm going take a skimmer out to the hovernaught and speak to Svenson face to face. It's the least I can do."

Reynolds thought about telling him that he had no reason to feel guilty and that there was so much more to do, but instead he just nodded and went in search of a fresh cup of coffee.

Yeoville opened the door to his darkened office and stepped inside. Closing the door wearily behind him, he sat down at his desk without bothering with the light switch. In the darkness he sat in troubled silence. His hand strayed to the silver-framed photograph of Mary Yeoville, touching, only briefly, the corner; not the picture itself.

Beau Svenson had been as proud and as solid as ever, to the point of near arguing with him over how stupid he thought his superior was being. He had then stressed that as soon as the King was clear he wanted Svenson to surrender immediately. At that, the big bald man had bellowed with laughter and said that he had no intention of dying yet and besides, he could not be gotten rid of so easily. Yeoville had smiled too then, and somehow, he almost believed him.

The smile had vanished the moment he left Svenson on the bridge of the hovernaught. On the short drive back to the base he could not help wondering just how scared Svenson must have really been feeling.

There was a light knock at the door. "Enter," he muttered, hardly aware that it passed his lips. Paul entered and offered the Major a warm smile. Catherine came in behind him and their eyes locked instantly. The smile he returned her was far more genuine than the feeble excuse he had managed for the King.

Paul witnessed the emotion in Yeoville's eyes and recognised it immediately. Stealing a glance towards Catherine revealed a mirror image. A smile crept across his face, despite valiant attempts to suppress it.

Catherine took a moment to compose herself and, still smiling, said, "We have an addition to the party." She stepped aside to allow Bradley's entry.

The young captain looked a little gaunt and pale, but he managed a salute that was as surprising as it was genuine. There was a change in his features that was less to do with his injuries. It was not exactly physical, more emotional. The mark of arrogance inherited from his father was less prominent, replaced by something that resembled sincerity. The salute had caused a flicker of pain, so Catherine, concerned, touched a hand to his shoulder.

"I'm fine," he said before she could speak.

Yeoville smiled at him with whole-hearted admiration. It was miraculous what a near death experience could do.

The morning sky was an angry grey and the wind stirred up the dark oily waters in the San Diego harbour, rocking the ramshackle array of rusted and bomb damaged boats, yachts and tugs.

A utility skimmer swung into view between deserted administration and Inspectorate buildings, jerking to a halt by the Navy pier. Yeoville was jumping out before it had even stopped. He could almost feel the time they had left ebbing away and he had the distinct feeling there was not a lot left. "This is it," he was saying as Reynolds dismounted with similar urgency.

Reynolds followed his finger until his gaze settled upon the rusted hull of a steamship lurking at the end of the pier. Listing slightly to starboard and with several broken windows in the upper deck, it appeared dormant and helpless. It was the largest vessel in the bay still afloat, but then only just. For a moment the Major was speechless.

Yeoville could not help but glance towards Point Loma to where he knew the blackened half-sunken hull of the once proud cruiser 'Victorious' lay. The ship had been one of the first major casualties of the war. Admiral Kurts, having been on the mainland seeing to official duties, had rushed back to his ship to re-group with the rest of his fleet. Unfortunately, as he reached the Point, he found most of the Pacific Fleet waiting for him. He had been trying to hail Rear Admiral Graceson in the fleet when they had opened fire. Victorious fought like hell but, outgunned and cornered, she quickly took several crippling hits and sank in a matter of minutes. Kurts and most of the six hundred and eighty strong Loyalist crew went down with her.

The survivors of Victorious, including her Captain—John Reach— were now visible on the decks and the pier around the old steamer. The crew were organising an array of machinery and equipment, including a crane.

"That wreck?" Reynolds finally asked.

Yeoville now jabbed the pointing finger. "That 'wreck' happens to be The Explorer."

"And?" He remained incredulous.

"The Explorer has seen more action than any other vessel afloat."

Reynolds now laughed cynically. "And it bloody well looks like it!"

Neither man spoke for some time, immersed in their own thoughts. It was Reynolds who broke the silence. "I was hoping for bad weather to help us sneak away, but this tub doesn't look like it could survive much more than a summer breeze."

"Captain Reach has the survivors of Victorious along with dockers and some volunteers working on her right now. They'll make her as good as new in no time."

Reynolds shook his head. "Don't go getting all adventurous on me. How about we just stick to keeping her afloat?"

Yeoville managed a smile, saying, "Have a little faith."

Within half an hour of the two majors scrutinizing The Explorer, more recruits had arrived to speed up its refit. Among them were Cobek, Swede and Cook. Rodriquez had been the only one able to evade the manual labour, having been assigned close protection duties to the King.

The Staff Sergeant immediately set about replacing the ship's defunct arsenal. With crews working fore and aft, the old primary gun was swapped for the nearly new twin barrels 'borrowed' from a badly damaged Rhino tank and mounted on an improvised housing. Where the fore and aft machine guns had been long since removed, new twin 20mms were locked into their predecessors mounts with minimal tinkering. Two additional 15mm MGs were attached to the rusted railings on both port and starboard sides.

The priority was to replace the dilapidated steam engine, and that too was already well under way. The first of two gleaming high-powered diesel engines were being lowered into position and the hole-ridden funnel now lay, partially collapsed, on the pier.

Civilian and military workers alike continued in unwavering harmony at a breathless pace to install modern radar and navigational systems—scrounged from a variety of civilian vessels in the bay. The hull was repaired and painted ocean grey and a sign painter risked travelling from Clairemont to paint the words 'H.M.S. EXPLORER' on her vastly improved hull.

As Swede finished locking the port-side MG into position, he took a moment to glance around the bustling ship. His fatigues were smeared with muck, grease and sweat and his face and hands even worse. He caught a glimpse of an equally grubby-looking Cook and shouted over to him, "Cooky, ya been drinking outta the latrines again?"

"Blow me," was Cook's witty response as he walked towards him, smiling. "Man, is this shit-bucket starting to look good or am I just so wrecked that I'd think even your mamma looked good right now?"

Swede feigned hurt and replied in a tone distinctly lacking in the masculine department, "Ooh, you're soooo cruel!" This set the two Guardsmen off in fits of laughter.

Cobek, on the pier, heard their laughing and yelled, "Will you two assholes quit screwing around!" He rolled his eyes at the grubby middle-aged marine engineer standing beside him, then looked back down at his clipboard.

The engineer—Dolan—continued his appraisal. "The hull and armaments shouldn't take much longer and the electronics, I'm told, we need to allow another five-to-six hours for. It's the engines and the rest of the mechanics that are going to eat up the majority of our time."

"I'll take your word for that, but we're quickly running out of it."

"Staff Sergeant Cobek?" a young voice enquired from behind him.

"Aye," he answered, without taking his eyes off his clipboard. "What's the problem?"

"Sergeant Elton, reporting for duty, Sir."

Cobek glanced up. The young NCO appeared to have been alone in the freckle line and so had received several extra portions. His eyes were bloodshot and his skin pale, but he was no weakling and stripes were not awarded lightly. The short private standing behind him lent a degree of credibility to the term 'bulldog chewing a wasp'.

"Where the hell you been, Soldier?"

"This morning I found out from headquarters that my older brother was killed up near Toronto." His voice remained even and his eyes steady, but Cobek saw all the anguish in a brief tremor in his cheek.

He was going to continue, but Cobek cut him off, saying, "I understand. I hear you're good with engines?"

"Yes, Sergeant."

"Good." Pointing to a man in jeans and tee-shirt on the deck, he said, "Go see that lanky Mexican up there."

Elton nodded, then introduced the motionless man behind him. "Picked up another helper along the way; Private Sargent."

Cobek cocked an eyebrow at him. "There's always one. Son, with a name like that you were just asking for trouble joining this man's army."

The private was used to similar comments, so his "Yessir" was distinctly lacking enthusiasm.

"OK, Elton, take Serge here with you."

The mess hall was sparsely occupied by small isolated groups. The atmosphere was both charged and pensive with everyone being scared (with every right), but at the same time impatient for the nightmare to begin. For some, there was an eagerness to get stuck in, but for the majority the thinking was 'the sooner it starts, the sooner it will end'.

Sitting with Reynolds in the corner closest to the door (intentional planning by Reynolds), Yeoville pondered over that last thought whilst pushing a piece of nondescript meat around his plate. Common sense would make one assume that, given the option, most people would prefer to linger in relative safety—however delusional—for as long as possible, but it was clear, that even he would consider death a viable alternative against prolonging the agony further.

There was, of course, only so much that even the strongest person could endure, and the San Diego garrison was so far beyond that point that the point itself had disappeared into legend.

"How's the steak?" Reynolds asked, eager to interrupt both of their thoughts.

"Damnit, I said no hints. It was on the tip of my tongue too." Both men smiled; it was light and pointless and just what they needed. Yeoville finally swallowed the chunk of meat and washed it down with some hot coffee.

Leaning back, he said, "So tell me, are there any miniature Reynolds' running about?" He had meant the question as another piece of light-hearted escapism, but Reynolds looked down at his half eaten mackerel a little too quickly.

"No," he replied, filling his fork with some fish and salad. After a moment he looked up at Yeoville. "A military career can be pretty demanding and so can women." Reynolds felt suddenly as if the ground was crumbling away under his feet, but he ploughed ahead regardless. "Samantha might've..." His voice trailed off.

"Samantha?"

"Samantha Gordon; the King's Personal Assistant."

"Oh," Yeoville muttered, knowing all too well what had become of the King's PA. He had stamped his foot right into it and now it was well and truly stuck there.

Reynolds continued, oblivious of Yeoville's distress. "Before she died I was sure something was happening between us. The way she looked at me; her smile. And when she died, she…" He took a hasty swig of his coffee and wished it was something much stronger.

Yeoville said nothing. He knew when to talk and when to shut up and Reynolds really needed to talk. The man of steel was at once very human with even a slight tremor to his voice.

"And you know what the worst thing is? Now that she's gone, I've started second-guessing myself, wondering whether I misread the signals, whether she cared a damn about me at all. Wouldn't you think that her being dead in a gutter somewhere would be the worst of it?"

Yeoville shook his head. "No, Rich, the aftermath is far worse. The questioning; the guilt; the doubt. I'd take physical suffering over mental anytime."

Reynolds nodded, but he was clearly unconvinced.

The nearby door chose that awkward moment to admit Bradley and Lee Farber. Both men saluted on seeing the two majors, the former albeit more carefully. Farber was carrying both their kitbags, much to the annoyance of Bradley.

"All packed?" Yeoville asked them.

"You bet," Bradley replied.

"Well, if you survive what they're serving here, get down to the Explorer and stow your gear."

"Yes, Sir." With that the two men headed for the service bay.

Relieved of the intrusion and eager to change the subject, Reynolds said, "He's changed."

"More like exorcised." They both allowed themselves the luxury of a little laughter one more time. They knew that it would be short-lived.

Barely an hour later, they were back in the Command Centre when the final assault began. A wave of renewed activity swept through the room. As sit-reps poured in from the field detailing enemy numbers and positions, Yeoville could immediately sense the rising panic. He knew the situation would nose-dive at a dizzying rate from this moment forward.

As operators and officers alike shouted and relayed orders, Yeoville turned to Reynolds and said, "Take the King to the ship and take Jones and Demoore with you."

Reynolds stared fiercely at him. "And you will follow?"

"I didn't know you cared." Yeoville slapped him on the shoulder. "Listen, don't worry about me. I want to hold the fort as long as I can here, then I'll be right behind you."

Reynolds reluctantly agreed and then called the two officers to his side. As they left, Yeoville caught worried glances from both Jones and Demoore aimed in his direction. As the door closed behind them, Yeoville slipped on a headset and spoke calmly, but quickly. In a moment he was speaking to Captain Svenson. "What've you got?"

The radio crackled, but the distant drum of gunfire and mortars was nonetheless distinctive. "It would seem they're hitting us from every angle. Those reports were not exaggerated."

"Staggered retreat; all sectors and ready the counter on my command. Then it's over to you, my friend."

"Roger that." The Captain's tone was grim, but resolute.

Standing on the Navy Pier, Staff Sergeant Cobek did not need to be warned about the advancing threat. Even though the fighting was still several kilometres away, the dull roar of battle was clear and it seemed to move closer by the second. As he barked orders at the frantic crew and workers, two T60s, heading north from Chula Vista in tight formation, flew low over the city firing rockets and cannon along the Loyalist lines. His gaze continued to sweep across the city, seeing also the last Loyalist gunship locked in a dog-fight with two Republican 'ships.

The situation was critical. "Move it!" he bellowed.

The remaining civilian workers were finally downing tools when a utility skimmer shot off Broadway and jerked to a halt on the pier. Reynolds jumped out from the driving seat, leaving the engine still idling, and Paul, Catherine and the two officers followed him.

Cobek grabbed the Mexican's hand as he strode off the gangplank. "We couldn't have done it without you, Miguel."

Miguel grinned. "Take it easy, hombre."

As the others quickly boarded, Reynolds stopped by Cobek. "We ready?"

"As we'll ever be. Cap'n Reach is powering up the engines as we speak."

Reynolds nodded and looked back at the city. The smoke was already thick above the skyline, obscuring, for the most part, even the darting aircraft that buzzed over it. He turned back to him. "We're waiting on one more."

Cobek was surprised, but said nothing. He was used to things being cut fine.

The last of the Command Centre's skeleton staff had just left, leaving Yeoville alone to his thoughts when Reynolds came over the radio.

"Yeoville, where the hell are you?"

The Major wearily shook his head and opened the channel. "I'm just tying up the loose ends. I'm walking out the door now."

"Don't walk; run! We're out of time."

Yeoville agreed and signed off. He took a moment to study the tac-com display and then hailed Svenson. "It's time."

"You got it. Take care, Dan."

Yeoville closed his eyes momentarily. There was so much he needed to say, but all that came out was, "You too, Beau." The link was severed and suddenly he felt more alone than any time in his entire life.

The room was silent and the few remaining working strip-lights were wholly inadequate. A couple of the few remaining terminals had been left on in their operators haste to exit, so now winking standby lights added to the atmosphere.

In the semi-gloom, images danced at the brink of the imagination. Yeoville thought he recognised one or two. Wes was there, he was sure of it...Lyn too. For a moment, he thought he saw Jones with them, but the image was gone before it had properly formed.

The thought that had been lurking just out of rational reach chose the perfect moment to leap out. He should not abandon his men; it was his duty to remain with them. And he could not be taken alive, not anymore, but then very few of his men would survive either.

Common sense struggled to intervene. He asked himself a simple question—where was he most needed? Ultimately, could he do any more here now or at some point in the future somewhere else? Of course, he would never know the answer.

He found himself hovering in the open doorway, his mind a cocktail of emotions with doubt and fear at the fore-front. Mentally, he wrestled for what seemed like an age, but was more like a minute. Images of first Catherine and then Mary fluttered past his mind's eye. They too fought for dominance. The room began to spin.

As he peered into the abyss, he felt the thump of artillery shells falling overhead and with that the lights flickered then died. With their passing, so the hysteria followed. He stood in the darkness and a new calm settled upon him.

A voice he knew better than his own seemed to drift in with the failing air-conditioning. It was Mary and her words were expressed rather than spoken and they made perfect sense. As his indecision vanished, so did her voice. Her words, however, would never be forgotten.

He turned in the doorway as a huge explosion rocked the base. The ceiling caved in with it.

Reynolds paced the deck of the Explorer and made no attempt to conceal his agitation. Catherine, Jones and Demoore stood in a close group near the gangplank. "Where the Hell is he?" the Major asked no one in particular.

"He'll be here," Jones assured, though his expression was far less convincing.

Cobek, the last person on the pier, walked slowly up the gangplank. Looking briefly over his shoulder, he said, "He must've bought it."

That was the final straw for Catherine. "Don't say that!" she cried. The composure that she had been so desperately clinging on to vanished and now tears started to well in her eyes. She was suddenly sick of trying to be discreet and wondered why she had done so in the first place. With grief came clarity.

Cobek hesitated short of stepping onto the ship. Clarity, it seemed, was infectious. He cursed himself for being so blind. "I'm sorry, Ma'am."

Reynolds cursed under his breath, then said, "I hate to say this, but—" He noticed a heavily dented civilian skimmer swing onto the docks and speed towards them. He knew instinctively who it was. "He's here!"

Catherine cried out in relief this time and rushed past Cobek to greet him. Cobek let her go and muttered, "Thank God."

Yeoville used the abandoned utility skimmer to help slow his hot-wired transport, slamming into the side of it. He was out and scooping Catherine into his arms in one fluid motion. Tears were streaming freely down her face and he too shed more than one.

"Thank God you're alright. Don't you ever leave me again."

Her words settled on him like a blanket and, without thinking, he kissed her gently on the lips and said, "I won't." There was no surprise on her face, just relief and uninhibited love.

They returned to the ship quickly and even as they stepped aboard, they felt the propellers kick in.

Smiling, Reynolds said, "You love to make a dramatic entrance." Then he saw Cobek draw his pistol and all pleasantries were forgotten.

Around a platoon of Republican troops converged on the dock in squads; an advanced recon unit given one way orders. They came through and from both sides of the Supply Centre and began firing immediately.

The remaining dockers, logistics staff and guards scattered for cover, but few survived the intense barrage.

Reynolds emptied his pistol at the attackers, as did Cobek and several others, and was satisfied to see half a dozen of the Republicans drop to the ground and stay there. "Move this tub of shit!" he bellowed towards the bridge.

With only Catherine's safety in mind, Yeoville swept her up and rushed below deck. As he deposited her in the corridor, he turned to dash back up to the deck.

"Don't go back up there," she pleaded.

On queue, the fighting intensified. He smiled at her and said, "You know I have to." Then he was gone.

As he reloaded, Reynolds noticed a nameless soldier take a bullet square in the chest barely two metres away. The man hit the deck hard on his back and did not move as a dark stain spread across his torn shirt. Without pausing, he resumed firing.

As Yeoville returned to the surface, the ship began to move with conviction. The Republicans, however, already had two large calibre machine guns set up and they renewed their onslaught with greater fervour. A seaman caught a round in the small of his back as another soldier lost his left arm below the elbow. The former squealed in agony and thrashed about on the deck as the latter, without so much as a sharp intake of breath, lost consciousness and hit the floor.

The deck then angled slightly as the full power of the twin diesels kicked in and propelled them along the bay. Cobek glanced towards the bridge and then back at Reynolds. They spared each other a flicker of a smile before both rushing to the aid of the wounded.

As the Explorer gained speed on course for the open ocean, a decidedly scruffy and dishevelled smuggler-cum-trader, standing by the closed gates of the Embarcadero Marina Park, watched in quiet contemplation. Sir Casey could see that they had cleared the immediate danger, but a sizeable chunk of the Republican navy lay in wait for them and the sky seemed to be darkening way too early.

His face was grimy and dried blood was smeared across his forehead, but despite not having a hit since before leaving the Samson—or maybe because of—the tremors had failed to return. He was parched and exhausted, but a smile touched his dry lips nonetheless. "We did it, Luke." He took a long slow draw off his cigarette and then dropped the butt onto the gravel. After stubbing it under foot, he let out a sigh and turned away from the docks.

Inland, the San Diego skyline was shimmering with smoke and flames and as the fighting lost some of its fervour, the fires seemed to poach it.

On the bridge of the hovernaught, Svenson, his first officer and the half dozen crewmen battled frantically to keep the heavily damaged vessel in the fight. The rest of his forces were scattered and routing and contact had been lost with all but a handful. The 402nd and their CO, Rowan Sleeper, had taken the brunt of the Republican might and been overrun in the first fifteen minutes of battle. A few isolated squads had since reported in, but there was no news of Major Sleeper himself.

Svenson rubbed his bushy moustache and said, "It's no good, they need more time."

His second, a chubby lieutenant, staggered against the central console with the jolt of another impact. He gripped one of the dangling support rings with one hand and with the other pointed towards the viewer, muttering, "We've got no more time to give, Sir."

As a fresh wave of rockets and missiles battered the floundering vessel. Several consoles exploded in a dazzling array of sparks and flames, casting two crewmen flailing across the floor, upper bodies ablaze.

While crewmates rushed to their aid, Svenson turned back to the viewer. "You're right, Weir," he admitted grimly. "Order the surrender. They're on there own."

As Shacks observed, and mere moments after Weir announced the surrender of San Diego, the hovernaught—already listing and engulfed in flames—was ravaged by a further wave of destruction which proved too much for the mighty warship. With its hull breached and a series of explosions ripping through it, the flagship of the San Diego Loyalist garrison crashed to the ground, obliterating several warehouses and a baseball diamond. The explosion spat high above all but the tallest of San Diego's buildings and its residual smoke hung ominously over the downtown area like a sulking thunderhead.

He turned away from the devastation and plucked out a battered pack of cigarettes from his torn and stained leather jacket. Two remained. "Shit," he muttered. He lit one and wearily trudged away from the marina.

The Explorer powered around the smouldering remains of North Island Naval Air Station and drew close to Point Loma. As the sky darkened and the water grew more aggressive, the jutting remains of Victorious dipped further below the turbulent waterline.

Everyone had vacated the decks apart from Cobek and the gunners. The Staff Sergeant felt a chill creep over him that had nothing to do with the wind that was steadily gathering momentum. It occurred to him for the first time in many years that sea travel was by far his least favoured form of transport.

Spray moistened his tunic and face. "It's gonna be a bumpy ride," he mused.

As grey bullet-shapes began to form on both the southern and western horizons, Swede shouted to his NCO. "This is nuts, Sarge! We'll never get through that fleet!"

Cobek did not have the inclination to glare. Instead, he just said, "Optimism, Swede, that's the ticket!"

Swede cursed under his breath and leaned back against his designated machine gun on the port side. He mulled over the mildly amusing notion that their NCO might indeed be a raving lunatic.

"Holy shit!" the private known as Serge yelled from his position on the starboard side. "Look!" In between Republican flotillas to their south and west, a huge wall of black storm clouds had appeared and was advancing eastward, like an army fresh out of boot camp.

For a moment all Cobek could do was gape at it, but he recovered quickly and said, "You wanted a way through the fleet, Swede. There it is."

With news of the loyalist naval assault on the northern elements of the fleet floundering, Reynolds and Yeoville, with Captain Reach's input, took only seconds to decide that what looked like the worst storm in Californian history would offer better odds than going head to head with the Pacific Fleet. It had been Bradley, however, who had adequately summed it up with the words, "We needed a miracle and we got one."

As the Loyalist corvette angled towards the storm, the Republican vessels picked up their speed, throwing caution to the wind, in a bid to stop them before entering the storm. As it turned out, the storm was sweeping in at an incredible rate of knots. The flotilla to the west was swallowed up before firing a single shot, but those to the south were closing fast.

Being too risky to maintain a presence on deck, Reach ordered the gunners below. As Cobek supervised the re-deployment, the first volley of deck guns roared out of the heavens. One blast tore a hole in the deck and mangled the railing and MG on the port side where Swede had been standing only moments earlier. A private, unlucky enough to be still near the stern, disappeared in the carnage.

With the jolt, Cobek lost his footing and hit the deck flailing. As his fingers frantically sought purchase, Explorer was engulfed by the storm. Its fevered embrace was violent to a point of disbelief. Huge waves crashed down on them and mingled with the driving rain. Visibility hit near zero in seconds and with the wind, the hurricane had a voice with which to express the true extent of its fury.

Sliding across the drenched decks, in the almost horizontal rain, Cobek grappled for something; anything to halt his ride into oblivion. Suddenly, as the ship rocked, all he could see in front of him was the thrashing grey ocean. Before he could even begin to digest the horror that closed in around him, he felt the jarring impact of the railings. The blow wrenched a cry from his taught white lips, but the pain was a welcome respite to certain death. Because the railings had been a similar colour to the water beyond them, he had not even seen them until the impact.

Wave upon wave crashed into him as he gripped the icy metal. He thought he saw a figure sweep past him, but he could not be sure. At times he was staring up into the sky, but it bore such a resemblance to its accomplice that, amongst the thrashing, telling them apart proved impossible.

Below deck, in the mess compartment, everyone similarly clung on to fittings for their lives, with the exception of Catherine, who held on to Yeoville. The Major held on to a hand rail by the vending machine for both of them. The only person missing was Reynolds who was on the bridge with Reach.

Yeoville had thought about making light of the situation, but the notion was instantly lost with another violent buffeting. It felt like a toddler, in the grip of the mother of all tantrums, had picked up their little toy-ship Explorer and was now making damn good use of it to vent his frustrations.

So the room remained silent, save for the incessant clattering of utensils and a couple of unlatched doors. To Bradley's near-amusement, everyone seemed to glance around the room looking vaguely embarrassed, like they were trapped in an elevator with an unwanted smell.

The thoughts of both men were jarred back to a semblance of reality when the Explorer struck a huge wall of water with a heart-stopping jolt. Captain Jones flew across the room with cartoon-style force and slammed into the opposite wall with a horrifying crunch. He broke several bones—including his neck—and died instantly. His twisted body lolled back and forth with the motion of the ship while the others looked on, helpless and aghast.

Unable to hear Catherine's tearful sympathies, Yeoville was transfixed by the look of mild shock on the man's face; apparently blissfully unaware of his impending doom. He could not draw his eyes away from the unnatural tilt of his neck or the angle at which his left leg jutted out from below the knee. So poor Dez Jones had drawn the short straw and joined Wes and the rest of the swelling ranks of men and women lost under his command.

Paul did his best to comfort a distraught Demoore but the thrashing of the vessel allowed only the briefest gesture. The tears rolled freely down her cheeks as she stared at her fallen friend. The Fort Wayne command had comprised of Yeoville, Palmer, Jones, Svenson, Bowman and herself. Now only two remained. Who would be left to mourn her? Despite being surrounded by her companions, a deep feeling of loneliness settled over her.

The death of Captain Jones dragged up a great deal of emotion that was not directly linked to the man himself. Paul, too, wondered if any of them were at all destined to survive their ordeal. Was it possible to triumph against such tremendous odds? Would America ever see peace again? As more and more questions formed in his mind, one fact shoved its way to the fore. When all is said and done, it came down to the simple and horrific fact that he, as the King and as a human being, was responsible for everything that had happened over the past months and years. He had caused all these deaths—including the poor man in front of him—which was precisely why he *had* to rectify it; no 'ifs' or 'maybes', just one hopeful conclusion—redemption.

Paul uttered a silent prayer for all their fallen and then wiped his tearful eyes.

On deck amongst the howling gale, rain and darkness, the railing Cobek held in a deathgrip began to give under the combination of the Sergeant's weight and the battering from the storm. With a drawn out groan, the steel buckled and sprung two rivets. A twang followed and several sections fell away into the darkness. As his section contorted the Staff Sergeant's scream reached new heights.

The mangled railing jangled against the side of the bucking ship over the very jaws of death. Driven by instinct alone, he clung on like a worm on a hook as his mind chanted repeatedly, *Not here...Not yet...Not my time...*

The boiling water below lapped at his feet and legs, almost mockingly, as if sensing that his escape was now impossible. In spite of its violence all around him, it seemed to touch him now with a newfound softness; like a lover's caress. It beckoned and even as his head shouted, 'Leave me alone,' his grip weakened and his fingers gave way one by one.

As he hung in the air for one final moment, he felt as if the ocean was parting beneath him. Then, as suddenly as he had lost his footing, he was yanked upwards and back onto the deck.

He lay in a crumpled heap for several minutes, oblivious of his saviour, heaving and throbbing from every muscle. Unaware that he was speaking aloud, he exclaimed, in one unbroken shrill babble, thanking everyone and everything for being alive.

Rodriquez let him finish and tried to memorize every legible word of it for reciting on future quieter occasions. Then, when he could hold back no longer, he said, "You look like shit, boss!"

Forcing himself into a sitting position, Cobek grabbed him with the little strength he had left and rasped, "Riquez, you sonuvabitch, I love you!"

Grinning, the private replied, "Cool it, Sarge. People'll talk."

It occurred to him then that, although the rain and wind was still lashing, the storm had lost much of its venom. The worst of the weather, along with the Republican Fleet, appeared to be behind them.

# Chapter 10
## Panama Canal

The atmosphere in the Presidential Conference Room was volatile to say the least. Lexus had shed his caged tiger outfit for the highly unnerving alternative of brooding silence. Usually, when angry he would pace, raise his voice, demand results etc, but this time he sat with his hands clasped together rooted to his chin, with his eyes downcast.

The fact that Silus was not with them, leaving only Halburd to share the brunt, further fuelled Namala's feeling of vulnerability. The General was obviously on a similar wavelength for, when their eyes met, he too was openly concerned. *This was not how the Republic was supposed to be.* It was more than just Grant's actions that were scaring him…it was his own thoughts too.

When Lexus did finally speak, his voice was even and devoid of emotion (a stark contrast to the turmoil within the confines of his mind). "Inform Admiral Graceson that if he does not apprehend and eliminate Frelon, he will be personally answerable and will take full responsibility. To that end he will be executed for gross incompetence and high treason."

The fact that it rolled off the tongue without a flicker across his icy features drove Namala a notch closer to hysteria. "Grant, Admiral Graceson has been unwaveringly loyal to the Republic, surely—"

"No," Lexus hissed, betraying a sliver of his fury. His voice was even once again when he continued. "If Frelon is not dead before setting one foot off that ship then Graceson will take his place at the block. Mark my words."

The two men nodded reluctantly, then left without saying another word. They both quite possibly would have agreed to the arbitrary extermination of their entire lineage to escape Lexus' seeping rage. They walked in silence through the ante-room. Two guards, deep in a Boston/Washington Rocket Ball debate, cut off in mid sentence to don their neutral 'on duty' facades.

Once out into the wide corridor, still garnished with paintings and vases from the previous owner, with the exception of all the pictures of the Royal family (those had been ceremoniously burned), Halburd grasped the Defence Secretary's arm and stopped in his tracks. "Zain, the guy is losing it."

Under different circumstances, Namala would have laughed at him, as it was, in its absence, anger stepped in. "Don't talk like that. You know the extreme pressure he's under; any other man—including you, Orson—would have crumpled by now."

The General did not release his grip. "Don't patronise me. I know precisely what he's going through, but I'm telling you now, he can't take much more. It's going to send him over the edge."

Namala's face grew crimson and he shook free of Halburd's grasp. "What *precisely* do you suggest we do?"

Halburd's gaze dropped to his empty hand and for a moment he said nothing. After releasing a sigh, he once again met Namala's glare. "I don't know what I'm suggesting; I just want you to here me out. I am as loyal to him as you are, heck you and I were in this from the beginning, but loyalty should lie with the Republic first. Everything we have fought for has been for a democratic Republic. For the good of that Republic I think he needs to take a rest, maybe step down, for a while at least."

Namala gaped at him and at last a laugh did escape his lips, but no humour accompanied it. "There is no way he would willingly give up his position. Anyone suggesting such a notion would be instantly arrested, especially in his present frame of mind. Besides that, the public support that we do still maintain would be thrown to the wind. In its current form Lexus is seen by the public as the face of the Republic, whether you like it or not."

He stepped forward to continue his journey, but first paused to state, "You had better watch what you say; for your own good, Orson." Further down the corridor, Namala turned and added, in the friendliest voice he could muster, given the circumstances, "Don't worry. He'll pull through."

Halburd neither replied nor turned to him.

Bradley leaned against a section of railing that had escaped the wrath of the storm and took a deep breath of fresh sea air. The sun was shining high overhead and the storm was long gone, leaving just a cool breeze and a scattering of white clouds. He looked out across the water to where he knew the coast lay just out of sight. "Welcome to the State of Southern Mexico."

Farber strolled up beside him and said, "From what I here it's in a right state."

Bradley laughed. "Anyone ever tell you that you've got a real negative attitude, Lee?"

"All the time. That's how come I'm outranked by you." The jibe came easy and both men were pleasantly surprised by it. Since narrowly surviving the mission in San Diego, the line between officer and NCO had blurred somewhat and neither seemed to be at all bothered. Both carried the scars and that seemed to more than justify it.

Unthwarted, Bradley said, "We should be dining in Panama by sundown."

"Yeah, I'll be glad to be off this heap, that's for sure. If I wanted to spend my time on floating coffins I'd have joined the Marines."

"She's not that bad; she saved our lives for one thing." He patted the railing and added, "Be careful, you'll hurt her feelings."

Farber looked at him and cocked an eyebrow. "You're nuts, Sir."

"That's how come I outrank you."

After confirming their current position with Captain Reach, Reynolds walked back to the hardcopy map splayed across the table to the rear of the bridge where Yeoville and Demoore waited. On his way, he made a quick mental calculation and said, "We should arrive at approximately twenty-two hundred hours. That'll time it just right to go in under the cover of darkness."

Still studying the map, Yeoville nodded and asked, "What about the Arion?"

"We rendezvous at Fort Walter; on the southern entrance. It's under the command of a Major Richly."

Yeoville looked up, quizzically. "Harry Richly?"

Reynolds nodded. "Major H Richly; so I guess so. You know the man?"

"Yeah, I went through the Academy with him. I haven't seen him since the reunion…must be nearly ten years or so. Jesus, we used to be thick as thieves and so damn competitive, yet it never once came between us." He had half turned to look out of the window, his expression wistful. "I'll be damned."

His colleague's dramatic mood change managed to get the better of Reynolds' usual 'no questions asked' attitude. "So, I'm curious. What happened?"

"Don't worry, nothing exciting. After graduating we received our postings and went our separate ways. We stayed in touch for a few years; a couple of visits to drink over old times and then we just lost touch. Funny how often that happens." He absently scratched his wounded shoulder and immediately winced, realising what he had done. 'Bastard' Harry, everyone had called him. Yeoville had been one of them, until, on a three day survival exercise in Colorado, the two had been teamed up and had been the only team to elude the hunters for the whole three days. In those seventy-two hours they had learnt all about each other, including the touchy subject of Harry's failed captain-turned-drunk father who had pushed too hard. After the exercise, the two became inseparable.

"Can we trust him?" Reynolds was asking.

"Without a doubt."

Yeoville stood with his arms crossed over his chest beside a humming Reach at the helm. He took a breath, then spoke into his headset. "Clarity, this is Wingless, do you copy?" Reynolds, the only other occupant, sat at the table, listening with interest.

A crisp young female voice responded almost immediately. "This is Clarity. Switch to…Echo Four on my mark…Mark."

Yeoville switched frequency, as requested, then said, "Priority message; code name Gabriel, over."

"Please hold, over." After a minute of silence, a new voice—male, hoarse—spoke, "This is Major Richly; bravo-delta-six-one-niner. Over."

Yeoville smiled as he responded with the secondary code. "Explorer; Pappa-Foxtrot-zero-one-zero."

"Roger; go ahead." Richly's voice remained utterly businesslike.

"I'm hurt that you don't recognise me, Bastard Harry."

A brief pause. "Desperate Dan, that you?" he asked sceptically.

"You bet."

"You sonuvabitch, they didn't tell me you'd be along! I should've known, you're always upstaging me, boy! How long's it been?"

"Too long," Yeoville said, leaning against the instrument panel, smiling. "What happened to you beating me to General?"

"You can talk, what are you? Wait a minute, it's Monday—so you're a major too, right?"

Yeoville laughed. "So you do care?"

"Enough to know that you've been soakin'it in California. How many bottles did that assignment cost you?" At that, they both laughed together and, for a moment, it seemed like they were back at Fort Ord.

Reynolds tactfully cleared his throat. Without turning, Yeoville waved off his impatience and asked, "So what happened to your voice, you're balls finally drop?"

Richly grunted with remembrance. "Fucking assassination attempt. Little bastard popped me through the throat; he was damn lucky to be blown away before I got my hands on him."

Yeoville cringed at the thought, but did not let it spoil his mood. "Still dabble in the torture techniques?"

"Damn right, it's great for easing away those tensions at the end of a hard day. Besides, it beats that Shing-Shong shit that you used to do!" As he laughed again, it turned into a coughing fit that resembled a speedbike with a faulty starter motor.

"You ok?" Yeoville asked, instantly concerned.

"Sure, sure," Richly replied, still half laughing-half coughing.

"Well, it was Shuai-Chiao and it's an ancient form of martial arts, you heathen."

"Whatever. We're all clear here, so you can bring her right in. And remember, you still owe me that drink."

Chuckling, Yeoville signed off and turned to Reynolds. "Can you believe that?"

"No I can't." Although his features were firm, Yeoville detected mild amusement hiding beneath his colleague's exterior. "OK, Reach, take us in."

Major Richly's office was light and roomy with a big blast-proof window offering a scenic twilight view of the parade ground surrounded by clusters of squat grey shapeless buildings. Beyond, was the wide expanse of docks, warehouses and offices at the mouth of the canal surrounded by lush green rolling hills. The swollen hull of a Texan freighter was slowly easing itself into the first of the giant locks.

The docks, as always, were a hive of activity. Just because there was a war on, it did not stem the flow of domestic and international commerce that swept through twenty four hours a day. The fact that the canal itself was civilian controlled and no one had tried to change this meant that, so far, the canal operations had remained completely untouched by the fighting (unlike Panama City which had seen a great deal of unrest and urban fighting between Republican, Loyalist, BFF and various gang factions). Neither side wanted a disruption to the maritime lifeline.

Unlike his room, the Major himself was dark and rather small. His broad and muscular frame, however, more than made up for his five feet eight inches in height. There had been several occasions in his colourful life where unsuspecting troublemakers had ended up with far more than they had bargained for by judging his strength, skill and sheer tenacity on height alone.

His black crew-cut with a generous sprinkling of grey was regulation length; not because he stuck to the book—he had a notorious disregard for rules, preferring to judge and act upon each new situation individually (unofficially, this stance had gained him a great deal of respect from his peers, despite his occasional loose cannon antics)— but simply because he liked it that way. One of his pet hates was long hair on men. His hard man look was completed with a messy three inch scar on his neck and a tightly cropped beard that reached cartoon-like heights at over-emphasizing his already imposing jaw line.

His olive-drab combat trousers and tee-shirt were damp with sweat and his ID tags dangled loosely around his neck as he leant across his desk to take hold of a bottle of '65.' He took a hearty swig then slammed it back down with less than half left. "April!"

The door opened to admit a young female officer. Lieutenant April Harris was two years out of the Academy and had already excelled herself both 'hands on' and tactically, but she was not renowned for her patience. She was tough and had the scars to prove it and if she caught anyone—sometimes of any rank—calling her ma'am, miss or any other 'girls' name, instead of Harris, lieutenant or sir—she could quite easily and quite often explode. She also hated the name April.

"Sir." She bared her teeth through a poor excuse for a smile.

Richly grinned at her and said, "I've been trying to raise Gould on the Kraken, but no dice; his damn set must be down again. Take a car and a com-tech and get down there.

"Aw fuck," she muttered, her southern drawl thick with her lack of enthusiasm. She shoved her hands deep into her trouser pockets and turned to leave.

"Hold it," Richly continued. "I'm not finished yet. Tell him to have the Kraken on standby and ready to move."

"Anything else?" Harris asked moodily, taking her hands out of her pockets and crossing them over her ample chest (a chest that she tried so hard to conceal).

"Yeah. Get a shave and put a shirt on; you look like shit."

April threw him a casual finger and glanced down at the Major's groin. She laughed as she closed the door behind her.

Richly shook his head then took another swig of '65'.

As the Explorer cruised into the Gulf of Panama, the mood onboard ship was that of silent apprehension. Although nobody actually spoke it, everyone was of a similar mind; their escape from San Diego and the subsequent journey down the west coast of North America had been too easy so far. Time had the extraordinary effect of either exaggerating or dulling historical events—never quite maintaining an even keel—thus their horrific battle through one of the worst storms on record had turned into just 'some bad weather'.

Amongst the quiet gathering on deck, Cobek scanned the horizon through image-intensifying binoculars. The half moon reflected off the calm waters, tempting tranquil thoughts out of all but the most hardened men onboard. The coast was illuminated only by a scattering of man-made sources and even they were softened by pockets of thin mist that clung to some of the low level areas.

The Staff Sergeant heard a disturbance in the water below him and looked down in time to see a long dark shape glide away from them just below the surface. *Out hunting, are we?* he mused, then instantly regretted the thought.

The mood of the crew began to lighten as they drew nearer and even Cobek loosened his grip slightly on his binoculars. Even the pessimists on board would not have entertained the notion of what happened next; not in their worst nightmares. Two frigates swung around from the back of the Isla Del Rey, high on their hydrofoils and raced straight for them.

Captain Reach's relaxed demeanour instantly vanished as they appeared. Cursing, he slammed the General Quarters alarm.

Yeoville and Reynolds jumped up from the table and rushed to his side. "Christ," Reynolds echoed. "Ours?"

"Walter's only got a Corvette and a couple of PPBs," Yeoville said, switching off the alarm. "Those are Orca-class frigates."

"Then we have problems, as usual." Reach was already executing the nautical equivalent of a U-turn.

Cobek saw the frigates approaching before the General Quarters sounded and knew what to expect. Instinctively, he grabbed a piece of railing and yelled, "Gunners standby! Non combatants below deck!" The alarm sounded in the next moment.

The deck pitched as Explorer swung about, catching several crewmen unawares. A gunner enacted an elaborate dance across the fore-deck in an attempt to stay on his feet. It seemed sure that he would be cast overboard, but instead at the last second, he managed to lunge against a fixed magazine housing.

Yeoville was poised over the radio when Fort Walter's CO burst over the airwaves. "Wingless, Wingless, get the Hell out of here!"

"Harry, it's Dan. What's happening?"

"Rep's everywhere; we're under heavy assault. High tail it, my friend."

"Sonuvabitch!" The Major slammed a fist against the console hard enough to flip a pen and clipboard onto the floor. "I'm sorry, Harry. This is our fault."

"Screw that!" Richly retorted, "We were in need of some target practice anyhow, so what the Hell. The Kraken's gonna draw some fire off your ass, so you make like a missile."

Still clenching his throbbing fist, Yeoville said, "Take care of yourself, Harry."

"You'll have to buy me that drink another time, bud." Richly severed the link before his friend could reply. He replaced the handset and glanced out of the window.

The night was illuminated by flashes from gunfire and mortars and thick smoke billowed from several fires within in the compound. One of the barrack buildings had taken a direct hit from a mortar, collapsing half of the roof and instantly turning it into an inferno. Half dressed soldiers frantically jumped through windows to escape the death-trap.

Looking past the carnage to where Explorer would be, he muttered, "Good luck."

As he pulled on his jacket whist heading for the door, the Republican spotters must have adjusted their fire for multiple explosions rocked the building so ferociously they seemed to jar it loose from its very foundations. The lights instantly went out, leaving the room illuminated by the silvery-orange glow from outside. Before opening the door, all he could hear was the muffled thump-thump-thump of mortar rounds. As it opened, screams and chaos spilled in.

The two frigates were gaining ground fast, but despite already being in range they still had not fired a shot. It was Reynolds who first spotted the small sleek craft emerging from the blackness behind the Republican vessels. "That the Kraken?"

Yeoville took the goggles and zeroed in on it as it raced terrier-like at two cougars. "Apt, huh?"

"Apt?" Reynolds snapped. "That corvette's only one gun off being a gunboat! She'll be cut to pieces by those Orcas."

With no where else to vent his rising frustration, Yeoville let off some of his own. "She's our only fucking chance! There's no storm to disappear into this time."

The two Majors lapsed into silence, leaving only the heavy breathing from Reach to punctuate the noises from the engines and the sea. It had a rhythmic feeling, not unlike distant drums drifting over a camp fire and it further fuelled their rising dread.

Their looks of dread turned to horror as one of the frigates launched a missile and veered off to intercept the corvette.

"Oh shit," Yeoville muttered.

Reynolds shot a glance over his shoulder to Reach and shouted, "Incoming!"

Explorer swung sharp to starboard as the missile hurtled towards them. Everyone on board held their breath and braced for impact. The ship to ship missile shot across the water at scarcely a metre from the tranquil surface, faster than the speed of sound. It hit the water twenty metres off the port side and its explosion lifted a vast fountain skywards, showering the Explorer with cold salt water.

The shockwave jarred the wheel out of Reach's big weathered hands, causing him to curse and suck one bruised finger, but everyone else breathed a sigh of relief.

They were given no further time for reflection. The Kraken launched all four of its missiles at the one frigate still giving chase to Explorer. Two splashed harmlessly, but the remaining two struck her in her lower aft deck. Twin fireballs ripped through the rear gun deck, causing a multiple of smaller explosions in quick succession. The fire and explosions then spread to the engine rooms and in moments the warship was dead in the water and floundering fast.

The Loyalists cheered as they soon left it behind, but their happiness was short-lived. A barrage of missiles launched from the undamaged frigate at close range totally obliterating the Kraken, scattering wreckage to the four winds. The survivors onboard Explorer fell silent as they watched the flaming remains of their saviour and her fifty-four man crew disappear beneath the waves.

The man-made illuminations dissolved into the horizon and the Explorer was left, once again, alone on the dark open ocean.

Below deck, the mess had suddenly transformed into a prison and Reynolds made no attempt to conceal his charged emotions. Once again, their plans had been well and truly scuppered, leaving their asses hanging in the wind. Yeoville had made the mistake of saying, 'At least we're still alive.' He had blasted him for it, which was pointless and counter-productive and now the guilt of which niggled at him. Yeoville still had a reason to feel optimistic; he, of course, did not.

Shattering the standoff, Bradley said, "So what options are open to us?"

"Not a whole damn lot," Reynolds growled. Bradley shrugged and leaned back in his chair.

Unperturbed by the previous outburst directed at him, Yeoville said, "You're going to wear a groove into the floor if you're not careful." His tone remained calm, aided by Catherine's hand that he held beneath the table.

With rage obliterating niceties such as tone, Reynolds spun on him and raised clenched fists. The gesture was easily misconstrued as threatening, but it was just another way of venting his desperation that was already at its peak. "How can you sit there and crack jokes? We're fucked, Dan old buddy."

"For crying out loud, Rich," Yeoville replied, feeling his composure rapidly dissolving. "We're not in that bad shape. Things could be a whole lot worse."

"How?"

The residue of self-control that he had been clinging on to rushed away in one quick burst. "Think of the men onboard the Kraken! Think of my fucking friend, Harry, you sonuvabitch!"

Catherine's hand tightened its grip. "Daniel, don't." Her soothing tone instantly cut through the red mist.

Reynolds stared at him, mouth agape at the sudden eruption. The former San Diego Commander was just as stressed as the rest of them. *Lay off him,* he warned himself. "I'm sorry, Dan." He searched for more words, but none came.

"Forget it," Yeoville said, his composure regained and embarrassed for his outburst.

As the room once again fell into silence, Paul continued to observe the proceedings with mixed feelings. Half of him wanted to intervene and force the situation into his control, but something held him back and kept his lips sealed. He wondered what the others might be thinking of his present impartial position—would they be judging him as cowardly or indecisive? He dismissed the thought before answering it; that was the old Paul thinking, suspicious and defensive.

In the silence, Yeoville glanced at Catherine for some moral support. Catherine sensed his readiness to renew the discussion and adorned a warm smile of encouragement. Feeling refreshed, he drew in a breath and, although addressing the room, he looked straight at Reynolds. "This may seem a little off base at first, but hear me out."

The Royal Guards Major, and recently appointed Knight, stopped pacing and folded his arms. "Alright, let's hear it."

"Right, firstly, let me tell you what I know about Ecuador. With it being the top leisure resort in the Americas, before the trouble started it already had a sizeable privately funded army of its own to ensure the celebs and VIPs were safe from the various terrorist factions that used to target it. Since the trouble, the Guayaquil Mayor, backed by some big businessmen, decided to set up an independent government. Now, with the rising strength of the BFF, backed by the Republic, they are under serious threat."

"I can see where this is going and I don't like it," Reynolds said.

"Give him a chance," Bradley injected sternly. Ever surprised by Bradley's change, Yeoville smiled at him before continuing.

"The Mayor—Fernando Maximillian—has been appointed President of their democratic system and has a great deal of local support. It has also become a safe haven for many of the Province's rich and famous. With BFF aggression imminent he would be receptive to negotiation. For example, in exchange for recognised independence and the backing of the Crown, I believe they would help us."

"Are you out of your mind?" The Major's face reddened despite all efforts to remain calm.

"No," Yeoville answered simply. Bradley could not stop a smile spreading across his face at the cool reply.

It was Catherine's turn to air her lack of patience. "Richard, just listen to him."

Yeoville leant forward, closing the gap between the two men. His tone was imploring. "Look, Ecuador are about to hit major troubles, there's no denying. The BFF have their ally; Ecuador's only chance of long term survival is to make some allies of their own. If we can offer them support—no matter how little—they would jump at the chance."

He sat back in his chair and glanced around the room before continuing. "I did not want to be the one to bring this up, but I think we have reached the stage where the Monarchy's long term survival may depend on some compromise."

Unexpectedly, Reynolds found his outrage ebbing away, but he still remained sceptical. "They could also double-cross us and use us to make a deal with the Republic to get the BFF off their backs."

"True, but one; any deal they could make would at best be a short term solution—even if they wanted to, the Republic would not be able to hold the BFF at bay for long—and two; I've got a gut-feeling about this. Common sense and gut sense can't both be wrong."

"Your common sense answer is still debatable and as for 'gut-feeling'—that's a helluva lot riding on a hunch." Reynolds turned to the King, his eyes imploring.

By way of reply, Paul said, "I have faith that both of you will agree on the final course of action. I will respect whatever decision you make." As the two debated further, he considered his own opinion on the matter. The word compromise lay heavily on his stomach; it was not something he had ever been used to, but what Major Yeoville said made sense. Pig-headedness and traditions, amongst everything else, were part of the reason why they were here in the first place. And yet, he himself had trusted his gut-feeling about Grant Lexus when his advisors had thrown up the warning signs. He had been wrong then…very wrong.

Reynolds threw up his hands and said, "Okay-okay, in the absence of sanity or a better plan, let's give it our best shot. He stood up and added, "I'll update General Somms and find out if he has any suggestions and whether he has any further information on Ecuador that may effect the decision."

The early morning sunshine was smeared by smoke rising from the charred buildings all around Fort Walter's parade ground. Bodies and debris lay strewn all around. Two skimmers, barely recognisable, lay torn apart by the felled gates along with a group of Republican soldiers watching with a distinct lack of interest. In the centre of the parade ground stood the fifty or so survivors of the battalion strong Fort Walter garrison and, set aside from them, stood Major Richly.

He had three soldiers from the 42nd surrounding him with their rifles trained on his gut, but he cared little about them and even less about the bleeding undressed wound on his thigh. It hurt like hell, but he was too angry about the younger faster soldier who got the drop on him to bare it the consideration it warranted.

As he waited, he wondered absently about April. He had only briefly heard from her at the start of the trouble and had not seen or heard from her since. She was not amongst the herded captives, so he could only assume the worst. The woman had had an untamed spirit and he had truly admired her for that.

His waiting seemed over as several assorted skimmers swung in through the entrance and came to an abrupt halt only a few metres away from him. Corallis jumped down from the lead utility skimmer and was immediately flanked by half a dozen troops from the truck behind. His grin broadened as he approached the Loyalist Major.

Richly spat at his feet and bared his teeth. He was in no mood for pleasantries.

"Your social graces have improved somewhat, Richly," Corallis said, his smile unwavering.

"Hello, traitor."

"A traitor is only ever on the losing side and—" he feigned surprise, holding his hands to his face, "Oh wait, aren't you being held at gunpoint with your men either dead or cowering with you? Didn't you *used* to command this pathetic little outpost?" Richly remained quiet, content to let him have his fun, for now. "That must make *you* the traitor!" His laugh was over-emphasised and to Richly it felt like a kick to the shin with a steel-tipped boot. He could not help but notice the smirks on some of his escorts' faces.

In an instant all trace of humour evaporated. Levelling his eyes, Corallis said evenly, "You know what the penalty for treason is?"

Richly managed to maintain an arrogant stance, but the twitch in the damaged muscles in his neck betrayed his true feelings. *Here it comes,* he mused. Through gritted teeth, he muttered, "I'll see you in Hell."

Corallis sighed and, in one fluid motion, drew his pistol and fired.

Lately it took a great deal to shock General Somms, but the news of Fort Walter's demise and the subsequent execution of its commanding officer did just that. For a couple of minutes all he could do was stare at the strat-com display at where the garrison used to be. The Republic were sending a powerful message—Fort Walter had been stable and relatively untouched by the conflict to date, now just hours later it was gone. Wiped out.

Colonel Drake waited patiently for a response while the General rubbed his eyes and uttered something under his breath. To Drake, his superior appeared calm, which was actually a miracle given the turmoil that raged just under the surface.

Eventually, Somms said, "Contact Decker and have him redirect into Belem."

"Belem was overrun, Sir. Major Frazer presumed KIA."

"I know. BFF forces are estimated at around a battalion; it shouldn't be difficult to retake." He paused for a moment and Drake mistook it for indecision. "Once secured, they are to fortify, leave the majority of his force there and, with the remainder, head inland up the Amazon and rendezvous with the King's party at Iquitos. If the King has any problems with Ecuador they can initiate a rescue and if not, they can link up as planned."

"Right," was Drake's simple response. The tension was palpable.

"Tell him to move fast; failure now is unthinkable." He stared hard at the Colonel and for once Drake had a brief glimpse of the depth of the man's stress. He was not given the chance to linger on the thought. "Have you got all that?"

"Yes, Sir."

"Well move it." Not waiting for a reaction, he strode away without another word. He went straight to his quarters without speaking to a soul along the way. As he entered, a synthetic voice said, "Welcome, there are…ZERO…messages."

The sitting room was in darkness and he left it so, heading through to the kitchenette. He opened the refrigerator and his hand fell instinctively on a bottle of beer. Letting it shut on its own, he slumped down on a stool at the breakfast bar.

He sat staring at the cold bottle in his hand for some time, unable to bring himself to twist the cap off. His mind was dwelling on deeper issues. Over the past few days it had occurred to him more and more that at the present time he was the one person who could stop this war and save the lives of thousands of Americans.

He considered that bold statement for some time. The King could eventually put a stop to it, but given his current predicament, it would take a great deal more time to filter down to the masses. Lexus, too, could end it if he called surrender—or even a truce—but it was possible that a large portion of forces would continue to fight regardless. Loyalist forces, he knew—discarding any prejudice on his part— would follow orders to the letter, if it came to it. So, if his logic was sound, he could end the war in the shortest possible time resulting in fewer casualties on both sides. Yet, even if that was the sanest most humane option, it was the one route that was impossible to take.

Was it just pure stubbornness that kept them fighting? Had they reached the stage that abolished all rhyme and reason so they now they just battled on purely to delay admitting defeat? The questions were ridiculous, but they nevertheless drifted amongst the more rational ones.

"I swore allegiance," he said out loud, his voice booming in the quiet room, but his sad tone unmistakeable.

The war had started off as right against wrong, of that he had been certain. But now, as if a frosted window had cleared in front of his eyes, his vision had become less distorted. It was just opposing views, which of course was what all conflict was ever about. Even Lexus, although he was a murderous traitor, still must be doing what he thinks is right. Surely nobody would do it purely out of spite or jealousy.

With that thought, he popped the cap and tried to wash down the bad taste in his mouth. The cold beer failed miserably, so instead, to take his mind off it, he concentrated on the faint resonance of enemy artillery shells.

The kitchen in the private wing within the Presidential Palace was lit only with a couple of low wattage wall lights, the main overheads remaining dark, lending an almost serene glow to the spacious room. The atmosphere was, in contrast, a powder keg.

Grant Lexus had not interrupted Namala as he spoke over the telephone in short nervous sentences, choosing to wait until he had finished his catalogue of blunders.

The dithering fool had rounded off on a sickly optimistic note that, in itself, left the President astonished for a few moments after it. He shifted the earpiece to his right ear, his expression unreadable. As he did, Namala obviously found the silence unbearable, saying, "Grant…Sir, are you there?"

When he did finally speak it was as heavy with undertones as it was lacking in emotion. "I am going to have a cup of coffee, get dressed and relocate to the conference room and when I get there I want you to have General Mendossa on the line waiting for me. Can you manage that?" He hung up before the Defence Secretary could reply.

He prepared the coffee maker then dressed as it bubbled away to itself. Using the glass on one of the kitchen wall cabinets as a mirror, he unhurriedly adjusted his tie. He could not help but notice the bruised areas around his eyes and the paleness of his complexion (exaggerated by the poor lighting).

How could it be so difficult to kill one man? His popularity had been steadily dwindling for a great deal of time; several years in fact, but now, for the first time in so long, initial reports were suggesting an increase. When he thought about it, it was only to be expected. It would be easy for the masses to think that a person so hard to bring to justice may in fact be the rightful ruler. But how wrong they were! The man was a walking disease that had infected the whole Province and would have destroyed them all if *he* had not stepped in to shout *Enough*.

For the good of every man, woman and child—his family included—he had to make sure Paul Frelon did not get another chance. But the masses were sometimes fickle and did not always grasp the big picture—the far-reaching consequences—no matter how much you educated them. In time, Satan himself could deceive the masses into forgiveness without someone taking the initiative. He had to do it; he knew the truth.

*I've come so far! We're so close; I can taste it…Yet, on the very brink of success they want to snatch it away from me. Orson, Kern— even Zain—they're just part of the masses with their heads planted firmly in the sand.*

His fist shattered the glass and, when he glanced down at it, was amused to see blood oozing from several cuts on his knuckles and fingers.

"Grant? Honey?" his wife's groggy voice drifted down the hallway.

Still looking at his hand, he replied gently, "It's alright, just an accident. Go back to sleep."

He entered the conference room, holding a steaming mug of coffee in his uninjured hand, the other wrapped in a dressing. Only Namala was waiting for him in the dazzlingly bright room. He noticed, even from the door, the winking red 'on hold' light on the communication set. Namala, he was pleased to see, was bleary-eyed and unshaven and looking worse than he did.

"Would you like it on speaker, Grant?" Namala asked by way of response.

Lexus nodded and sat down a couple of seats away. As Namala switched the com-set to speakerphone, Lexus sipped his coffee; Brazilian, if his memory served him correctly.

"General Mendossa, good of you to talk at such short notice."

"Mister Namala expressed a great deal of urgency, President Lexus." The native Brazilian's tone seemed almost mocking.

Lexus disliked the leader of the Brazilian Freedom Fighters. He was crooked and bordering on psychopathic, but, for the time-being, he was a much needed ally in the anarchy of the south. Another thing Lexus disliked was asking for favours. "Well, it is good to speak to you again, General. How are you?"

"Cut the pleasantries, we are both very busy men. What is it I can do for you?" There was more than a hint of distrust in his voice. The feeling was, of course, mutual.

"As you have no doubt heard, the fugitive King—Paul Frelon—is still at large."

"Yes, despite that confusion some time ago." This time sarcasm garnished his tone.

Lexus continued unthwarted. "He has become quite a nuisance. So, to cut to the chase, I would like your assistance in a joint operation to eliminate him once and for all. He should be landing by ship on the east coast of the southern continent very shortly. We will have concrete reports of where and when soon."

"And what would I gain for such a service?"

*Oh, what a surprise,* Lexus thought with a smile. "It is unconfirmed at present, but we expect that he will go to Ecuador for help. I assume a Loyalist backed and far better organised Ecuador would not be high on your wish list. Especially if unforeseen circumstances meant that you had to cope with less assistance from over-stretched allies."

The General easily recognised the less than subtle undertones. Angry, he said, "I can handle Ecuador, Lexus. With or without your help."

"Of course you can," Lexus replied, changing to big brother. "But with the former King still stirring up unrest in the north, I'll have to start reallocating resources to compensate, severely hampering our aid to you in your other endeavours. And given the troubles you're having with the Guyanan Guerrillas, the Recife Bandits and Paraguay Command to name a few, it could prove costly. Oh, and did you manage to sort out those annoying internal problems yet?"

Mendossa was silent for a moment, before saying, "The difficulties we're experiencing are minor and are being addressed."

*Yeah? How about I add the Republic to your problems, Rico?* Lexus thought, rapidly losing what thread of patience still remained. No, he could not push him too hard. Far better an ally kept than an enemy gained. He strained to further lighten his tone. "I'm sure you are quite capable of dealing with whatever problems arise. All I am saying is that this particular problem has now become a joint one and we, being allies, should work together to eradicate it. All I ask is a little co-operation, Ricardo."

The BFF leader once again fell silent. His thoughts formulated just out of earshot. When he spoke, his tone was back to its default setting of smug. "Once again, my friend, you are right. What do you need from me?"

Lexus smiled.

After enlightening the BFF leader, Lexus rose from his seat and arched his back in a lingering stretch. His manipulation of Mendossa had revived his somewhat flagging spirits and even though it was not yet light, he felt equipped to deal with whatever was thrown at him for the rest of the day. "Make sure Corallis gets his Panama strike force along with the rest of the 42nd into Bogotá on schedule; I won't tolerate delays."

Namala nodded slowly. He did not share his leader's newfound zest. "I'll make sure of it."

"You had better." He took the edge off the threat by releasing a genuine smile, then added as an after thought, "I assume that Admiral Graceson has been executed as ordered?"

Namala nodded again, but could not bring himself to make eye contact.

# Chapter 11

## Allies in the South

The lush Ecuador coast was shrouded in early morning mist set against the stark uncompromising backdrop of the Andes. Explorer appeared to be a mere pin-prick on the calm ocean as it glided silently towards the more turbulent waters near the shore. As they grew closer, the mist began to melt away, revealing the domed city of New Guayaquil.

The humidity and light gave the domes an opaque look despite the fact that they were actually transparent and even invisible in certain conditions. The sight inspired all who saw it. Of the two people aboard who had seen it before, Paul and Catherine were no exceptions. What they saw from the bridge of the Explorer that cool morning was far more powerful than either of them had ever experienced. As unconventional as it may seem, it was that first sight of Guayaquil that confirmed Paul's beliefs that they had indeed made the right decision.

It took several long minutes for the Guayaquil radio controller to agree to put his supervisor on the line and then several more to convince the supervisor to get the operations manager.

Whilst speaking to the middle-aged woman with an unpronounce-able name and strong opinions, Reynolds showed great strength of character in concealing virtually all traces of impatience and annoyance. But he did have his limits. "I cannot go into any more detail over an open channel. Please, this is of the utmost urgency. All I ask is that you grant us permission to dock and speak with an advisor to President Maximillian or whom ever you feel appropriate."

Whilst listening to the operations manager, he glanced around at the anxious faces of Paul, Yeoville and the others. In the King's case, his mood was misinterpreted; it was actually anticipation. As he massaged the back of his neck, he said, "Yes, I'll hold." To the others, he said, "I think we're in."

Paul nodded, but said nothing.

After a further couple of minutes, the radio bore life once more. "Right, I understand. Thank you. Over and out." He pulled off the headset and, smiling, gave the thumbs up. "Let's go."

"Well done, Rich," Yeoville said, slapping him on the back.

Paul smiled. To him, it had felt like a foregone conclusion.

Explorer was guided into a secure covered dock by two sleek hydrofoil gunboats. Awaiting their arrival was a middle-aged suited man who turned out to be the President's personal assistant and a platoon of soldiers fully kitted out for urban combat. Their dark visors and motionless formation was intimidating, but not unexpected. Apart from an operator sitting in a booth operating the umbilical (in most other ports restricted to first class use, but as nobody travelled to New Guayaquil in any other class, the state-of-the-art Umbilical Boarding Aid (UBA) was fitted as standard in every dock), the dock was otherwise deserted.

From there, Paul was to be whisked away to a secret rendezvous with the President. At that Yeoville immediately expressed his concern, but it was Reynolds who pointed out that they had already past the point of no return. The King was allowed one companion and in that there was no argument. Yeoville knew his place was with the ship, the crew and Catherine. Reynolds knew his place was by Paul's side; no matter what.

They were driven in a black unmarked vintage wheeled limousine with two escorting speedbikes along wide spotless roads lined with perfectly spaced palm trees. There was a large police presence on foot and in an array of heavily enhanced cruisers and speedbikes, but what military was on show was low-key, discreet.

Paul glanced to his left and saw a row of huge stylised mansions, each one entirely individual to the next. To his right at the engineered lake partitioned by a sweeping footbridge complete with a concoction of vines and climbers elegantly disguising almost every inch of metal and stone. He remembered this street from his visit before the revolution and it had not changed one bit.

Guayaquil was perhaps one of the last havens still untouched by the war. The King attempted to draw solace from that, but instead harboured the conclusion that even this sanctuary would soon be a battle ground with its clean streets awash with American blood. He did not look at the scenery again.

The limo pulled into a theme park, its tyres crunching on gravel. The gates were opened by two men in suits and dark sunglasses, but the park appeared otherwise deserted; Reynolds knew better. They stopped outside an office building disguised as an Egyptian pyramid and were ushered inside to its cool air-conditioned interior.

Reynolds was politely asked to wait in the reception area with four more men in suits and the President's assistant, leaving Paul to enter the luxurious office alone. The Knight smiled politely at the burly bodyguards while sizing each one up and making a mental note that three were packing sidearms in left mounted shoulder holsters and one in a right. Their faces remained stern, but at least the assistant offered him a coffee.

There was one occupant waiting for the King. Fernando Maximillian was a big round man with dark leathery skin and bushy black hair and beard. Despite a prominent hooked nose, his face portrayed the deep warmth of a family man.

"You are a wanted man, Your Majesty." His tone was neutral, but he offered his hand and Paul took it, neither eagerly nor with reservation.

"That I am," Paul agreed. "As long as I live, Lexus will see me as a threat."

Maximillian had met the King once before, but did not get the opportunity to shake his hand. He was a great believer in instinct and first impressions and the man's grip felt good. He did not reveal it, instead saying, "And are you?"

"I have learned a great deal from what has transpired and feel that I can, given the opportunity, finally correct that which I have done wrong and ensure the American people get the future they deserve. For that I will do whatever it takes." He had to take a breath to stop himself leaping headlong into a ranting speech. After a moment, he said simply, "Yes, I am a threat."

Maximillian gestured to a couple of nondescript chairs and as they sat said, "The war is not going too well for you."

"We have suffered defeats and a lot of Americans have died and if it came to a war of attrition, the Republic would currently appear to be in the stronger position. However, I would rather surrender now than allow this war to continue much longer and I have no intention of surrendering."

"So you plan a swift victory?"

The sadness Paul had become so accustomed to, settled over him once again. "My conscience is burdened enough. This war has to end at its earliest, otherwise once again I would have failed our people and that is something I do not intend to do again."

Maximillian leaned back in his chair and spread his spade-like hands. "And in what way could Ecuador help? And why?"

"I would like you to aid my friends and I on a journey into Peru to meet up with Loyalist forces. In return Ecuador will receive full Loyalist support and recognised independence."

"There are no Loyalists units left in Peru."

"There will be."

The President of Ecuador revealed a smile that only a loving father could possess. "You show true spirit and compassion, Your Majesty, and possibly just a small amount of insanity. But then the world is an insane place, so one could not hope to survive without just a little madness."

Paul matched his smile. He felt as though the man in front of him was a close friend and had been for years and he sensed the feeling to be mutual.

Both men rose in tandem and Maximillian said, "Of course we will help you. Partly because of the support you can offer us, but mainly because, in the end, I believe you will succeed." He grasped Paul's hand and shook it firmer than ever.

It crossed Paul's mind that he should at least remain wary, but the thought was dismissed instantly. He felt that he could trust him equally as much as Richard or Daniel.

An escort comprising of a company of soldiers with transporters, utilities and scouts was hastily assembled in the grounds of the Guayaquil Armed Forces HQ, which happened to be an imposing 300 year old fortified chateau, complete with its own coffee plantation. Amongst the frenzy of activity, Cobek organised the Loyalist survivors and their assigned transportation. Being back on dry land put the Staff Sergeant back in his element.

Reynolds stood with Explorer's skipper, aside from the commotion. "We couldn't have pulled it off without you, John."

Reach shifted his cap to the back of his head and, chuckling, said, "I wouldn't have missed it for the world, Sir Rich."

"Well take real good care of yourself and her." He cocked his head in the direction of the docks.

"You can count on it." They shook hands then Reynolds strode over to his designated utility skimmer. As he joined Yeoville, Paul, Catherine and Bradley, Reach yelled, "I'll be seeing you soon!" Reynolds waved before boarding with the others.

Once they were all secure, Reynolds leaned over to the forward compartment where Farber was sitting in the driver's seat along with a private beside him. "We're ready, Sergeant."

As Farber spoke on the radio, their attention was drawn to an assault helicopter thundering overhead. They all looked out to see President Maximillian hanging out of the open side door. Secured with a safety harness, he had a loudhailer in one hand and waved furiously with the other.

"Good luck, my friends!" he yelled. "God be with you!" He continued to shout best wishes even after his voice was drowned out by the roar of all the skimmers igniting their engines. Then, as the column slowly pulled away, the helicopter veered off and was gone.

Laughing, Yeoville said, "That guy's crazy!"

"Only a little bit," Paul said and smiled.

The convoy detoured through a residential district of Guayaquil and to their surprise the streets were lined with hundreds of spectators. And what seemed even more surprising was the fact that they were cheering. There was uncertainty on the faces of some, but the majority seemed overjoyed at their new allies.

"We didn't need to come through the city," Reynolds muttered. "This has to be Maximillian's idea."

"He checked with me first," Paul answered. "We were agreed that secrecy was no longer an issue given that the Republic would've known of our arrival almost immediately. And this way boosts morale."

Bradley turned to them with a smile across his face and said, "They love us!"

"No kidding!" Farber added.

"It is nice to be wanted again," Yeoville said and slipped his hand around Catherine's. She smiled and edged closer to him.

"Well," Reynolds injected, "we've got about another eight hundred kilometres to go. Let's see if they love us where we're heading."

"You must be great fun at parties," Bradley muttered and was pleased to hear a muffled cough-cum-laugh from Farber.

Reynolds chose to ignore it, mainly because he found it amusing too.

As the kilometres swept by, the journey grew more monotonous. They had left the luxury and safety of Ecuador and were now heading parallel with the Tigre River, having detoured from the more conspicuous central highway route. Their progress was slow and frustrating as their chosen minor road that zigzagged through the jungle was in bad condition at the best of times, but now the trappings of war and unrest had worsened it still.

A burnt out vehicle or cart lay around almost every bend and several times they came across dead bodies sprawled by the roadside; not just of men and women. They passed a bus, fully submerged bar its roof and tail end, in the Tigre's murky depths. The Company Commander, an Amerindian called Major Garthea, assured them that his scouts had thoroughly searched it and had found no survivors, only several 'restless souls'.

What living survivors they witnessed, shuffling along with meagre possessions, tended to duck away into the undergrowth. It was often where life was already at its most fragile where war took its greatest toll.

With dusk heavy in the cloudy sky, the convoy was ordered to a sudden halt. A utility skimmer pulled up alongside the King's and Garthea jumped out at the same time gesturing for Reynolds to do the same.

They stood between the two grumbling vehicles on the pitted road. Garthea remained silent for a moment, his head angled to the treetops. The humming, clicks and squawks from all around them were shrill, even over the rumble of the vehicles, and the Amerindian seemed to focus on them for a while, before airing his concerns.

"Sir Reynolds," he said finally, "my scouts have spotted a group of Guyanan Guerrillas; approximately one platoon. I'm afraid this will interrupt our journey for a short time."

"Alright." Reynolds did not like it, but he did not want to cause tension in challenging his judgement. The Ecuadorian was worried, but surely not of thirty or so poorly equipped guerrillas? There was something else. "How long?"

"They are preparing a camp—as we would have being doing in an hour or so anyway. My men will wait until dark and then strike." Trying to sound reassuring, he added, "We will get an early start tomorrow. Do not worry, Sir Reynolds."

*Do not worry?* Something was definitely wrong. "I'm not worried, but you seem to be."

Garthea ignored the remark. "I will assign Captain Clasos and two platoons to escort you and your people back five kilometres to an area my scouts located earlier. They have reconned the area thoroughly, but stay alert." The Major did not say another word, but with his expression he revealed his true feelings and its translation was unmistakable; we're being watched.

As the convoy—reduced somewhat in size—doubled-back to the campsite, Reynolds updated the others. They remained quiet until his final comment. "One more thing," Reynolds continued with reservation, "he's under the impression that we're being monitored."

Yeoville was the first to speak. "Is it such a good idea to split up then?"

"Tactically, it makes sense; if either team are compromised, the other has the opportunity for counter-measures. Also, if there is a hostile force out there we don't want to alert them to our concerns."

It was Bradley's turn. "Do you trust him?"

Reynolds did not need to think about his answer; he had already dwelled upon it since the start of their journey. "As a matter of fact, I do. I'm not so sure about some of his subordinates, though, but of Garthea I'm staking our lives on it."

Night descended upon the Loyalist/Ecuadorian camp quicker than seemed possible and with it, the jungle came alive. All around them, insects preyed upon insects that were preyed upon by small mammals that were preyed upon by larger mammals that also preyed upon each other. In the midst of the bloodbath of nature, man was no exception.

The clamour of the jungle was matched by the eruption of distant gunfire and explosions. It captured the attention of everyone in the camp as they listened intently for several long minutes. An uneasiness creeped in from the jungle, seemingly carried in with the aroma-rich humidity.

The firefight reached a climax and then quickly tapered off to an occasional lonely discharge in a sea of silence. Then it hit them— silence—the jungle had as one suddenly held its collective breath. Not even the constant drum from the insects remained.

Reynolds whipped open the flaps on the tent and stuck his head in, searching the darkness for Yeoville. The others were sleeping—Paul restlessly—but Yeoville was sitting upright next to Catherine.

"Something's wrong," Yeoville whispered in the dark.

"I know, get everyone up and ready to roll. I'm going to speak to Clasos." He ducked back out of the tent before Yeoville could reply and headed for the Ecuadorian Captain who was standing in the shadow of a transporter talking to one of his officers. As he walked briskly towards him, Clasos appeared to have the same idea and met him halfway.

"Something's not right," Reynolds said. "I'm preparing my men to move."

"A wise decision, Sir. I am doing likewise. We must be on our guard for the jungle could easily consume us."

Reynolds stared at the slim man as he scanned the tree line. *Consume us?* If he were anywhere else...

"Major Garthea has informed me that they have eliminated the guerrillas apart from a few stragglers—they are hunting them now. His tone confirmed that he too is deeply concerned. He will be joining us shortly to eat and interrogate the prisoners. That is if we do not have to vacate this location for one with a more suitable feel—" The captain stopped abruptly and the colour drained from his cheeks. "Get your people out of here. Now."

Reynolds went cold and started to speak. Mortars hit them before he got the chance.

The camp was instantly thrown into chaos as the barrage rained down upon them, obliterating everything in their path. One shell landed dead centre in one of the small campfires, blowing cinders as well as shrapnel into the eight men huddled around it. They fell away, in flames and screaming. Another shell punched a hole in the roof of one of the transporters. A soldier was scrambling out of the rear doors, half dressed, when the explosion picked him up off his feet and hurled his broken body half way across the camp.

Reynolds sprinted through the smoke and screams in the direction of the King and the others. He numbed his mind of everything except his goal as the destruction closed in around him. As his eyes began to stream from the smoke, he slammed into a young Ecuadorian soldier. The smaller private fell to the ground, crying out in fear rather than pain.

Without thinking, Reynolds hauled him up by his collar and dragged him along with him. As they struggled on towards the cluster of two utilities and one transporter that had been supplied to them by the Ecuadorians, one of the utilities exploded in a ball of flames, scattering several figures.

With renewed urgency, Reynolds ignored his searing lungs and pushed on. Even when a shell landed far too close for comfort, knocking the two of them off their feet, he was scrambling again as his hands hit the ground.

Awareness that the mortars had stopped struck him even though their fury still rung in his ears. With that, came the realisation of what would follow. He struggled to pull the two of them to their feet, but suddenly Cobek was beside him, lifting both of them with one sweep of his free arm.

The Staff Sergeant all but carried the two men back to the frantic group of Loyalists, powering onward like an enraged bull. With the massive influx of adrenaline came strength and determination stronger than he had felt in all his years. Swede had been among the poor bastards who went up with the skimmer, along with Elizabeth Demoore and two others.

After hauling the two men into the remaining utility skimmer, Cobek ran around to the transporter and scrambled in. As he did, gunfire seemed to erupt from all directions at once, adding orange flashes to the smoke and flames.

"Let's go!" Yeoville yelled as he helped Reynolds into his seat.

The two skimmers lurched forward and sped out of the clearing. Two heavily camouflaged soldiers dove out of their way, but a third did not quite make it, his head impacting off the sloped front of the utility skimmer and disappearing amidst a spray of blood.

"What about the Ecuadorians?" Bradley was saying, his head turned back to the clearing.

"There's nothing we can do!" Yeoville shouted. "That's a fucking Republican assault if I've ever seen one."

"How the hell did they find us?" Bradley asked, somewhat numb. Before anyone could answer, a volley of bullets ripped into the side of the lightly armoured skimmer. Catherine screamed as they swerved, crashing through thick foliage to one side of the thin track.

Ignoring the gaping wound in the driver's cheek and eye that was pouring blood all over the controls, Farber threw himself onto the dead man's lap to regain control of the hurtling vehicle. Leaves and vines flashed by, whipping the grubby windshield and catching in the shattered side window.

Yeoville was holding Catherine; her screams were not merely of panic, but pain. As Yeoville tried to sooth her, Paul bent over and tugged aside her bloody shirt. The wound below her ribcage looked surprisingly neat, but was bleeding profusely. Gently leaning her forward, he found that it had luckily made an equally clean exit, but without adequate knowledge, he could only fear the worst.

He pulled out his handkerchief and vainly tried to stem the flow of blood. The small piece of silk was instantly soaked.

Catherine's screams had turned to a soft whimper and Yeoville, feeling utterly helpless, could only hold her and whisper in her ear. "I love you...Don't leave me...please..."

"I love you too," Catherine replied with a whisper, her lips barely moving.

Reynolds had been checking on the Ecuadorian Private who was cowering on the floor with his grubby hands over his head and only now noticed the situation with Catherine. He moved towards them only to be thrown back again as the skimmer swung into a tight bend. He slammed against Bradley who was rummaging through their scattered equipment, expelling an "Ooff!" from his tight lips.

"Catherine," Reynolds managed as he clawed away from him.

"I know," Bradley muttered, not looking up.

Reynolds reached Catherine on his second attempt and roughly pushed Paul aside, muttering, "I'll handle it. Keep down."

At first Paul shrank away, but he stopped, hovering over his seat. "No," he said finally. "I'm sick of hiding, damn it. I'm going to bloody well help!"

Reynolds glanced at him; it was enough to see the King's face red with determination. He nodded and turned back to Catherine. "Alright, see how Farber's doing."

"Thank you," Paul said with sincerity. It took him a moment to find and release the catch to open the partition between the two compartments.

Sensing help at hand, Farber whipped one hand from the controls to stab a couple of buttons. The driver's door slid open, letting in a rush of air and the second button released the dead driver's safety harness. Whilst grunting and attempting to squeeze out of the way, he said, "Push the bastard!"

The King gave the body one hard shove and watched, briefly, the dead Loyalist disappear into the green/brown blur. Then he hastily crammed himself into the passenger's seat and, trying hard to ignore its stickiness, tugged on the safety harness.

Farber was doing likewise, but his seat was infinitely worse.

In the back, Bradley had finally located something useful; an assault rifle and a couple of spare clips. He looked up towards Catherine, his eyes bloodshot and watery, then they were all thrown to one side as Farber threw the skimmer around another sharp bend, clipping some mangroves in the process.

"Be careful, you idiot!" Reynolds snapped. "Who the hell's trying to kill us here, you or them?"

"He's doing his best," Bradley injected, then, brandishing the rifle, added, "This is all I could find."

"Keep it handy," Reynolds answered, only taking his eyes off Catherine for an instant. He had the remnants of a field medical kit strewn around him as he worked unceasingly on the bullet wound.

Bradley stole a moment to glance out the back and was greatly relieved to see the transporter still behind them. It was dented and bullet-ridden, but as long as it was still moving it was help. Its occupants must have sensed his attention, for Reynolds' headset crackled into life.

"Sir Reynolds, it's Cobek. Do you copy?"

Reynolds was both shocked and annoyed that being so wrapped up with his immediate problems he had completely neglected his few surviving men. He did not stop applying first aid to Catherine, but he was quick to answer and divert some of his attention. "Go ahead, Cobek. What's your status?"

"We've got company; I count four scouts in pursuit. Likely more on the way. How'd you fair on the exit?"

"Couple of wounded. How about you?" He finished off the field-dressing and motioned for Yeoville to apply pressure to the compress.

"We started with sixteen, but we got cut to ribbons on leaving the clearing. We're down to ten, including wounded."

"How's the old unit?" Reynolds tried to pose the question casually, but failed.

There was a slight pause before Cobek said, "Swede bought it back at the clearing. Rodriquez and Cook are fine. Don't worry about us, Sir. We can still kick Rep ass."

He did not actually say it, but his meaning was clear; they would die trying. "Can you lay your hands on some explosives or rockets?"

"A pack of RAXXLA, two RACE disposables and some grenades do ya?"

"Keep a few grenades back in reserve, but throw everything else at those scouts. Our only chance is to disappear before their backup arrives."

"You got it. Anything else?"

"Just...good luck."

Cobek considered throwing back the old one of how they didn't need luck, but he knew that would have been bullshit to the extreme. Instead, his tone unnaturally soothing, replied, "You too, Sir. Out."

"How we doing?" Yeoville asked. Since Catherine had been given a pain-killer and her wounds had been tended to, he had managed to regain some small element of control.

Reynolds sensed that Yeoville had spoken, but his mind was focusing elsewhere. A scene had formed, drawn from some dark recess. It was the day they had received their orders to escort the King out of Washington to a secret location. He had gathered the whole thirty-three man platoon in the training hall and given them the news that they had to move out in sixty minutes and, as usual, were not allowed to speak to anyone outside the unit. It had been like any other briefing, even ending with a couple of wise-cracks from Cook, but it occurred to him now that it had been the last time the whole unit had been in the same room at the same time. It had been a frenzy of activity since and now, thousands of kilometres down the road, only Cobek, Rodriquez and Cook remained. Luke, Anderson, Kennedy, McGuire, Swede…all gone.

*Leave it, damn you,* he told himself. The job had not changed and neither had his responsibilities. They had not died in vain; The King was still alive, so there was still hope. He opened his eyes.

Yeoville had seen that distant look before—in the mirror, among other places—so he did not press Reynolds for an answer. Instead, he found himself thinking of Elizabeth. Since their hasty escape, he had not lingered upon her death; he had not had time. She had been a good friend, as Wes had…

"They took a few knocks but Cobek's still got a few men with him," Reynolds was saying. "They're going to attempt to take out our pursuers."

The high speed chase continued for several long minutes with gunfire and explosions casting demonic shadows on the black jungle around them. In places, the jungle was close to reclaiming the track altogether, so the skimmers often had to plunge headlong into a sea of green and in those instances luck alone played the largest part.

Abruptly, the battle ended with the fireball of the last pursuer. A volley of bullets struck the stream-lined nose of the scout and it exploded instantly. As the Loyalist vehicles swung to follow the winding track, the mass of flames and metal carried on into a cluster of balsa trees and shredded them and itself in the process.

"That was the last one," Cobek said over the radio.

"Good going," Reynolds replied. "Now step on it."

"You heard him, Lee," Bradley yelled. "Open up throttle!"

The two ravaged skimmers continued through the darkness for the best part of an hour, before Reynolds gave the order to slow down to a crawl. All adrenalin from the chase had long since dissipated, leaving only exhaustion for company. They drifted on for several drawn out minutes, before Reynolds noticed a break in the trees to their left.

It turned out to be a disused track that was heavily overgrown. It may have only been since the start of the conflict that people had stopped using it, but the jungle was quick to reclaim that which it had lost.

They picked their way carefully through the dense foliage until they came to a small clearing where a dark wooden cabin sat near the edge of the track. It was showing some signs of disrepair, but was in remarkably good condition, except for the missing door and smashed window. The cabin—and its owners too—were probably more victims of the conflict. Even right next door to nowhere was still someone's target.

Cobek sent the majority of the remaining men who could walk out in twos to scout the immediate area; among them were Rodriquez, Cook, Elton (with a leg wound), Private Sargent and the Ecuadorian Private whose name turned out to be Jivaro from some distant musical heritage. The Staff Sergeant, Reynolds and Bradley searched the cabin.

It turned out to be a two roomed affair with presumably outside conveniences. The larger room consisted of a solid fuel stove and fireplace, stainless steel sink, crude balsa furnishings (table and three chairs, sideboard and trunk), a patterned fabric sofa and a viewer. The second room was cluttered with two single beds and several smaller items of furniture and had a number of garments strewn about it (men's work pants, simple but pretty dress and small boy's leisure shoes among them).

The viewer and lights turned out to be powered by a cheap solar generator. Any power it had stored, however, had long since ebbed away.

Reynolds felt like an intruder, but he said, "This'll do. Post four sentries and cam-up the vehicles. I want everyone to bed-down in here except for one person in each of the vehicles."

Cobek nodded and turned to leave.

"One more thing," Reynolds added.

"I'll get Yossession to take a look at Miss Frelon," the Staff Sergeant said without turning.

"Smart ass," Reynolds muttered, but offered a fatigued smile all the same.

While guards were posted and the vehicles were checked over and camouflaged, Yeoville, with the help of the medical corporal, Yossession, moved Catherine and the two more seriously wounded soldiers into the bedroom. Once settled, Yeoville kissed Catherine's forehead and left the medic to his duties.

Reynolds, Bradley and Paul had gathered around the table in the main room with a hard copy map of the Southern Continent splayed out before them.

"OK, so we can't get in touch with Detroit or the Arion," Bradley was saying, "So where does that leave us?"

Reynolds was mulling over Bradley's brief re-cap when Yeoville joined them. "How is she?" both he and Paul asked in unison.

Rubbing his greasy face, he replied, "She's resting. Yossession says she should be OK as long as we can keep any infection at bay." He attempted a smile, but it was closer to a grimace. He looked haggard, as they all did, but he appeared deeply anguished with it.

Reynolds felt for the man and wanted to console him, but instead he just offered him the best reassuring smile that he could muster and continued with the business at hand. "To answer your question, Bradley, that just leaves us with the original plan."

"That's going to be pretty difficult with Republicans and the BFF swarming all over the tri-state area," Yeoville pointed out. "The Arion may already have been compromised, captured or even wiped out by now. At the very least they've probably had to pull right back or go to ground due to all the activity. That Decker's crazy but he's not stupid."

"What happened to Dan the optimist?" Reynolds asked, shaking his head. "Decker will execute his orders to the letter. He knows what's at stake and there's no way that the Cheyenne could take out the Arion in these conditions, even with the help of the BFF; Decker's a slippery sonuvabitch and this terrain is far more suited to the Arion than it is the Cheyenne."

Yeoville remained silent for a moment, then said, "I hope you're right."

After observing the two men, Paul felt compelled to speak. "Daniel, you must not lose hope. All is by no means lost and Catherine, although hurt, is *going* to be alright." He paused, briefly, then addressed all three men. "This journey of ours has been a treacherous one and is not over yet, but we have each other and, although it may not seem like it at times, we have many friends; General Somms, Colonel Decker and the Arion Elite and more recently President Maximillian, to name a few. I am sure there are also allies out there that we have yet to realise." He considered that last statement for a moment and, on reflection, wondered why he had not known that all along.

That night Paul slept restlessly. A thick fog clouded his dreams, revealing only dark frantic fragments, both teasing and terrifying with possibilities and tainted with a deep underlying feeling of urgency.

*Trees without bark and withering leaves. Faces he recognised as friends...terrified. Something crouched in the dark, stalking, drawing nearer. Trees now just charred stumps. Walls closing in. Hot breath, but no face. Growling—low at first—but growing louder (animal or human?)...Flames gushing out of the ground...Friends ablaze and screaming...Booming thunder...Fork lightning spitting amongst the burning trees...Flames all around...Growling turning to laughter... Right behind him...Can't move...Hands on fire...Arms...Blistering face...Screaming (Rain?)...Screaming (Arrows?)...*

Paul sat bolt upright, a gasp caught on his lips. His survival bag had slipped down to his waist, exposing his damp bare chest. The air was heavy and the night was still. Still groggy and filled with images from the dream, panic consumed him. His eyes scoured the room—piercing the darkness—to reveal a lurking enemy poised to kill.

Then Reynolds was crouching beside him, a flashlight in his hands aimed at the floor. "Are you alright, Sire?" he whispered with marked concern.

Without thinking, the King replied, "Bad dreams are a sign." And then, almost as an after thought, added, "We must get out of here."

The Knight's eyes widened. He had felt uneasy, but had not been able to place it, but even before Paul had finished, everything instantly fell into place; it was the same as the clearing, only more subtle this time. An underlying feeling of dread. "Wake the others." He almost fell in the doorway in his haste to leave.

Everyone was ready in two minutes flat. They were throwing the last of the equipment into the vehicles when Reynolds addressed the hushed group. "OK, same positions as before. We'll keep the speed down to cruising unless we hit any trouble. Lets..." His voice trailed off as his attention was diverted to Private Jivaro who had turned pale and was backing away from the rest of the group. "Jivaro?"

As the rest of the group turned to him, he threw up his arms and fell to his knees. "Don't kill me! I'm sorry! Please!"

A wave of realisation washed over the congregation. Rodriquez shot forward and thrust a knife to his throat in one fluid motion. "You motherfucker! Wired!"

"Carve the bastard up," Cook growled.

"We get out of here—right now—is what we do," Reynolds ordered, grabbing Cook's shoulder.

The gesture appeared to signal the Republican attack. Rockets and gunfire erupted from all directions. As the Loyalists started to scatter, the transporter took several hits and exploded in a dazzling inferno. Serge died instantly in the forward compartment.

The remaining Royal Guards began laying down suppressive fire as the others scrambled for cover when a rocket shot through the shattered window of the utility skimmer. Farber felt searing heat and a whoosh and glanced to his side quick enough to see the rocket enter the cabin window and blow a huge hole in the back wall. Reacting, rather than thinking, he applied thrust at the same time as two grenades rolled under the vehicle.

Flat to the ground, near the cabin door, Bradley had a perfect view of the two grey cylinders. He started to yell a warning as, simultaneously, the grenades exploded and the skimmer shot forward.

The force of the blast tossed it onto its roof, but although black smoke bellowed up from the battered remains, miraculously it did not explode.

In the chaos, Jivaro snatched his chance and made a run for it. Rodriquez was vaguely aware of his escape, but he knew all too well that the person who had sealed their doom had of course sealed his own and, as if to prove it, the young Ecuadorian was cut down before clearing a couple of metres; killed by the very people he had aided and for reasons that would never be known.

From a kneeling position, Cobek fired short rapid bursts in a wide arc at the undergrowth on the other side of the track. Glancing around, he saw that at least Reynolds and the King had made it back into the cabin, whether that was good or bad would soon be revealed. Yeoville and Catherine were nowhere to be seen, so they were probably in there too. The smoke and darkness made it difficult to be sure, but he thought that Rodriquez, Cook and the chunky medic were still returning fire, but anything else was pure guesswork.

"'Riquez, Cook, cover the back of the cabin!" he yelled and could only hope that they were 1. still alive, 2. able to hear and 3. able to act.

"We're fuckin'dead, man!" someone cried. Cobek did not recognise the voice, but, after a scream, it was silenced permanently. Then he noticed someone stumbling out of the back of the burning remains of the transporter, hands pressed to his face in a futile attempt of a shield.

On top of everything else, the sight of one of his men in flames became the straw that broke the camel's back. "Jesus," squeezed from his lips, then he was up and running to his aid.

Elton had appeared in the cabin's doorway with a pistol in his hand. He recognised the bounding Staff Sergeant immediately and yelled, "Cobek! NO!"

The human torch fell to the ground at Cobek's feet and even in the poor visibility, he knew it was too late. With rage carved into his face, he planted his assault rifle firmly against his hip and opened fire. His lips were forming obscenities that only he could hear.

A bullet came from nowhere and struck him in the chest. He screamed, spraying a mixture of blood and spittle, but continued firing, only pausing to reload. A second bullet slammed into his abdomen, then another clipped his shoulder. He was still firing when a round smashed one of his shins.

"I'm not afraid!" he cried as he lost his balance and started to topple back. Two more bullets struck his torso before he hit the ground.

Rodriquez came running around the side of the cabin, intuition more likely playing the biggest part. His exceptional eyesight picked out the Staff Sergeant's still form instantly and he rushed over, oblivious to any danger.

"Sarge!" Rodriquez exclaimed as he dropped to his knees beside him. "No, man, you're invincible. You can't die!" He shook the man's limp form by his webbing, refusing to believe what he was seeing. Staff Sergeant Cobek was already dead.

After physically throwing Paul back into the relative safety of the Cabin, Reynolds drew his pistol and looked to Yeoville who had followed him in, carrying Catherine. Elton was the last to join them.

Yeoville and Paul eased Catherine into a prone position under the table, then Yeoville said, "Sire, I'd be grateful if you would take care of Catherine for me."

Paul placed a hand on her forehead and replied, "Don't worry. Go to Richard; he needs you." The former San Diego garrison Commander nodded and stood up. As he approached Reynolds and Elton he too drew his sidearm.

The battle outside was becoming one long deafening roar with only the gunfire and occasional explosion distinguishable.

"Elton," Reynolds said, "You guard the door and keep an eye on Cobek and the others." The Sergeant nodded and limped over to the door.

The two Major's stood in the gloom for a moment, neither man wishing to speak. Smoke hung in the air from a rocket which had smashed a hole in the far wall. It had not started a fire, but now more smoke was spilling in from outside, causing both men to cough.

Between coughs, Reynolds said, "We'd better cover the back wall." Yeoville did not bother to agree, he just walked quickly over to the charred hole. As they positioned themselves at either side of the opening, Reynolds said, "They've probably had a good couple of hours to close us down on all sides. Yeoville just nodded; he was not in much of a mood for talking.

"The one thing in our favour," Reynolds continued, "is that they'll have orders to either take the King alive or at least identifiable otherwise the public would dismiss it as another stunt. So they haven't got the easy option of just levelling the building."

Yeoville finally spoke. "We're dead, aren't we?"

"It doesn't look good."

The moment the utility skimmer came to a rest on its roof, Bradley started to crawl over to it. Although it had not travelled far, he quickly fell out of range from the shouts of Cobek and the others. As he reached it, he could clearly see shapes emerging from the trees and undergrowth both from the other side of the track and from both ends of it. He silently cursed then looked into the battered forward compartment to see Farber upside down and struggling to unbuckle his harness.

The Sergeant sensed his arrival and turned to him. "Alright, Sir?" he asked accompanied with a smile.

"Quit hanging around. We need all the help we can get."

With Bradley helping, they soon had him free. Farber paused only to reach back for his rifle. Once out, Farber said, "If I'm not mistaken it's time for a bit of payback."

"Damn right," Bradley replied.

There were more than a dozen visible targets cautiously approaching them. They fired sporadic bursts, but not directly at them, so they were still oblivious of their presence.

"You ready?" Bradley asked.

"Always." The two men took aim and opened fire.

Elton hobbled over to Yeoville and Reynolds, his rifle dangling loosely from one hand.

"What's the situation?" Reynolds asked as he drew nearer, only taking his eyes off the opening for a moment.

"Bad," Elton said and sounded somewhat numb. "Cobek's dead...So's most of the others. Rodriquez went berserk and I don't know about Captain Frelon. The only other person I am sure about is Yossession; he's pinned down out front. What're we going to do?"

Reynolds did not reply for a moment. The last of his men were gone; laid prematurely to rest. He had outlived them all—even the bull himself, Cobek—but not for long. He considered his options, then inwardly laughed when he realised that he, of course, had none.

Seeing the Knight's hesitancy shoved Elton one step closer to the edge, but he remained quiet and waited all the same, trembling slightly. The events of the last few days were spinning around his mind, intermingled more frequently with thoughts of suicide.

Yeoville was about to speak and tell the poor young Sergeant anything at all rather than let him suffer a second longer, but Reynolds beat him to it. "Try to get Yossession in here and the both of you take up defensive positions at the door. There's nowhere left to run, so we end it here."

The finality in his words caused Elton to take a step back. Yeoville, too, stared at him, shocked at his calm resignation. The Royal Guards Commander and Knight had truly had enough.

"Move," Reynolds prompted. Elton was pale and had legs like jelly, but he nodded and limped back to the door.

Yeoville looked back into the jungle. Figures were starting to take shape all along his field of vision. "So this is it," Yeoville said, his own voice remarkably calm. There was only one thought filling his mind; Catherine. He prayed that she would not suffer any more.

"Yes," Reynolds replied. Yeoville turned to Paul.

Paul, despite being acutely aware that he should be, was not actually afraid. Instead, he smiled warmly at the Major then returned his attention to his niece. Then Elton returned with Yossession right behind him and the moment was lost. The two men settled down beside the door and readied their weapons.

For several long seconds the battle died down to just a few isolated exchanges, then the final assault began. Gunfire tore at the cabin from all directions. A plastic canteen was blown clean off the work top beside the stove. Several rounds struck the viewer and showered the room with glass and sparks. A round grazed the side of Yossession's head, tearing his ear clean off, but in a flash, with blood pouring down his face, he was returning fire once again.

Countless bullets appeared to be whizzing right past Yeoville's head. The walls were being peppered with small holes and wood splinters showered down on him. He glanced sideways at Reynolds and saw that the man was not flinching at all, just firing continuously into the darkness. *If anyone survives this, it'll be him,* Yeoville thought absently.

The bedroom door was blown open from the force of an AP grenade smashing a hole in the outer wall. More smoke bellowed in. Reynolds was on his feet in a flash. "Keep this end covered," he shouted at Yeoville then, half crouched, rushed over to the bedroom. Out of the corner of his eye, he noticed Yossession doing likewise. As his body reacted, his mind considered the events in a kind of replay mode. The Republicans were doing one of two things; either diluting their defences or going in for the kill. Given the weight of the opposition, it was most probably the latter. He would find out all too soon.

Reynolds reached the door just ahead of Yossession, but two Republicans dove through it before either man could react. It was luck alone that decided that one of the Republican rifles jammed as the other one opened fire.

Several rounds hammered Yossession's chest, driving him staggering backwards until he struck the back of the sofa and toppled over it. Whilst one soldier feverishly attempted to un-jam his rifle, the other trained his on an oblivious Elton.

A fraction of a second was all Reynolds needed. He fired twice, hitting both men in the head. Both were dead before they hit the floor. There were more Republicans scrambling through the smouldering hole in the bedroom, so the Major emptied his pistol into them, then dropped to his knees and grabbed Yossession's killer's rifle.

Two more soldiers appeared in his sights and they, too, followed their comrades, then something totally unexpected happened. All Hell broke loose. The battle outside suddenly rose to an all new level of intensity, so much so that when Reynolds yelled out to Yeoville to ask what was happening, he could not even hear himself. And, beneath the

gunfire and explosions, was something scarcely distinguishable...
*whoosh-whoosh-whoosh.*

Both Yeoville and Elton edged away from their respective
positions, barely able to suffer the sheer volume of the battle. Reynolds
joined them near the centre of the room and, as he did, a single wooden
arrow struck the floor just inside the doorway. All three men stared at
it with amazement.

Reynolds moved closer to the door and, from his vantage point,
witnessed scattered groups of soldiers fleeing in all directions. Arrows
were cascading out of the sky like a tropical storm, felling Republicans
by the dozen and instantly throwing them into total disarray. Then *he*
appeared.

It was not an armour-clad soldier Reynolds saw, but a painted
warrior dressed only in a loincloth and holding a finely crafted bow
rather than a rifle. He had emerged crouching and, after appearing to
briefly sniff the air, he focussed on Reynolds. Even with the smoke,
darkness and distance, Reynolds knew he was looking straight at him.

The sniff had, undoubtedly, been a signal, for half a dozen
'warriors' appeared behind him, armed only with bows and spears and
with the same green/brown paint that allowed them to perfectly blend
in with the foliage. As the sounds of battle diminished and the whoosh
of arrows was silenced, more groups emerged from all sides of the
clearing, but remaining at its edges, waiting.

A figure stepped in backwards through the hole in the back wall. All
three men swung weapons to bear on the intruder, but Reynolds
immediately lowered his, saying, "It's OK."

Cook waited until he was right inside the remains of the cabin before
glancing at his fellow survivors. "I don't know about this native shit,
Sir."

Paul had joined them and he was smiling.

"I guess, Sire, you're getting more of this than the rest of us?"
Reynolds said with uncertainty.

"I'm not sure...maybe," he replied.

Then a more familiar group of men entered the clearing next to the
original scout and headed straight for the cabin. It was not until the lead

man was in the doorway that both Reynolds and Paul recognised him. Colonel Decker was heavily camouflaged, but his death-head grin was unmistakable.

Cocking a thumb over his shoulder, he said, "Have you met our Aztec friends? Not very talkative, but great at parties!"

"You like cutting it fine, Sir," Reynolds said, powerless to contain a smile.

"Not on purpose, I assure you." The Colonel looked him up and down briefly and clicked his tongue. "Reynolds, you look terrible." He then noticed the King and immediately thrust a fist to his chest. "Your Majesty."

Paul stepped closer to him and held out his hand. "Michael, you and the Aztecs have saved our lives. Thank you." He grasped the man's hand and the look of shock on his face quickly turned to pride.

As three more people were herded through the doorway, Decker added, "Do these belong to you?" Bradley, Farber and Rodriquez were caked in blood and muck, but were smiling like it was Christmas.

# Chapter 12
## The Duel

Decker's utility skimmer drove the King and his party to a rundown and abandoned village where the Arion Elite had set up a temporary base camp. Outside the village, in a hastily hacked down coffee field, Aztecs and Arion alike surrounded a couple of hundred captured Republicans and Brazilians. The guards were hardly necessary, given the weary and defeated looks on their faces. The skimmer pulled into the centre of the village and onto an overgrown grass strip with an aged wooden bench set back on it overlooking a simple stone-built church.

Decker led them into the church, the interior of which had been transformed into a field operations centre. Several officers and technicians were crammed into its cool confines, surrounded by portable terminals, communications equipment and generators.

"What's the final count?" Decker asked the captain who had turned to greet him.

"Two hundred and forty three, including six officers. Mostly Republican."

"I would like to speak to the officers," Paul injected, stepping in from behind the Colonel.

The Captain, somewhat startled by the King's sudden appearance, stammered, "Yes, Sir-I mean Sire."

The Cheyenne officers were brought in front of the church; three lieutenants, one captain, one major and Lieutenant Colonel Zed Corallis. Two guards stood at all sides, except the front, where Paul, Decker, Yeoville and Reynolds stood at the church doors.

Decker delighted in the hate-engorged stares Corallis received from the two majors, but was somewhat surprised to see what resembled pity in the eyes of the King.

Paul took a moment to study the Mexican standing defiantly before him. This was the man who executed Elias and Fredrick and countless others. Was he not supposed to feel hate or disgust?

He drew in a deep breath and said, "I have decided to send you and your men home, but before I do, I would like to offer you another option." A mixture of fear and hope on the faces of all except Corallis; only contempt from him. *Why such loathing?*

"I will give you all one chance to renounce the Republic and join us; we need good men like you. Or you can be shipped home, and that you have my word on. The decision is down to each of you individually and will also be put to your men." He caught a sideways glance from Decker and added, "I know what you're thinking, Michael—we'll end up fighting these men a second time—but if that is the case; so be it. I will not permit the execution of fellow Americans and that is final. I have made such grave mistakes in the past; I have no intention of repeating them."

At this, the prisoners glanced at one another, being careful not to catch a glimpse of the fury etched on Corallis' face. After a couple of minutes of silence, the Captain stepped forward. After clearing his throat, he said, "I, Captain Gabriel Hicks—one-four-six-nine-three-eight—renounce the Republic and ask for the honour to serve my King again." He then knelt down on one knee and held a fist to his chest and uttered, "Forgive me, Sire."

"Hicks, you fucking coward," Corallis growled, then spat at the Captain's feet. The Captain did not turn to meet his former superior's stare, but his face showed neither shame nor regret.

Paul stared at the Lieutenant Colonel and their eyes locked.

"Zedayal Corallis," he said evenly, "you have a third option, but we shall leave you till last."

"I can't wait," Corallis muttered sarcastically.

Focusing on the others once more, Paul said, "Now, have the rest of you decided?" Two of the lieutenants rather sheepishly renewed their allegiance to the Crown then Paul returned his attention to Corallis. An emotionless indifference settled over him that threatened to transform him back to how he had been before the conflict, but given the subject, he found it impossible to quell it. "And now your third choice."

"And what might that be, you son of a whore?"

At that, Reynolds could contain himself no longer and stepped forward, baring his teeth. "Why you—"

"Wait," Paul interrupted, raising a casual hand to stop the Knight in his tracks.

"That's good, *Paul*," Corallis sneered. "Can he roll over too?"

"I'm going to kill you, Corallis," Reynolds spat, all restraint completely used up.

"Good," Paul said, "Because the only way this can be settled is the old fashioned way; a duel. It would certainly offer you, Corallis, far more of a chance than you gave my brother and nephew and the others you executed. A fight to the death with quarter neither asked nor given."

"Him?" Corallis jabbed a finger at Reynolds.

Paul looked questioningly at the Knight. Reynolds did not take his eyes off the Republican, he just nodded slowly and smiled.

The fight was staged right in front of the church, but not before a group of Republican and BFF NCOs had been brought along to bear witness along with their officers. Amongst them, in a grey BFF Master Sergeant's uniform, was Carlos. His auburn eyes appeared downcast, but in fact they scrutinized every detail around him.

Reynolds snatched a six inch combat knife from its sheath on an Arion guard before he could protest and strode into the centre of the makeshift arena. Corallis walked more casually, but his eyes were equally venomous.

Then a blade came from nowhere, flashing through the air and landed with a whisper, jutting out of the dirt right at the feet of Corallis. The Republican looked down at it and was amazed to see a dagger no less than fourteen inches long, perfectly honed and with an ebony hilt carved into a screaming face.

With eyes like a hawk, only Decker glimpsed it owner. "Laws, seize that man!" he bellowed, pointing at Carlos. A burly sergeant stormed over to the smiling black BFF soldier. Two other guards converged on him from other directions.

"Search him," Decker ordered. "I'd like to know how in the Hell he managed to hide a fucking sword like that in his jacket! Heads will roll for this one!"

As the Loyalist yanked at his clothing and snarled in his face, Carlos remained silent and smiling, further fuelling the Sergeant's vigour. "He's clean," Laws shouted.

"He better be. I'll want some answers about this, but now's not the time."

In the commotion, Corallis had picked up the Soul Dagger, under the watchful eye of Reynolds, and had tested its weight. Its balance was perfect and it was far less cumbersome than it looked.

Decker walked over to the Republican with a standard issue combat knife in his hands, but Reynolds stopped him in his tracks by saying, "It's OK, Sir. It suits him." The Colonel studied him for a moment, before shrugging and turning back to the King. Reynolds did not watch him walk away; his eyes were fixed on Corallis.

As the two fighters stood face to face amidst a blanket of hate, Paul's reservations grew. Five minutes ago he had been certain that it was not only the best course of action, but the only one. Now, although he still felt his decision to be sound, he was no longer certain. The nobility of it had been lost in favour of savagery. He felt compelled to speak, one last time.

"Now that you are prepared, I will ask once, are both parties still agreed to this duel?" He addressed both men, but meant it only for Reynolds. The brutal dagger Corallis held in his casual grip seemed to be mocking him. It was at best a bad omen, but at worst something far more sinister. The only two people who could stop the fight, however, merely nodded.

Paul sighed, then said, "May justice prevail. Let the battle commence."

Reynolds instantly flew at his opponent, his anger overcoming his better judgement. The Republican side-stepped and whipped his blade round in a narrow arc, aiming for the Loyalist's throat.

Wrists clashed and locked an inch from Reynolds' exposed neck. The two fighters growled and strained for a couple of seconds before Corallis struck again, slipping a foot around the Knight's ankle. The struggling forms pivoted and fell to the ground.

Reynolds rolled away as Corallis lashed out. The huge blade narrowly missed the Loyalist's arm, striking the dirt instead. The two men were on their feet in the next moment, dusty and breathing heavier and sweat standing out on their foreheads, but as yet unscathed.

"Keep coming, traitor," Corallis hissed, gesturing for the Reynolds to come forward. "Come on!"

Reynolds roared and sprang at him. Corallis aimed high, but the Loyalist anticipated the move, ducking low and swiping out at his abdomen. The Republican jumped back in the nick of time, but Reynolds' momentum carried him back into range and this time, using the hilt of his knife to add force to his blow, he slammed his fist into the Republican's face and was rewarded with the satisfying crunch of teeth.

As Corallis staggered backwards, his mouth a bloody mess, Reynolds bore down on him again, this time ramming his shoulder into his chest. They both collapsed in a flurry of arms and legs, dust and muck thrown up around them

Their frantic movements were scarcely distinguishable by their audience. Paul had not been sure of what to expect, but he was surprised when he became vaguely aware that there was no clapping or cheering; the Loyalists and Republicans alike were just watching in muted fascination.

One arm suddenly came free of the struggle and, for a moment, held the Soul dagger high over the two bodies. Then it plummeted down into Reynolds' back just below the shoulder blade.

The injured man arched his back, wrenching the dagger out of the Republican's hand and leaving it embedded into his flesh. His cry was both of agony and rage.

Yeoville stepped forward from the crowd, drawing his pistol, but Decker grabbed his arm. "No. You can't intervene—" The Colonel's voice was lost as Reynolds' cry transformed into a more familiar snarl.

Whilst sitting astride of the Republican's thrashing form, Reynolds gripped his knife with both hands and plunged it straight into his chest. There was a sharp crack like a bullet, then silence. Zedayal Corallis was dead even before Reynolds had fallen off him. The duel, as short and frenzied as it was, was over.

As Yeoville, Decker and several others rushed forward, Reynolds lay still, gasping and muttering indistinct words. Paul stood back from them and turned his eyes from Reynolds to where the Soul Dagger had dropped when the Major hit the ground. It was no longer there.

In a wave of panic, Paul shot a glance towards the BFF Sergeant. The smiling black man was no longer there either, but an Arion guard was; dead on the floor, a trickle of blood oozing from the side of his contorted mouth.

The King shouted the first word that came to mind. "Richard!"

Yeoville and Decker both turned around. It was not what he had said, but the way he had said it. The word was thick with unadulterated fear. As they focussed on him, they immediately understood. Carlos was standing directly behind the King with the Soul Dagger in his grip.

Yeoville and Decker reacted as one, drawing their sidearms, but Carlos was already angling the bloody dagger towards the King's throat.

Paul only realised what was happening when he heard the whisper of the blade cutting through air. He started to throw himself forward, but it was far too late. He was also vaguely aware that both officers were not going to be quick enough either. And yet as he felt—rather than saw—the blade draw right up to his throat it was suddenly flying away from him and, glancing over his shoulder, he saw his would-be assassin toppling sideways, blood gushing out of a neat bullet hole in his own throat.

Rodriquez was standing around twenty metres further down the street with a smoking pistol still in his hand. His expression was calm, even thoughtful.

Dozens of people seemed to crowd in on all sides around Paul and Carlos, including Yeoville and Decker. "Sire, are you okay?" someone was saying.

Paul's head was spinning and he had one foot hovering in hysteria, but he managed to shout, "Richard…What about Richard?"

"Don't worry," Yeoville said, "he's being seen to. Are you alright, Sire?"

"I'm fine, I'm fine," Paul replied absently as he pushed his way through to the fallen assassin. He knelt down next to the dying man's face and said, "Who are you?"

The man's auburn eyes focussed on the King. His lips moved, but at first no sound emerged. Then, though thick and gargling, he said, "…can call me Carlos of Haiti; Bokor and charged with your destruction."

"Lexus—the Republic—sent you?"

"No…Is my next target. So I have seen, so it will be…"

"What the hell is he talking about?" Decker injected. "Bokor what?"

"He's a Voodoo Sorcerer," Rodriquez said, his voice drifting through from the back of the crowd.

"Sorcerer or not, I don't think he can quite manage to kill Lexus now. More's the pity," Decker said.

Paul ignored them, he saw and heard only Carlos, but as he watched, the Bokor's eyes rolled upwards and glazed over, then he muttered two more words, "Yes, Papa." He died with the last syllable on his lips.

"This is bullshit," Decker said, straightening up. "He's a Republican assassin, or paid by them, at least."

Yeoville was still staring at the dead man, but then he turned to Decker and said, "Yeah, but why lie?"

Decker shrugged. "I don't know. To keep us off guard?"

"Sir," Rodriquez said, "He said 'Papa'—that could be a reference to

Papa Legba—a Voodoo God—the Guardian of the Gateway to the Other World. Also known as God of Crossroads."

Decker looked angrily at him. "And what would you known about it, Soldier? Voodoo's been dead for centuries."

"With respect, Sir, that's not the case. It is very much alive in isolated communities, like the one I grew up in on Puerto Rico. My uncle was our village Hungan and although I left for the mainland when I was young, he still taught me a thing or two."

Paul finally stood up and tore his eyes away from Carlos. "There are other forces at work here. I fear we have not seen the last of Carlos and his kind."

The President's private study seemed rather cluttered, despite its size. On every spare section of wall there was either a heavily laden bookshelf or scenic oil paintings or family photographs. Some of the paintings were by sought-after artists, but a few had been painted by the fair hand of his wife. A professional family portrait of husband, wife and son held centrepiece on the wall opposite the imposing mahogany desk.

Grant Lexus sat at the desk in silence with an unopened file in front of him. He had been studying its cover, which was bare apart from the two bold words, 'TOP SECRET', for some time, without so much as looking up once at Namala, Halburd and Silus, standing rather awkwardly in a row in front of the desk. When he did finally speak his voice was guttural and his eyes remained downcast.

"What is happening?"

Halburd searched for support first from Namala and then Silus. Neither offered any. "Well, it…it seems that somewhere in the region of ten to twenty thousand people in the northern regions of the Southern Continent have taken up arms against Republican and BFF forces—"

"Get to the point," Lexus muttered.

Halburd took a deep breath. "Employing guerrilla tactics and combined with their numbers, they managed to break down command and communication in the area."

"Civilians?"

"IO point to an underground movement known as the Aztecs with help from the Arion Elite."

Lexus finally looked up and his eyes burned through each of them in turn. "So, if I may summarize, Frelon has now managed to link up with his prized special forces and, as well as allying with the Ecuadorians, he has now gained the support of thousands of Aztecs whom, as I recollect, were previously considered a low-risk band of brigands. Have I pretty much covered everything?"

The three men wisely remained quiet, as Lexus expected them to. Shaking his head in feigned amazement, he said, "Order Corallis to pull back to Bogotá and re-organise."

Namala felt that the next piece of news was best heard from him. So, fighting back the natural urge to cringe, he said, "I'm afraid Corallis is dead, Sir."

The volcano Lexus was harbouring appeared to subside; an event infinitely worse than an eruption. Under the desk, his hand sought the small alarm button and depressed it. Then, staring straight at Halburd, he said, without emotion, "I entrusted you with the defence and security of the Republic, General Halburd. You have failed me and, most of all, the Republic for which you serve."

Halburd gaped at his leader as the door opened to admit two security guards with sidearms already drawn. He glanced from the guards to Namala then to Lexus in quick succession. "Wait a minute, it's not my fault! I did everything I could, for Christsake!"

Lexus ignored him, saying, "Guards, take Orson Halburd into custody."

"Yes, Sir," the more senior of the two guards replied and grabbed the General's arm.

"Grant, please—" Namala began, but was silenced by a glare from Lexus.

Anger replaced Halburd's previous fear and he surged forward to the desk, growling, "You bastard!" The two guards yanked him back before he could do anything more and manhandled him out of the room.

Lexus waited until the door had been closed and then calmly asked, "What is the current situation in the Southern Continent?"

"The erm…42nd have been reduced to a few scattered units—no figures available yet—and the BFF survivors are withdrawing back across the Amazon in disarray. Our strong holds remain intact." As Namala spoke, he could not quell the image of Halburd, enraged and terrified, being dragged out of the room.

"Well, as I said, regroup the 42nd at Bogotá. We will organise a counter-offensive from there, but we will need to pull more units from the north to assure success. Kern, where do we stand in the public's eyes?"

With the President's attention and possible wrath aimed at him, Silus felt a sudden surge of panic, but he kept his voice remarkably stable. "I have no figures yet, but indications show a significant drop in support for the Republic. Demonstrations and acts of violence against the Republic are also on the increase."

Lexus turned his chair away from the two men and stared out of the window at the cloudy evening sky. "Leave me," he muttered.

# Chapter 13
## Turning Tide

Bell Somms entered his office and was immediately struck by the change in atmosphere. It was no longer tarnished with claustrophobia or a place to harbour fears and anger. It was as though someone had opened a window and let in a cool breeze, even though there was no window and the gale that was blowing in off Lake Erie held an icy breath.

He sat back in his chair and, for the first time in months, revelled in its comfort. After releasing a long sigh, he glanced over at the picture of his wife and touched it briefly. A reflective smile hovered on his lips.

*The tide is turning*, he thought absently. Along with their successes in reaching the King unmolested and gaining allies in the bargain, he had just found out that a power struggle had flared up in the BFF hierarchy which had resulted in General Mendossa having to flee into exile, leaving their delicate balance of control blowing in the wind. The Republicans, too, had been left reeling from defeat in the South.

Having allowed himself the luxury of enjoying a long overdue victory, he now forced himself to consider the path ahead. It held no assurances or certainties, except that there would be far more bloodshed before the day was done.

Their victories, although far from meaningless, could yet be in vain. He pressed the TRANSMIT button on the intercom built into his desk and said, "Arianne, can you hail Colonel Drake and ask him to join me A-sap?"

"Sure thing, General."

As he awaited Drake's presence, he re-examined every detail of the plan that he had kept concealed in his head all these weeks. It had not gradually formulated, but instead had arrived in its entirety in a moment of solitude. For so long now he had kept it hidden in the only place he was sure no prying eyes could find it, waiting for the perfect time to reveal it. The time had come.

"You wanted to see me, Sir?" Drake asked on entering.

"It's time we sought an arrow."

Standing at ease in front of the desk, Drake frowned. "Sir?"

"An arrow," Somms continued, "that we can shoot right into the heart of the Republic. One single action that would shake the entire Province."

"Yes, Sir, but what?"

"The heart in question is the Capital; Washington DC."

"Sounds pretty ballsy," Drake replied, smiling. "What you got in mind?"

"It would be extremely high risk, so much so that Lexus would never entertain the possibility that we would attempt it. At the start of the war the DC garrison comprised of around ten thousand with armour and air support. It has since been diluted to half the original numbers."

"That's still one helluva defence force, General, and they've got the fortifications and natural defences to back them up. I don't see how we could muster the resources for it."

Somms smiled. "You're right. But I know a man who does."

Realization spread across the Colonel's face and he thought, *Maybe...*

The King, together with the Arion Elite and some five thousand Aztec warriors, made quick and easy progress to the newly secured Loyalist outpost of Belem. On the journey, Major Reynolds slipped in and out of consciousness as his body was racked by a fever that baffled both Loyalist medics and Aztec healers.

They encountered only sparse disorganised resistance from a few Republican and BFF units along the way and, by the time Belem's ancient battered battlements were in sight, news had reached them of the BFF's collapse. On entering the city, more than a thousand had been added to their number from civilians, rogue units and former Republican and BFF units. As they marched in as one multi-uniformed army, it seemed as though nothing on Earth could stop them.

The commercial port and the ancient Naval Base on the Para River estuary were teaming with vessels of all shapes and sizes. There were three more notable ships; two were old Delaney class frigates and the third was the Explorer. Amongst them were fast attack craft, gun boats, freighters, trawlers, liners and leisure boats.

Within an hour of arriving, the boarding process began and as soon as one vessel was at capacity it would weigh anchor and head off at full speed to the staging area.

The King and his party (except for Reynolds, who was transferred straight to the Naval Medical Centre) were taken into the base Command Centre and through to a briefing room that had a number of officers already waiting for them.

The newly appointed Belem garrison Commander, a stocky Brazilian Major named Tabrico, offered introductions. Also present were Captain Slattery (Commander of the frigate, *Sister of Mercy*), Captain James (Commander of the frigate, *Dawn Warrior*), Captains Potter and Wilhem (Arion Elite) and a face they already knew—John Reach. Tabrico then handed the briefing over to Colonel Decker.

Decker thanked his fellow Arion Elite officer and walked around to the head of the table in front of a huge projection screen. Despite the enormity of the task ahead, the mood was evoking excitement and eagerness.

Picking up a remote control, he said, "Right, you all know the basic idea. I'm going to put some meat on the bones. I'll go over the overall plan and objectives to all of you as a group first and then brief each of you individually." He stepped aside to give everyone a view of the screen as a murmur of acknowledgement rippled through the room.

He initiated the visual sequence as he spoke. "December 5, the strike team, under the command of Major Yeoville, will be deployed under the cover of darkness into northern Rock Creek Park where they will proceed to designated strategic targets in the downtown area. Their objectives are to disrupt communications and transportation and cause diversions to the occupying forces." He looked at Yeoville who, in turn, gave his approval with a quick nod.

The animated map panned back to show the Potomac Basin and Chesapeake Bay area with symbols representing the Loyalist armada moving into positions. "December 6," Decker continued, "the task force, under my direct command, will converge on Chesapeake Bay, whereupon our escorts—Sister of Mercy, Dawn Warrior and the fast attack craft—will break off from the fleet to confront the Republican Naval presence. The rest of the fleet will then head up the Potomac straight to downtown DC to initiate the landings.

"In coordination with the naval assault, we have acquired a couple of civilian airliners which will have scheduled arrivals into Washington National Airport, but will instead divert to Bolling and Andrews AFBs." The display showed the two aircraft moving towards their targets. "Once in position, they will drop cluster bombs followed by Arion paras. Captain Potter will lead the Bolling assault and Wilhem, the Andrews assault. I also hope to get a couple of T60's in from Bermuda to hit Fort Belvoir, but they are yet to be confirmed and their limited range would mean that they would have to land at either Bolling or Andrews or they'll have to ditch."

He plucked a Cuban cigar out of his breast pocket and stuck it in his mouth. "That, my friends, is the plan."

Everyone filed out of the room in high spirits, leaving Paul and Decker alone. The Colonel sucked on his as yet unlit cigar, sifting through his notes. Paul watched him in silence for some time, before saying, "Casualties are going to be very high, aren't they?"

The officer's notes were forgotten in an instant. He looked up at the King with sombre eyes. "No mistake, Sire. The journey up the Potomac is going to take a lifetime and we're going to have to contend with shore gun emplacements, the navy and air strikes; even if Bolling and

Andrews are complete successes, they'll still most likely be able to launch one attack on us, and that's not to mention gunships and possible strikes mounted from further a field."

He took the cigar out of his mouth and seemed to scrutinize it for a while, before looking up again. "Our losses before even establishing the beach-head could be as much as fifty percent."

Paul walked over to the screen that held the now still image of the target area. His eyes fell instinctively on Washington DC and he muttered, "My God."

Now that he had started, Decker felt he had to get everything off his chest. "Once our men are on the ground, they'll still be up against a heavily fortified force with armour, air and logistical support. It may still be our country, but to all intents and purposes we'll have all the problems of a foreign invading army."

Paul continued to stare at Washington as he said, "Do you believe in this plan?"

Decker considered this for a while, then sighed and said, "I believe it's our best shot."

Paul finally turned to face him. "Tell me the truth; do you think we can win? Because I'm not going to stand by and allow thousands of men to be sacrificed for nothing."

"General Somms wouldn't have put this plan forward had he not thought it possible." His chiselled face relaxed somewhat. "But to answer your question; yes, we can win. It's going to be the toughest fight in American history—far worse than your brother's fight at the Battle of Atlanta—but it's not impossible. Our men fight with unparalleled determination. And you've had firsthand experience of those Aztec warriors—those guys are unbelievable. On top of that, we've also got the Arion Elite, for Godssake!"

Paul smiled. "That's right, I forgot." He took the man's hand in his and shook it hard. "Thanks, Michael."

As he walked towards the door, he turned one last time to say, "One more thing, once you have finished with the briefings, I'd like to hold a separate ceremony for you and Daniel to ordain you both into the Knighthood." He left Decker speechless, his cigar drooping from his lips.

After the individual briefings had concluded, Catherine, weak but well on the road to recovery, went in search of Yeoville. She knew instinctively where to find him. After discussing the incursion in great depth with Decker, he headed straight for the Medical Centre.

Catherine found him at Reynolds' bedside reiterating the plan even though the Royal Guardsman—and soon to be fellow Knight—was unconscious. That seemed to be beside the point. He was not aware of her presence, so she watched in silence.

The private room was quite, save for the beeping of the heart monitor and Yeoville's hushed words. A woman laughed from down the hall at the nurse's station. It was a flirtatious giggle, the response to a young man's joke. Not for the first time, it struck Catherine as amazing how, regardless of the crisis, life and love continued no matter what.

She tentatively touched the throbbing wound on her side and smiled despite the pain. She was no different. "Daniel," she whispered.

He turned and his face lit up. Despite his obvious delight at seeing her, his face then frowned. "You're supposed to be resting."

"We haven't got much time," Catherine replied, walking to him. "I had to be with you." She crouched down and laid her head on his lap. Yeoville's hand gently stroked her long silky hair and she felt his chest rise and fall with a deep sigh.

Looking up into his eyes, she said, "Take me back to my room."

They talked until late into the night. Their surroundings, officer's quarters that appeared never to have been lived in, were hardly romantic, but their eyes never strayed from one another long enough to notice. Yeoville managed to 'acquire' a bottle of wine and some sandwiches, so they sat on the single bed—dressed with a brown blanket and a white sheet—sipping wine from plastic cups and eating ham and pickle triangles.

Catherine, sitting cross-legged, brushed a few strands of hair out of her eyes and then said, "Make love to me."

"I—" Yeoville began, but she lent over and placed a finger on his lips.

"Don't say anything."

He nodded and brushed her damp cheek as she lent closer to kiss him. That night they made love and afterwards they both cried in each others arms before drifting into a restless sleep.

Rain was hammering against the window when Yeoville awoke early the next morning. He washed and dressed in silence as Catherine continued to sleep. It was still dark and the rain had brought with it a shroud of humidity that caused sweat to glisten on his freshly cleaned face.

As he slipped into his tunic, he felt sweat rings form in his armpits. He felt a twinge of homesickness for the dryer warmth of San Diego.

Once dressed, he bent over Catherine and kissed her on the cheek. She awoke instantly and threw her arms around him, tears immediately welling in her eyes.

As Yeoville and Paul drove over to the airfield, the rain intensified with the murky light. They found the rest of the strike team already assembled in the hanger as they pulled into it. Amongst the eleven men were Bradley, Farber, Rodriquez and Cook. They all appeared fairly relaxed, but that was probably a long way from the truth.

Paul shook each man's hand and wished them all good luck. "Take good care of yourself," he said to Bradley. "Your Father would be very proud."

Bradley smiled, despite the painful memory it conjured.

Paul then clapped Yeoville on the back. "You take good care too, Sir Daniel. I'm looking forward to the wedding."

The King's blessing was given quick and easy, but Yeoville was shocked all the same. "Thank you, Your Majesty," was all he could think to say.

After an unceremonious farewell, the strike team boarded the small Uni-Am StateHopper and settled down for the flight.

Their journey took them north-west up the coast of South America and then out over the Caribbean Sea. Before they hit the Florida Keys, the small shuttle dropped down below radar and then sought an airstrip on Little Pine Key.

The small island comprised of the airstrip, a cluster of dilapidated one storey wooden buildings (some of which had been destroyed by a hurricane at some point) and a wooden pier. It was deserted apart from a fishing trawler at the pier and the dozen men it had brought. As soon as they had landed, the men busied themselves with wheeling out fuel drums and mounting routine checks on the aircraft.

Yeoville and his strike team left them to it and made themselves as comfortable as possible in a rundown beach tavern. There, one of the trawler crew brought out a banquet the likes of which none of them had seem since before the war; fresh fish and vegetables and fruit for dessert.

They stayed on Little Pine Key for two days before continuing up the East Coast to their drop off point.

The night was cold and windy and a blanket of grey clouds threatened to open up the heavens above them. After concealing their parachutes in the undergrowth, Yeoville's strike team crouched together in the wild grass and bull thistles surrounded by skeletal trees and darkness on all sides.

He picked out the blackened faces of each man in turn, hoping to draw courage from their resolve. As one, Bradley, Farber, Rodriquez, Cook and the other seven Arion commandos held the same look of determination and focus.

There was a physical change to Bradley, as well as a mental one, that was all the more apparent squatting in the dark undergrowth. The petulant teenager had been completely replaced by a courageous man. His jaw was set and his eyes were focussed. The stress and pain of their journey from San Diego was written all over his face, but all it had achieved was to make him stronger and more determined than ever.

Farber was by his side, inseparable and totally loyal ever since their baptism of fire in San Diego.

Yeoville had initially thought that Cook and Rodriquez would take issue with him commanding them instead of Richard. But he had found out later that they had been outspoken in their relief that he would be leading them instead of one of the more than capable Arion officers. On

Little Pine Key they had even suggested, albeit light-heartedly, making him an honorary member of the Royal Guards.

He had fine men with him, but he wished that Reynolds was with him too.

"OK," he whispered, "Riquez take point."

As they picked their way through the parkland, heading south into the Capital's nucleus, the first spots of rain descended upon their blackened faces. By the time they had made it to their first target—the Naval Observatory and Communications Centre on the outskirts of the Park—the rain had turned into a torrent, reminding him of his departure from Belem.

The following evening was still grey, but the rain had eased off to an icy drizzle. The Loyalist Fleet, now comprising of some three hundred vessels, converged on the entrance to the Potomac. Sister of Mercy and Dawn Warrior, along with their flotilla of Fast Attack Craft fanned out to await the Republican Navy while the troop carriers began their slow accent up the river towards the Capital.

The lead vessels were ten kilometres past Cornfield Point when the first enemy warships were spotted, swinging out from behind Smith Island and into Kedges Strait. Two frigates, and behind them, a destroyer. Then, passing Goose Island, the bulk of the Atlantic Fleet appeared, missing only the carriers, the support vessels and a skeleton escort. The remainder of the four battle groups and three PhibRons raced towards the pitiful Loyalist defenders.

Sister of Mercy swung about and ploughed headlong into the 2nd Fleet's main body, letting fly a wave of missiles. Three struck home on two separate targets, lighting up the dark horizon with flames. The Republicans were quick to return fire.

The force of their strike was devastating with more than a dozen missiles finding their target. The thunderous roar was gone in an instant, like a final agonised cry, and with it went the cheery Captain Slattery and the lives and crew of the Loyalist frigate. The possibility of survivors was negligible.

Dawn Warrior beat a gradual retreat, scattering wave upon wave of missiles behind her. The attack craft flung themselves at the onslaught, only to be swatted like flies from enraged giants.

At the helm of one such attack craft was Dewson, a veteran of a few pirate encounters with the scars to prove it. He angled the small hydrofoil so that it was running parallel with one of the other attack craft on a course between two frigates, heading straight for the cruiser, RAS Absolute.

Speaking into his headset, he said, "Echo, this is Bravo, copy?"

"Go ahead, Bravo."

"You thinking what I'm thinking, Echo?"

"Damn right, Dewson. Let's take this up with Papa Bear. Last one in's a sissy!"

"Roger that!" Dewson smiled, revealing several gaps in his teeth. He gunned the engine to maximum and turned to the young midshipman standing nervously beside him and said, "Here we go."

Bravo edged ahead as they raced in between the two Republican frigates, one in flames from a missile hit to its fore decks. Their main armaments were directed elsewhere, but that did not stop their machine gunners from having some target practice. Gunfire spat at them from all directions as they ran the gauntlet. Bravo shot out the other side, but Echo was not so lucky. The heavy calibre machine guns from both ships zeroed in and ravaged the small craft. A brief flash signalled its loss of propulsion, then, dead in the water with its deck gunners valiantly fighting on, it was torn apart until only a smoking hull remained that quickly slipped beneath the waves.

Dewson and his crew did not have time to mourn the loss, as they approached the cruiser, one of its laser-targeting forward guns picked them out and opened fire with both barrels. Dewson reacted as the gun barrels recoiled. The two shells splashed down only metres off the starboard side.

"Charlie, aim the launcher and the gun at the bridge and give it your best shot when I say the word. We'll only get one crack at this!"

The chief gunner acknowledged immediately.

Dewson swung the craft in a wide arch, being careful to avoid machine gun fire from another frigate and the big gun from Absolute. Then, he angled her on a collision course with the huge cruiser. As the gap quickly closed, a second gun revolved to attempt to eradicate the nuisance.

Dewson threw the craft from side to side as both guns blazed at them, then as the gap closed further, Dewson yelled, "Give it to'em!"

Bravo's single missile tube and deck gun fired simultaneously. Both hit their mark, blowing two holes in the bridge and belching flames out of all the windows.

Dewson and his crew rose up in a united cheer. The mighty Absolute was out of the battle, brought down in classic David and Goliath fashion by a humble fast attack craft. Their joy was short-lived.

As Bravo powered away from the stricken giant, they were struck amidships. The single shell was enough to tear a gaping hole right through the small craft. She dropped to water level and drifted for several seconds before sinking fast.

Dewson man-handled his petrified crewmate out of the door ahead of him, yelling, "Abandon ship!" After shoving him over the railing, he glanced once over his shoulder at his smouldering vessel, then followed. As he jumped, Bravo snapped in two and disappeared.

Only a couple of fast attack craft remained when Dawn Warrior took a hit astern. Explosions ripped through her rear compartments, crippling the last of the Loyalist defences. She struggled for several agonising minutes to keep her nose above the water, then a second missile struck her radar dome, scattering flames and debris onto the frightened survivors assembling on deck. A third struck the waterline amidships and that signalled a fast demise.

With the last of their escorts obliterated, the Loyalist Fleet's rear vessels, a couple of ancient minelayers, began scattering their loads behind them.

Two strike aircraft out of Bolling joined two from Andrews over Wicomico River and fanned out in attack formation as they approached the mass of loyalist vessels. As they passed Cobbs Island they opened fire with everything they had before banking off over St Mary's and heading back to reload. Their Air to Sea warheads obliterated everything they touched.

A freighter off Explorer's port bow took one hit in the central upper level and erupted in one enormous fireball. The entire ship was gone by the time the smoke started to clear. A luxury yacht, a passenger liner and a trawler followed. Explosions plumed in all directions.

The 2nd Fleet, gaining fast, stole further casualties; one of the minelayers and a tug. Gunships joined the melee from installations across both States. Buzzing amongst the ships, they emptied every rocket and every round they had. Small arms fire, along with a scattering of deck guns and shoulder mounted launchers took their toll, but they still managed to cripple several more of the smaller vessels.

As the Loyalists approached Blossom Naval Station, Republican Fast Attack Craft leapt upon the depleted Fleet. One of the largest ships of the fleet—the luxury liner Emerald—had already taken a hit from the earlier air strike; its leisure deck a flaming ruin. The small Republican Attack Craft picked her out of the crowd, like lions to a wounded calf and launched themselves mercilessly at her. A few smaller vessels, including one of the last remaining gunboats fought in vain to draw their fire.

The liner took multiple hits and started to list. She then did what nobody expected; she pulled sharp to starboard and ploughed straight into the harbour wall of the Naval Station. Even before her once sleek nose had finished buckling, her survivors, mainly Aztecs, were pouring out to attack the Station's guard detachment. Quick thinking by the crew had managed to save most of the 1,000 strong compliment, enabling them to storm the Naval Station in force.

As the Fleet passed the battle raging in the Naval Station they came into range of the Grayton Sea Defence Battery, whose huge long range guns immediately began pounding. Even amidst the utter carnage on the Potomac, their distinctive *thump* was clearly audible.

Several smaller vessels broke off from the main body of the fleet to race ahead and attempt to land marines to put the guns out of action.

Captain Potter's airliner had successfully lined up for its bombing run on Bolling Air Force Base. He conferred one final time with the pilot, then hurried back to the main cabin where his men were already lining up in full kit next to the exits.

"All set, Spears?" he asked a wiry Staff Sergeant.

"Just waiting for the green light, Sir. Then it's time to kick some."

Potter smiled, causing his moustache to arch comically. "You better believe it!"

The bulky tri-winged aircraft came in low under radar, so was on top of the AFB before they realised they were there. The cargo doors slid into the fuselage and where cargo pallets would usually be were racks of free fall cluster bombs. The racks flipped at the touch of a button and hundreds of small bombs cascaded Earthwards.

As the aircraft banked for its second pass, explosions rippled through the base, tearing holes in buildings, runways, vehicles and scattering ground crew and soldiers. As chaos spread, the Loyalist airliner dropped into position and Potter's troops dove into the affray.

Scarcely half of the Loyalists paratroopers were descending when a SAM locked on to the transporter. The pilot registered the warning light and threw them into a sharp bank, but the civilian airliner was no match for the heat and laser guided missile. It struck the tail engine and, in a blinding flash, wrenched five metres of tail clean away from the rest of the aircraft. The pilot blacked out as it dropped out of the sky like a stone. The passengers and crew, including Captain Potter, were thrown about like rag dolls as the aircraft spun towards the parkland surrounding the base.

The airliner hit a picnic area nose-first and exploded on impact. Flames and fragments of twisted metal swept outwards, igniting trees and a nearby ranger cabin.

Captain Wilhelm's men had better luck at Andrews AFB, but their transporter met with a similar fate. It lost a chunk of wing after releasing its entire cargo and belly-flopped into an industrial estate in District Heights. The packaging plant it struck burned for three solid days before fire crews finally brought it under control.

A young black Corporal, Ben Creed—Joker, to his friends—had been one of the first out of the aircraft over Andrews. He plummeted to the drop zone like a bullet, his small stealth chute allowing for a far more rapid descent. He gripped his sub-machine gun with the certainty that it alone would save his life once his feet hit the ground. Despite the hurtling fall he was able to recognise a couple of his fellow jumpers only metres away.

"So this is economy class!" he yelled out to nobody in particular. His smile was ridiculously exaggerated by the rushing wind.

The warning buzzer sounded in his helmet, forcing him to prise a hand away from his SMG to unclip a smoke grenade from his webbing. As he dropped it, he glanced down and realised how close the tarmac was.

He gulped in cold air and dropped a second smoke grenade just as the warning buzzer sounded again. "Three...Two...One..." The thrusters built into his backpack ignited for one bone-jarring second the moment before landing. His feet struck the ground as if he had just stepped off a curb.

After releasing the pack and chute, he crouched down to survey the scene. There was gunfire in all directions and the smoke from dozens of grenades, combined with several burning buildings from the cluster bombs, lent perfect cover to their landing. More Loyalist paras were landing all around him. "First Platoon, Second Squad; on me!"

It had been against Decker's advice, but Paul had insisted that he accompany him on the Explorer. Now the King stood on the bridge with Decker and Reach and, for the first time, regretted his decision. It was not through fear of his life, though he was scared, but because of the sheer magnitude of the butchery he now bore witness to. He had known that it would be bad, but nothing could have prepared him for the slaughter now surrounding him. He described it simply as soul destroying.

An old merchantman up ahead of them burst into flames, the cause unknown, but the result saw burning figures on deck desperately hurling themselves into the broiling river. Its engines lost power and drifted, dead in the water. All three men turned to watch the burning wreck as Explorer passed without even slowing.

"Like shooting fish in a barrel," Reach muttered and turned away in disgust.

Decker was about to reply when his headset caught his attention. After listening for some time, he said, "Understood. Carry on." He turned to Paul and said, "The Bolling assault was unsuccessful. Andrews continues on."

Paul considered asking about Captain Potter and his men but, given the circumstances, he remained silent. Decker, a man usually possessing ample qualifications in emotion concealment, was clearly agitated.

Instead, the King closed his eyes and prayed. As they passed a blazing yacht, the flames played across his troubled face. The gentle face of Jennifer formed in his mind, banishing for the briefest moment the carnage all around him. The desperation to be with her and to finally mourn the death of their son together was unbearable. Jason was gone, but he had scarcely had any time to think about it…it had been so detached from his frantic reality, leaping from one crisis to another. *Jennifer, we will be together soon…I promise.*

Sir Richard Reynolds awoke with a start from his fevered sleep. Sweating and panting, his eyes slowly refocused to take in his surroundings. The private ward was in near darkness, apart from a night light on the wall above his bed.

Squinting to see the time on the wall clock, he realised that the assault had begun. He heaved himself into a sitting position and took a sip from a glass of water at his bedside.

Despite the cool fluid, his voice was gravely as he whispered, "God be with you, my King. Take care, Dan. You make sure you get back to Catherine in one piece." With that he eased himself back down on the bed and closed his eyes. His mind took him back to a moment with Samantha; their brief embrace. It had been a perfect moment that would be with him for as long as he lived.

The Republican gunship swept low along the turbulent waters of the Potomac heading out of Washington DC. Even in the dark with the drizzling rain, the flames, tracer rounds and explosions up ahead were plain to see. The battered Loyalist Fleet grew ever closer to their goal.

As the lead vessels came into range, the gunship strafed with rockets and guns. A fishing trawler took a direct hit from one of the gunship's rockets, blowing the cabin apart and casting several crewmen and passengers into the icy river. More figures were seen scrambling onto the deck to leap overboard as it quickly slipped between the waves.

Yet more Loyalist vessels fell prey to the onslaught from land, sea and air. It became increasingly difficult to navigate between floating and sinking wreckage. Then, after what seemed like a lifetime, the lights of the Capital city came into view and shortly afterwards the landings began, stretching from Georgetown University to West Potomac Park.

Dug in Republican troops were waiting for them. Trenches, sandbag walls and barbed wire defences had been prepared, even in front of the King Luther Memorial in the west end of the Park. Machine gun nests on the bridges and Potomac Island tore into the crammed decks of the Loyalist ships, killing and maiming countless soldiers before even setting foot onto the Capital's soil.

The sloped banks of the Chesapeake & Ohio Canal harboured more enemy defenders. A column of Rhinos drew to a halt on the raised section of freeway overlooking the Potomac, giving them a perfect view of the passing vessels.

Despite the overwhelming Republican presence and the natural and engineered defences, Loyalists of all guises—Arion, regulars, Aztecs and civilians—poured forth into Washington DC. The first wave of attackers were all but annihilated. The second wave suffered heavy losses but managed to hold some ground. A couple of Arion Demolition Techs managed to get underneath the freeway and, with a few well placed charges, brought two huge sections of it crashing to the ground and most of the Rhinos along with them.

A rocket struck the sincere granite head of King Luther and blew it apart while several smaller vessels diverted into Little River and pulled up on the opposite shore of Potomac Island. Loyalists surprised the machine gun nests and an artillery battery and quickly overrun them.

Lacking the armour and machine gun support, the beachhead was finally secured and the Loyalists swept into the city. Fighting was fierce and without mercy from either side. The Republicans, faced with a major frontal assault along with insurgents playing havoc behind their lines, lost ground fast.

Lexus called in reinforcements from all over the Province, but he quickly discovered that they would never make it in time. Paul's rebels had gone on the offensive, something he had known would happen given the time, but he had not realised that he had ran out of it. It suddenly became clear to him that his rule was drawing to a close. Given that devastating conclusion, he felt strangely calm, perhaps even relieved.

As he spoke to his frightened secretary, his tone was relaxed. "Could you ask Zain and Kern to join me, Bernie?" He drew his hand slowly away from the intercom, then guided it to the top draw in his desk. There, it fell upon an automatic pistol.

Namala was first through the door. He was angry and scared and his face was flushed with exertion. "Grant, we'll lose control within the hour. There's a helicopter—" Lexus lifted the pistol into view and aimed it at the Defence Secretary's chest. "No!" He threw his hands up instinctively.

Lexus pulled the trigger and shot him through the heart. Namala died before he hit the carpet with disbelief etched into his face. Silus appeared in the doorway and looked from the body to the barrel of the gun then into the President's eyes. Horror drained the colour out of his cheeks.

The State Secretary felt hot urine jet down his leg and then a hammer-blow to the chest. As the room faded, Silus stared at the indifferent face of Lexus. Then he, too, vanished.

The President's eyes remained on the bodies of his dead colleagues only briefly before turning to the window. He heard cries down the hall from Bernie. Despite the sound-proofing, he also heard the dull drone of the battle drawing nearer, now mere blocks away.

He looked down at the gun in his hands; a wisp of smoke was still drifting out of the barrel. From there, he turned his attention to the small pewter framed photograph on his desk of Fiona and Adam. After a moment's contemplation, he pressed it to his temple and muttered, "I'm so sorry."

There was a dark figure standing behind him—more like a shadow really, but it had not been there a moment ago—but the auburn eyes were unmistakable and so was the smile that broadened as Lexus squeezed the trigger.

# THE END

# Appendix I

## History

**Frelon Family Tree**

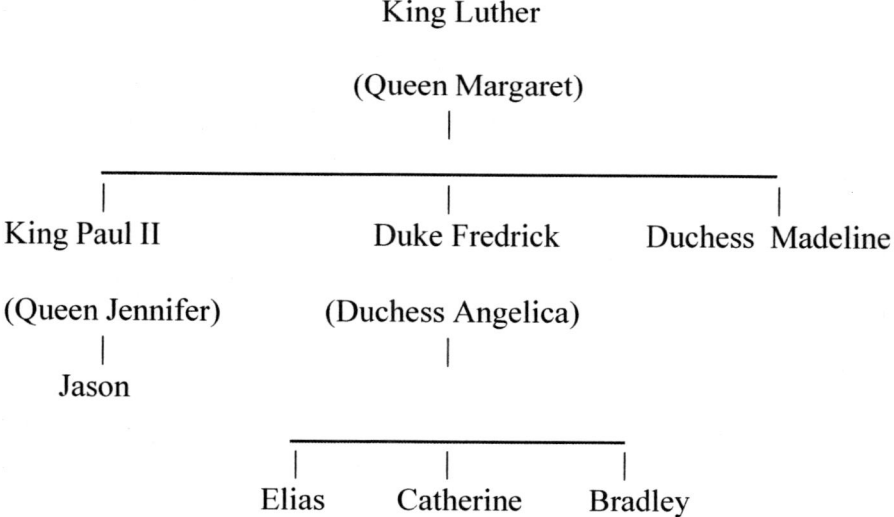

King Luther

(Queen Margaret)

| | |
| King Paul II | Duke Fredrick | Duchess Madeline |

(Queen Jennifer)          (Duchess Angelica)

Jason

Elias          Catherine          Bradley

## The Great War

The apocalyptical war over 500 years ago that ended the 21st Century civilizations and plunged the world into years of chaos and tribal war. After a century of darkness, one man rose up to unite the Americas and restore civilization. Seth Frelon became Seth the Uniter and the first King of America.

## Fort Wayne, Detroit

Loyalist stronghold and headquarters for the exiled Monarchy. Named after the famed war hero from before The Great War, John Wayne. Records are sketchy of this mythical icon.

## Duke Fredrick of Atlanta

The title 'Of Atlanta' was awarded when, towards the end of the four year war with the African Warlords, he led six hundred men of the Knoxville Light Infantry Battalion into battle against the Kanaga—an invasion force of five thousand—at the battle of Atlanta. A mere twenty eight men survived the carnage, but they induced such great losses (no accurate figures available) upon the Kanaga that, instead of marching on a virtually defenceless Washington DC, they withdrew back to their New Orleans beach head. The withdrawal gave American forces enough time to amass an army substantial enough to finally overcome the Kanaga in the Easter war.

## Louisiana and Mississippi Riots

A month prior to the beginning of the civil war, nearly one hundred thousand people in these poverty stricken states took to the streets in protest against government policies towards the poor and disadvantaged. The demonstrations started out as a peaceful one, but when militia forces moved in to disperse the crowds, fighting broke out. The riots lasted right up to the start of the war. In that time, approximately five hundred civilians and one hundred militia and military personnel were killed.

### Arion Elite

So named after their first Commanding Officer, Major Charles Arion. The unit's formal title remains 101st Assault & Insertion Battalion (the only such unit serving in the American Armed Forces). Specialists in land, sea and air assaults. After the death of their unit's founder in the Easter War, they adopted the crest of the powerful stallion, Areion, from Greek mythology, to honour his name.

### The Order of the Provincial Knights

The Order was first established out of the twelve strongest and most loyal chieftains who aided Seth Frelon in uniting the Americas and to become the first King of America. The Order maintained only ever twelve members at any given time for its two hundred and fifteen years of existence, until being disbanded by Paul's Great Grandfather, King Thomas.

### Fort Walter, Panama

The base was established by Sir James Walter, a Provincial Knight and personal friend to King Seth, after he made his heroic stand against the Del Toros rebels in the early years of the Monarchy.

# Appendix II

## Glossary of Terms

| | |
|---|---|
| **'65'** | Alcoholic beverage popular among the Central American States. Named after it's alcoholic content. |
| **AA** | Abb. Anti-Aircraft. |
| **ADU** | Abb. Area Defence Unit. |
| **AI** | Abb. Artificial Intelligent. |
| **APC** | Abb. Armoured Personnel Carrier. |
| **AT** | Abb. Anti-Tank. |
| **Bokor** | Voodoo Sorcerer. |
| **C&C** | Abb. Command and Control. |
| **Carama** | Ceremonial robe (green, yellow or grey depending upon rank) worn by the Queen's bodyguard. Specially made to balance femininity with close protection effectiveness. |
| **CinC** | Abb. Commander in Chief. |
| **Click** | Military jargon for Kilometre. |
| **CO** | Abb. Commanding Officer or Commissioned Officer. |
| **Com-Headset** | Abb. Communications Headset. |
| **CP** | Abb. Command Post. |
| **The Great Boroldus** | Famous magician and escapologist |

**Grunt**  Slang term for Infantryman.

**Harvey Wallbanger**  Slang term for the Harvey MK2 Assault Pistol that combines the strength of a shotgun with the automatic capability of a pistol. Popular among travellers in the less hospitable states of the Southern Continent. 0.5inch calibre. 8 round clip.

**High Council**  Hastily established government body consisting of twelve departmental secretaries and chaired by the President with the power to veto any marginal decisions. The basis of the new American Republic.

**Hovernaught**  Viking Industries heavy battle skimmer. Largest battlefield assault vehicle in existence. 24 crew plus one platoon of combat ready troops. Armaments include a six gun battery of 240mm cannons, two quad 120mm cannons, one quad AA missile launcher, two quad AT missile launchers and an array of light weapons.

**Hungan**  Voodoo priest.

**I-I**  Abb. Image Intensifying

**IO**  Abb. Intelligence Office. Also known as 'The Agency'.

**KIA**  Abb. Killed In Action.

**LC**  Abb. Lance Corporal.

**Lion Cross**  Medal for 'Valour beyond all expectations.'

**LT**  Abb. Lieutenant.

**Mammoth**  Tracked vehicle used in the early colonial years for long distance transport through treacherous territory. 1-5 crew plus a further 12-36 passengers depending on cargo configuration.

**MBT**  Abb. Main Battle Tank

**MIA**  Abb. Missing In Action.

**NCO**  Abb. Non Commissioned Officer.

**PASH**  Powerful synthetic narcotic swallowed in capsule form.

**PFC**  Abb. Private First Class.

**PPB**  Abb. Plastic Patrol Boat (a light-weight lightly armed patrol boat).

**R&R**          Abb. Rest and Recuperation.

**Rack, The**    Moody rock group, infamous for hallucino-rock.

**Rocket Ball**  High velocity ball sport, of which the team consists of two forward blasters, three mid blockers and two rear blockers. The League consists of teams from most major cities throughout the American Province and is also gaining popularity throughout the rest of the world. In the last few years it has steadily grown far more popular than the 'classic' sports.

**SAW**          Abb. Squad Automatic Weapon.

**SO**           Abb. Special Operations (Intelligence Office unit).

**Speedbike**    One seater light-weight skimmer built for speed only. The racing circuit is dominated by the Speedster Supanova MKII, the Whitely Corsair and the Lazer 350.

**Strat-Com**    Abb. Strategic Computer.

**T60**          Ground Support Aircraft nicknamed 'Flying Tank.'

**Tac-Com**      Abb. Tactical Computer.

**Tonnelle**     Voodoo ceremonial hut/building.

# Appendix III
## The Other Provinces

### European Province
King Alexander of the Brittons has ruled the Province for 18 years. His father King Edward ruled for 32 years before him after seizing control, relatively peacefully, from King Otto the Second of the Heinrichs after a family reign of 94 years. A state of mutual cooperation has existed between Europe and America since the Heinrich period. The European Province has, on the whole, remained stable since the uniting of the European Monarchies 160 years ago.

### Asian Province
There are many warring factions in this volatile land, but the principal ruler is recognized world-wide as The Khan, Mougrel the Slayer. Opposition exists from rival Indian, Arab and Chinese factions. During the wars between America and Africa, the Khan heavily aided the African Warlords by first cutting off American trade routes and giving weapons and supplies to the Africans and later actual military intervention, attacking American overseas forces close to Asian borders. The most notable attack was the massacre of the Masoom-bi Trading Post and Marine supply depot. A full scale war was narrowly averted after intense negotiations (including Europe's threat of offering full military support to America) ended in the lifting of all

trade restrictions between Asia and America and the promise of much needed medical aid to help combat a typhoid epidemic. It was later named the Bangkok Treaty.

### African Province

A number of tribes (the exact number is not known due to the constant merging and breaking up of larger tribes) rule this harsh famine-fraught land, the larger ones being the Nubian (broadly covering Egypt across to Morocco), Kanaga (South Africa as far as Congo) and Oumbossa (Kenya across to Nigeria). The Kanaga united the rest of the Province against America in a war that lasted four years after America set up a small experimental colony near the Kanaga's territory in Angola. The Kanaga reacted fiercely to these 'invaders' and slaughtered every man, woman and child; 103 in all. America promptly declared war. The fighting came to a head when, with Asian backing, many tribes united under the single Kanaga banner invaded the American mainland. Heading to the Capital, they made it as far as Atlanta and then were forced back. They were finally defeated (lack of supplies due to Asia's withdrawal from the conflict along with a European blockade of the Gulf of Mexico being root causes) at New Orleans in the Easter War.

### Oceanic Province

There are many independent countries within this Province (the larger ones consisting of Greater Australia, Queensland, Victoria, New Zealand and Papua) but all are united by the Oceanic Defence Treaty. Although there are occasional squabbles between member nations, the Treaty has held strong for nearly fifty years. Their policies, although generally insular, do extend to positive diplomatic links with Europe and America and a neutral stance towards Asia.

### Artic and Antarctic Provinces

No recognized regimes. Small towns have emerged in these cold inhospitable areas, but they are inhabited in the main by pirates, profiteers and people that, for one reason or another, are unable or unwilling to live in the more governed Provinces.

Printed in the United Kingdom
by Lightning Source UK Ltd.
110613UKS00001B/126